T0300735

A NEW SEASON

Ray Paul

authorHOUSE®

AuthorHouse™
1663 Liberty Drive
Bloomington, IN 47403
www.authorhouse.com
Phone: 1-800-839-8640

First published by AuthorHouse 12/17/2009

ISBN: 978-1-4490-4149-6 (sc)

Printed in the United States of America
Bloomington, Indiana

This book is printed on acid-free paper.

DEDICATION

For Jo Marie, the love of my life for fifty-one years and a peerless editor.

ACKNOWLEDGMENT

I am deeply grateful to the following: Christine DeSmet, my wise and talented mentor. Our daughter, Laurie Kelly, for her writing insights and the cover art for *Between the* Rows and *Shards* and our granddaughter, Shannon Nicole Kelly, for her cover art on this book. Additional thanks to David McCarty, MD, Mary Doyle, RN, Mary Ellen Devorak, Kristin Hollinger and The Troubadours Writers' Group.

ABOUT THE AUTHOR

Raymond L. Paul was born in St. Louis, Missouri on February 25, 1936 and has been a resident of Rockford, Illinois since he was four. At West Rockford High School he was a top student, three-sport star and an All-State football player. He attended the University of Wisconsin on a football scholarship, majored in insurance and finance and graduated after four years with a Bachelor of Business Administration Degree.

Immediately following graduation in 1958, he passed up an opportunity to play minor league baseball in the Dodger farm system choosing instead to marry his college sweetheart and begin a career with Massachusetts Mutual Life Insurance Company. Fifty-one years later he is still smitten with Jo Marie and proud of his ongoing relationship with Mass Mutual.

Ray's writing career had its genesis in college where he eschewed his business electives for creative writing classes. Though this period primed his heart for creative writing, fighting for a toehold in the financial services industry and being a good father to three daughters precluded any serious involvement. His hiatus from fiction writing lasted almost forty years.

Fourteen years ago Ray finally reached a comfortable stage where the demands on his time and energy were diminished. Their older daughters had moved away and started families of their own, and he and Jo Marie had weathered the crisis of losing their youngest daughter to meningitis. With his golf scores soaring and time on his hands, he needed a new challenge. Two college writing classes and a couple of workshops later, he had found a new avocation. With the first click of the keyboard, he began writing himself toward retirement.

In the past seven years, Ray has written *Cabbage Requiem,* the sequel, *Between the Rows* and now *A New Season,* the finale of the George Konert trilogy. In addition, he has published *Shards,* an eclectic collection of his best short stories, some twenty-two of which were previously published in a variety of literary journals and magazines. Ray also teaches writing classes at the Center for Learning in Retirement at Rock Valley College.

A NEW SEASON

CHAPTER ONE

"We're going to die anyway. Let's get it over with."

George Konert scanned the room. He noted the trite combination of light blue walls and pink accents in the curtains and pictures. The use of baby colors had to have been some decorator's ill-conceived attempt at turning an ordinary waiting room into a shrine to motherhood. Still, he had to tip his hat to the unknown talent. He, or she, understood the market value of ambiance. Virtually every chair that lined the walls, each presumably just as hard and uncomfortable as his, was filled with laughing, talkative women in various stages of rotundity.

He and his wife, Catherine, were sitting side-by-side when he took a sheepish glance at her. They were in the waiting room as a result of her positive mammogram, but she was the one who was enduring the ordeal far better than he. That made him feel both weak and uncomfortable. While she appeared to be placidly reading a vintage magazine, it bugged him no end that his stomach was responding to his wife's predicament with a gut-filled dread that had made its appearance the first moment he'd learned about her abnormal test.

Fifteen years earlier, his first wife had died of breast cancer. While George assumed a jury would excuse him for not jumping in and catering to Catherine's needs, he was more harsh and less forgiving of himself for not wanting to face it. During his first marriage, he'd thrived on Grace's guidance and directions. After she left him, he had eventually healed, but not until he'd spent far too many years scratching away in his garden looking for solace. During that time he'd been wary of all human contact, avoiding it whenever possible by staying alert for the slightest movement toward him and fleeing to safety at the mildest of advances. Then Catherine entered his life, and he regained all the richness he'd given up. Now, thinking of an existence without her, he wasn't sure he could ever cope again. In fact, just the thought of another bleak future filled him with terror.

Catherine carefully placed the open magazine across her lap, reached over the chair arm and grabbed his hand. Her move startled him. Then, upset him. He should be the one reaching out to her, not the other way around. Before he could form any meaningful response, she said, "I'm just as worried as you are, George."

Not thinking to soothe her worry, he blurted, "Yeah, but you handle things better than I do."

"It's all a facade. Underneath, I'm a nervous wreck."

"Me, too. Do you suppose it's contagious?"

His ridiculous wisecrack brought a smile to her lips. Yet, before he had fully castigated himself for being a complete oaf, he felt her hand tighten its grasp. That's when he knew that no matter how he might disguise his love for this woman, she could read his heart and knew he had no intention of letting her face her problem alone.

A white-clad tugboat holding a chart emerged from the door to the inner sanctum. Between glances at the clipboard, her eyes swept over the faces of the maternal crowd, past Catherine and him and on to the remaining younger women. Two octogenarians, actually one, since Catherine was only seventy-five, among all those kids. The nurse appeared flustered as she again consulted her chart. Hesitantly, she called, "Catherine Konert?"

Egad, he thought, if her age was on the chart, surely she can pick a grandmother out of this bevy of impregnated youths. Or, perhaps she couldn't distinguish Catherine from among the other expectants because his wife was so well-preserved. Still, that was silly. As beautiful as Catherine is, no one but a sightless person could believe she was still young enough to conceive.

Just as he reached the peak of his disbelief, Catherine solved the nurse's mystery by standing, and the woman flashed a relieved smile. Rising, he quickly caught up to Catherine and accompanied her to the spot in the center of the large room where the tugboat was moored. In his mind the whole purpose of his being there was to hold Catherine's hand and generally comfort her while the doctor ran through his diagnosis and explained what was going to happen next. As usual, he was wrong. Before skipping off with the nurse, Catherine placed her palm against his chest and stopped him in his tracks.

"Can't I come, too?"

"Let me find out what's going on, George. I'll fill you in later."

He tossed a plea toward the nurse who was studying her clipboard. She either didn't notice him or chose to ignore him. Reaching out a tentacle, she snared his wife's arm and attempted to move her toward the door.

"But, I want to be with you, Catherine."

"I know."

"But, there's nothing to read, and the chairs are so darned uncomfortable, and...."

"Please," she whispered. Then she followed after the tug and marched through the forbidden gateway to the doctor's offices.

Once the door closed behind her, George briefly studied the floor, aware that the drama had entertained the whole room. Gathering up his shattered ego, he slunk back to his chair where he began squirming like a five-year-old and feeling sorry for himself. After a few more moments, he picked up first one, and then another magazine from the table before returning them unread.

George found the whole setup foreign, but he wasn't oblivious to reality. Gynecologists didn't market their services to eighty-one-year-old men. So why would the doctor or staff running this place give a darn about catering to his comfort. Still, even if he was stuck here, he wasn't without options. Maybe he should spend the duration of the appointment in the men's room. In the end he decided to quietly endure the ordeal.

So, why was he here, anyway? That was an excellent question. The answer: he'd come to support his wife, but she hadn't let him, and now he was all alone in this dreadful feminine enclave. George glanced around the room. The place was alive with the sound of young mothers-to-be yakking with each other. They also talked to the babies in their swollen bellies or to the whole room in general, which seemed to be the case for one whose kernel was about to pop and who had a voice as loud as a ball game beer vendor.

The racket began to depress him. With all these words to share with each other, wouldn't you think someone would aim a few at the decrepit old guy who'd accompanied his wife to the doctor to share a prognosis that began with a flawed mammogram? All these life bearers had seen his wife abandon him. They'd also seen him turn tail and slink back to his chair, his face red from anger and embarrassment. Yet, would one of them shut up long enough to console him? Hardly. They all seemed offended by his taking root in their sanctuary.

A soft female voice encroached on his thoughts. "Excuse me. You seem really, really agitated." He'd felt the light touch of her hand on his sleeve and had been soothed by it even before she spoke. Then he heard the caring in the sweetness of her young voice and was swept away. Tears came involuntarily, gratefully washing away all the clutter in his head. Clutter that concealed his hurt and disguised his worry about Catherine.

He turned to her. "I am agitated, and I really appreciate your interest. My wife had a problem with her mammogram, and we're here to see what has to be done."

She pointed to the portal leading to the inner sanctum. "Is she already in there with the doctor?"

By the way she asked the question, he felt obliged to explain why he wasn't with Catherine. "I got up to go in with her, but she stopped me. No explanation. You probably saw her put her hand against me so I wouldn't follow." He laid out his hurt to the young woman. "Why wouldn't she want me with her?"

"I don't know," she said. "There have been times when I'd rather not share with my husband. He scares easily." She grabbed his arm. "I'm sorry. Don't get the idea I think you're like my husband, or that all men are alike. It's just that...well, maybe she wants to hear the diagnosis and then filter it to you. That way she can absorb the shock before you two talk about it."

"That's nutty. I know all about breast cancer. My first wife died from it."

"Oh, God. No wonder you're upset." Then she brightened. "Fortunately, now they can diagnose tumors earlier. Plus, they have so many new treatments." She smiled at him. "I'm sure it will turn out fine. I hope so, at least."

"Thank you," he said, returning her smile. For the first time he studied the young woman. She had a pert little nose, dimples when she grinned and a cute blond haircut that made him wonder if she combed it with a Mix Master. She was also showing a lot of baby. "When are you due?"

"Six more weeks."

"Your first?"

"Yes."

"And, you're doing fine?"

"Physically, yes. Emotionally, not so hot. I have mixed feelings about giving up my career. My husband thinks I should stay at home with the baby, and I agree, except I've finally earned the head marketing position I've always wanted. I've invested a lot of time, effort and education to get it. I hate to just walk away."

"What company wouldn't keep your job open for awhile?"

"Mine. We're too small, and I can't do justice to the job on a part-time basis."

George immediately thought of his oldest daughter, Jill. Although there were mitigating circumstances in addition to her need for career achievement, Jill chose to work through her childbearing years. When her first husband died, she remarried a man with two terrific teenaged sons whom George immediately accepted and loved. Still, he felt like the world had been shortchanged because no child would ever inherit Jill's spectacular genes, and that was too bad.

Swinging his thoughts back to the about-to-be mother, George hesitated for a few seconds, then plunged ahead. "I hope you don't mind my asking you something. Do you need the income?"

"What? Oh, gosh, no! My husband is a successful dentist. Money's not the issue. It's my fear that after raising kids, I'll never be able to catch up and recover what I've lost."

5

Now George was faced with a dilemma. In the last few moments he'd really taken a liking to the young woman. Not only because she'd started a conversation with him, but she seemed so straightforward and honest. The last thing he wanted was to turn her off by giving some unwanted advice. "Do you have a grandfather?"

"No." She said cautiously. "Not anymore."

"Then, are you open to a little advice from one?"

She grinned. "Oh, yes. I haven't had any for a long time."

"Here's my take on your concern." He leaned toward her. "Bringing a new life into the world, caring for it and educating it until it can pass on to others all the things you've taught it, is the least appreciated but most important and satisfying career you can possibly have. Moreover, you only have a few short years to work on this project, and that time is now. Some women pass by this opportunity and then spend the rest of their lives regretting it. If you consider how long we live nowadays, you've got a lot more time for a career than you have raising kids. So if you ask me, and you didn't, you are doing exactly what you should do. Plus, I'll bet your parents agree with me, too."

At first it seemed she was rejecting his message. So, he blathered on, "But, of course, I am an old fogey, and all my ideas may be as extinct as the dodo bird and not have a place in your young life...."

"No, no, you're right, especially the part about my parents. Or, rather my father. My mother died of can—my mother died last spring. My dad and my husband are in complete agreement about my being a stay-at-home mom."

Sadly, the nurse chose that exact moment to hold open the door with her back side and call, "Pamela Turner?"

"That's me," his new young friend said as she quickly collected her jacket and purse. She then took his hand and said, "Thanks so much for reinforcing my basic conviction. I have my doubts sometimes."

"You should have doubts. I've had doubts every day for eighty-one years."

"That makes me feel better," she said as she waddled toward the nurse.

"Good luck," he hollered after her.

She waved back. "You, too."

George glanced at his watch. How much longer would Catherine be behind closed doors? Besides being worried about her, he was still angry and a bit embarrassed at being turned away. He repositioned his butt to better fit the rock-hard, fabric-covered wooden chair. Did all doctor's appointments require interminable waits? While it seemed illogical that anxiously waiting was part of the cure, many of his experiences with the medical profession seemed to suggest it. He tried to recall whether he'd ever been treated immediately upon arriving at a medical facility. While there must have been a few, he failed to come up with a solid number, except for the time he'd driven himself to the emergency room with chest pains and ended up with four bypassed arteries. His memory of that event had ended with his passing out at the ER door. Although he couldn't prove the hospital staff had acted promptly, he suspected they had. Otherwise, had they dallied, he darn well wouldn't be here today anxiously waiting for Catherine.

Prior to his conversation with Pamela, who upon reflection now reminded him more of his homemaker daughter, Anne, than his executive daughter, Jill, George had eyed the water cooler at the other side of the room. He'd felt dry, parched. He still did, but, how to get there without being scrutinized by every one of the mothers-in-waiting? They'd titter when he stood up and paused to let the blood rush to his head so he wouldn't faint. Then, crossing the room to the cooler, they'd grin at his creaky gait and probably laugh their heads off when the cool drink dripped down the wrong throat precipitating a coughing jag. With those thoughts impinging on his thirst, he'd blinked away the sight of the cooler. After what Catherine did to him, why suffer any more abuse?

Now, glancing around the room, George definitely sensed a change in the atmosphere, and remarkably, it felt like it had shifted in his favor. When his eyes lighted on their young faces, he received a smile in return, and the smiles gave him courage. Perhaps now would be a good time to fetch that drink of water he'd considered earlier without feeling cowed. George tossed the year-old *Readers*

Digest he'd been perusing onto the side table and stood up. Pausing to clear his head, he strutted to the water cooler, purposefully downed the liquid from the small paper cup, poured and drank another and had the temerity to return their gazes.

However, when he returned to his seat, his boredom started up again. Grasping for relief, he began making calculations based on tummy size as to the prospective due-dates of each about-to-be mother. When his eyes lighted on one sweating woman in full bloom, he thought about breaking his silence by hollering something like, "Hey lady, you better call an ambulance, or you're going to have that kid right here."

As it turned out, his warning wasn't necessary because within moments the nurse began nudging the engorged woman toward the door to the doctor's office.

From there his imagination soared. What if the whole setup was a sham? Perhaps there was no doctor behind the door at all, just a hologram. Or, if there was a physician, perhaps the man was merely sipping cocktails and popping hors d'oeuvres instead of examining patients and handing out advice and prescriptions. Worst yet, what if Catherine was in on the joke and was back there partying with the man in charge, while her stupid husband was worrying about her diagnosis and crippling his back on the hard chairs.

What seemed like an hour, but was probably closer to twenty minutes later, the overweight nurse escorted Catherine to the center of the waiting room. He creaked to his feet and rushed to her. "What did Dr. DeHaven say?" Before she could or might have answered, George spotted several pairs of prying eyes. Instead of waiting for an answer, he took her arm and whisked her toward the door. "You can tell me in the car," he whispered.

He guided the Buick from the lot and pointed it toward home. Glancing over at his wife, he saw her closed eyes. She was tight-lipped and frowning. Not good, he concluded. The diagnosis must have been bad. Otherwise, why would Catherine be hoarding all the information she'd gleaned? If the news was good, she'd be spitting out medical jargon as fast as he could absorb it. Instead, silence. Yep, the news had to be very bad.

Rather than interrogate her, he decided on a ploy to open up a dialogue. Passing the park, he commented on the beauty of the turning leaves. "It's definitely autumn, isn't it?"

Catherine didn't bite. The stony silence continued.

With a degree of trepidation he decided to broach the subject directly. "What did you find out?" When she didn't respond immediately, he followed up with, "Catherine, talk to me!"

They were stopped at a red light when she snapped at him. "George, you always think you can fix everything. You couldn't prevent Kevin from dying, and you can't fix me. Let me handle this."

The harshness of her words jolted him. Why stab him in the heart? He was just trying to share her burden. Instead of eliciting his sympathy, her comments triggered his exasperation, which happened to turn to anger simultaneously with the greening of the traffic signal. He peeled away from the intersection like a hot rodder.

"George! You'll kill us both," she screamed.

"Good. We're going to die anyway. Let's get it over with."

Moving along a little above the speed limit on the familiar boulevard with the side streets passing in rhythmic succession, his temper cooled. Yet, the bitterness of their exchange remained. He took a deep breath. Whether his wife appreciated it or not, he had been working on controlling his temper from the beginning of their relationship. Now, he only lost it on rare occasions—okay, on many occasions—like now when his frustration became so great the dam broke, and he was flooded with more than he could contain. All he'd wanted from the moment they'd arrived at the doctor's office was some insight into her situation so he could be helpful and understanding. While he disliked being angry, how could he be criticized for wanting to know what was happening to her?

Then an ugly thought entered his head. Could she be trying to aggravate him for some reason? Maybe because he couldn't come up with any meaningful conversation when they first showed up for her interview with Dr. DeHaven. Still, to lash out at him about the circumstances surrounding Kevin's death was abject cruelty. He loved the boy, and he'd tried to make him wear his helmet when he rode his bike. The boy just hadn't listened. Even more puzzling was bringing it up now and coupling his death with her breast tumor. He peeked at her. Smug as a thug on a drug. If making him mad was her intent, she was certainly succeeding.

He made the turn onto their short street, headed toward home and pulled the old Buick into the driveway. He decided to make one last appeal. "When we get into the house, you will tell me what the doctor said, won't you?"

She sighed. "Yes, of course I will, George."

Maybe he was better off with the silence and the anger, because the quaver in her voice rekindled all his fears.

They were seated at the kitchen table. George had made a pot of coffee while his wife had changed into slacks and a sweat shirt. She held the cup between her two hands, warming them, staring out at the bright autumn afternoon. "You're right about the trees, George. The colors are especially vivid this year." He nodded, staring at her, trying to drag her eyes back from the window so he could hear the verdict. "I thought they were rather dull last year, didn't you?"

"I can't remember last year. I can't remember yesterday. I only remember a doctor's appointment earlier today. I'm worried sick about it. Do you happen to remember anything that was said there?"

She removed one warm hand from her cup and placed it on top of his. "Okay. The second mammogram shows the same fairly large calcification in my left breast. The good news is it isn't on the chest wall. The bad news is that calcifications that large are usually malignant. Especially when it hasn't shown up on any tests in previous years."

He covered her hand with his, leaned forward and asked, "So what are they going to do? Grace had treatment as soon as they found the original tumor."

"And, she died."

George took a deep breath and exhaled slowly. "It spread."

"That's the problem. Cancer often returns. Dr. DeHaven thinks the best course is to have a radiologist do a needle localization where they follow the needle down to the tumor and remove it. While he's in there, he'll also remove some of the sentinel nodes–those are the nodes closest to the tumor–to see if the cancer has already spread. Then, they send everything to the lab and have it analyzed. If it's cancer free, they'll keep testing me periodically."

"So, it might not be malignant?"

"He says that's fairly unlikely. Hopefully, the nodes won't be affected and removing the tumor will be the end of it. For now, anyway."

"That doesn't sound so bad."

"Of course not. It's not your breast."

"Catherine!" he said in a hurt voice.

She gripped his hand. "I'm sorry, George. I'm just afraid they'll find some abnormal cells in the nodes. Then, I'll have to have chemotherapy or radiation and feel sick all the time."

"Let's try to be positive. Maybe they won't find any abnormal cells at all. Or, if they do, they'll be confined to the tumor and the doctors can remove it, and the cancer will be gone."

"I'll buy that. Still, even if everything is fine, I might feel safer if I had a mastectomy."

"But, isn't that cutting off your nose to spite your face?"

The suddenness of her laughing startled him. He smiled back, not sure if she was laughing at or with him since the absurdity of his analogy hadn't yet struck him as humorous. "Although a mastectomy seems extreme, after my experience with Grace, I'm for whatever works. I don't want to lose another wife."

"It's all about you, isn't it, George? Do you think I want to be taken down by breast cancer?"

"I'm sorry, Catherine. That was a thoughtless remark. It's just that it never occurred to me you might die before me. By rights, I should go first. I'm older and a man, and ever since we've been together I've become so dependent on you for support, I doubt I could live alone again."

"This conversation is the very reason I wouldn't talk in the car. The whole subject is loaded with emotion neither of us can handle."

"I can handle it, Catherine. I just don't want to."

"Well, I have to, and based on your reaction, I think I'm going to have a mastectomy."

"Why?"

"I was leaning that way even before your sweet confession."

"If there's no cancer in the nodes, why do it?"

"At my age it's worth giving up a breast to live worry free for a few more years."

George drew her hand toward him and kissed it. "I'm one-hundred percent behind any treatment that keeps us together. I'm just a lost soul without you."

Catherine stared steadily into his eyes before breaking into a grin. With the grin, George felt the somber mood lifting. Her next words made it official. "Okay, George. Cut the crap!"

Recognizing the devilish glint in her eyes, he chuckled and said, "Catherine! How can you say a thing like that to the man you love?"

"I wouldn't say it to *him*."

"Oh, no! You aren't still making it with the butcher at Kroger? You said you weren't shopping there anymore."

She winked at him. "I didn't for awhile, but he enticed me back with his kielbasa."

"I never thought they had good sausage there."

"You have to ask for Sam. He knows what he's doing."

George decided to keep on with the game. It sure as hell was an upgrade from the prior discussion. "When I'm out today, maybe I should get some."

"You could, but I doubt you'll get the same attention he gives me. He says I'm special."

He gathered himself and stood up. "You are special, Catherine." He kissed her lightly on the lips. "I love you so much," he said. "We'll get through this thing together."

"I hope so, George. You're the best thing that ever happened to me."

"Better than Sam?"

"Oh, yes. Except, he does have better kielbasa."

"I should hope."

CHAPTER TWO

"If you expect old age to be easy, don't bother going there."

The next day when George rolled out of bed in the morning and took his first step toward the bathroom, a sharp pain shot through the arch of his right foot. His first reaction was, "Ouch!" His second, concern. First time pains always create anxiety. But why panic? A foot isn't a vital organ. It wasn't like a chest pain, bad headache or a sharp stab in the abdominal area which might portend a life-threatening event. Still, it was something to consider.

A foot did have some value. It wasn't like an appendix or a tonsil that could be disposed of with little consequence. A foot kept old folks mobile, and when it hurt it was like any other pain that took some of the fun out of living another day. He pulled out his litany of worries. Why did he have the pain? Was it as bad as it would get? How long would it last, and what had to be done to get rid of it?

He took a few more agonizing steps. Since he couldn't ignore it, he needed to do something about it. But what? Try to get an appointment with Dr. Jabor? If he did, he'd probably end up with a prescription or some free drug samples to go along with a sage diagnosis such as, "It's just a sprain, George." Or, "It's just your arthritis, George." Then he'd get the benefit of Dr Jabor's cutting-edge treatment. "Put moist heat on and stay off it, George. If it isn't better in a week, come back and see me again."

Since he already knew the drill, he decided to handle it like he did most other non-threatening pains. Take two acetaminophen every four hours and try to figure out why he was visited by the foot ogre in the first place. If a week went by, and he wasn't any better, that was the time to bring the doctor into the plan.

After shaving and before getting dressed for the day, he flopped onto the chair in the corner of the bedroom and watched Catherine sleep. His wife was making her usual ruckus. The snorts and wheezes that often woke him or kept him from returning to a sound sleep helped keep his mind off his foot. In addition, whether it was the pills or his not asking his foot to bear weight, he was far more comfortable now than when he took his first steps. Maybe, after his wife woke up, he'd ask her to rummage around in the closet and find the old cane he used following his knee replacement. He'd look for it himself except he'd probably wake her in the process. If the princess lost her beauty sleep, he'd also be a loser. Besides, after the tension of the previous day she needed all the rest she could get.

As he lounged in the half-light, he remembered a fellow who worked with him at Kerr. What was his name? Harold–Hal– something like that. Damn, it was frustrating not being able to remember names anymore. Anyway, the old guy had an assortment of aches and pains he liked to share with anyone who'd listen. Unfortunately that *anyone* was usually good old George. Hobbling around the office, the guy would complain about his sore back or knee, or his favorite, a stiff neck. Sometimes he'd go into a full rant against the medical profession who always let him down and never made him feel better. While George had a degree of sympathy for people in serious pain, he found it difficult to come forth with even a few crumbs for that guy, especially since Hal's moaning and groaning gave *him* a pain in a certain part of *his* anatomy.

Their connection trudged on for years until the old fart finally packed up all his complaints and retired to Arizona. Along with all his earthly possessions, Hal also took the tired admonition he repeated to George several times a day. "Getting old is no picnic." George groaned. As far as he knew, Hal was still alive and miserable as ever. I wonder who's listening to him now, he thought.

Although he'd always found ways to challenge Hal's complaints, he'd never been upset enough to bring out the show stopper. "If you expect old age to be easy, Hal, don't bother going there."

Despite his annoyance with the man's act, George did gain something of value from the relationship. He used Hal as a sort of negative role model. Remembering how the man had irritated him, he swore he'd never, ever bore others with his own piddly problems. Over time the vow served him well. He never felt avoided or merely tolerated. Moreover, whenever a person let George into his life, he always felt welcome. He was proud of that fact because, in his experience, not many old-timers shared that feeling.

George looked over at Catherine and smiled. Softly, so he wouldn't wake her, he said, "Please shoot me if I ever turn out like Hal."

That was it. Saying *Hal* out loud extracted the old goat's full name from the nether regions of his brain. Hal Robinson. How could he remember so much about him without having his name on the tip of his tongue? He could always recall Kermit Townsend's name from college, and he'd only downed too much beer with him one night and thrown up in an alley. Could it be that one night of dissipation with Kermit was more memorable than a decade with Hal?

Although he was sometimes frustrated by his inability to extract details from his brain, George was elated that all the information he ever needed was stored in there. So, maybe he was a little forgetful. That wasn't so bad. A lot had happened in his life he'd just as soon forget. Nevertheless, having a mind that mostly worked was mighty comforting since it relieved him of his major worry about getting older. Given a choice, he'd take pain any day. To be saddled with Alzheimer's or suffer a stroke and not be able to communicate would be terrible. He just hoped he could continue participating in the lives of those he cared about and never be a burden.

George watched Catherine battle with the light blanket that covered her. It was difficult to judge who was winning. Probably his wife. If he knew her, she wasn't about to let a good fight wake her up at seven AM. Not his Catherine. She had at least another good hour of sleep in her. He tucked away his envy, limped to the closet and struggled into his bathrobe.

By the time he reached the head of the stairs, his foot, rather than being a cause for alarm, had become a minor inconvenience. Since it was most likely a cramp, he'd probably be fine without attempting to compare his pain to the little yellow smiley-faces on the chart in Dr Jabor's office. "Rate your pain on a scale of one to ten, one being a big smile, ten a deep frown," the nurse would say. George was amused at this recollection. It was another reason to avoid a day at the clinic. Why see the doctor when he could conjure up the chart in his mind and make his own analysis? Earlier, he'd been an eight. Now, he was a tolerable two.

With that satisfying information tucked away, the descent to the bottom of the stairs was even less daunting than expected. He entered the kitchen, made a pot of coffee and popped two slices of bread into the toaster. By the time he'd finished breakfast, he'd developed another theory. Unlike other men his age, maybe he was able to tolerate more pain. Throughout his life he'd had his share, beginning with the knee injury in college that robbed him of his athletic skills. This was the same knee he'd faithfully and painfully rehabilitated after it was replaced several years ago. Even the pain of his heart bypass hadn't fazed him, because he was so grateful for the extra years it afforded him. Maybe it was mind over matter. Or, perhaps he was just lucky not to have some excruciating affliction that made life a living hell.

Along the way he'd been taught that there was always a physical reason for pain. Usually it was a warning that his system was experiencing a breakdown. With that in mind, maybe he should be more susceptible to it. Without an early warning system in perfect order, he'd never be alert to all the maladies that could kill him. He reached down and touched his foot. "Don't let me down, foot. If something's really wrong, warn me."

After clearing the table, he rinsed his plate in the sink and placed it in the dishwasher. Then he poured himself another cup of coffee, put on a jacket over his bathrobe and headed for the screened porch. The morning was sunny, but quite cool for October. Without reconsidering, he sat down on the chaise just as he had thousands of times before over the last forty years. He studied the silver maples swaying in the breeze. Their partially yellowed leaves clung tenaciously to the branches. He wasn't sure whether the branches were unwilling to release them or the leaves reluctant to fall, but unlike other years, only a few appeared on his lawn.

He glanced at the two large patches of black earth. After Jim and Rachel Alexander had cleared away the spent foliage last month, the bare plots were all that was left of their garden. Until this past year those plots had contained his own vegetable garden. He'd planted it, weeded it and picked it. In the autumn he'd cleared it, and in the winter he'd studied the seed catalogues to plan the next year's crops. Before he married Catherine, this was the center of his existence.

That all ended last spring with his promise to stop the time-consuming, backbreaking labor so they could spend more time with each other. For a few months, despite some regrets, he'd been able to live with that decision. Separation anxiety aside, he found out the earth still revolved around the sun, and he and Catherine enjoyed the additional time together. In fact, with the exception of the weeds that took root in the fertile soil, their relationship flowered compared to the fallow plots.

Then, Kevin Alexander got thrown from his bike and died.

Days later in the midst of his own bereavement, George tweaked his promise to his wife because Kevin's older brother, Jim, was inconsolable and miserable. Since the boy seemed to be a kindred gardening soul when he helped George during previous summers, George suspected that once the boy again experienced gardening's simple pleasures; hoeing under a hot sun with a summer breeze drying his damp skin, outwitting garden pests of all sorts–animal, insect and weed–and eating the fruits of his efforts, he would be distracted from his sadness. In addition, George hoped the disconsolate teenager would revive his spirit by experiencing the wonder of creating abundance from a small seed nurtured in rich soil. That's when George offered up the healing power of his garden to alleviate the boy's grief.

As it turned out, Jim quickly accepted full responsibility for the two barren patches of ground and turned them into an Eden. Thus, by the time school started in the fall, the boy had emerged from the darkness scarred and saddened, but otherwise functioning well.

George looked out over the barren ground and gave the garden gods their due. Once again they had worked their magic. Yet, their healing power hadn't been restricted to the young man. By guiding Jim, gardening had helped George work through Kevin's death as well.

George pushed himself up and glanced around the grounds. While last year's garden belonged to Jim with a little help from his sister, Rachel, this year because of that promise to Catherine, there wouldn't be one at all. Disappointment clung to him like velcro. Life without a garden sounded like another death knell.

While he shuffled from the chaise toward the door to the kitchen, a couple of crows mocked him. He turned and raised a fist and shook it. His effort didn't have much effect because they continued cawing. However, his reaction kept him from becoming increasingly maudlin. Despite Kevin's death, and despite his own concerns about the length of the path he was traveling, he wasn't going to let the specter of despair blur his vision like a pea soup fog. Catherine needed him. The Alexander's did, too. So did his daughters and step-daughter, Gert. Even his "homeless" friend, Reuben, craved his company. The need to be needed gave his life purpose. For that reason alone it was worth hanging around.

Though he'd never really considered it before, he could only think of one drawback to maintaining all his faculties and living to a ripe old age. He'd have to endure a lot more sadness burying friends and loved ones. That was the singular curse of being the last one standing.

Catherine was looking out the window by the sink in her ratty pink chenille bathrobe when he returned to the kitchen. "You're up early," he said.

"Are you being sarcastic?" She pointed at the wall clock. "It's almost nine."

"I must have been out on the porch a lot longer than I thought." He moved next to her and gave her a kiss on the cheek. "When I first got up, I sat in the chair by your bed and watched you sleep. I felt so much love for you, I wanted to kiss you. However, I guessed you were in the middle of a dream so I didn't want to wake you."

She turned, threw her arms around his neck and leaned into him. He took her by the waist and held her close, not speaking, not kissing her, just holding her tight to him. The moments passed as they embraced until Catherine whispered in his ear. "George, I was just plain cruel to you yesterday. I should have let you come in with me to talk to Dr. DeHaven, and I made that inexcusable remark about Kevin. I'm so sorry. Please forgive me."

His answer carried a message he didn't really feel. "My love knows no bounds, my dear. All's forgiven." They slipped apart, and he led her to the kitchen table where he held a chair for her.

"George, I'm being sincere here. Don't dismiss my apology. I know I hurt you."

He sat down in the chair next to her and reached for her hand. "I felt more helpless than hurt, Catherine, but hurt will do." Then he smiled. "However, I don't want yesterday to spoil today. I have an agenda in my head. First, we discuss your problem rationally, think through your options and make some plans. Then, we'll have some fun. We could go shopping. Maybe buy you a new bathrobe."

"There's nothing wrong with my robe, George."

"Except it's a hand-me-down from your mother."

She laughed. "It isn't, but it could have been. Okay, it would be fun to have a new robe. Then, while we're at it, let's get you a new grey cardigan sweater."

"I like my grey sweater."

"It's full of moth holes, and it's too small."

He pointed an accusing finger at her. "You washed it in hot water and shrunk it."

"I'm sorry about that, but it wasn't wool, and it smelled. I don't think it had been washed in twenty years."

"It was sort of washed when I got caught wearing it in the rain once." He sighed. "When I lived alone, I was kind of a slob."

"I guess you were, but that's not going to happen on my watch. We're getting you a new sweater."

"Whatever you say, Catherine. It's your day."

She tilted her head back inviting his kiss. "Good. Maybe we can find time to cuddle a little?"

"And maybe play some gin rummy," he said accepting her invitation. "To tell the truth, before you began spending all our money on a sweater, I was planning on taking you out for a fancy lunch or dinner and a movie."

"That sounds great."

"Now, it's going to be the senior special at the Mayfair and then home with a DVD. I can't afford a fancy dinner and a sweater, too."

"You're the boss, big spender. Whatever you decide is fine with me. Just so we leave time for some intimacy."

"Well, I guess I can afford that."

George creaked to his feet and began limping toward the coffee pot when he realized his foot no longer pained him. Well, possibly it hurt enough to rate a one on the smiley-face scale, but it certainly didn't hurt enough to be limping or worrying Catherine about it. He retrieved the pot and filled his wife's mug to the top before pouring himself a half cup. Settling in next to her, he said, "Okay, Catherine. It's time to discuss your options." He reconnected his hand with hers. "What are you considering?"

"I've decided I'm going with the needle localization. I'm going to pray there's no cancer at all or it hasn't spread."

"No mastectomy?"

"Not unless it's absolutely necessary. I've become rather attached to my breasts."

He grinned. "I'm sure I'm supposed to come up with a clever response to that comment, but for the life of me, I can't. When are you scheduling the procedure?"

"Unless a phone call won't fit into your plan for the day, I'll get hold of Dr. DeHaven's office this morning. Hopefully they can make an appointment with the radiologist for me some time very soon. This whole thing is really weighing me down."

"You're not the Lone Ranger. My future is tied to your future."

Her hand lingered in his as she pushed away from the table. "I believe you, George."

Glancing at the pink robe heading toward the telephone, he smiled and said, "While you're calling and grabbing some breakfast, I'll get dressed for our outing. That way I can complain about always having to wait for you."

"I'm not always last."

"Yes, you are Catherine, but this time you have a good excuse."

They were driving toward the mall in his gray, ten-year-old Buick. Catherine was decked out in the vibrant red, yellow and blue jacket she'd purchased on their last shopping trip. He also thought her navy slacks were new, but he wasn't sure. There had been so many trips and so many new outfits in the three years since they'd met, he couldn't keep them all straight. Not that he minded the expense. She was tall, thin and beautiful. It only made sense to enhance the endowments God had given her. It was flattering to watch all the old geezers ogle his piece of eye-candy whenever they were out in public. Trailing in the wake of their own faded mates, he sensed their admiration as they tossed him a knowing smile.

Of course, he may have only imagined all this attention, and that was okay, too. It was even possible the young ones viewed them as just another doddering couple to push aside as they raced on to their next task while holding a cell phone up to a multi-pierced ear. Or, maybe the old men with their diminished sight couldn't see, or if they did see, didn't dare compare their aging bundle with his prize. The truth was he really wasn't out to make them feel bad. It just felt good to know Catherine was drop-dead gorgeous, and she was all his.

They were pulling into the lot when he posed a question. "Do you think I'm cheap?"

"Absolutely not. You're very generous."

"Then, why do you sometimes call me a skinflint?"

"It's just a running joke. You're always saying we can't afford things, like a new sweater, when I'm sure we can. Or, you say we have to eat at five o'clock because of the early-bird special. Then, like the other day when you broke a shoestring and said you couldn't afford another." She laughed. "I don't know your finances, George, but I'm sure you can afford new shoestrings."

"I'm German. We don't waste money on nonessentials."

"Like shoestrings?"

"Like sweaters, when I have a perfectly good one to knock around in."

"Don't buy one, then."

"I have to."

"Why?"

"You'll think I'm cheap. I don't want my beautiful wife to think I'm cheap."

Catherine grinned. "In that case after we shop, why don't we eat a late lunch at the Tea Room and then go to a real theater to see a movie?"

He frowned. "Don't push it, Catherine."

George had just pulled into a parking place and turned off the engine when his wife scrunched closer to him and laid her head against his shoulder.

"What's that for," he asked.

"I just love my big, strong, handsome *generous* husband."

"Oh, Lord. I've bred a viper! Now we're eating at the Tea Room and taking in a movie.

CHAPTER THREE

*"Character is developed by suffering the ire
of an enraged spouse."*

On the day following her procedure, George and Catherine were sitting at the small kitchen table. They were finishing up a little late lunch that looked a lot better than it tasted. The home-grown tomato filled with tuna salad, which always tasted so good when they consumed it on the porch in the summer on white bone china plates, hadn't passed muster. The pretty store-bought tomato had all the flavor of fresh cardboard. Plus, when he'd prepared the salad, he'd used too much mayonnaise so it tasted like a grease pit.

To top it off, they were both in a rotten mood because Catherine's daughter, Gert, hadn't answered the phone for two days. In fact, no one had. Catherine had called and left messages, and so had he, yet no one returned them. Several times George offered to call Gert's husband, Roundy, at his company, but she'd said no. "If there was a serious problem, I'd have heard by now."

George groused. "Why does she have to be sick or maimed to call us? Isn't it common courtesy to return calls?"

She nodded. "Yes, but please, George, just give her a chance to call back."

"We have, Catherine. I'm sick of her of playing hard to get. It's time to call Roundy."

"No!"

"What if she's in the hospital? Or, he is?"

"George, give it up. You're making me nervous. Someone would have let us know."

"Sure, like your friend Amy did, when Gert was young. Good god, Catherine. Gert didn't contact you for two whole years."

"Yeah, because she was seventeen, pregnant and had run away from home, and because she had a drunk for a father and a mother who was too self-absorbed to be of any help to her." Catherine glared at him. "You are such a...such a...damn it, George. Why would you bring that up now when I'm worried sick about her. What if she's drinking again?"

"Talk about bringing up the past. She hasn't had a drink in thirty years."

"Don't be flippant, George. Alcoholics can start again anytime."

George sighed. He was losing this irrational battle, and he had no strategy for turning it around. It was a good thing he'd earned his living in manufacturing, because he would have made a terrible general. Plaintively, with a touch of resignation, he said, "Then why is it I can't call Roundy?"

"Because I don't want you to."

Studying his wife, he saw the perspiration glistening on her forehead. A few tiny drops appeared on her upper lip and flushed cheeks. He'd unintentionally gotten her all worked up and knew he should let the subject drop, but he couldn't resist forging on. "Why are you overreacting like this?"

"I'm not overreacting."

"You are, too."

"I'm having a mother's normal reaction to a crisis."

"Catherine, we don't know there's a crisis, because you won't let me call Roundy."

"So, I guess that means there is one until they tell us differently, and I intend to overreact until I'm shown there isn't."

To which he responded with a shrug, "Okay, then!"

George clasped her clammy hand and led her into the living room. He'd thought briefly about sitting on the porch with her until she simmered down, but realized even though it was only mid-

October, it was too chilly without a wrap. Plopping onto the couch, he watched as she found a place at the opposite end. He shook his head. Oh, great. As far away from him as possible. Would he ever understand persons of her gender?

After all, other than Gert, he was her sole support system, and, of all times, he would have thought that now she would want to be one with him and help him understand why he couldn't call Roundy.

George sat back, closed his eyes and decided to let her bring the game to him—a great idea except she'd already quit playing. Within the time it had taken to quell his agitation, her arms had dropped to her sides, her eyes had closed and her sleep snorts had begun. He smiled in disbelief. How could this wonderfully strange and enigmatic woman morph into a lump of spent emotion before his eyes. Once again she'd displayed her uncanny ability to control her stress by dumping it all onto him. Now, he was left with the worrying. Darn woman. She hardly ever caught the stress bug, but she sure was a carrier.

After a brief snooze, George looked over at Catherine to gauge the depth of her sleep. Judging by the regularity of her breathing, it was pretty deep. That left the coast clear to consult his wristwatch. It was two-fifteen, a good time to sneak in a call to Roundy. If he was in town, he should be at the office. Quietly, so as not to disturb her, he rose to his feet and tiptoed toward the phone in the kitchen. Whether Catherine wanted him to call or not, someone had to see what Gert was up to.

He found the number for Gerlach Machine and asked the company operator to connect him with Mr. Gerlach. Instead of his son-in-law's, the next voice he heard was that of Roundy's assistant and George's old friend, Ann Marie.

"How nice to hear your voice again, sir."

Ann Marie was always so formal. Even when he hugged her on his recent trip to the company, she still called him *sir*. "It's George, Ann Marie. Not *sir*. I've never been knighted."

She laughed. "I'm sorry, George. Old habits are hard to break. Your old friend, Mr. Gerlach senior, wanted me to be formal with everyone. His son could care less."

"I think it's the times. Everyone is more casual now. You see a lot fewer coats and ties at church."

"And, in my world," she said. "It's not just the men. Women are even wearing shorts and slacks in our hallowed halls. I don't like it, but it's what it is."

"I never saw a bare belly until after the Korean War, and that was at the beach," George added. "Now, all I have to do is go to the grocery store."

"Formality is definitely out, George."

He chuckled. "Do you suppose we're showing our age, Ann Marie?" In answer to his question, the phone went dead for a moment. "Are you still there Ann Marie?"

"Yes, and I might suggest, Mr. Konert, that commenting on a lady's age in polite conversation is just as inappropriate as it ever was."

"Sorry, I should have said *my* age."

"I was just kidding you, George. I've always liked you too much to be offended." She paused. "Mr. Gerlach is free now. I assume you called to talk with him?"

"Yes, please."

Just before transferring his call, she said, "Come see us again before winter, George. I'm ready for another hug."

"Maybe this afternoon?"

"Oh, George!"

While he waited, he poked his head around the corner to make sure his wife was still sleeping. Though dismayed by his need to make a call to Roundy in secret, he felt better knowing Catherine wasn't going to be the first to hear Roundy's explanation. Perhaps it was a needless fear, but he had a premonition that something was terribly wrong, and if that turned out to be true, he wanted to be the first to know so he could soften the blow for Catherine. Still, the call wasn't fully an unselfish act. Although Gert was his stepdaughter, he loved her right up there with his own daughters, so his need to know she was okay was more than just nosiness.

He took one last look at his slumbering wife and waited for Roundy to pick up. Though hardly aware of it, his foot was tapping to the rhythm of his heartbeat. And the beat seemed to be gaining momentum.

When Roundy answered with a rousing, "Hi there, George. What's on your mind today?" he relaxed. Roundy's tone of voice didn't match the bleak account he'd been anticipating. So instead of dread, he conjured up a picture of the stout, middle-aged executive speaking to him from his unusual stand-up desk in the center of his modernistic office. Funny how our feelings change over time. When the man first began squiring Gert, he'd been leery of him. Since then, he'd grown to respect him to the point of admiration, plus he considered him a good friend. He also suspected the feeling was mutual, and that had a bearing on why he felt comfortable calling him on a personal matter in the middle of a workday.

"I'll just take a second of your time, Roundy. I know you're busy, but..."

"You should never be reluctant to call me. Nothing I do is so important I can't find the time to talk with you or Catherine, and I really mean that, George."

"You've said that before, and that's why I took you at your word and called. Roundy, we're worried about Gert. She's not returning our calls. If she were going out of town, she'd call her mother to let her know. Is she sick or something?" He noted the silence emanating from the other end of the line. "Please tell me she's okay?"

"She's fine, George, really. It's just...." George began tapping his foot again. Roundy tended to interject long pauses into his conversations. The tougher the response, the more verbal squirming. "Excuse me for dancing around the reason. Also, I apologize for leaving you guys hanging. I was home and wanted to return your calls, but I couldn't."

"Couldn't? I don't understand."

"The reason is too childish to admit. I didn't call because Gert told me not to let her mother know what she was up to."

George mumbled, "Those two!"

Roundy said, "I didn't hear you, George."

"I started to say, those two have the strangest relationship. I don't know why they treat each other the way they do. One day they're all hugs and kisses, and the next they're keeping secrets."

"I know."

George lowered his voice. "Certainly, you're not forbidden to tell me?"

"I'm afraid I am."

"I'd be sworn to secrecy. The Brotherhood of Husbands demands it."

"I hadn't thought about that. Moreover, the tenants of the Brotherhood require me to tell you. It's in the oath. *Share thy wife's secret with a brother.* Isn't that the way you remember it?"

"Yes, I believe it is. It's the Second Admonition. Right after *Always have a cold beer in the fridge.* Also, the creed of the Brotherhood states: *Character is developed by suffering the ire of an enraged spouse.*"

"Then by all that is worthy in a man, I choose to proceed."

"I will stick by you to the end," George said solemnly.

"All right, then. Here's the skinny, George. You are aware that Gert has registered with an organization that matches up children with their birth mothers?"

"Yes. She told Catherine and me about it several months ago."

"Well, she was contacted by her son two weeks ago. He lives in St. Louis. She's been there the last few days. I don't know much else other than she's flying back to Cincinnati tomorrow night, and I'm picking her up. I expect to hear all about it on the drive home. If all went well, I assume you and Catherine will get the details soon after that."

"And, if it didn't work out, she'll keep everything to herself."

"That's my guess. I know she wouldn't want Catherine to get all excited over nothing."

"My wife is very good at that." He paused to let Roundy concur in some way, but his polite silence kept the ball in his court. So, George responded with a thank you for filling him in.

"Wild horses couldn't have dragged that information from me, but the Brotherhood...."

"I know," George responded. "What a marvelous organization!"

George carefully hung up the phone, slowly let out a breath and quietly slipped around the corner into the living room. Catherine lay in waiting. She eyed him sharply. "What did Roundy have to say?"

"Roundy? What makes you think I was talking to him?"

"I heard you say his name."

"Oh! Well...ahh...we were just talking about the Bengal game on Sunday."

"George?"

"Yes, Catherine."

"You're full of it."

George remained mum during the grilling. He stayed strong throughout the browbeating and stood firm despite Catherine's array of threats. In fact, it wasn't until his wife's tears flowed like a waterfall that he weakened. Unable to hold out any longer, he gave in and told Catherine where Gert was and what she was doing. After giving up the few details at his disposal, his wife fixed him with a perplexed gaze and said, "Why in the world would you men..."she spat out the word *men* like a cobra strike..."want to keep something that benign from me?"

George shrugged offering no defense. Inasmuch as he'd withstood telling her the part about Gert not wanting her mother to know about her activity, a shrug was the perfect response lest it slip out now. Let the Brotherhood take the rap. He'd learned Gert's whereabouts while protecting the important part of her secret, and that's what counted.

That next evening at the dinner table he and Catherine were enjoying the gourmet chicken casserole they'd prepared together. In addition, the two of them had tossed a lettuce salad with an aromatic vinaigrette dressing. The culmination of their efforts, an apple crisp dessert cooling on the counter, filled the room with a cinnamon fragrance. Surprisingly, the preparation had been performed without incident. Even with Catherine nipping on some Riesling, or maybe because of it, they'd been able to work side by side in the kitchen.

Considering the complexities of the meal and the personalities involved, George admitted this smooth sharing of effort was quite rare. Catherine, as the woman of the house, always assumed *her* kitchen was part of *her* domain and totally under *her* control. He, on the other hand, who brought his new wife to live in *his* house after their wedding sometimes took issue with this arrangement. After all, he'd developed significant cooking skills during his years between wives, and he liked to display them. But, tonight with the wine flowing freely and each bite a delight, there was no backlash from the meal creation. Not only did each savor the results of their perfect creation, both seemed awed by the absence of casualties.

After cleaning up and saving the leftovers, also without incident, they held hands on the way to the living room. Unlike earlier in the day, he let her find a spot first and then once she was comfortable, moved in next to her. From there he proceeded to put his arm around her shoulder and pull her toward him. She responded by kissing him passionately. Suddenly, they were two rabid teenagers in the back seat of a car at a drive-in movie, panting and pawing, intertwined as much as their full stomachs, stretched tendons and aching joints allowed.

Suddenly, Catherine pulled away. "I'm getting a stiff neck, George."

"I know what you mean. Do you think we should continue in the bedroom?"

"Are you up for it?"

"It may be a steep climb for nothing."

"Even though we may not reach the summit, it's never nothing, dear. Let's go for it."

Later, when they were back on the couch playing gin rummy on the cushion between them, George said, "I'm so glad your breast tumor wasn't malignant. What a relief not to have to worry about it."

Catherine placed her cards in her lap and studied him. Finally she said, "What planet do you live on anyway?" His shocked expression served as a catalyst for Catherine to raise her voice. "I thought the doctors made it clear that my tumor was cancerous." When George slowly shook his head, she continued, "Both the radiologist and the gynecologist said there was clear evidence of a malignancy, but they were positive they got it all. You must have misinterpreted that to mean there wasn't any cancer. It hadn't spread because the nodes surrounding my breast were cancer free. That must have been the part you heard."

"I guess that's what I picked up on. I must have mistaken your elation to mean there wasn't a malignancy."

"I like your version better, George. But, I fear we haven't seen the last of my breast cancer."

CHAPTER FOUR

"Unfortunately, you're also not saying anything."

The morning after she returned, Gert popped in on them unannounced. The visit sent a signal to George that the connection with her son had gone well. However, from Gert's conversation, he and his wife would never know it. She was rambling on about everything and anything except what she'd been up to the last few days. Since they'd agreed not to implicate Roundy, neither he nor Catherine could come right out and ask how things went in St. Louis without betraying his trust. Not known for patience, Catherine endured Gert's monologue by sprinkling in a bunch of eye-rolling and a lot of fidgeting. Finally, out of desperation, she suggested they move from the kitchen to the living room so they'd be more comfortable. However, any hope the different venue might encourage Gert to change the subject vanished when she picked up her non-stop soliloquy exactly where she left off.

Now, George joined in Catherine's agitation. He started to interrupt, then coughed, then made a big thing about getting coasters out of the end table for their coffee cups. When this distraction only served as a catalyst for more meaningless words, he plopped back down on the couch and tried a new maneuver. Instead of continuing to feign interest in what she was saying, he began to stare at her. Soon, Catherine picked up on his tactic and did the same, offering no reaction to anything Gert said.

When her self-consciousness finally kicked in, Gert's face reddened, and she began squirming in her chair. "What?" she asked stopping her monologue in mid-sentence.

"Oh, nothing," George said nonchalantly.

"Sorry, I guess I am monopolizing the conversation."

"Yes, dear, you are," her mother said. "Unfortunately, you're also not saying anything."

Gert grinned sheepishly. "Most *old* folks like you wouldn't pick up on that."

Catherine emitted a light hearted groan. "Those are fighting words. Don't ever underestimate me, Gert. I'm not so old I can't discern babble from substance."

George jumped into the fray, although he had trouble keeping a straight face. "That goes for me, too, Gert. I'm quite sure you didn't come clear across town to discuss the weather and ask your mother how to get Roundy's underwear clean. We both have had enough exposure to you to know you have something else on your mind."

His wife followed up the accusation. "You do, don't you, dear?"

Gert smiled. "Actually, I do, but I don't know where to start."

"You might try the beginning," George said.

"That's very good, dear," Catherine said.

"Thank you, sweetheart, I thought it had substance."

Squinting, Gert appraised them. "What's with you two?"

"Nothing, dear. We just want to know what's with you."

Gert didn't begin immediately. She pushed herself up from the couch and began pacing. The action perplexed George. If her experience with her birth son had been all positive, he would have thought she'd launch right into one of her wildly animated speeches or at least some enthusiastic re-enactment of the events of the last few days. But she didn't, and that suggested she had reservations about her experience.

He shared a glance with his wife and read her concern. He also heard her say sarcastically, "I know you've lost a bunch of weight and are proud of your new figure, Gert, but stop modeling and say something!"

"All right. I've been in St. Louis, and I met my son, Todd." Following that admission, she resumed pacing and began a new non-stop account. At Lambert Field, she'd spotted a handsome dark-haired young man just outside of security and knew immediately he was her son. Remarkably, he'd had the same insight, and they'd each waved to one another simultaneously. "When I reached him we embraced, and I cried, and he cried, and then he took my hand, and we walked hand-in-hand all the way down the concourse to retrieve my luggage."

Looking up at her from the couch, George smiled as she described Todd. "He's quite tall and well-built, unmarried and intelligent. He also has a Ph.D. in applied psychology, teaches at Washington University and does research." She then described his large well-appointed apartment, and how he fixed her a great shrimp dish with saffron rice and artichokes. "It was to die for," she said. Then she grinned and added, "We finished the meal with home-made custard fruit tarts and coffee.

"While he was making dinner, he apologized for not serving wine. Can you believe he's also a reformed alcoholic like me? This revelation led to a long discussion, and we talked about everything we'd gone through to resolve our mutual problem. Before we met, I'd been worried about telling him for fear he'd be upset about his heritage, but once we opened up, I think it made it easier to bond. He'd gone through what I'd gone through, and we were in perfect sync." Tears formed in Gert's eyes. "We hugged and cried a lot after that."

With Catherine and George egging her on, Gert described the great meal they ate the next night at a famous Italian restaurant on The Hill where conversation flowed freely, followed by a new musical at the Fox Theater. She then said, "The next afternoon when Todd took me to the airport, he promised to come to Carlisle soon. 'I just have to meet my birth grandmother, Roundy and George,' he said. Before I boarded the plane, he apologized for not introducing me to his adoptive parents. He told me they're wonderful people, but might feel hurt by his searching for me. Also, he was sorry I couldn't meet his partner, Charles, because he was at Johns Hopkins giving a paper."

George rose to his feet and gave Gert a silent but powerful hug. Loosening his hold he smiled and said, "I'm so happy for you, Gert."

They both fixed their gaze on Catherine, who hadn't moved. She said, "That's a lot to take in."

"I know, but he's really a neat guy, Mom," Gert said in a reassuring voice.

"I don't doubt it for a moment. For years I was upset over never having a say about your putting my grandson up for adoption. Now that you've found him, I'm going to love him to pieces."

"Oh, me too, Mom. Me, too."

George smiled. "You two are something else." He gave Gert another squeeze and again sat down on the couch with his wife. After kissing Catherine on the cheek, he asked Gert, "Is Todd a gardener?"

Catherine rolled her eyes. "And here I thought we might get through a whole conversation without the *G* word raising its ugly head. You're obsessed, George."

"All I want to do is relate to the man, Catherine, and see if we have similar interests. Gardening is not one of the seven deadly sins, you know."

Gert rushed in to change the subject. "His research area is the mind-body connection. His specialty is geriatrics."

George grinned. "That will work for starters. He can study me. I'm old, and I have a mind and a body."

Catherine smirked. "Neither of which works very well."

"Maybe that will make me even more interesting to him. What else does he do?"

"He and Charles are ardent fishermen," Gert offered.

Catherine gently nudged him in the ribs. "George fishes. I saw a picture of him sitting on a rock fishing with a cane pole and a bobber."

"I had to be about ten when my father took that picture." He looked up at Gert and shook his head. "I've fished since then. In fact, I used to fish a lot with a guy I worked with at Kerr. The poles and a tackle box are somewhere up in the attic."

Catherine looked perplexed. "How come I've never seen them?"

"I'll get them and prove it to you."

"You don't have to go that far," Catherine said. "I can't imagine you'd fib about something like that."

"I wouldn't. You just haven't seen the fishing stuff because it's back in the post-war section."

"Which war?" Gert asked facetiously.

"I don't remember exactly, but I'm pretty sure I last saw it hanging around the Lava Lamp and the original Chia Pet."

"That would be Vietnam," Catherine said with authority. "I had a Lava Lamp."

He sighed. "I really don't care how old it is, Catherine. I need to find my fishing tackle so I can connect with my brand new step-grandson."

George moved over so Gert could squeeze in between them. She said, "Relax, you two. If Todd's like most ardent fishermen, he'll have enough tackle to supply an army platoon. I can't imagine he won't lend you some of his."

"Good point, Gert," George said. "It makes no sense to be worrying about it now."

Another wifely eye roll. "I guess! You're already going fishing with Todd when you haven't even met him yet!"

George peeked around his stepdaughter and snapped, "Gert is helping this conversation, Catherine. You're just being snippy." Then he reached across Gert's lap and patted his wife's hand. "I'm sorry, I guess I am, too."

Even though the weather was unseasonably crisp for late October, George thought it would be a good idea for the two of them to walk. "We need the exercise, don't you think?" His wife's agreement settled it. Pulling on sweaters, they changed into their walking shoes and slipped into windbreakers. Then, they began fighting the bracing breeze as they walked past the O'Hara's house.

Next door, where the Colemans had lived until recently, some workmen were repairing the siding. His mind rewound and then began playing out his experiences with the former occupants. The first confrontation had involved Brad, their beastly teenager. The second was a scene with Brad's brutish father. Both incidents were the result of the punk raiding George's garden and pulling up all his tomato plants in retribution for his intervening in a disagreement with O'Hara's young son, Shawn. The argument with the father came about when George stormed their fortress and accused the son of performing the terrorist act against his tomatoes. Since Brad was the poster child for all the over-protected, spoiled brats who were never held responsible for any of their misdeeds, George had known even before he left home, the confrontation would be fruitless. Actually, it had gone even worse than expected; so bad, in fact, he returned home angry, frustrated and seeking revenge.

That's when he retaliated. Following his request, George's now deceased farmer friend, Tom Wembly, dumped a load of manure on the Coleman's driveway in the middle of the night. Although his counterattack was extreme, George felt totally justified in his action. In addition, he got a big kick out of surreptitiously watching his hairy nemesis sweating up his undershirt as he worked to rid himself of the offensive smelling pile of waste.

The afterglow of his revenge ended a few months later when Brad and a hoodlum friend of his stole a car and, in an attempt to elude the police, ended a high-speed chase by crashing head-on into a large oak. Both died instantly.

Maybe it was guilt that drove George to the visitation, or sorrow that one so young had to die before he could turn his life around, but, suddenly, most of his animosity toward the parents disappeared. It was plainly obvious to him that like most parents, the Colemans had made some serious mistakes while raising their only son. He also believed their errors weren't made by design, but out of misguided love.

Still, his new understanding didn't drive him to befriend the Colemans or even be neighborly. Before Brad died, he'd often noticed the father puttering around the yard in his undershirt trying to keep the property in good repair. Since Brad's death, the place had fallen into ruin. Not only had the grass grown knee-high, but the weeds competed with the foundation plantings and the paint on the siding showed peel. As a result of what he observed and the fact George hardly ever saw them anymore, he made the assumption the Colemans were choosing to live behind locked doors and windows to keep the memories of their only child from escaping.

Then, one day not too long ago, he noticed the moving van in the driveway as he drove by. The realization that they were moving on forced him to explore his feelings more deeply, and he immediately came to a surprising conclusion. He just didn't care.

George took one last look, grabbed Catherine's hand and plodded on. Judging by the workmen, it was apparent the new neighbors were going to fix the place up. Maybe they'd be more friendly, too. Then, giving one final thought to the Colemans, George dismissed them with the hope they might find solace in a different place far away from him.

He and Catherine rounded the curve and headed down the street past the Alexander's. There was no reason to stop. Mary was working full time now at the accounting office. On one of their earlier jaunts before she'd returned to work, they'd stopped, and Mary had said, "I can't stay in this empty house all day with Kevin gone and Jimmy and Rachel in school. It's too quiet and depressing."

They'd understood, and Catherine had hugged her, and said it was a wise decision. Then not wanting to be left out, he'd said without thinking, as Catherine would remind him later, "If there's anything we can do to help?"

That brought him a hug, and Mary's response, "You've both already helped more than you'll ever know."

After they left, they'd barely made it down the driveway to the sidewalk by the street when his wife began gently chastising him. "What else could Mary say, George?"

"What else could *I* say, Catherine? You tell me. You're the keeper of the words."

"Well, I hate when someone says, 'If there's anything I can do to help.' It seems empty and dismissive. I think if you can't find something that will help, you keep quiet."

He'd let her have the last word that time, although he'd tried like heck to come up with some profound defense on their silent trek home.

Today they walked by Gert's old house. After she married Roundy, she'd sold it to a young couple with a teenage daughter. George still hadn't made an effort to meet them. However, with their doors shut, the shades drawn and no signs of life, he could forget about trying to welcome them to the neighborhood today. Instead, they headed toward the corner where the stop sign beckoned. Then, retracing their steps, they walked past Gert's, the Alexander's and their own house to the cul du sac at the end of the street. They circled it and began a second trek to the stop sign before returning home. "A mile," George insisted, but he'd never actually measured it.

On their second trip around, Catherine said, "I'm so happy for Gert. Not every mother is as pleased as she is after meeting a long lost son for the first time. He sounds very kind and interesting. It also sounds like he has an important job in academia."

"But, aren't you a little surprised...?"

"What? That he's a reformed alcoholic? Not in the least. It runs in families. His mother is one, and his grandfather was one. Booze controlled his grandfather's life because he never had the backbone to admit he had a problem."

"But what about..his...ah...lifestyle?" George asked.

"I don't want to discuss it. He's my grandson, and I'm just thrilled to know I'm going to get to know him after all these years."

"But, Catherine, I'm not judging him for being gay. However, I think you should acknowledge it."

"Mention it again, and I'll murder you in your sleep."

George laughed. "Well, okay then."

CHAPTER FIVE

"Sorry, my mind is on something else."

Several weeks later George broke his tooth chewing on an ice cube. Even though ages ago his first dentist, old Doc Weinstein, had warned him of the damage he could inflict on his teeth, it was a habit he'd had since puberty and wasn't about to break. Why should he? He'd long ago given up most of the other pleasures of that exploratory time. His cave drawings had been obliterated, and his pets, like the wooly mammoth, had long been extinct. Moreover, since ice had been invented during his teenage years, he felt a need to hold on to this one remaining connection. As long as he still found joy in cracking a cube and feeling the chips melt on his tongue, he decided fixing a tooth was a small price to pay.

He held the piece of broken tooth between his thumb and index finger. While it was only a millimeter or so in diameter, the hole left behind by its departure seemed like a vast abyss when he explored it with his tongue. Although he felt no pain, the damage sent him scurrying to his Rolodex to look up the number of his vintage dentist, Dr. Arnold.

When the name appeared with a line drawn through it, he was struck by an unnerving thought. Had Dr. Arnold retired? George seemed to remember the elderly dentist had sold out his practice shortly after his last checkup which happened to be about the time he began courting Catherine. Whew! That was over three years ago. When had he ever gone that long between visits. Still, he did recall an announcement to that effect, and he'd casually tossed the embossed card after noting the successor's name in the back of his brain instead of his address book. A foolish mistake. Now the name was irrecoverable, and one quick trip through the *Yellow Pages* confirmed it. It was time to explore other options.

He could ignore the tooth until it gave him some trouble, or he could drive to Dr. Arnold's office building, take the elevator up to the office and plead emergency to the receptionist. If the dentist was still at that location—a big if—he could probably conjure up some sympathy and a treatment date. But, the problem was pleading an emergency. If he had no pain, where was the emergency? George shook his head. He was not about to resort to a ruse. There had to be a solution that didn't offend his sense of honor.

Suddenly, just as he was about to ignore the darn thing, a whole new approach to the problem came to him. Instead of his trying to find a new dentist, he'd turn to the font of all knowledge in the man who could always come up with a perfect solution. That would be his next door neighbor and legal expert, Mike O'Hara. Mike was the kind of guy who'd buy him a dentist if the price was right.

Of course, he was kidding. O'Hara was his beer drinking buddy. He could always depend on him to tip a couple with him on his porch in the evening, as long as the weather was in the temperate range, and George had some expensive foreign brews stored in his fridge. Sadly, Mike was about the only male friend he had left to occasionally pal around with, and he had one major flaw. He couldn't be talked into learning to play cribbage. For awhile following the death of his farmer buddy, Tom Wembly, George filled the cribbage void with Reuben. But now with each visit he found Reuben's acuity slipping fast. Unfortunately, Catherine was unwilling to learn the game because she enjoyed dominating him at gin rummy. That left O'Hara. If he'd only learn to play, George wouldn't have to give up the game altogether. But, he'd refused, and though George was slightly upset with him for awhile, he realized Mike was the one younger guy who'd drink beer with him and trade insults.

This was a far-cry from how other younger men treated him. Perhaps they were showing their respect for him when they were benignly pleasant. Or, maybe it was their way of honoring the aged, and he should feel flattered. But, he wasn't. He felt patronized. That's why he liked O'Hara so much. His neighbor wasn't afraid to practice his deprecating wit on him. Nor did he mind if George fought back with a few jabs of his own.

Actually, their clashes gave him a glimpse of his younger days when he was pretty darn good at throwing a barb around. At Kerr he was known as the king of caustic comments. The man who could always rise to the occasion with a perfect putdown. That was quite an honor in a workplace that ran rampant with mouthy wannabes. It also meant that everyone in the place saved their best material to throw at him. Sadly, except for O'Hara's efforts, those days were gone forever.

In a way, Catherine also helped keep the tradition alive. She was mouthy and funny. However, she really didn't count. Wives had been trained since birth to improve their husbands. Mothers passed on the skill to daughters who only qualified as wives if they could verbally challenge their spouse with a gotcha. While he appreciated Catherine's efforts, she still wasn't nearly as accomplished as his neighbor. She could be clever on occasion, but her retorts never had much sting. Mike O'Hara knew the drill and reveled in it, and George liked having him stop by to entertain him even if his taste for foreign brews pushed him over his beer budget.

George flipped through the Rolodex again and found the number of O'Hara's law office. If he was available, he'd promise him an extra Becks for the name of his dentist. Then, if Mike was acting in character, the lawyer would call the receptionist for him and play on her sympathies. Somehow he'd finagle an immediate appointment for 'the poor pathetic old man who lived next door to him.' That was Mike's genius. He'd always find a way to get the job done.

The name of his dentist was Dr. Jack Turner. He was relatively new to Carlisle, but O'Hara liked him and thought he was competent. His only concern was his instant popularity and the fullness of his practice. "I'll call and make an appointment for you, but I'm not sure how soon I can get you in. I may have to pull a few strings."

George poured it on. "Oh, would you *really* do all that for *me*? You are so nice to take time out of your busy day to help an old man."

"George?"

"Yes."

"You knew I'd call for you, didn't you?"

"I was hoping." They both laughed. "Maybe it will help if you tell the dentist I won't bother him often, and because of my age, there probably won't be too many future visits."

"I doubt those are good selling points. Let me figure out what to say."

"How about that I'm friendly and talkative?"

"Not worth much with his hand stuck in your mouth."

"I pay my bills on time."

"Now there's something I can work with. It's usually all about the money."

Mike got him the appointment for nine-thirty the next morning. After he thanked him, and Mike informed him that he'd tack the time onto George's next legal bill, George reminded him that he'd be collecting from Catherine because he didn't intend on needing any more legal work until it came time to settle his estate. When Mike didn't have a comeback, George felt the warm glow of victory.

The appointment was a breeze. Since the nerve wasn't exposed, Dr. Turner appraised the damage and ground down the rough edges of the broken tooth. As he finished, he did suggest George make an appointment with the hygienist. "You've gone a long time without x-rays, and your mouth could be cleaner. I think you'd be happier with a little less plaque."

"I'd be happier?"

"Okay. I'd be happier. I like to prevent tooth decay and gum disease."

"I'm with you, Doc. I'll set up the appointment on my way out."

While Dr. Turner was removing his gloves, George pointed at a 9x12 picture of a new baby. "Is that a current picture?"

"Yes. Thanks for asking. That's my son," he said proudly. "He's almost a month old."

"Your first?"

"Oh, yes. Pam and I waited awhile until I established my practice. Plus, she had a great job she was reluctant to give up. Since our son was born, Pam seems completely happy being home with him. We both feel our lives are richer knowing we've added to the continuum; that there will be someone after us to carry on our name and values."

George smiled at the exuberant father and said, "Amen."

Suddenly, an unexpected revelation sent him searching the walls of the cubicle for affirmation. When he saw the familiar face smiling from the picture frame, he asked, "And, that's your wife?"

"Yes, that's Pam."

"I know her."

"Really! She's not from Carlisle. Did you know her from her job?"

"We met at the gynecologist's office."

"Where?"

"It's a long story. I was there with my wife. Anyway, I just want you to know, she was so kind to me at a moment when I was really down. I've never forgotten her. Pamela Turner! I'll be darned. So you're her dentist husband. What a small world."

"I'll tell her I had you in my chair, Mr. Konert." Then he slipped seamlessly into his sales pitch with a wry smile. "And, that you'll be coming back soon to see my hygienist."

George grinned. "I'll be a good boy, just as long as you give Pamela my best wishes."

"Oh, I will. I definitely will."

On the ride home, George considered the enormity of the coincidence that brought him to the husband of the young woman who'd made such a profound impression on him a couple of months earlier. The odds of their reconnecting were so astronomically small, it was downright spooky. *I break a tooth, ask O'Hara about his dentist, get an immediate appointment and voila, the dentist is the husband of the pregnant stranger I sat next to at the only gynecologist's office*

I'd ever entered. That thought set him to wondering about their original encounter. Could that unlikely meeting have involved more than coincidence? Was it significantly more than two momentarily needy people accidently sitting next to each other in a crowded room? What if they had been led there to serve some higher purpose than a mutual anxiety cleansing? And now? Was his needing Dr. Turner destiny calling, or some sign he was supposed to acknowledge? Although George wasn't prone to such whims, the facts seemed too strong to ignore. He felt drawn to see Pamela again.

Once before, when he hadn't heeded his gut instinct and occasionally let Kevin Alexander get off without wearing his bike helmet, the consequences were devastating. Not that he felt any such dire premonitions driving his desire to see Pamela again. He'd liked her the only time he'd met her, and his curiosity was enough. To heck with the metaphysics. He didn't have to rely on cosmic forces for them to reconnect.

By the time he swung the car into the driveway and waited for the overhead door to rise, his mind was made up. He intended to see her again.

Just as he exited the Buick, a concern popped into his head. How was he going to handle the obligatory baby gift one always brought to a new mother? The idea brought on a sudden hot flash. Picking one out was way beyond his meager abilities, and asking Catherine to purchase one for him could subject him to all kinds of questioning. Or ridicule. Or, what? Jealousy? Ha! Didn't he wish! Still, she'd have a field day with the question of why an old goat like him would have a thirty-something young mother on his radar. That would be tough to explain.

After he got out of the car, George carefully navigated his way between it and the garage wall to keep his coat from rubbing against the dirty fender. While he really should take the car in for a wash, it wasn't as high on his agenda as being able to have a sane conversation with Catherine about Pamela and talk her into picking out a baby gift. Entering the kitchen, he examined his long all-weather coat. He found just one small spot of grime which he easily wiped off with his hand.

Since he smelled coffee brewing, he deduced that Catherine was up. She should be. It was near eleven. He spotted her at the kitchen table, poured himself a cup and joined her.

"By the looks of things, you haven't been up too long," he said gently.

"Is that a problem?"

"No. You can sleep as long as you want."

"Do you think?" She pulled her new azure blue robe more tightly around her, flashed a smile and said, "I don't recall the wedding vows saying anything about promising to be an early riser."

He laughed. "That's a good thing, isn't it?"

She rolled her eyes and said. "I don't see the virtue in it, but evidently you do." She raised the coffee cup to her lips and took a sip. When she placed it back on the saucer, she looked up at him and asked, "So, how did it go at the dentist?"

"Fine," he said absently while his mind tried to find a way to work Pamela into the conversation. "And, how did you sleep?"

"Fine," she mimicked him. "Actually, I didn't sleep at all. I was awake all night."

He didn't answer at first, and when he did, he wished he'd kept quiet. "Still, you don't look as bad as you do some mornings."

"That certainly makes me feel better."

"Sorry, my mind is on something else."

"Really! I'm glad you told me, or I'd never have known."

At that point George excused himself to use the bathroom, which was part reality and part cover-up to steal a few minutes to get his own thoughts straight. There was one thing he'd already figured out. This wasn't the best time to discuss his plan for seeing Pamela with a cranky wife made crankier by his actions. What was the point of fighting heavy traffic when he could park behind the locked bathroom door for awhile and hope things would be different later in the day.

CHAPTER SIX

"George cheats, you know!"

George made a decision in the quiet of the bathroom. Today, based on his first contact with Catherine, he determined he lacked the guts to discuss shopping for a baby gift with her. However, he did devise a backup plan to escape the house for awhile. He'd visit Reuben at The Willows. Thus, when he came out of hiding and reconnected with Catherine at the kitchen table, he meekly checked his idea out with her, and she grunted her agreement.

About one-fifteen he found himself rummaging through the closet looking for a nicer pair of slacks to wear for the visit with the now demented old poacher. In the process, he reached over and picked up one of his good black lace-up shoes. These were the ones he always wore with his blue serge suit to fancy occasions, like weddings, banquets, funerals and such. By his reckoning the darn things had to be at least thirty years old, yet the shiny black uppers still looked as new as the day he bought them at the department store in Columbus with his first wife, Grace.

His mistake was turning the shoe over and examining the bottom. The heel was worn round and the sole paper thin. He let out a surprised whistle. Since the wear couldn't have occurred overnight, he tried to remember when he'd last worn them. Had it been Tom Wembly's funeral three years before or another one? He wasn't sure. His own wedding? The answer to that was, no. Catherine had made him rent a pair along with the tux. When had it been then? Surely he'd worn them sometime during the last five years. Or had he? Time sure had a way of flying by when one was old. Shaking his head, he picked up the other shoe and noticed the same degree of wear. Suddenly, a reason came to him. Catherine was sneaking into his closet and wearing his good shoes when he wasn't around. He laughed. On another day when she was in a better mood, he'd have to have words with her.

Meanwhile, he should have the damage fixed. While the wedding invitations were now a mere trickle compared to the past, the funerals were popping up at a furious pace. He just might need them sometime. Of course, he could continue to wear them as they were and hope they'd expire about the same time he did. Since the uppers looked so good no one would ever know that his socks might be soaking up water on a rainy day. Of course, he could buy a new pair. But why? Even taking into consideration the poorer quality of the modern shoe, the curve of the mortality table made it quite clear he'd hardly get the footwear broken in before they'd be sent to the Goodwill along with his other earthly belongings or adorn his feet in the casket for all eternity.

Another option was to wear a pair of his comfortable shoes, like the tan suede loafers or the high-top work shoes. He'd seen lots of old codgers wear non-conforming footwear and get away with it. One guy actually wore his bedroom slippers to a visitation. However, he also remembered hearing the snickers and noticing the sly smiles as the old boy moved out of earshot. No, the slipper solution wasn't for him. He had too much pride to try it.

That left one solution. Take the shoes to old Tony, the Italian man on Front Street, and have them repaired. Over the years he'd always taken his shoes to Tony. His workmanship was first rate and his prices quite reasonable. Only one thing bugged him about going to the man's shop. *Old Tony* was a good fifteen years younger than he was.

Dressed in the same gray slacks and maroon sweater he'd worn to the dentist, George headed down the stairs carrying the shoes. He came across Catherine in the living room. She'd finally moved from the kitchen and was now reading a romance novel. She looked up and smiled. "Where are you going?"

"I'm going to drop these shoes off to be fixed before I play some cribbage with Reuben. As long as I'm out, I could stop at the store on the way home. Have you started a grocery list?"

"Not really. This book is so titillating I hate to put it down."

"Well, I like titillating better than grumpy." The minute the words escaped his mouth, he wanted them back.

However, rather than escalating anything, Catherine smiled. "I'm sorry about earlier, but you must admit, we both have our moments."

"I'll admit it. So, how about this? You read your book, and I'll cook the dinners for the next few nights. You always get stuck with the meal planning and the cooking."

Catherine placed the book in her lap and pleaded, "We could go out."

"We could, but I'd like to cook for you. Maybe put some variety in our meals."

"Frankly, I get kind of bored with what I pick out, too," she said. "So, that sounds fine. And, you'll clean up afterwards, too?"

"Don't I always?"

She rolled her eyes at his ridiculous attempt at a joke.

George left the living room for a moment and returned with a pad of paper and a pencil. "Let's see, I think I'll buy some calf's liver. I haven't had any for ages."

"No organ meat, George. It's not good for your cholesterol."

"Well, okay. My mother used to make fresh tongue. I love tongue."

"You're kidding me?"

"No, I'm not. When I was young we had it at least once a month. The leftovers make great sandwiches. Shall I get one?"

"Not if you want to stay married to me."

"Ring bologna?"

"Ish."

"Spareribs and sour kraut?"

"Nooo."

"City chicken legs?"

"I don't even know what those are." Catherine snapped her book shut, and with George's help, rose to her feet. "Now I know why I plan all the meals."

"Me, too. However, you do not have an adventuresome spirit."

"Maybe not with food. In the areas where I am adventurous, you don't perform like a trapeze artist anymore," she said slyly.

George put on an exaggerated pout. "That hurts, Catherine. Until now, I never realized you and I were so incompatible."

"Not incompatible, George. Incapable of changing. There is a difference."

"I've changed a lot. I gave up my rousing single life to marry you."

"Yeah, you were so-o-o happy."

"That's not the point, Catherine. The point is, I changed."

"All right, I'll show you I can change. Buy a big fat ugly tongue, and I'll cook it for you."

"Do you know how?"

"Now you're missing the point, George. This has nothing to with whether I can cook the darn thing. This has to do with my willingness to change."

"Maybe it shows your willingness to change, but the real point is, if you're going to ruin a perfectly good tongue because you don't know how to cook one, I don't want you to change." He sighed. "Since I can't think of anything different that we'll both want to eat, I'll get some chicken breasts."

"But we have those every week."

"Exactly, Catherine. Because we know how to fix them."

"But, aren't you bored with them? I know I am."

"Yes, I am Catherine, but I would never ask you to change."

That's when she ripped the pad of paper from his hand and said, "I'll go to the store and find something different."

"But, what about your book? I thought it was so good."

"It is good, but it's so steamy it doesn't relate to my life. I'd rather go to the store than sit here and realize my life is devoid of bodice ripping."

George reclaimed the list and laughed. "Catherine, I hate to say it, but you're just too old to read books like that. I'll bring home the chicken breasts later."

After dropping the shoes off on his way to The Willows, George recalled the previous fall when he'd laid eyes on Reuben for the first time. He was sitting on his porch when he spotted the elderly man. With some amusement and some irritation he'd watched as Reuben foraged through his spent garden picking the remnants of his tomato and cucumber crop. At the time he wasn't sure if he was a dangerous lunatic, a drunken marauder or just some old guy who liked to steal vegetables. What he found out when he confronted him was Reuben was a runaway from the best retirement home in Carlisle, The Willows. Forced from his home and into The Willows by his son over concerns for his health and security, Reuben rebelled. He wasn't ready for the regimentation, the planned activities or the safety of his new surroundings. So, he took to the streets for a few days and ended up a scavenger in George's vegetable garden.

Rather than calling the police or even scaring the man off, George had been solicitous of him that day in the garden. The result was a friendship that helped ease Reuben's adjustment into retirement home life and changed George's negative opinion of such places. It also created one of the most rabid cribbage competitions known to man.

Recently, George had begun to worry about his friend. Each successive visit gave evidence that Reuben was crumbling mentally. It started with his cribbage playing. Time and again, he'd make mistakes playing his cards. Sadly, these were not the subtle errors that good players make on occasion. These were elementary errors, stupid mistakes, like putting fives in an opponent's crib that would have embarrassed a competitor like Reuben had he been aware he was making them. To keep the game progressing, George would either correct the mistake in a way Reuben wouldn't perceive or ignore it totally.

Although their competition had deteriorated into a game where George was in effect, playing both hands, there still had to be a winner. They were men, after all, and men, no matter how old or senile, play for the thrill of victory. Knowing this, George would pick a spot to end the game and declare one or the other the winner. When Reuben lost, his sadness was evident by his downcast eyes and pouting lips. However, when he was the announced winner, he'd hoop and holler and taunt his opponent with derisive comments about his poor play. Reuben's behavior did more than amuse George. It challenged him to stay sharp for Reuben's sake. Thus, even though the games were played in this altered state, they still provided the conduit for them to stay connected and his friend to maintain his dignity.

Besides Reuben's deteriorating cribbage skills, George observed him grasping for lost words or thoughts. At other times he'd phase out in the middle of conversations or go off onto long-winded verbal excursions unrelated to reality. Although it was painful to see the dementia eating away at his friend's nobility, George was insistent that burying a friend before he was dead was unconscionable. So, he kept up his periodic visits and continued to treat him as he knew him when they first became acquainted.

When he arrived at the upscale retirement complex that afternoon, one of the three ladies that acted as a receptionist informed him that Reuben had been moved to the assisted living center. George wasn't surprised. He'd be watched more closely there. Since George had visited others in assisted living, he turned down her offer of directions and proceeded to the room number she'd given him. To his surprise, a middle-aged man answered Reuben's door. He was about to apologize for trying to gain access to the wrong room, when he saw his friend through the cracked door sitting on the edge of his bed dangling his legs and talking with a woman.

Since the man wasn't about to let him enter without scrutinizing him for criminal or deviant tendencies, George stood in the hall and waited. With his scowl indelibly in place and suspicion ruling his voice, he said, "I'm Sheldon Goldstein. Who are you?"

George reacted immediately to the guy's accusatory attitude. He didn't like his tone of voice. He didn't like his swarthy looks, and he didn't like being kept out of his friend's room. Even if he was Reuben's son, and with the same last name he probably was, George wished he wasn't there, period. Still, he managed to remain civil.

"I'm Reuben's friend, George Konert. I visit him periodically, and we play cribbage."

The man surveyed him suspiciously before saying, "My father can't play cribbage anymore."

George bristled. "What do you mean, he can't? We play all the time, and he does just fine. He enjoys playing with me."

"I'm his son, I know his brain's shot, and he can't play. You have no business making a fool of him."

While George was thinking, *I'm only aware of one fool here,* Reuben spotted him and hollered, "Hi there, George. Do you want to play cards?"

George took a moment to revel in the look of astonishment on the son's face before waving back and saying, "If you want, Reuben."

"But, Mr. Konert, you're interrupting our visit with my father."

George smiled. "I'm not in a hurry. I can wait until you go."

The woman with Reuben said, "Why don't you come in? My husband is famous for his bad manners."

With that utterance the barricade came down, and he slipped past Sheldon who continued to stand sentinel at the door. George pulled up a chair in front of the bed next to the woman who introduced herself as Sybil, the daughter-in-law. After a few pleasantries with Sybil and Reuben, he relaxed. She appeared to be as sweet and caring as her husband was hostile. He felt relieved. At least his friend had one decent heart in the family.

Imagining the son staring holes in his back, George made an attempt at understanding his antagonistic attitude. If he could find any reason at all, he'd use it to excuse the lout. Perhaps Sheldon couldn't handle the strain and heartbreak of seeing his father lose his personality to dementia. Few people can. Then again, mental afflictions can be extremely embarrassing for those unable to cope with the changes, or terribly scary when uncertainty becomes the norm. Few sons or daughters are capable of handling the transformation from follower to leader and pupil to teacher without a firm grip on their own psyche. How hard it must be to see the man who was your role-model and the object of your admiration regress to a child-like being with a faulty memory. So, if these were the reasons, George could give him a pass.

Glancing over his shoulder at the man, he wondered if any of his made-up excuses were on the mark. Judging by Sheldon's look of disdain and the tightly folded arms across his chest, George realized that maybe the son was just an ornery SOB who wasn't decent to anyone. Didn't Sybil's opening comment to him suggest as much.

When George finally focused on Reuben, he took his eyes off his son and grinned at George. "Can we play cribbage, now?" he asked.

"Maybe some other time," George responded. "You have guests to entertain."

"I don't want to entertain. I want to play cards."

George shrugged. Sybil placed a hand on George's and smiled. "It's okay. Dad doesn't ever want to talk with us."

"I'm sure that's not true. I should go. I can come back another time."

"I think that's a fine idea. Mr. Konert has already overstayed his welcome...."

"Sheldon!"

"I mean it, Sybil. My father doesn't know where he is or how he got here or how to keep his pants dry, so he sure as hell doesn't need some card sharp coming between him and his family."

"Excuse me?" George said. "Are you suggesting I'm somehow taking advantage of your father?"

"Maybe."

Reuben let out a sharp whistle. George glanced at him and saw the agitation and frightened expression. He also noticed the box of cards he was nervously passing back and forth from hand to hand as he sat on the edge of the bed. Then he said petulantly, "I want to play cribbage."

"Dad, you're not going to play cards with this man while Sybil and I are here." Sheldon moved behind George's chair with the intent of having him stand and leave.

"Yes, I will," Reuben yelled. "Tomorrow and the next day and the next day and the next day."

George was on his feet now, caught between wanting to push the man aside and knowing his staying would only make things worse for Reuben. Sheldon had taken George's now vacant chair and was absorbing the abuse Sybil was piling on him. Slipping into his windbreaker, he couldn't wait to evacuate the bizarre scene. He'd taken a few steps toward the door when he heard Sheldon suddenly cry out, "Ouch!" He turned and saw him covering his cheek with his hand. Seduced by the sudden hush, George watched the tableau unfolding before him. Reuben was sitting on the bed with a proud smile covering his face, Sybil looked startled and one bastard of a son was dabbing the corner of his mouth with a Kleenex to staunch a trickle of blood. Near his feet lay the vicious weapon that caused the injury, a boxed deck of playing cards.

George took a few backward steps toward the door pleased by his friend's retaliatory blow. Although he was sure Reuben had no concrete idea why he'd thrown the cards, George preferred thinking it was the result of a father's disapproval of a misbehaving son. While George stood by the door mulling over his conclusion, the son must have come to a similar one. For as he slowly reached down and picked up the box of cards, George could see he was crying.

"I'm not good at any of this, you know," he said with a quavering voice.

Between glances at Reuben and eying the son silently fingering the unusual weapon, George felt his own anger dissipate. In its place came empathy, not so much for the man who'd treated both he and Reuben so badly, but for all the sons and daughters who had to deal with mentally challenged parents.

Before George was out the door, Sheldon jumped to his feet and walked toward him. "I'm sorry for my ghastly behavior, Mr. Konert. My father obviously wants you to stay." Then he added, "I'd like you to stay, too. Maybe then you won't think I'm such a complete jerk."

He agreed to hang around and at Reuben's insistence, they played cribbage. Surprisingly, Sheldon helped his father avoid the mistakes George usually corrected, and Sybil sat behind George and watched so she could learn the game.

They were pegging on third street during the second game when Reuben blurted out, "George cheats, you know!"

George glanced at Sheldon to make sure he wasn't buying into the accusation. Then he answered, "You're my friend, Reuben. I'd never cheat you."

"Yes you do, George. I've seen you switch the cards around so I can win."

George grinned, "Oh! Well, maybe once in awhile."

"All the time. I know when you do it, so I make a big fuss about beating you and brag about how good I am, because I know that makes you happy."

"You sneaky old goat."

Reuben began to laugh. "You can't fool me. I know when you do it. I know when you let me win. You can't fool me."

That's when his son smiled at George and mouthed, *Thank you.*

CHAPTER SEVEN

"Hi, Pamela. This is George Konert."

When he asked Catherine to help him buy a baby gift for Pamela's little boy, she was actually quite reasonable about it. She hadn't protested or questioned him. She was just helpful and understanding. "I can see how you'd want to reconnect with someone who showed such kindness to you. She obviously had a big impact on you that day when I was so stressed out and awful to you. I'd be happy to try to make amends by selecting a gift for the little boy."

"You could also come with me when I see her."

"I don't think so. My presence might be stilting, George. Maybe another time."

So, they'd gone to the department store, and Catherine picked out a little blue outfit with yellow and red trucks on it marked twelve months. "So the baby can grow into it," she said. "Mothers get lots of tiny baby things that they can only use for such a short time. I think it's kind of a waste."

With the word *waste*, George had latched onto the outfit like he'd thought of it himself. He'd carried the bag to the car and into the house, and even put his finger on the ribbon to help Catherine tie the bow after she wrapped the package. Later, after getting the telephone number from information for the Turner's new home, he slipped into his recliner and began practicing his phone conversation with Pamela out loud. *"Hi, Pamela. This is George Konert. You know, the old man who sat next to you at Dr. DeHaven's and gave you some grandfatherly advice. As you probably know from your husband,*

I saw you and your son's pictures at his dental office, so I bought a little present for Timmy and would like to drop by sometime and give it to you. When would be a good time?"

He was in the middle of polishing the third revision when Catherine popped her head around the corner and began listening. When he finished, he asked, "How does it sound?"

"Just fine. When I first heard you mumbling to yourself, I was afraid you'd gone over the edge. But now that I know what you're up to, you suave devil, I'll bet you'll sweep the girl right off her feet."

"That's not the purpose, Catherine. I just want to have a brief visit with her. I remember how busy new mothers are."

"I have one question, George. When you were courting me, did you practice before you called me?"

He laughed. "Heavens no, Catherine. Old ladies are so grateful for male companionship, I could have said almost anything, and you'd have been ecstatic."

With a groan of disgust she abruptly turned her back on him and headed for the kitchen. He shrugged. Apparently his answer did not meet her lofty expectation.

Around four, rested from a short nap and full of confidence, he picked up the phone and tapped out Pamela's number. When she picked up, a baby's crying accompanied her abrupt, "Turner's."

He launched into his prepared approach talk. "Hi, Pamela. This is George Konert...."

"Who?"

"George Konert. You know...."

"No, I don't know any George Konert, I'm busy, and I don't want to take these kinds of calls."

"But...."

"Don't you know I'm on the Do Not Call Registry? Did you check it?"

Plaintively, he said, "Didn't your husband tell you about my visit to his office?" It took a moment for him to realize the silence on the other end was a clue, a clue that his protestations were of scant interest to a dead phone.

George was stunned. Then, mortified. Before he was forced to explain or tell a white lie to his wife about what had just happened, he trudged upstairs to the quiet of the bedroom. Other than the basement, which would have required passing near Catherine on the way, their sleeping emporium was the most remote spot in the house he could think of. Dropping into the soft chair across from the bed, he rested his head against the back and fought back tears.

As he'd aged, tears were a constant companion that could make an appearance at almost any moment. Any heart-rending remembrance could dampen his cheeks, as well as a deep sadness, like Kevin Alexander's death a few months before when his twelve-year-old neighbor crashed his bike and died. That loss was washed in tears because he and Kevin had a relationship that any grandfather would envy, and now it was over. So he'd cried for Kevin, he'd cried for Kevin's family, and he'd cried for himself.

Still, it didn't take deep grief to bring on the rain. Tears had a way of showing up during a tender scene on TV or a poignant spot in a movie. Sometimes they even appeared when a smile or laugh didn't fully express his deepest joy. While he could usually place the source of his tears into recognizable compartments, the liquids that resulted from his call to Pamela were stinging as they escaped his eyes. Since these tears were so different from any he'd recently experienced, they were tough to categorize. Yet, they needed a label, so he named them after his feelings. He called them the tears of a fool.

And, a fool he was. It was ridiculous for him to think a young mother like Pamela would have time for him in her life. Their one conversation at the doctor's office which he'd found so meaningful was probably just an amusement to her. She'd had a choice between worrying about her upcoming delivery, perusing a vintage magazine or talking to the old guy sitting next to her, and she'd chosen him as the lesser of evils. He now realized he'd been reading far more into her friendliness than she'd intended. He was just a blip on her life's screen, a person so insignificant she didn't even remember his name. Oh, what a fool! All those thoughts of imagining her being directed to him, two lives destined to share something of importance, they were just so much hogwash.

Worst of all, he now had to dispose of a dumb baby outfit. If for some odd reason the store wouldn't take it back, he'd have to dump it on some charity. In fact, he could only think of one positive aspect of the whole ordeal. Now he wouldn't have to go ga-ga or "ooh and aah" over the child, who from the picture he'd seen at his father's office, looked just as ordinary as any other new baby he'd ever seen.

In reality, the aborted phone call was probably a good thing. He had enough people in his life without adding Pamela and her baby. What's more, he was actually too busy to visit them.

That brought a pause. What was all this busyness exactly? Since it was almost November, and other than their usual trip to Chicago to visit his daughter, Jill, and her family over Thanksgiving, there wasn't much for him to do. Sure, he could fill the void playing pretend cribbage with Reuben or lose at gin rummy with Catherine. Or, perhaps something around the house might break and he could fix it, or possibly, some distant acquaintance might die of old age, and he could fill an evening and a morning with the visitation and funeral. Whatever way he cut it, he had to be damn lucky to fill the looming void until his Thanksgiving trip to Jill's.

George stretched out his legs and lounged in a near-prone position. He knew before long his back would rebel, and he'd have to get up. Meanwhile, he hoped that by roosting a bit longer he might find something truly positive in the blow Pamela had inflicted upon him. Or, at the very least, he wanted to be able to put a spin on the whole fiasco to make Catherine think what happened was of no consequence.

When he finally pulled himself up from the chair and headed toward the top of the stairs, he repeated out loud, "You may be able to BS others, George, but you can't BS yourself."

Catherine was waiting for him in the hall at the foot of the stairs. "What were you doing up there all that time?"

He hung his head. "Feeling sorry for myself because I'm such a fool."

"I figured it had something to do with your calling Pamela. What happened? Didn't she want to see you?"

"Worse than that. She didn't remember who I was and hung up on me."

She encircled him with her arms and pulled him close. "You must feel terrible. You had a lot of emotion invested in meeting that woman." She took his hand and once they were seated next to each other on the living room couch, George spilled out the aborted conversation with Pamela. When he took a breath, she asked, "Is there something I can do?"

His answer came quickly. "Yes, there is, Catherine. Would you go out to dinner with me tonight? Someplace nice."

"I certainly didn't see that coming. I've got chili cooking on the stove, and I'll have to change clothes. It's already getting close to dinner time. Why tonight?"

"Who knows. Fools are hard to understand." Then his tears returned, and he added, "Catherine, I love you so much."

An hour or so later, they were gussied up and enjoying a spectacular meal with wine and dessert at Alphonso's. Catherine also added insight into his hurt feelings that made the injury disappear. In return, George focused on Catherine, held her hand between courses and left his usual quips and barbs at home. Then, later in bed as he held her close until she fell asleep, he hoped the love they'd shared that evening would always be part of their lives. It also occurred to him that being a fool might not be so bad after all.

The next morning he was down in the basement sorting old paint cans into two piles. Those he knew he might use to touch up some spots, and those he should have thrown out years ago. By comparison to the first pile, the second was enormous. As he worked, he stacked the keepers on the newly found shelf space and began carrying the losers up the stairs and out into the garage to be hauled to the toxic waste site on the south edge of town. On one of his forays when he entered the kitchen from the garage, Catherine handed him the portable phone.

"Who is it?" he asked her.

She just smiled and held out the receiver until he had no option but to take it and say, "Hello?" The voice on the other end startled him. "Hi Mr. Konert. This is Pam Turner, and I am so embarrassed.

When you called yesterday, the baby was crying and I couldn't hear too well, and I had it in my head you were a salesman. I never knew so many salesmen called during the day. I was never home before, so anyway, if I'd known it was you, I'd never have been so rude. Then last night my husband finally told me you were in his office. I could just die. I'm so, so sorry."

"It did sort of ruin my day," he said with a faux chuckle.

"That makes me feel even worse."

"I'm exaggerating," he lied. "But, my wife and I did buy a gift for the baby. That's why I called. I was wondering if there was a time when I could drop it off? I wanted to see the baby and you, of course."

"Gosh, that's certainly nice of you guys. By the way, how is your wife?"

"They found a cancerous tumor, but the doctor thinks they got it all."

"That must be a big relief." There was a pause, then she asked, "Were you thinking of bringing her along, too? I'm sorry, I forgot her name."

"Catherine."

"Yes, I remember now. Any day in late morning works for me. I'm nursing and napping when I can. That's the one time I can be pretty sure we could chat for a few minutes. How about next Tuesday?"

As Pam was talking he grabbed Catherine's attention by waving his arm, pointing at the phone and beginning an elaborate pantomime involving driving a car and going to Pam's house with him. She answered by vehemently shaking her head. "Tuesday's fine for me, but Catherine will take a rain check."

"That's too bad. I'd like to meet her."

"There'll be another time, I hope." George heard crying in the background and said, "You better tend your baby."

"He's hungry all the time, or needs a diaper change." Then she added, "Again, I'm sorry I screwed up yesterday, Mr. Konert. Tuesday seems far away, but the days all run together for me now. I look forward to seeing you again."

"Me, too. But, you will have to explain to me what a 'Do Not Call Registry' is."

"It's Tuesday, then."

"Okay, then as Clint Eastwood said, 'Thanks for making my day.'"

"He didn't say it quite like that, Mr. Konert."

"Well, he should have."

After he'd hung up the phone and before he clomped back down to the basement, George noticed his wife eyeing him. Although she was rolling dough for some still unannounced delicacy, her eyes were definitely on him. In addition, her expression had all the elements of a *cat that swallowed the canary* grin. While he felt a certain foreboding that whatever she was holding back might not mix with the joy he was feeling over the sudden turn of events, he still needed to know what she was thinking.

"So, you're going to the young woman's house after all," she teased.

"Never overstate the obvious, Catherine. You were hanging around through the whole conversation."

She turned toward him and stuck out two puckered lips. "You can kiss me now, because I helped make the whole thing happen."

"You didn't call her?"

"You know I'd never interfere like that."

"I wouldn't have thought you would," he said as he took her into his arms and kissed her, oblivious to the two floured hand prints now residing on the back of his sweater. "You were certainly sweet to me yesterday when I felt so miserable."

"I hate it when you're down on yourself." After wiping the remaining flour from her hands on her apron, she began rubbing the white patches from his sweater. "Don't you want to know how I got you two together?"

He smiled. "I sure do. Tell me."

"I prayed to my spirit guides. I asked that Pamela would figure out her error and have the courage to call you." She grinned. "I also prayed that you would accept her explanation and get over yourself."

George reached out for her and planted another kiss on her. "Thanks, Catherine. Maybe there is something to all that stuff you believe in."

She stopped him with an open hand that eventually found its way to his chest. "Don't misunderstand, George. I just asked my guides to help. I didn't make it happen."

When he returned to the basement to finish up his paint can purge, his mood was high. All he had to do was carry up the throwaways, three or four trips at most. Ten minutes tops. That's when the solitary lawn chair propped against the wall beckoned. Why rush the job when he could bask in the quiet of the empty basement. He unfolded the chair in the middle of the room, plopped into it and began sorting through the unanswered questions that bombarded him.

With all his moaning and groaning about Pam hanging up on him, why hadn't he thought to pray for a reunion with her? Maybe if he'd prayed about how much he wanted to see her instead of being so concerned about his wanting her to want to see him, the painful rejection might never have happened. That led him to a larger question. Why was he so reluctant to pray? He believed in the power of prayer. He believed in God, well, most of the time, although on several occasions he felt he'd been treated shabbily by Him. Otherwise, why would He have taken Grace and young Kevin from him. He could even accept some of those tragedies as part of a plan that brought Catherine to him, and allowed him to help Kevin's brother, Jimmy, get on with his life by working with him in his garden. Still, he wasn't always sure why he was chosen to work through those ordeals. As the guy in *Fiddler on the Roof* said, 'Please God, couldn't you choose someone else once in awhile?' or words to that effect.

His thoughts suddenly shifted to the cancerous tumor the doctor removed from Catherine's breast. While in the eyes of the medical profession, she was cancer free, evidently his wife wasn't completely convinced. On several occasions she'd stated, "We haven't heard the last of my breast cancer." Since he wasn't sure whether the comment reflected an unfounded worry or some inside knowledge from a higher level, he always felt helpless in the wake of her pronouncements. Knowing his first wife died of the disease, Catherine's worries tapped into his fears and left him only hollow words of encouragement to offer her. Now that he knew she'd had some success with her prayer for him even though it was spirit guides, it was time for him to work on her behalf. Maybe if he made a practice of praying for Catherine's well-being, God would make sure she stayed healthy for years to come.

CHAPTER EIGHT

"I'm so glad our lives intersected when they did."

Two things of note happened on Tuesday morning. His older daughter Jill called and invited the entire family to Chicago for Thanksgiving weekend, three weeks hence, and he got lost trying to find Pamela's house. He never got lost in Carlisle, well almost never, except once in awhile when he was exploring, and since his daughter's contacts with him, excluding e-mails, were few and far between, these two events made the morning far more significant than most.

As usual, Jill's invitation was generous and detailed. She'd buy the plane tickets and email the record locator along with the weekend's agenda. Also, someone would pick them up at O'Hare Airport. In the past that someone was usually Carlos, the company limo driver for KTR where Jill had been CFO. While he and Catherine had grown fond of Carlos, George was resigned to not seeing him again. Jill had left her executive position with KTR to join her husband's company, and he doubted their fledgling venture needed nor could afford a driver. Most likely Carlos stayed behind with KTR. Aside from the conjecture about Carlos, one thing was a certainty. If his daughter said they'd be picked up, they'd be picked up, be it Jill, her husband, Curtis, or some total stranger.

In his mind, Pamela Turner and Jill had a lot in common. Each had been a corporate executive, although Jill worked for a large enterprise while Pamela's company was more modest. However, that's where the similarity with Jill ended. As George would find out, when it came to directions, instead of sharing Jill's talent for geographical detail, the young woman had more in common with his younger daughter, Anne, who could get lost in her own driveway. Apparently, neither had enough GPS in their DNA. Moreover, it was his belated recognition of this fact that caused him to become hopelessly lost in the new part of town where she claimed she lived. Unfortunately, while he admitted to being at fault for taking for granted he'd find her house, when he called her from a pay phone for explicit directions, he found out she didn't have the least notion of how to guide him to her.

Fortunately, someone did. The old guy who worked in the gas station/convenience store that housed the pay phone knew most of the streets in Pamela's subdivision and drew a map for him on the back of a small white paper bag. Not only was he pleased the proprietor could help him, but the bag itself reminded him of times past. Had he stopped at almost any other store, that little white bag would have long ago been replaced by plastic.

As a reward for the man's help, George bought two Butterfingers for future consumption and placed them next to the baby gift on the front seat of the Buick. Then, he began following the map. Turn right at the stop sign, follow the curvy street past three intersections. After two short dead-end streets on the right and just before the cul-de-sac, turn left. The street sign should say Carpalia Way. To his amazement, it did. Turning into Pamela's street, all he had to do was find number 3115.

Then he saw the marked mailbox and turned into the driveway. Before exiting the Buick, he glanced and then gaped at the new two-storied, white pillared, red brick edifice. It was a damn mansion!

Except for a few older homes in the upscale section of town down by the river, he never realized Carlisle had such huge places tucked away in its new subdivisions. Rather than studying the impressive architecture, his mind reflected on the cost of building the place. When he built his three-bedroom frame home fifty years before, he'd paid twenty-eight thousand for it. Pamela's monstrosity had to have cost at least twenty or thirty times that. Who had that kind of money? A young business tycoon maybe, or George's MD, but certainly not a new dentist like Dr. Turner. In fact, based on how little the young man charged him for his recently chipped tooth, he wouldn't think the dentist could afford to buy George's own home at today's inflated prices, never mind the one staring him in the face. He shook his head. No, for Jack and Pamela Turner to have built it, someone in one of their families had to have some big time wealth they either bequeathed or gifted them. Or, perhaps the mortgage company had so much excess cash laying around to lend, it just decided to take a chance on a young professional.

Pamela met him at the door with a handshake and dragged him into the foyer. "You're here! Thank goodness! I'm sorry you couldn't find me. We've only lived here three weeks, and I'm terrible with directions. So far, I can get from here to the grocery store and that's about it. Otherwise, I'm temporarily dependent on Jack to take me places."

"It's my fault. I've lived in this town all my life, and I took for granted I'd find you easily." He tapped a finger on his temple. "Quite obviously some of these newer subdivisions have yet to be programmed up here." Sweeping his hand at the opulent front entryway with the huge chandelier hanging from the two story high ceiling, he said, "This is quite a place." Then he smiled at her. "Now that I've found you, it was well worth getting lost."

"You're very nice, Mr Konert. Thank you. By the way, would you be offended if I called you George?"

"Of course not. Along the same vein, I noticed your husband referred to you as Pam. Is that his pet name or is that your preference?"

"It's my choice for friends. However, Pam can sound a little cutesy in a business setting. That's where I'm more comfortable with Pamela."

"I never had that problem. George is George. There's not much you can do with it. Except for my stepdaughter, Gert. She calls me Georgy boy." When she smiled, he kept on. "Now my father, on the other hand, was Adolph Arnold Konert. He went by Arnie and Dolph as well as either of his given names. He was a completely humorless, stuffy old Kraut. However, he did have a saying he used when people were confused by what to call him. He'd say, 'Call me anything you want except don't call me late for dinner.' I never thought it made much sense, but it would bring a chuckle from some people."

He glanced at Pam. To his relief, she still had a grin on her face.

The whole time he was story-telling, as Catherine would call his ramblings, he was studying the young woman standing before him. The pert nose, exuberant smile and sweet voice were exactly the same. So were the deep blue eyes. Reconciling the much narrower Pam in the loose-fitting navy blue blouse with the vivid image of the Pamela he remembered with the large belly, butt and waddle when she walked, was more difficult. Fortunately, the same disheveled blonde hair gave her away. He smiled. Yes, this was the same young woman he remembered from his only other encounter with her.

While they chatted, he followed her into a large, high-ceilinged room. Light streamed through a wall of picture windows overlooking a large expanse of brown earth that he presumed at some future time would be sodded or planted with grass seed. The room smelled of new wood, plaster and paint all blending into what he remembered as *new house smell.* Once, long ago, his house had the same scent, and he loved it.

However, like everything else he'd ever experienced, it was transitory. In many ways there was an analogy between houses and people. *New house smell* was like the sweet smell of a baby's head, even dirty diapers or a tiny whiff of spit-up. Middle-age homes smelled of what the inhabitants cooked and ate unless they were diligent with their room air-fresheners and mouthwash. He smiled, old people, excluding himself of course, smelled just like the houses they lived in, moldy.

"It's a beautiful room, Pam." Although he'd spotted a bassinet against the long bare wall opposite the windows, he preferred focusing on the house rather than exploring the contents of the baby's abode.

She said, "I think it has great potential, but it needs some professional help. I need the time and money to furnish it. Still, I keep telling myself 'Rome wasn't built in a day.' We have a big house, and we just haven't been here long enough to even think about finishing it. One of these days we will."

Then she said the feared B-word, "Would you like to see the baby?"

"Of course," he said disguising his ambivalent feelings. Just then he remembered the package keeping the candy bars company on the front seat of the Buick. "I brought that gift for him and stupidly left it in the car. Maybe I'll go out and get it."

"That's very sweet of you, George, but don't bother about it now. Let's visit Timmy."

The child was stirring slightly as they looked down on him sleeping in the bassinet. "He's going to be hungry shortly, and I'll to have to feed him. We may as well get him up now before he gets fussy." She reached down and carefully picked him up, sliding one of her hands under his head. Then she extended her arms a little so George could peek at his tiny face.

Instead of feeling pressured to come up with something unique to say, to his surprise, he was swept away by the glorious pairing of mother and child. "Beautiful!" he said.

She grinned. "Would you like to hold him?"

She must have read his mind, because that was exactly what he wanted to do. Despite some reluctance about his ability to do so, he wanted to hold that precious gift close to him and coo and nuzzle and do all the silly things adults do in the presence of such perfection.

"I'm not too good at holding. Maybe if I sat down."

"We'll go into the other room. There are two chairs. You can hold him until he's ready to be nursed. Then you can hand him off to me." Although the nursing part caught him off guard, he followed her to a small library where they settled in. At first she helped him cradle the tiny child in his arms, but when doing so became a bit fatiguing, she laid the baby on his lap so he could look down at Timmy and smile while having a totally nonsensical man-to-man conversation with him.

Later, with George's wisdom fully imparted, the little tyke let out an ear-piercing shriek that announced his demand for some milk.

"Oops!" Pam said. "He does that sometimes. I should have warned you. She took the baby from him, and while he busied himself cleaning off his glasses with a handkerchief, she threw a lightweight crocheted blanket over her shoulder and discreetly secreted the child under both her blouse and the covering. She grinned at George. "He'll stay busy for awhile, so now you can slap some more of that grandfatherly wisdom on me." He was about to comply when she frowned and exclaimed, "Oh, dear! I never thought to ask if this would make you uncomfortable. Does it?"

Watching Pam with her child conjured up so many avenues to follow, he just let the words come out. "You won't believe this, but I've never knowingly seen a woman nurse before. Everything I've ever heard tells me it's the best thing to do, though. When my kids were babies, the obstetrician discouraged Grace, that was my first wife, from nursing because she was having trouble with it, so she never did. Then my daughter, Jill, never had kids, and my younger daughter, Anne, couldn't have children for the longest time so they adopted a little girl, Lily, from China."

"Lily! That's a lovely name."

"It fits her perfectly, too. She's almost four now, and I love her to pieces. Then two years ago, Anne had a miracle baby, Gregory George. They called him that for my benefit for a year or so until reality kicked in. They realized that none of his friends would want to repeat a mouthful like that so rather than having them call him, Hey You, Butch or Buzz, they started calling him Greg. It's really for the best, but I'm a little sad not to have another George in the family."

"Maybe he'll have all your good traits. That's better than just a name."

"I hadn't thought of that." George stroked his chin. "Now that I think of it, Anne might have tried to nurse my grandson for a short time, but if she did, I never saw her do it. By the way, they live up in Columbus, so we don't see them too often. My son-in-law, Brett, is also a successful dentist, just like Jack."

"I wonder if they know each other?"

"Brett would be somewhat older than Jack."

"Still, dentists tend to keep track of each other. Who knows." Pam laughed. "I think it's because they're the only ones who have any interest in what they talk about, like mouths, teeth and gums. Pretty boring stuff."

"That brings up an interesting thought. I wonder what proctologists talk about away from work?"

"Mr. Konert!" Her laughing momentarily ruffled the baby so she did some tucking and calming under the protective covering. Then she added, "I guess it could be worse. Jack could be a gynecologist. Or a urologist. I can only imagine what they talk about."

"When I have an appointment, all my urologist talks about is golf."

"I'm sure Jack does that, too. He loves to play."

"He never mentioned golf to me. He must have sensed my dislike for the game. Of course, with his hands and tools in my mouth, I couldn't have responded anyway."

She laughed. "That's why they become dentists. They can lecture without anyone talking back to them."

Since Timmy was still ostensibly sucking away, George felt comfortable slipping the conversation into another topic. "I want to ask you about something you said to me over the phone."

"Oh George, what I said to you was inexcusable. Even the pushiest salesman doesn't deserve the treatment I gave you."

"I wasn't going there. I forgot about it the minute you called me back. However, I was going to make an observation about some of the expressions women use. Like your saying, 'I could just die!'"

"I didn't expect to be taken literally."

"And, you weren't. But what you said is a good example of the kind of graphic phrases that your gender seems to rely on to express feelings when they do something dumb. 'I'm going to kill myself,' or 'I'm going to die,' or similar words. I always assume they aren't serious, but I find those expressions disconcerting nonetheless. We men, on the other hand, are usually more self-deprecating. 'What an idiot!' or 'How dumb can you be!'" He smiled. "And you call us the more violent sex?"

"Wow, I really struck a nerve. I'm sorry. I've never thought about the meaning behind the actual words because they were never used with intent. It does sound awful."

"It was just an observation. Actually, I have a couple of others on my list that are quite funny. Once a really diligent gal at work misplaced some paperwork and said, 'I'm going to fall on a knife.'"

"That's graphic!"

"However, I think the cleverest one I ever heard was spoken by a young neighbor friend of mine when her son did something stupid. She said, 'I should have eaten him when he was young and his bones were soft!'"

Suddenly his smile faded, and George felt his eyes tearing up as it dawned on him the words were Mary's, and the reference was to Kevin. He dabbed at them with a knuckle, but try as he might, he couldn't stop the flow.

Pam threw him a quizzical half-smile. "That was clever," she said, "but not funny enough to bring tears."

"These are tears of sadness, Pam. The boy was my buddy, and he was killed in an accident last spring."

After that they sat in silence while the baby finished dinner. They glanced at each other and smiled occasionally, and all the time George was castigating himself for taking the conversation over a cliff that was now too steep for a return climb. Talk about being stupid. He really liked Pam and enjoyed getting to know her better, but, oh no, he had to douse her with a bucket of gloom. Maybe he should go, or maybe *he* should just fall on a knife.

After Pam burped the baby, she placed the now-sleeping child in George's arms and left the room. Since he was rooted in a chair with arms anyway, the sudden gift of warmth kept him from contemplating leaving. It also made him realize Pam wasn't particularly upset with him. If she were, would she have entrusted him with her child while she was gone from the room?

After a time he heard her voice from another room. "Soup's on, George. It's way past noon, so you may as well join me for lunch."

He looked down at the child and shook his head. If the surprise call to lunch wasn't accompanied by some help, she was going to be eating alone. There was no way he had the agility to rise from the low chair holding her baby. Fortunately, she must have realized his predicament, because before he had to holler for help, she was in the doorway and then rushing toward him with hands outstretched saying, "Here, let me take Timmy from you so you can get up."

By the time he'd risen to his feet, Pam was already headed toward the bassinet in the large sun-filled room. With the baby tucked in, she caught up with him in the hall. Then she grabbed his arm and guided him toward another room. "We're going to eat in the kitchen," she said. "I hope you like corn chowder and brie cheese on crackers."

"They're my favorites," he said, although he wasn't sure he'd ever had either. Then he said, "I didn't expect lunch."

"It's no bother. Friends have been wonderful dropping food off. The soup and cheese are both leftovers."

She led him into the biggest kitchen he'd ever seen outside of the country club where he'd worked as a teenager. At one end of the space was the heart of the kitchen; seemingly endless cupboards on three sides with a refrigerator, two sinks and a built in dishwasher. The top of the center island contained an enormous stove and grill. At the open end where they seemed to be headed, sat a large round wooden table surrounded with comfortable looking chairs. On the table were two place settings of black handled flatware framing two black bowls centered on two larger black and white checkered plates. They rested on bright orange place mats set next to each other about twenty-five degrees apart. George also noticed that the bowls each contained a creamy goo. Another black plate held a small wheel of white cheese next to a plate of round white crackers. If the room weren't so modern and bright, the entire table scene made him think of two ghouls about to share a Halloween meal.

Yet, Halloween was over and his hostess was saying, "Pick your spot and tell me what you want to drink. Lemonade, soda or water."

"Lemonade, please."

When Pam returned with the drinks, he joked, "I'm not sure I can enjoy lunch in such cramped quarters."

"Like everything else, it's way too large, but there's a reason. We're going to fill it with kids."

"You're kidding! I thought you were going to go *one and out* so you could get back to your job."

"I was hanging onto that plan by a thread when I met you. Then, you gave me your grandfatherly advice at exactly the right time, and now I'm planning on fielding a basketball team of Turners."

"Like the Jackson Five?"

"I didn't know they played basketball," she said laughing.

"Michael and Janet were pretty small to be competitive, but they could jump around pretty well."

She patted his arm. "You're a cool guy, George."

"We called it hip in the middle-ages. When I was young, the cool people listened to Guy Lombardo."

"Who's that?"

"Ask your great-grandmother."

"I can't."

"He was a race car driver."

"I don't believe a word you say."

He grinned. "That's very perceptive on your part."

They settled into eating mode, silently sipping the corn chowder and placing bits of cheese onto crackers that quickly found, filled and silenced their mouths. When their bowls were empty, Pam pushed back from the table and said laughing, "Now, back to me."

"Not until I say how much I enjoyed the lunch. Everything was delicious." He nodded. "Now, proceed."

"While we were eating, I was thinking about how a chance meeting with a nice person can change the direction of one's life. Before I met you and had Timmy, I really believed I'd be back at work after my maternity leave. However, I now realize I'm as good at mothering as I ever was at my old job, and it gives me a whole lot more satisfaction. Unlike some families, we don't need my income so the set-up is perfect. I can go through the stages and grow up with my kids. From awestruck New Mother, nursing, cuddling and wondering how I could have produced such a sweet child, I can go on to School Mom, packing lunches, being a room mother and doing homework, and then to Little League Mom and all that involvement. Wow! Every bit of it looks wonderful from here, George."

He looked into her radiant face and caught a glimpse of his daughter, Anne, after adopting Lily and giving birth to Greg. Rather than rebutting a few of Pam's fantasies by reciting some of the frustrations Anne continually encounters raising his grandkids, or bringing up the heartaches some parents suffer when their kid's lives go horribly wrong, he smiled back at her and said, "I'm so glad our lives intersected when they did."

After helping Pam clear the table, they went to check on the sleeping child. Then George remembered the gift and the time. "Old people need their naps and so do new mothers."

"You can't leave yet. I have one more thing to show you." She rummaged through a drawer and returned with a handful of photos. "My father took these over the years," she said as she handed them to him one at a time. "He was a fabulous wildlife photographer. Not only did he take splendid pictures of birds and animals in the wild, but his forte was showing nature interacting with man. There is a lot you can read into his shots. Many actually tell a story."

She was sitting on the arm of his chair now. "See this one with the man holding a huge hawk by the wings? That magnificent creature actually flew through a window of a fishing lodge and was banging his enormous wings against the walls scared to death and trying to get out. The man holding him is a Native American fishing guide. Moments before Dad took the shot, he'd captured the hawk with the help of a large muskie net. You can see that at the moment the flash when off, the bird has his wings fully extended and the guide is holding it away from his body so it can't sink its talons into his arms or face. It must have been quite a struggle. The fishermen rightly assumed the guide's next move would be to take the bird out through the door and let it go. There you can see the guy holding the door ducking out of the way. Anyway, the guide took the hawk outside–there used to be another picture of that, but my dad still must have it–and much to the horror of the fishermen, he quickly broke the huge bird's neck. See, here's a shot of the guide throwing the hawk in the garbage can."

"Good god, that's awful!"

"Terrible!"

"Why would he do that?"

"I really don't know, but the whole scene gave me an idea. Do you know what I want to do, George?"

"Photograph nature like your dad?"

"No, paint it. Use some of his pictures to start with, then find my own subjects."

"Are you an artist?"

"At heart, but I need to develop a lot more skills than I have. The plan is to take some classes while the baby is young and before the others come along. Then, I'll just work during the quiet times on perfecting my craft. What do you think?"

"I think if you want do it, you can and should. I hope I'll be around to see the results."

"I'd better get cracking, then."

"And, I'd better get going," George said. "Catherine will wonder what happened to me."

They walked through the hallway, and she hugged him in the open doorway. Then, instead of sauntering toward the Buick, he stopped and said, "What's this Do Not Call Registry all about?"

She laughed. "All right then." They stood in the hall with the front door open as she explained it to him. "Anyone can place his or her name on a list to keep from being annoyed by unsolicited phone calls at home from sales people pushing their products. They're supposed to consult the list before they call someone."

"I never get those calls anymore. Apparently, I'm so old no one cares whether I buy anything or not."

"Consider yourself lucky, George. Before the Do Not Call Registry, we were bothered every night–bank credit cards, siding salesmen, cell phone companies. The worst were people peddling timeshares. We couldn't eat dinner without one of us having to get up and answer the phone. To have a few moment's peace, we even thought about leaving the phone off the hook, but my husband gets an occasional emergency call so we couldn't even do that. When the Registry became law, and we put our name on it, it was like a miracle. We stopped being bothered."

"I should get my name on that list. I still get a lot of annoying phone calls from organizations asking for donations."

She laughed. "We do, too. However, there's nothing you can do about them but hang up. Charities and political organizations are exempt from the Do Not Call Registry. As long as they call you before nine at night, they can pester you for money all they want."

"That figures," George said. "Certainly, no self-respecting politician would ever cut off his own money supply."

"You got that right, George." Then, as he turned and took the few steps down to the walk, she said, "Don't be a stranger."

"I won't. God willing, I'll be seeing you again."

It wasn't until he'd driven the three block stretch to the corner that he noticed the gift lying on the seat by the Butterfingers.

CHAPTER NINE

"Don't interrupt when your mother and I are talking to you."

George was relaxing in the tipped-back lounge chair and amusing himself by searching for the familiar cracks in the ceiling plaster of the living room. A few months before, he and Catherine had discussed a new paint job to cover them up, and now it seemed they were gone. He knew she hadn't hired a painter to come in while they were gone because he managed the checkbook and hadn't been presented with a bill. Could Catherine have painted over the cracks herself? Certainly she was both capable enough and sneaky enough to do it even when she'd promised not to climb ladders. But, when? They were seldom apart, and he never remembered any paint smell.

Squinting up at the unmarred whiteness, another more sinister thought crept into his consciousness. To respond to it, he gathered himself and stood up. Standing on his tiptoes, he tilted his head back and stared up at the ceiling. From that elevation, the cracks were clearly visible, especially when he turned his head sideways and studied them from the periphery of his eyes. The revelation sent a jolt of fear to his solar plexis. The mysterious disappearance wasn't his wife's doing at all. It was his eyesight that was to blame. Now what was he going to do. Being blind was unthinkable. He sighed. Damn, if living in an old body wasn't just like driving a beater car. One was always going to the shop to get things fixed.

He should call Dr.Martin, his ophthalmologist, at once because it could take months to get in to see him. However, he wanted to talk with Catherine first, and she was next door substituting in

Cheryl O'Hara's bridge club. Anyway, he rationalized, it might not be anything serious. It was probably just some old age thing that could be corrected with stronger lenses. So that was where he left the issue, sort of, as he relaxed back into his chair.

Ever since he'd learned he was going to have an unencumbered afternoon with the house empty, he'd been looking forward to putting the time by himself to good use. He wanted to immerse himself in some much needed reflection. Now, instead of doing what he'd set out to do, he'd end up fussing about his new revelation. For some reason, finding unfilled voids where he could get in touch with his thoughts had become much more difficult since he'd married Catherine. Not that it was her fault. He'd chosen her to fill the void in his heart and rid him of the long empty days of his widower years. However, the problem wasn't the lack of voids. It was his inability to accept a gift of time and nurture it by blocking out the siren calls of trivial time-consumers. Not that going blind was trivial. It was just so blasted annoying.

During his unmarried years he'd listened to other seniors commiserate with each other about always being so busy they never had any free time. Now that this busyness was a proven fact in his own life, it only served to make the claims of his peers more believable. Unfortunately, when he closely observed his own behavior as well as theirs, he couldn't fathom why everyone was so rushed when they were accomplishing so little.

Of course, he knew the answers to that question. He and his fellow travelers placed undue importance on completing minuscule undertakings that in their earlier years they might have ignored altogether. Whole days could be consumed performing meaningless tasks, like sorting paint cans or searching for long lost items that no longer held any relevance except they were lost and needed to be found.

Another space-filler was remembering, and when possible, connecting with the remaining old acquaintances who'd played a role on his march toward eternity. When he ran into these old-timers at visitations and funerals or sometimes the grocery store or mall, he enjoyed reminiscing with them. Then, there were those like

Reuben he'd visit at the retirement home. That was enjoyable, too. Mostly, though, George's connections were through his memories: Mrs. McConnell and her chocolate chip cookies; Cement Head and their altercation at the tavern; and Tom Wembly, his farmer friend, who willed him his roto-tiller. Since these folks and so many other old acquaintances were now dead, George had long ago taken responsibility for keeping alive his connection with those who were still around. Soon enough, they and he would be memories for the living.

After wiping away a sudden tear with his sleeve, George switched his attention from his departed friends to his family. His older daughter, Jill, came to mind first. If he had to find the best word to describe his feelings for her, it would be admiration. Of course, love would fit in there somewhere, because she was a product of his loins and fathers loved their daughters for better or for worse, whether they admired them or not. A case in point was his younger daughter, Anne. Like Jill, loving her was easy. He enjoyed her company and liked how she raised his grandchildren. However, she always seemed to fall a little short of fulfilling her full potential in his eyes. While George tried hard not to rank his girls on their achievements, he did occasionally do just that, even though he knew he shouldn't. In practice, he attempted to keep the ledger balanced, and on his application for the next life, he'd swear his love was equal. However, if God didn't buy it, his plea would be simple. How could he judge both of his daughters equally when Jill was so doggone exceptional?

George glanced at his watch. Catherine wouldn't be back for at least an hour. With his musing list nearly scratched off and his eyes growing weary, a little nap seemed inevitable. Furthermore, since his feet were already resting comfortably on the raised footrest, and his head lay flat against the lowered headrest, he was in the perfect position to have one. Except, he had a few more thoughts to examine; like how would the grandchildren react to him on this visit to Winnetka, and would Curtis' sons, Kyle and Peter, still think he was cool? And what about Anne and Brett? Would the scars of her indiscretion still be visible? And who would fetch Catherine and him from O'Hare Airport?

Slowly, his eyelids closed and the room darkened. Rather than struggle to contrive answers to his questions, he decided to let his subconscious work on them while he dozed. His sleep deepened to a level where even the sound of the front door handle turning passed through his senses without waking him. In fact, it wasn't until he felt a presence hovering over him and the sensation of a kiss on his forehead, that he opened his eyes to view Catherine perched on the arm of the chair with an amused look on her face.

Smiling sheepishly, he said, "I took a little nap."

After deplaning, George and Catherine played guessing games about who would pick them up at the baggage carousel at O'Hare Airport. Catherine, who was the first to step off the escalator, began waving to a figure holding a sign that said, *KONERT.* Rushing ahead, she hollered, "Carlos!" and flung her arms around the young man's neck. Amused by her exuberance, George said to Carlos, "I haven't seen Mrs. Konert this excited since our honeymoon. You certainly bring out the best in her."

Catherine grinned. "It's nice to know someone can."

Carlos freed a hand and offered it to George and said, "Mr. and Mrs. Konert, how wonderful to see you again."

"You too, Carlos," Catherine said. "Since Jill left her job with KTR, we were resigned to not seeing you again."

"It's a long story, but a good one. We'll talk about it once we get on the road. For now, let's get your bags."

From the moment they'd greeted Carlos, George had been attempting to shift his carry-on to his other shoulder. The short muscular driver noticed his struggle and easily lifted the bag to his own. George moaned. "Sometimes when you're older, Carlos, the simplest things become so difficult."

"Thank goodness! Otherwise, what would I do?"

While they were driving north on I-294, George slipped out of his reverie upon hearing Catherine restate her pleasure at seeing

Carlos again. "We really weren't expecting you to pick us up," he said.

"I don't work for KTR anymore either, thanks to Mrs. Axelson."

"Jill got you fired?"

Carlos laughed. "Oh, no, Mr. Konert. I have my own business now, and she helped me get it started."

"Whew! That sounds more like Jill."

"Yeah, first she convinced the person that replaced her at KTR that the company would be better off contracting my limousine services than having all the expenses of owning a limo, paying a salary and providing me with benefits. However, before the new arrangement was struck, she took the time to teach me how to price and market my services, finance my vehicle and keep good financial records. She also called a lot of her business contacts and told them about me. I'm so indebted to her. But, that's not all. When I got too busy and had to turn down rides, she encouraged me to buy another vehicle and line up some part-time drivers to fill in. That's when the bank got concerned and refused to finance a second limo. She solved that crisis, too, by loaning me the money at market rates."

George replied, "Since Jill doesn't make many bad business decisions, I'd say she has a lot of confidence in you, Carlos."

"I think so, too, and I'm greatly complimented." Then, he added laughing, "She also understands how to deal. She knows I'm so grateful for all she's done for me and my family that I'll drop whatever I'm doing to help her...at discounted rates, too."

"Now, that sounds like the Jill I trained for the big, bad world," George said.

"No disrespect, sir, but I'm convinced that persons with Mrs. Axelson's business genius and managerial skills are born with them."

"I can go along with that, Carlos." Then, George chuckled. "So, unless you know something I don't know, I had a little something to do with that, too."

The conversation continued after they turned east off of I-294 and eventually found themselves in the circular drive of the old

Axelson family mansion Curtis inherited. It had been almost a year since they'd last visited the place, strolled the manicured grounds and admired the Tudor architecture. Although his daughter's family had visited Carlisle in the summer, he was anxious to see and talk with her about Carlos' new venture and her part in it as well as her own role in their new family business.

What George didn't know was he'd have to wait until the Friday morning after Thanksgiving for the two of them to have a quiet chat. That was when he learned the full extent of Jill's business acumen, and the friction it was creating between Curtis and her. She and George were sipping coffee in the sun room overlooking the side patio encircled by the neatly trimmed boxwood hedge. The mob of family members had dispersed leaving them alone. Her husband, Curtis, and his two sons, Kyle and Peter, along with George's other son-in-law, Brett, had taken off about a half-hour before to go bowling. The women, with Catherine leading the pack, had left moments before with Anne's two little kids, Lily and Greg, to go department store shopping for post-Thanksgiving bargains.

As for himself, George had opted to sit the morning out mainly because his head was still pounding from the wine, which he seldom drank, and the intensity of the Thanksgiving dinner and accompanying noise. He hoped a quiet morning would rejuvenate him so he could get through the afternoon board games with the boys and a noisy restaurant meal that evening. Jill, for reasons known only to her, stayed behind as well.

Actually, he was glad she'd decided to stay home with him, because he wanted to talk with her. Not that he was nosy, but he'd noticed a few outbreaks of tension between Jill and Curtis the previous day and hoped Jill might want to open up to him. He observed that once, when they were setting the table for dinner, Jill had snapped at her husband, "The knife goes inside the spoon, you dolt." Then later during the meal, Curtis had said sarcastically, "Jill, we've been out of gravy for ten minutes now. Should I ring for the kitchen maid, or are you going to fill up the gravy boat?"

At the time, since each remark had gone unchallenged, no one but George seemed to notice the hostility. Perhaps the general bedlam that accompanied the meal covered up the guerilla war, or more likely George reasoned, if others had noticed, they'd been discreet and kept their observations to themselves. However, he knew entertaining a mob of guests could, on occasion, make any host snap at a spouse. Heck, even without guests, he and Catherine bickered, and they couldn't love each other more. Still, it was strange to see Jill upset, because she was always so cool and in control. Moreover, he'd never seen Curtis show any pique when speaking to his daughter on any previous visits.

He broached the topic directly when she was standing in front of him in the marble-floored sunroom holding a hot cup of coffee. He looked up from his arm chair, smiled and patted his thighs. "Do you want to sit on your old man's lap and tell him all about it?"

The action bloomed an innocent smile. "Tell you about what?"

"I thought you might want to tell me why you and Curtis were snapping at each other yesterday. I've never noticed that before."

She looked down at her cup. "I wish you hadn't noticed it now, Daddy."

"I wouldn't have except it seemed so out of character."

Since she was hovering over him, he glanced around for a better place to continue their conversation. Her eyes followed his to the paisley love seat. Placing her cup on the end table, she proceeded to lend a hand and pull him to his feet.

Once he was situated in the larger space, he patted the seat next to him hoping she'd plant herself there and continue the conversation.

She didn't disappoint. "It's a business thing," she said, "and it's encroaching on our personal life, just as you predicted when I first quit my job to stay home and help Curtis with his company."

"I didn't mean to...."

"Interfere? You didn't. You just wanted to warn me that I might screw up our relationship because I'm so damn success driven."

Noticing her eyes fill with tears, George placed his arm around her and pulled her toward him. Soon, her head lay on his chest, and George heard and felt her sob for the first time in over fifty years. Instantly, every stored image of the brilliant, tough-as-nails, female executive disappeared. His little girl was in trouble, and the revelation left him numb.

While she cried herself out, George let all the questions he wanted to ask die on his lips, whereas moments before he wanted to pepper her with them like buckshot. What had gone wrong? Was the business in trouble? Had she miscalculated her influence on the results of their joint venture?

Instead, she looked up at him and said softly, "You are so wise, Daddy."

"I'm not wise. I'm old. There's a difference."

"No, you're wise because you knew exactly what would happen when I joined Curtis. You said regardless of how successful we became, he might resent my involvement. The business was built on his ideas, it was his sweat and tears that helped it survive, and all his manhood was tied up in its success. In addition, whether the business was doing well or not, his identity came from being the head of it.

"Well, we struggled for awhile until I implemented a few changes and followed those up with a few innovations, and suddenly we were off and running, and the money rolled in and for all intents and purposes I was the leader and Curtis became the sales manager, and our relationship turned to shit. That's business terminology for awful, Daddy."

"I knew it was a golf term. I didn't realize it had a business application." He looked at her down-turned mouth and eyes still red from crying and said, "I'm sorry. This isn't the time for levity."

"It is a time for levity. It's just that nothing's funny." She groaned. "Ironically, one thing is amusing. Here we have a business run by two angry partners living together on this estate. We have a world-wide group of sales reps out selling our product like mad. We don't have to worry about manufacturing or distribution because everything is subbed out, and to top it off, a large reputable venture capital firm just offered us six million for the operation. And, here's the funniest part. Curtis turned them down even though a year ago he couldn't have given the business away."

George said, "Without knowing anything about it, that sounds like a lot of money."

"It is, but Curtis doesn't look at it that way. He sees it as something he's built all by himself, with a little help from me, and he's going to make it bigger."

"Is he right?"

"No. Our success was a fluke, Daddy. All the stars lined up to get us this far, but once other companies figure out what we're doing and how easy it was for us to succeed, we'll have competition, and then, if we can't stay on the cutting edge, we'll die. Technology businesses like this are just one innovation, one patent, one miscalculation away from bankruptcy. We should sell, invest the money, start another business, anything but hold on."

"What if you're wrong?"

"A reality. The very nature of business is making a decision that could turn out wrong. In fact, in this case no matter what I say, I'm wrong. If the business prospers after we sell, I'm wrong. If we keep it and it flops, I'm wrong. Even if we sell and it goes down the tube, I'm wrong because Curtis finally found a job he enjoys, and I sold it out from under him. So you see, I should have listened to you in the first place and not become involved."

George studied his daughter. Once again he marveled at her innate ability to analyze a large problem and sum up all of the alternatives. What paltry advice could he offer her even if she was foolish enough to ask? He grinned. Then he said, "You've got yourself a six million dollar pickle."

"Daddy, you have to help me!"

"I don't know anything about modern day business. Any advice I might give you is suspect."

"Business is people working together for a common cause. You're the experienced one when it comes to people. Help me."

He took a deep breath and let it out slowly. "Okay, let's approach this like your mother would, from the inside out."

"I don't understand."

"Of course, you don't. You're an accountant. Your mother never carried that burden, but she had great analytical skills." Although he seldom consulted her anymore, George looked up toward the ceiling like he did anytime he wanted a chat with his deceased first wife. "Come on, Grace, come through for your older daughter."

"Daddy, this is weird."

"To an accountant, maybe. But, not to me."

He laid his head against the back of the couch and pulled his glasses down so he wasn't looking through his bifocals. "You told me the last time I was here that you were a wealthy woman in your own right. I think I recall you mentioning a variety of investments and a large conservatively managed retirement plan. Does that still hold true?" When she nodded, he continued, "So, if you and Curtis lost his business, would you guys be on welfare or need to turn this place into a B&B to survive?"

"Of course not, Daddy. We'd be fine financially, and we'd both find something challenging to do. That's not an issue. The problem is...."

"Don't interrupt when your mother and I are talking to you. Just answer the questions."

Jill grinned. "Okay."

"Now, let's discuss your relationship with Curtis. You love him very much?"

"Oh, yes, Daddy. Other than this problem of working together which is spilling over, he's so good to me, and we're so compatible, and I love his boys. Yes, I love him very much."

"Six million worth?"

"Well...sure."

"Great. Can you get me a beer? I think my work is done here." He looked up at the ceiling. "Thank you, Grace. I'll be talking with you soon."

"Wait a minute. I don't understand."

"When I do a good job, I'm usually rewarded. Go get me a beer while you think about what I said."

"Wait, you're saying I should just let Curtis run the business into the ground?"

"You said so yourself, it could eventually be worth more."

"Not likely."

"But it could, so give the guy a chance to try. Help him, but let him have his fun and his pride. Maybe he'll come to the conclusion to sell on his own. Treat him like a partner and support him. Don't treat him like an employee."

She wrinkled her brow. George could tell she was having trouble buying his advice, yet her smile told him she wasn't rejecting it either. "But, this is such poor business strategy."

"It's easier to fix a business than find a good husband like Curtis. Money's not everything, kid. Now, are you going to be a good hostess and get your father a beer, or are you going to make him find one on his own?"

She laughed. "I'm going! I'm going!"

A fleeting thought crossed his mind while she was out of the room. Why was it Carlos was so grateful to have Jill help him grow his business, while Curtis bristled at her participation in his? Did it say something about the two men? Maybe Carlos, who started with nothing, and Curtis, who came from wealth, valued success differently. To one, Jill was a lifeline, to the other, a competitor. Or, maybe in the case of Jill and Curtis, friction was bound to occur when two strong-minded spouses tried to work together. Since he suspected the latter, he'd try to butt out of any further discussions.

George and Catherine were driving back to Carlisle from the Cincinnati airport following the family Thanksgiving weekend. Although the plane landed at 5:10, and it was now only an hour later, it was pitch dark except for the smattering of lights along the roadway. As George drove, he listened attentively to his wife's observations and stories from her expedition to several malls with Anne and his grandchildren. While he didn't go into detail about his chat with Jill, he did some bragging about beating Anne's husband, Brett, and Curtis and his teenage boys at UNO and Monopoly after they returned from bowling. Although he'd had a great time hanging out with the "boys," Catherine's enthusiasm for his grandkids made him wish he'd taken more time to hold little Greg and have a big person conversation with Lily. At his age, he needed to make the most of every opportunity to bond with the little ones because they were rapidly growing up, and he was galloping toward the finish line.

The same was true of his adult children. While he'd been able to interact with Jill on a one-on-one basis, he never had an equal chance to sit down with Anne. This oversight bothered him a lot. He should have taken charge of that. After all, it wasn't as if Anne lived next door where he could pop in and chat with her anytime he wanted to. She lived a full two hours away in Columbus. While the road did run both ways between her home and his place in Carlisle, for her to visit him meant bringing the kids and packing all their paraphernalia. Moreover, if the kids missed their naps, they arrived cranky and out of sorts. The same was true when he and Catherine made the trek to Columbus. Without naps they arrived tired and cranky, too.

While his younger daughter actually reminded him a lot of his new friend, Pam, something about that friendship gnawed at his gut. There was no reason he should be investing more in a near stranger than his own flesh and blood. That was wrong. Even though they were continuously busy with activities at Jill's, he certainly should have corralled Anne when they were billeted in the same house. Just knowing he'd blown an opportunity to seek out his younger daughter left a bad taste in his mouth. Next time he'd drag her somewhere to have a quiet talk with him. Next time. Hopefully, there was a next time.

"That Lily," Catherine was saying. "If she doesn't end up doing something exceptional during her lifetime, I'll be surprised. She makes up intriguing little stories that her mother writes down in a book and they both illustrate. Did she read you the one about the giant who grows huge plants with large red fruit that are so big only the giant can carry them? It was quite impressive."

"You know that story was all about her grandpa."

"My, my! Someone else has a wild imagination."

"It's possible, Catherine. I make quite an impression on children."

"That's very true, dear," she agreed. "I always say, it takes a child to really know one."

"I'm proud of my childlike qualities. In reality, I'm a perfect blend of carefree youthfulness and adult power. Youngsters respond to my charm and respect my authority. Did you notice how quickly Greg climbed onto my lap when I motioned him over to the couch?"

"George, you coaxed him with a cookie."

"I wouldn't have had to except I leave nothing to chance."

A vehicle rounded a curve on the two lane road and blinded him with its headlamps. He winced. Lately, whenever he caught a glance of an inconsiderate high-beam or what might only have been the normal beam of a pickup or SUV, he began to have second thoughts about whether he should be the one aiming his car down the highway at night. Whereas a few years before, such flashings annoyed him, now, because of the momentary blindness that resulted, he was beginning to realize that night-driving might be too dangerous to continue. When he finally gets in to see Dr. Martin, he'll ask his opinion. With or without it, he still felt strongly that no prudent person should expose Catherine and himself to this unnecessary risk. With his reflexes slowing, and his eyes needing extra moments to refocus long after the vehicle passed, he should be riding not driving. At his age there were already enough hazzards to kill him and Catherine without adding more.

He glanced at his wife and cringed. Oh, Lord! If he quit driving at night, she'd be his natural successor. While her sight was superior to his, he'd have to invest a lot of hours and patience to help bring her driving skills up to highway standards. Even then he'd have to navigate because Catherine seldom knew where she was. Heck, she could get lost going to the bathroom. All things considered, they'd be more likely to survive a trip with a blind man behind the wheel than his wife.

However, this was not the time to expose Catherine to his concerns. Since they were already halfway to Carlisle and having a good time, why get her worked up?

Rejoining Catherine, he asked, "Since the last time we saw them, didn't Brett seem more settled?"

"Yes, and Anne, too. She seemed unusually devoted to him. The difference was like night and day. Of course, she's always devoted to our grandchildren."

"You know, Catherine, I'm always amazed at how the human soul regenerates. If you give the process time, old wounds heal and damaged relationships can be restored."

She patted his leg. "But, that only happens when the parties involved want to make things right."

He clutched her hand, moved it to his lips and kissed it. "I agree, and I give Brett and Anne a whole lot of credit. They both cared enough to stop blaming and arguing and started loving again."

"Is that a message for us, George?" she asked sweetly.

"I don't believe so, Catherine. Yes, we do bicker periodically, but I can't think of a thing to stop blaming you for."

Before she replied, he heard her laugh. "Well, George, I have some things I might blame you for, but I'm too tired to get into it."

CHAPTER TEN

"I don't want to hear this, Jim."

George's young buddy and neighbor, Jim Alexander, showed up unannounced around ten on Saturday morning. Just seeing the boy standing on his front stoop through the peephole raised the level of his excitement a few notches. What if Jim was about to tell him he was going to accept his business proposition. George had made the offer a few weeks before, and Jim had promised him a response after he talked it over with his mother.

In George's mind, the deal he'd offered was fair. In return for a handsome hourly rate, he'd place the boy in charge of tilling, planting and weeding his backyard garden the following growing season. He knew Jim needed to start saving for college, and if Jim and his mother found the deal as enticing as he hoped, the arrangement would solve his most vexing problem. He couldn't live without his garden and yet, sadly, he was getting too decrepit to do all the back-breaking work. In a way, the boy could be his savior. If the plot were to lay fallow, the spiritual lift he always received from its blooming existence might be lost and that loss just might force him into an early grave.

George laughed. Where did these melodramatic thoughts come from? A garden wasn't a life and death matter. However, not having one signaled change, and he hated change. Deep down he knew he would survive without his garden. He just wasn't so sure he wanted to.

He opened the door. The day was freezing cold even for early December, yet the boy wore a light jacket and jeans. Rather than comment on the skimpiness of his attire, George looked past the gangly youngster to check out his mode of transportation. Now that Jim was driving on a learner's permit, he'd seen him driving past the house several times, although never without Mary, his mother, sitting next to him on the front seat. That was the law and ever since his brother's tragedy, his parents had become sticklers for doing things right.

Today, there was no car and no bike lying on his blacktop drive. Deftly using that information, George determined that the young man must have walked the two blocks from the Alexander house. Jim's action earned George's highest esteem. In an era of overweight, couch potato, computer-addicted teenagers, it showed that he was a throwback to an earlier era. If further proof was needed, Jim also was a thin, physically fit fifteen-year-old with an unfried brain who spoke in understandable sentences full of comprehensible words that George could understand. No wonder he found him so refreshing.

As the boy entered the foyer, George said, "If I'd known you were coming I'd have baked a cake." Judging by Jim's blank expression George realized the old song lyrics had made as much impact on him as if he'd said, "Tippecanoe and Tyler, too." For some reason the famous Whig saying from the 1840's led him to recall Theodore Roosevelt's famous summation of President John Tyler's career, "Tyler was called a mediocre man, but this was unwarranted flattery. He was a politician of monumental littleness." George laughed to himself. What else from his American history classes was locked in his brain straining to come out?

He glanced at Jim. The poor kid had the puzzled look of a person who'd accidentally wandered onto the funny farm. Trying to recover some dignity, George pulled out an appropriate greeting from his selection of hip expressions. "So wuz up? Are you here to discuss your wages for working in my garden next summer?"

There was a pause and a nervous grin. "Not exactly, Mr. Konert. My mom and I are still discussing it."

"I'll raise my offer fifty-cents per hour. How does that sound?"

"It sounds great. I'll tell my mom."

"All right, then," George said, showing some disappointment. "If you're not here about the job, what do you want to talk to me about?"

Jim shuffled his feet and glanced at the floor. "I need to talk to you. We've talked before. It's about women."

The sudden shift in topics caught George by surprise. However, it was a pleasant surprise, so he placed his arm around the boy's shoulder and guided him toward the living room. "You've come to the right place, young man. Do you want me to share all my expertise or just offer you a quick fix?" He ignored the derisive, unwarranted and unappreciated groan that emanated from the kitchen where Catherine was cleaning up after lunch.

"Please keep it simple, Mr. Konert. I'm pretty dumb about girls."

"I understand completely. I have so much experience to share. Actually, Jim, more mature men than you have come to me for advice about the fairer sex." He nodded toward the kitchen. "Perhaps we should take a trip to the basement where we won't be disturbed."

With Jim following close behind, George tiptoed down the hall toward the door to the basement stairs. As he was turning the knob, Catherine said, "If you're going to take the boy down to that dismal basement, at least see if he'd like a soda or hot chocolate or something. I even think there's some cherry pie left–and ice cream."

Since Jim had overheard the offer, George couldn't very well deprive him of his bounty. He led him through the kitchen door to face Catherine. "Do you want some pie?" she asked.

With a dimpled smile, Jim vigorously nodded his head.

"Do you want some ice cream on it? Maybe a soda?" Since the head kept bobbing, she grinned and pushed past George to give Jim a grandmotherly hug.

"Can I help?" George asked, somewhat dismayed by how easily Jim had been distracted from sipping from his font of knowledge.

"No, George. Just sit down with your protege."

George was in the process of glumly pulling out a chair, when Jim asked, "Mr. Konert, aren't I a little old to be a protege?"

George thought for a moment and answered. "No, Jim. You are a young student, trying to learn all you can from a brilliant teacher..." He sighed as he glanced toward Catherine. "...who if he listens carefully will eventually become as wise as his mentor."

"Oh!" Jim said with a straight face.

Since he'd lost the struggle with his wife, George chose silence as she placed a plate holding a large slice of pie with two scoops of vanilla ice cream on top in front of Jim. Then she scooted off and returned with a large glass of cola for him. When she finally finished fussing over the teenager, she playfully nudged George and asked sweetly, "Are you sure I can't get you something, dear?"

He groused. "You're going to give the boy diabetes."

"I don't think a little splurge once in awhile will hurt him. Anyway, look at him. He can handle a few more pounds."

"I'm lean, too, but all that sugar would end up hanging from my middle."

"I assume that means you don't want anything?" she said smugly.

Realizing he'd been trumped by a cunning example of female trickery, the very type of manipulative behavior he intended to warn Jim about, George nodded and meekly waited for the kid to woof down his adversary's treats.

Then, with a flourish intended to render him completely powerless, Catherine marched toward the door to the hall. "All right, men, you'll have to get along without me now. I've some woman's work to do upstairs."

"Thank you, Mrs. Konert," Jim said.

She returned to tousle his hair. "You're welcome anytime, Jim." Then as an apparent afterthought, she added, "Since I'll be awhile, don't bother going down to the basement. Just sit right where you are and have your manly talk."

A few steps into the hallway, she turned again and said, "Now, Jim, make sure you listen carefully to everything Mr. Konert says. He has all the answers about women."

George frowned. "Thank you, Catherine. I'll handle it from here if you don't mind."

Jim finished his treat and then carried his dish and glass to the sink, leaving George to wrestle with how to regain a degree of self-respect after his embarrassing defeat. He began by sitting up straight on the hardback chair and gazing intently at the boy. "So, Jim, how can I help you?"

"Do you remember telling me to check out the cool chick that moved into the house where Mrs. Gerlach used to live? You told me it was a lucky house because that's where you met Mrs. Konert."

Considering the scene with his wife that just played out, he wasn't so sure the house was lucky at all. "Yes, I remember saying that. Last fall I suggested you take a bag of vegetables from the garden to give to the person that answered the door. Did you ever do that?"

"Yeah, Jenny's mother came to the door...."

"Did you already know the girl's name was Jenny?"

"Yeah, I'd checked her out at school a few times. She's got long blonde hair. Anyway, her mom, who's real cool, too, came to the door in her bare feet with her hair wrapped in a towel. I told her my name, gave her the bag and said I lived across and down the street. She took it and said, 'How thoughtful,' and thanked me. I was about to leave when she looked me over and said, 'I think my daughter, Jenny, would like to meet you.' I said, 'sweet.' Then, she called upstairs and told Jenny she had a guest, and I went into the living room to wait for her."

George smiled. "Very clever so far, Jim. It always helps to get to the daughter through the mother."

"I guess. Anyway, before long Jenny came into the living room. She was all dressed up in jeans and a tight top with a little sweater over it and her hair all awesome and smooth. I guess I was gawking at her, because she flashed me her great smile." Jim blushed. "Did I tell you, she has a real cool figure, you know...hot."

"I get the picture, Jim. Even though I'm old, I think I still know what a cool figure looks like. Plus, I've seen her, and she is very attractive."

"Anyway, Mr. Konert, I asked her to go to a movie, and she said, 'Okay.' I didn't tell her it was my first date. My mother even let me drive to impress her."

"You can't drive without an adult in the front seat."

"I know. My mother was there both ways. Jenny rode in the back."

"Oh!"

"We saw a funny movie about a family of girls and how they kept frustrating their father."

"I can relate to that."

"It wasn't Disney or anything, but it wasn't full of sex and violence either. My mom okayed it. I thought it was great."

"I'm impressed. Go on."

"During the movie we held hands, and Jenny kissed me on the cheek." When George didn't react, he continued. "Since then, we study together in Jenny's room or sometimes in our den, and we hold hands, and sometimes she kisses me on the mouth. I really like that."

"Aren't you a little young for that?" George said. "I'm not sure studying in her room is such a great idea, either." However, George's weak nod was all the encouragement Jim needed to continue.

"Last Thursday night Jenny called me and said her parents were out for the evening, and I should come over and study. So, I did."

"Did you tell your mom her parents weren't home?"

Jim hung his head and mumbled something that meant no.

"So, you went over there, and...."

"She met me at the door in her nightgown. I could see right through it."

"For heaven's sake, you didn't have sex did you?"

"Mr. Konert! I'm not even sure how to have sex."

George sighed. "Believe me, at your age, it's easier than you think." He paused for a moment and stared at the startled young man. If he didn't have sex and if the girl hadn't put him in some compromising position, why was Jim seeking his advice? Although at first, he was complimented by the boy wanting to talk with him, he was now wondering why Jim wasn't talking with his dad about such a delicate subject.

George placed the back of his hand on his neck to see if his overreaction had sent his arrhythmia into orbit. When he was sure his heartbeat wasn't going to disintegrate into some spastic dance, and he'd apologized for his outburst, George decided on an intelligent action. "Have you and your father talked about this?" When Jim shook his head, George took up a listening posture and waited for him to move on.

"I told Jenny to go get dressed, or I'd have to go home."

"That's perfect!"

"Yeah, perfect. She hates me. She kicked me out of her house that night, and she wouldn't talk to me whenever I saw her at school on Friday, and she wouldn't sit with me on the school bus. Just perfect! I should have been a man and seen what I could get, but I was chicken."

Suddenly, George had a great thirst and asked Jim to get him a glass of water. That was the difference between Catherine and him. If she wanted to buy some time, she'd get the water and see if Jim wanted some, too. Since he usually thought more clearly in a sitting position, he'd send the kid after the water and hope for the arrival of a quick dose of insight during Jim's brief absence.

With half a glass ingested and the other half held in reserve, he began. "This is a very complicated situation, but we're going to work through it, and I think you'll like the outcome."

"Really?"

"Yes, really." He wanted to go off on an exaggerated "Because I am the all-knowing seer whose answers have been helping MANkind for years," but the problem at hand was too important in Jim's mind for silliness. This was serious business, and to maintain his relationship with Jim, he had to treat it as such. "Let's start by looking at this through Jenny's eyes."

"Okay."

"Do you suppose she'd greet someone she didn't like at the door in her nightgown?"

Jim shook his head. "I know she liked me then. The problem is she doesn't like me now."

"Could it be she's embarrassed by her behavior? She knows she acted like a...like a...well, she didn't behave like a nice girl, and she knows it, and she can't face you."

"If I'd done something other than tell her to get dressed, you know, kissed her or something, she wouldn't be so hurt."

"Maybe not, but you'd probably both still be embarrassed. As it is, at least you did the right thing and should feel proud. It's never wrong to be a gentleman and treat a woman with respect. That's what you did, you know."

"Maybe, except she probably thinks I'm a dork, and all the guys think I'm stupid."

George raised his voice. "If you told any guys about this, you are stupid. That will ruin her reputation as well as yours."

"I didn't, Mr. Konert."

"Good. I can guarantee Jenny didn't say anything to anyone."

George finished off the water and pushed the empty glass toward Jim. Needing a few more moments to summarize what had taken place and move on, he said, "A half glass this time, please."

Jim took the glass and returned with two. His own was filled to the top. During the minute or so while Jim was at the sink, George mused about how unbelievably forward girls were these days.

"Mr. Konert, how can Jenny and I be awesome friends again?"

"I'll answer that with a question. Let's say you had followed up on her obvious invitation and done something you both would have regretted. Could you have remained friends?"

"I don't know. That's why I'm asking you."

"Well, in my opinion, you're both too young to be serious, or go steady or get married...."

At the word married, Jim began to laugh. "We're both fifteen. We can't get married."

"That's exactly my point. If you aren't mature enough to get married, you aren't mature enough to get involved sexually."

"But other guys my age are."

"Maybe they are, or maybe they just say they are. I don't really know or care. They didn't ask me how to continue a friendship with a female. You did."

George finished the water to let his words sink in and encourage Jim to say something. When he didn't, he pushed the glass toward the boy. "More water, please."

The youngster tossed him a perplexed look but dutifully made another round trip to the tap. By the time he returned, George was ready with another question. "You do realize you're way too young to have sex with anyone, don't you?"

"Yeah, I guess."

"I also hope you realize that declining her offer, whatever it might have been, is not the reason she's avoiding you. The truth is, had you acted on impulse, no matter how much you may want to stay friends, the emotional baggage might be too heavy to carry. But, Jim, you didn't act foolishly, so there's no reason you can't still be friends."

"Yes, there is. Jenny won't talk to me."

"This is where you have to trust my experience, Jim. I think all you have to do is stop over and ask her to take a walk with you. Don't call on the phone. Go to her in person. Then, when you're with her, tell her she's the best friend you have, and you want to spend time with her and study with her and sit on the school bus with her. My guess is she'll go for that walk, and you'll be friends again."

"What if you're wrong?"

"Then, I'm wrong. My old boss used to say, 'There are two distinct philosophies for getting along with women, and neither one works.'" George grinned at the recollection.

Jim stared at him and narrowed his eyes.

"There's also an old story I used to tell my salespeople when they were reluctant to make a sales call on a tough purchasing agent. I'd say, 'Before you call on the purchasing agent, remember you've got a big oak door between you and him. He's in his office, and you're on the outside. Now, let's assume you knock on that door, and he opens it, sees it's you and slams it shut in your face. What's different about your position?'"

Jim shrugged.

"'Nothing, I'd tell them. 'He's still in his office, and you're still outside the door.' Jim, you're in the same boat as the salesman. The only way to get back with Jenny is to pound on that thick oak door."

His eyes lit up. "How did you know her door was oak?"

"You've missed the point of the example, Jim." Then, he groaned. "You're putting me on, aren't you?"

Jim kept a straight face for a moment before he broke into a grin. "I know it's not about what the door is made of. It's about making a move."

"Exactly. You need to overcome your fear and attempt to see her. She'll admire you for trying."

"I think I got it." He flashed a smile. "You know a lot about women, Mr. Konert."

"I'm going to level with you, Jim. A novice backyard astronomer knows as much about the universe as any man will ever know about women."

"So, you don't know why Mrs. Konert always gives me a treat when I come over?"

"I have no explanation for anything Mrs. Konert does." Then he smiled. "My guess is, she serves you pie and ice cream because she likes you a lot and wants to show it."

"I like her a lot, too, but I'm sure she isn't as good as you are at man-to-man talks."

"Considering the strength of the competition, Jim, I accept that as a compliment."

After Jim thanked him at the door and began walking toward his house or maybe Jenny's, George trudged up the stairs to see what *woman's work* Catherine was involved in. A search of the bedrooms revealed nothing. Only the open attic door gave a clue to her whereabouts. "Are you up there?" he hollered. "And if so, why?"

"Why don't you come up and see what I've found?"

"The stairs are steep. Can't you tell me?"

When the answer was "no," he struggled up the wooden steps and found his wife in a circle of dim light put out by the single bare bulb hanging from a rafter. She was hovering over a pile of his old fishing tackle that included four poles, a fly rod, a casting rod and two spinning rods. In addition, she'd found his old tackle box, a landing net he used for walleyes and bass and the old boots he used when he fished for catfish from the muddy shore of the local river.

Catherine said, "You told me all this stuff was up here, so I went looking for it. I was really surprised to find it, because I was often up here when we were redecorating before we got married, and I never saw it."

"You're surprised. I'd be shocked if any of it was useable after moldering in the attic since I last fished. That's been at least twenty years."

"Well, you better get it organized and throw out what's no good, because one of these days my new-found grandson is going to invite you to fish. I want you to be ready."

"First of all, Catherine, what makes you think Todd wants to fish with an old man like me?"

"He will. I know it for sure."

"Well, there's no hurry until I know what kind of fishing he does. If he's a fly fisherman, I'd just be in his way. I never was any good at it, and I'm too old to learn. The same with ice fishing. Plus, Catherine, if he were to fish this time of year, he'd probably go to Arkansas, or Louisiana or even someplace real warm, like the Florida Keys. If that were the case, it would take too much effort and far too much money to tag along."

"Well, I don't know anything about fishing, but I have this gut feeling my grandson is going to want to impress you."

"Why? I'm not even related."

"Because Gert loves you, and I'll bet Todd has picked up on that. Believe me, you're going fishing so you need to be ready."

George picked up one of the spinning rods and whipped the tip through the gloomy attic dusk. "This was my favorite." Then he added, "I suppose if he wanted to try Lake Erie in the spring or summer, it might be feasible for me to go."

Tugging on the monofilament line, he wasn't surprised when it broke easily in his hand. "Ten pound test doesn't break like that unless it's rotten."

"So, what are you telling me, George? That you're so particular about your fishing you won't fish with Todd except on your terms? If so, you might as well throw all this junk out."

"No, Catherine, you have it all wrong. I'm saying that since I won't be fishing until spring at the earliest, I have all winter to rejuvenate some of this stuff. Especially, if Jim won't do my garden work for me next summer."

"He hasn't taken you up on your offer yet?"

"Nor my new offer. I'm afraid instead of reading seed catalogues, my only winter project will be refurbishing tackle."

"You better read your catalogues because if I know you, whether Jim helps or not, you'll have a garden."

"I sure wish I had your confidence. At the moment, if Jim doesn't come through, I'm out of options. Rachel is too young, and I'm just too old."

Holding the pole in one hand, he wrapped his other arm around his wife. "But, I'm not too worried, since I believe that living is all about adapting. If fishing with Todd does come to pass and Jim backs out, I'll just fill our bellies with fruits of the sea, instead of feeding us from the earth's bounty."

"I'd be satisfied with fruits from the supermarket. My hope is that fishing is a way to get to know our grandson." She drew away and kissed him. "Still, I'd be super surprised if you didn't find a way to have a garden, because a garden helps you believe in the future."

"That's truly profound, dear. Did you read that somewhere?"

"No, I learned that living with you, and I still believe Jim is going to help you this year."

He kissed her again. "I sure hope you're right."

Giving the fishing rod a few more wristy flicks, George set it down on top of the pile of gear. "Thank you for finding this stuff, Catherine. Whether I ever use it or not, refurbishing it gives me something to do this winter."

She rolled her eyes. "Besides reading seed catalogues?"

He stepped around the pile and took her hand. "Have I ever told you how much I hate winter?"

"Only a few thousand times."

"Well, maybe after I fix this stuff, we'll go somewhere warm and use it, like Florida or South Texas. You could cook what I catch. How does that sound?"

"I'd rather go on a cruise and let the chef cook the fish. In fact, I'll make you a deal. You take me on a cruise, and if Jim doesn't work for you in the spring, I'll help you plant your garden. How does that sound?"

This time he took her in his arms and kissed her passionately. When he let her loose, he said, "I really like the sound of that."

Later, after coming down from the attic, Catherine joined him on the couch in the living room. "By the way, how'd it go with Jim?" she asked. "Apparently his little girlfriend from down the street is real cute."

"You know about her?"

"Gert told me all about her. She says she's a real femme fatale."

"Since I'm his advisor on women, I wish I'd known that."

"With all your female expertise, I assumed you would have realized it the minute Jim started talking to you about her."

Why was it his comments to Catherine always came back to bite him?

The next Saturday Jim stopped over to give George a progress report on Jenny and him. Jim had done exactly as George had suggested and Jenny agreed to take a walk with him. They'd talked and held hands, and they even slipped into the grove of trees around the corner on Blackberry Trail where he kissed her.

"So all my wisdom paid off. You're friends again."

"Yeah, I even told her how much I enjoyed looking at her awesome body through her nightgown."

"You didn't!"

"Yes, I did, and I said if we were older...."

George put his hands over his ears. "I don't want to hear this, Jim."

Jim smirked. "Just kidding, Mr. Konert, and so was the part about kissing her in the woods."

"Whew! You had me going there!"

"I actually kissed her standing on the porch. Really." Then he said, "Oh, and Mr. Konert, I want to be your gardener next summer."

"Really?"

"Yes, really."

He threw his arms around the startled youngster and said, "Oh my, thank you, Jim."

CHAPTER ELEVEN

"Did they get mad when you caught all the fish?"

George was dozing in his easy chair with the newspaper tented on his lap when he heard a loud pounding. Since he was not mired in the depths of unconsciousness, he immediately realized the unwanted racket emanated from the front door. He also quickly deduced that if he wanted it to end, he would have to answer it because Catherine either wasn't nearby or didn't care enough about the noise to get rid of it.

He began unfolding from the chair and creaked to his feet. The banging stopped. Pausing in mid-step, he considered returning to the lounger only to be jarred by a new annoyance, a persistent clanging of the door chimes. Evidently, whoever wanted in had all the patience of a octogenarian on laxatives. Now his curiosity drove him toward the door.

Suddenly, the mystery ended when the door flew open, and he was attacked by a middle-aged, wild-woman in hair curlers who wrapped him in a bear-hug and practically hoisted him off the floor. "He's coming, George. My son, Todd, is coming to visit on Saturday."

"You're squeezing the breath out of me, Gert. Let me loose before I pass out."

"I'm sorry. I'm just excited."

"Really! I'd never have guessed."

She looked past him down the hall into the kitchen. "Where's Mom?"

With a straight face, he said, "I don't know, and, frankly, I don't care. I find it upsetting to take all this physical abuse when you're actually looking for her."

Gert grinned. "Poor, Georgy boy. His life just isn't fair." Then she added, "She must be here somewhere. The garage door is up, and the car's in there."

"That's good. At least she's not out maiming people with the Buick. My guess is she's upstairs in the bathroom."

With George following her, Gert pirouetted to the foot of the stairs and placing her thumb and forefinger in her mouth gave an ear-piercing whistle. She followed that up by yelling, "Are you up there, Mom?"

Seconds later, Catherine appeared at the top of the stairs holding her robe shut with her hand. "Is that you, Gert?"

Good grief, George thought! Who else could it be?

"Todd is coming on Saturday and is staying through Sunday," Gert hollered. "You'll get to meet your grandson!"

"Fabulous!"

Since his stepdaughter was already on the first step, George said, "For heaven's sake, stop yelling, Gert. Go upstairs and talk with her."

She returned his entreaty with a wry smile.

After she'd climbed to the top, George slipped into the kitchen and pulled out a couple of tissues from the box on the counter. Then, just for fun, he tore up the tissue into several pieces, rolled them into two large wads and stuffed them into his ears. While it wasn't his cleverest stunt, he could always count on the women for some reaction. Returning to the living room, he dropped into the lounger and waited with glee for them to descend.

Besides the anticipation of a laugh at the women's expense, George discovered his little joke had a side benefit. It muffled the yakking that tumbled down the stairs and allowed him to muse in peace about his new relative.

By Gert's account, George had been led to believe the young man was The Second Coming. Given her past struggles, this was understandable. Todd's presence represented something tangible, a reward of sorts, for all she'd overcome since her youthful pregnancy. Moreover, now that 'Georgy boy' had been relegated to comic relief, and Roundy's status had been downgraded to that of a mere husband, Todd's showing up was a perfect time to add him to the family circus.

That Catherine had caught the fever from her daughter was no surprise. She still carried a load of guilt whenever she revisited her mothering years. Not unlike a baseball umpire with three blown strike calls, she'd never forgiven herself for her mistakes. Strike one was believing her drunken creep of a husband was a decent father to their oldest daughter. Strike two was letting Gert run free without a mother's guidance and not even being aware of the trouble she'd gotten herself into. Strike three was perhaps the most insidious mistake of all. In spurning Gert, she gravitated toward her younger daughter, Marianne, and showered her with the love and attention she should have dispensed more evenly.

As for himself, from the first moment he heard that Gert was contacting her son, he had only one fervent hope. Whether the kid was rich or poor, brilliant or slow-witted, interesting or a bore, the important thing was he'd be considerate of his mother and wouldn't hurt her in any way. To date, his wish had been granted, and he felt secure in that knowledge.

While Gert's over-the-top reaction didn't surprise him, Catherine's did. Although she hadn't even met Todd, she was almost as giddy as Gert. Considering her delight, it was possible it might have come from observing Gert's joy. Still, knowing his wife, he was sure there had to be more to it than that. After tossing around a few ideas, he concluded that she was just plain infatuated with the concept of meeting an adult grandchild for the first time.

By comparison, his own enthusiasm for Todd was more subdued. While it would be nice if he and the young man got along and a bonus if they really liked each other, their relationship was more or less inconsequential. The more important part of the equation was how Todd and the women felt about each other.

There was one thing about the whole situation that especially amused and at times irritated him. It was Gert's fear, voiced by

Catherine, that somehow because Todd was gay, George might make an ass of himself. He'd been able to ignore Catherine's empty warnings and threats because they had no substance. However, her unwillingness to let him express any ambivalent feelings was annoying. What did she fear? That he was some crotchety old homophobic who might somehow offend her grandson? First of all, he wasn't, and second, he wouldn't, and furthermore, her attitude seemed to indicate she might not be as settled on the subject as she'd like him to think she was.

With no apparent threat of an interruption from the upstairs maidens, George hunkered down into his lounger to further explore his own feelings about Todd being gay. To start with, he admitted to knowing a bit about some of the stereotypes, but little if anything about any particular gay man. In truth, he'd lived in the dark a long time without a cat of that persuasion crossing his path. So, this was as good a time as any to have the experience. Not only was Todd Gert's son, but from all accounts, he was intelligent, apparently caring and a willing conversationalist. Plus, he worked as a researcher at Washington University in the area of geriatrics. That was fortuitous. George was old and actively conducting his own research on a day-to-day basis. By verbalizing his own experiences, George could probably give Todd first-hand insights into what physical and emotional battles an oldster has to fight. Maybe by combining their efforts, he might help the young man become a geriatric guru of sorts. That was an enticing fantasy.

So, why was his wife bugging him? She had to be delusional to worry about his embarrassing her or himself. Why would he harbor any strong opinions about another man's sexuality when at the age of eighty-one and taking a beta blocker, his own libido was decidedly stalled?

About thirty minutes later, after Catherine and her daughter had apparently talked themselves out, Gert came skipping down the stairs. From his lounge chair George watched her approach. To her credit, instead of ragging him about the tissue sprouting from his ears or commenting on the idiocy of his outlandish stunt, she remained closed-mouthed. Silenced by her silence, he sheepishly smiled up at her. Then her *coup de grace.* She bent down, kissed him on the forehead and backed out of the room without saying a word. At the edge of the hallway, she gave a little wave with her fingers and slipped out the door.

Later, when Catherine came down, she rooted herself in the chair opposite him. He waited for her to voice her first command so he could pretend his earplugs kept him from hearing. She didn't disappoint. After a few moments of quiet, she raised her voice a few decibels to a level that could penetrate a concrete block wall and said, "Take those silly papers out of your ears. We need to talk."

However, he wasn't ready to give up the game. "What did you say?"

"You know as well as I do we need to talk about Todd."

"Why?"

He said it with enough innocence to trap her into responding. "George, you can be such a pain in the you know what!"

With that, he pulled the plugs from his ears and replied, "Why talk about Todd? You have nothing to fear from me, Catherine. That is, unless your grandson turns out to be a despicable character who treats you or Gert poorly. In that case he and I will be at odds. If not, we'll get along fine. Now, you might ask, 'Will you still feel the same if he doesn't like you?' Well, Catherine, that is the remotest of all possibilities. Everyone likes me."

She gave him an exasperated look.

"You know that's true. I'm friendly with everyone from the young to the senile."

"Well, then how do you explain your feud with the Colemans?"

"Their son ripped up my tomato plants, for gosh sakes. Why would I want to get along with them?"

She looked at him quizzically. "You *do* know Todd is gay?"

"I don't live under a rock, Catherine. Of course I do, and I don't have any problem with it. Unless...."

"Good. End of discussion." She pulled herself up from the chair. "I'll start dinner."

"Hang on a second. I'm not finished. Unless he turns out to be militant. I've butted heads with quite a few union guys who picketed my company to further their ends at the expense of everyone else. I've also watched people march on TV attempting to force their agenda down the rest of our throats. My feeling is ideologues make lousy friends."

"So, you're planning on not liking Todd?"

"Did I say that?"

"You intimated it."

George shook his head. "I never did. I've never looked askance at anyone because he was different from me. Unless...."

"I don't think Todd's a marcher," Catherine said in a tone filled more with doubt than authority.

"We'll find out, won't we."

She nodded.

"If he chooses to be some kind of symbol, he's all yours. If not, he and I will get along just fine."

"That's so self-righteous," she complained. "Todd's my flesh and blood grandson. I want you to love him to death."

"I probably will, but what I don't understand is why you're trying so hard to love Todd when you already have flesh and blood grandchildren in Seattle. I don't notice you straining to love Peter or Nicole."

Tears formed and her voice quaked as she moaned, "Oh! What a terrible thing to say! You know my relationship with my daughter, Marianne, has become compromised over the years. I don't feel like I'm a part of their lives anymore. Plus, they live so far away."

"I know all your excuses, but we could travel to see them anytime. They're neat people, and Nicole and Peter are definitely your grandkids."

"What does that mean?"

"Nothing. I guess I still don't see why Todd has ascended to godlike status at their expense. He's probably a good guy, but you've never even met him."

She wiped away the tears with a tissue. "I only know Todd is Gert's son and the grandchild I never expected to see. This is a wonderfully different experience for me."

"I'll take your word for it. Just so you're not overcompensating."

Seeing a brush fire of emotion breaking out further, he added, "Honestly, Catherine, I will not ruin anything. I know this is a big moment for you and Gert, and I will honor it."

"Sometimes I hate you," she said as she ran off to the kitchen.

Once again George wished he'd kept his unsolicited editorial to himself.

Todd arrived in Carlisle sometime Saturday morning. George assumed that by the time he and Catherine showed up at Gert's home about four, the visit and bonding between mother and son had gone well, and that Roundy had been brought into the fold. Thus, while Catherine and Todd were intertwined in an embrace that exceeded the normal time limits, George glanced past them toward Roundy. Gert's husband answered his unasked question with an upturned thumb, and the positive opinion bolstered George's outlook before his turn came to meet the husky young man. He thrust out his right hand and said, "I'm George. It's nice to meet you, Todd."

With a strong grip, Todd grabbed his hand and shook it with enthusiasm. "You're exactly as I pictured you from my mother's description, Mr. Konert. I'm looking forward to getting to know you."

George grinned. "Then you'll have to get past the 'Mr. Konert' thing. From now on, I'm George, okay?"

"You got it! George."

He laughed. "Perfect. You're trainable." Then, attempting to sound as sincere as he felt, he added, "We're going to get along just fine."

With his words matching his music and the young man smiling at him, George knew instinctively their strong beginning boded well for a solid relationship. That possibility sure as heck should make the women happy. Rather than an ordeal to be endured, Todd's visit might even be an event to be savored.

The four of them were in the middle of dinner, each talking loudly and often without any concern about interrupting one another in mid-speech. George was amazed. All this social interaction had erupted without the aide of the forbidden elixir used by most hosts to loosen tongues. Perhaps it was Gert's delightful dinner presentation consisting of a Waldorf salad and a delicious chicken and rice curry casserole that kept their spirits high. Or, the smoked salmon with capers and grated raw onion she served as a starter. Whatever the reason, the absence of wine or cocktails never curtailed or even hindered the group's merriment. That is, until Catherine picked one of the few quiet moments to ask Todd, "When are we going to meet your boyfriend?"

Suddenly, a hushed silence enveloped the group, as each person had a sudden need for another sip of liquid or bite of food. George glanced at Catherine. Her face had taken on the color of a day at the beach before sun block. The poor thing. She was trying so hard to be "Grandmother of the Year," she had a brain cramp. George tried to think of a lifeline to throw her, but couldn't. He sighed. At least *he* hadn't been the one to mess up.

Suddenly, Todd broke the silence. "Hey, folks, you don't need to walk on eggs with me or Charles when we're both around. We don't march at the head of the parade, and the things that offend us are exactly the same things that would offend you." He smiled. "In other words, just be yourselves."

Instead of staring at his plate in silence like the others, George asked, "So, when is Charles coming to Carlisle?"

"Depending on his schedule, my partner will probably come with me for Christmas, if that's all right?"

"You and Charles are welcome anytime," Gert gushed.

After that, for the most part everyone relaxed and the smiles reappeared around the table. That's when George peeked at his wife as she slipped her fork under a remaining bite of casserole. As she lifted it to her mouth, he noticed her hand was shaking.

All at once Gert announced, "Now it's time for the mystery dessert."

Although her cooking history was spotty at best, George found his anticipation growing as Roundy and Catherine helped Gert clear the table. George assumed the dessert would be the usual large glob of vanilla ice cream with chocolate sauce she typically served, but the secrecy surrounding the upcoming offering, along with Gert and Roundy's weight loss and new healthy eating regimen, suggested something else. Partly to impress Todd with his mother's exploits, George turned to him and said, "The dessert should be great. As you can tell by the dinner, Gert's a marvelous cook."

"That's what puzzles me," Todd replied. "When she was at my apartment in St. Louis, she kept saying she was such a terrible cook, kind of apologizing in advance. As if I really cared."

George said, "That's Gert. She doesn't want you to be disappointed with her or anything she does."

"I pegged her as outgoing and not the least careful about what she says. That's one of the things I liked about her."

"You're right-on there, but she's not always as self-confident as she appears." George sat back in his chair and studied Gert's son. "You, as much as anyone, ought to understand what I'm about to say. You can try to pack a person in a cardboard box, but don't be surprised if some body part hangs out."

Todd smiled. "I've never heard that before."

"I just made it up."

"Well, it's profound. None of us are easy to peg. Just about the time we think we have someone down pat, they do or say something that contradicts our impression of them."

"Like Catherine?"

"Oh, no! She's exactly the grandmother I expected and wanted her to be."

"I like that comment. She wants so badly for you to like her."

Todd raised his hands in benediction. "So who could ask for more than that?"

Soon Roundy and Catherine returned to the table and took over the conversation. They were going strong when Gert entered from the kitchen.

"Ta-da," she announced as she carried a tray with cups, a pot of coffee and five perfectly formed caramel colored flans covered with burnt sugar. "The third time was the charm," she stated. "I messed up big-time twice before I got these little suckers perfect. The mistakes didn't go to waste, though. Roundy and I finished them off, didn't we, hon?"

"You bet. If the final result is half as good as the errors, you guys are in for a real treat."

Afterwards, when consensus was reached on the delightful custards, there were no dissenting votes, just compliments. Then, as before, the conversation continued to ebb and flow from spot to spot around the table until the last sip of coffee was drained.

When the chef, host and waitress once again deserted them leaving the young man and George alone, they switched to a new topic.

"I understand you're a fisherman," George said.

"Charles and I have been known to drown a few worms."

"Then you aren't fly fishermen?"

Todd shook his head. "Far from it! I know fly fishing has its devotees, but I'm not one of them. I always figured it was a method used by a fishermen to avoid catching fish they'd have to clean."

George laughed. "My sentiments exactly. Personally, I enjoy the feel of the fish on my line, but I don't mind some fish in my cooler either."

"Right. How often do you fish, George?"

"About every twenty years," he dead-panned. "Actually, I used to fish quite often with a couple of buddies from work, but I've been retired for sixteen years, and they retired before me. Both of them moved away a long time ago and most likely have died by now. However, even though it's been awhile, I haven't lost my desire to fish, and I doubt I've lost my skills. Just my opportunities."

"Did you own a boat?"

"No. My friends each owned one, and I freeloaded. I guess I never cared enough to want all that expense, bother and responsibility."

"We don't have a boat either. Charles and I go on a Lake Michigan charter about every month from April through October. Also, we've been threatening to fish Lake Erie for walleye and smallmouth bass forever. We just haven't gotten around to it. Which would be easier for you?"

George made a mental calculation. It took four hours to drive to Cincinnati and fly to Chicago, and about the same amount of time to drive to Sandusky where most of the fishing charters originated for the western part of Lake Erie. "It doesn't make much difference to me."

"I was thinking Lake Erie would be easier, but don't you have a daughter living in the Chicago area?"

"Winnetka."

"Definitely easier. We'd pick you up in Winnetka and the guide in Lake Bluff. You get in some fishing and still have a nice visit with your daughter."

"So, you're inviting me to go fishing with you? That's great."

"Absolutely! We'll shoot for April, but it might be May. Some of the uncertainty involves the weather and Charles' schedule. As we get closer, we'll make concrete plans. The nice thing about using a charter guide is you don't need any tackle. He supplies it all."

George rubbed his hands together. "Todd, this is very exciting. Now all I have to do is make sure I'm still around in April and able to go."

"It could be May."

George grinned. "A bigger challenge, but I should be able to hang on 'til then. I'd better be here. I've got a young neighbor boy hired to put in my garden about then."

Later, while Roundy had disappeared to make a phone call and Gert was upstairs for a few minutes, George and Todd were sitting in the living room with Catherine. Todd said, "I've been thinking, George, and something concerns me. This morning I asked Roundy about going on a little fishing excursion, but he didn't think he wanted to. Now that you're planning to go, do you think Roundy will feel left out if I don't invite him again?"

Catherine jumped into the conversation. "What excursion?"

George silenced her with a look and turned back to the younger man. "I don't think Roundy likes to drown worms."

"Drown worms!"

"Catherine, please don't interrupt. We men are talking."

"I'm not invisible, George. You can't just ignore me."

Todd asked Catherine, "Is it okay if George goes fishing with us?"

"Of course, Todd. If you can stand him. But first he has to get his tackle organized."

"He doesn't really need his own tackle," he answered politely. "The charter captain supplies it."

"Oh. I didn't know that."

"Anyway, Charles and I would love to have him go. Fishing is a great way to get to know someone."

George raised his hand like a student eager to ask a question. Todd smiled and acknowledged him. "Wouldn't asking Roundy to go with us depend on how many people comfortably fit in the boat?"

"These are fairly large boats, George. They usually hold up to six. Since Charles and I now hire out the whole charter, there will be plenty of space for Roundy if he wants to go."

George tossed him an inquisitive glance. "Why wouldn't you want other guys on the charter? Did they get mad when you caught all the fish?"

When he noticed Todd's grin, he added, "If that's the case, I'm not sure I want to go either."

"No. It's just that we got tired of all the drinking and obnoxious conversion. You know how guys get when they've had a few too many."

"I know exactly. Those scenes aren't my favorites either," George said. "Now as far as Roundy is concerned, why don't you ask him again? If he doesn't want to fish, he'll be glad he had an opportunity to say, 'No thanks,' and if he does fish and decides to go, I'll have company on the trip, and you'll be glad you asked him because he's a great guy."

His wife popped into the conversation again. "Isn't it pretty cold to be going fishing?" "Catherine, we're not going until April or May!"

"That's a long way off. Anything can happen by then."

"I already acknowledged that, Catherine. I'll see that you're informed on a need-to-know basis."

"Yes, *sir*," she said as she snapped a salute.

Todd glanced from one to the other, grinned and asked, "So, is this what married life is like?"

They glanced at each other, laughed and replied in unison, "No. Sometimes it's worse."

CHAPTER TWELVE

"So, how are you really, Reuben?"

In the days following Thanksgiving, George frantically made the rounds intent on fulfilling every obligation and every need before he tore the last sheet of the year from the calendar. He began with a stop at Pam's to see her and baby Timmy. When she greeted him at the door with a hug, he handed her the gift he'd forgotten on the previous visit. The de-ribboning started a two-way cascade of words that continued throughout his stay.

Besides his weekly visits with Reuben at the nursing home, George readied his Christmas cards for mailing. A few late afternoons each week he also monitored the O'Hara's driveway. When he spotted Mike's car, he'd march over carrying an empty beer mug and knock on the door. Besides enjoying Mike's company, his calculations showed that O'Hara had consumed more beer on his porch during the year than he'd received at the lawyer's. He was intent on balancing the ledger by year's end.

Early December was also a time to make up for other shortfalls. A few weeks before Christmas, George and Catherine drove the two hours to Columbus. While the trip was billed as a grandchild fix, George planned the trek to assuage his guilt for not setting aside time for a one-on-one conversation with Anne while they were at Jill's over Thanksgiving. Not only did he closet himself with Anne and share some good in-depth conversation, he came away satisfied that the scales with Jill and Anne were back in balance. That felt good. So did getting down on the floor to entertain little Greg with his toys and reading with Lily on the couch.

With his eyes continuing to bother him, and driving at night and reading becoming a chore, George phoned his ophthalmologist for an appointment. Miraculously, Dr. Martin's scheduler gave him an appointment on the Friday after New Year's day. Since the next available date was in May, he eagerly gobbled it up. However, the earlier date forced him to rethink his plans for a seven-day Carribean cruise with Catherine in early February. If there was need for a follow up appointment, he decided it wouldn't be wise to have a trip scheduled that might have to be canceled.

Since Catherine was the driving force behind taking a cruise in the first place, he expected a big show of disappointment. However, to his surprise, she totally understood and agreed with his decision. So, George began looking at a ten-day Panama Canal cruise in March to replace it. After consulting the blank calendar pages and weighing the additional cost for the ten-day trip, George turned to his wife and said, "We're only young once, girl! Let's do it."

"If you recall, neither of us are young, George. However, I am still much younger than you."

"I know, Catherine. If you weren't, I'd have thrown you back long ago, and gone trolling for another chick."

She eyed him. "I believe you troll for fish, George. Typically, chicks come home to roost."

One of the things that bothered George most about winter was the uncertainty of his daily exercise regimen. With sleet, snow, freezing rain and extreme cold always a possibility, walking outside from December through February seemed dangerously foolish for a man with four bypasses. To solve this problem, George concocted a plan. The idea was simple, but ingenious. While some folks walked inside the mall for exercise, he decided to walk inside the super market instead. Usually, when he shopped at Schnucks, he arrived carrying a list of what he wanted to purchase laid out in the order he'd find each item in the huge store. Produce was first, then on to aisle two for canned goods and so on ending with dairy and beer. With a well-planned list, he never doubled back nor took any needless steps on his journey from the entrance to the check-out counter.

One miserable day when he was feeling especially glum because he couldn't take his usual walk outside, he rearranged his shopping list before traveling to the store. The revised list forced him to start at the farthest point from the entrance and then backtrack by crisscrossing from aisle to aisle hitting all the distant points until he was finished. After initiating this convoluted route, George confirmed its validity in a couple of ways. His walk was considerably longer than before, and due to the greater distance between items, he could move at a faster rate of speed while taking care not to crash into anyone. Thus, he raised his heart rate to a healthful level, picked up the items he needed and didn't freeze his butt off, all without journeying to the mall and being laughed at by the bare-middled, baggy panted, paired-up teenagers.

Meanwhile, Catherine went to Curves for her workouts.

Despite his new exercise regime and his continual string of activities, George still moped around the house during his unfilled moments.

"I just hate winter," he complained to Catherine.

"I know, dear. You tell me that every day."

"I get depressed when I have nothing pressing to do."

"But, sweetheart, you're busy every minute, and much of it doesn't include me. Don't you know I'm miserable when you're gone?"

"I guess I never realized that, Catherine."

"It's true. I feel almost as miserable as when you're here."

George stared at her, a smile building as he processed a retort. Finally, he said, "Do you remember when we were up in the attic and you offered to work with me in the garden?"

"Yes, but I never really meant it. I was just trying to make you feel better until Jim accepted your offer to work."

"Now that I've given it some thought, I'm going to fire Jim and accept your offer. We'll work together planting and weeding and picking. It's the perfect plan for bringing us closer together."

"But, George, I wasn't serious."

"Well, I am. We'll call it the Catherine and George Garden."

Catherine sighed. "Oh, my! Shoot me if I ever open my big mouth again!"

The day George chose to visit Reuben at the nursing home dawned dark and gloomy and deteriorated into a windy, bone-chilling morning. It was one of those winter days where any sensible octogenarian would have settled in by a blazing fire instead of challenging Mother Nature. Undaunted, George spurred the old Buick and drove to the grocery store. There, he picked up a short list of non-essentials while completing his walk. Then he drove to The Willows before conditions worsened into a winter melange of sleet, snow and ice.

The full idiocy of his plan hit home when the cruel wind buffeted him on the short walk from his parking place on the circle drive to the front door of the nursing home. Ironically, based on his last few visits, there was little reason to believe Reuben would even recognize him when he arrived or remember his being there after he left. Reuben was on a downward spiral, and all he could do was witness it. Still, rather than return home, he turned up the collar of his heavy wool overcoat and pressed on.

Despite his wishing otherwise, their bittersweet connections had become more challenging than uplifting of late. The two of them couldn't play cribbage anymore or carry on an intelligent conversation, and now, even the silliness of Reuben's off-center ramblings that had so often amused him were buried under the weight of his disintegrating personality.

When George found the room and entered the partially opened door, he spotted his pajama clad friend sitting with his back against the headboard of the bed holding his knees. Summoning up some enthusiasm, George asked, "How are you doing today, Reuben?"

He barely looked up, "You tell me, you're the doctor."

George wasn't surprised by the reply. He'd encountered it before on previous visits. Evidently some misfiring neurons in his friend's brain had recently transformed all males into doctors and all females into nurses. This failing was one more in a long list of reasons why George clung to the hope his own life would end before it deteriorated to the point where he had to be handed off to an institution.

"Are you feeling well?" George asked.

"You tell me, you're the doctor."

"Well, this doctor says it's stifling in here." He could feel the sweat building on his forehead and under his arms, so before he began to puddle his friend's room, he shed his coat and sweater. Piling the unneeded outerwear on the foot of the bed next to where he'd thrown his hat, George made his way to a chair by the window.

"So, how are you really, Reuben?"

No answer.

He tried more questions. Then a chatty monologue about the severe weather.

Still no answers. In fact, there was no reaction to anything he said.

After a few more minutes of frustration, George quit talking. He realized that gabbing with his mute friend and trying to draw him out wasn't going to work for either of them. Reuben was too far gone to benefit from his presence, and he wasn't receiving a thing for his failed efforts other than fulfilling some unspoken promise that he'd see his friend through to the end.

As he thought about it, George did see one advantage to his being secluded in this room full of silence. There was nothing to distract him from his thoughts. So, for the next few minutes he compared Reuben's dementia with that of his old cookie-baking neighbor, Mrs. McConnell. Maybe contrast was a better term for their individual situations. While he had reservations about the old lady's daughter leaving her to fend for herself in her own home with only a few cognitive tools, Mrs. McConnell had managed to cope quite well with most of her daily challenges including the baking of her famous chocolate chip cookies. At times she talked. Sometimes, she didn't. But whether she was lucid, or her thoughts were locked away, she seemed more alive in her familiar surroundings than Reuben did in the antiseptic environment of the assisted living section in The Willows where every minute detail of his existence was programed and monotonous. Maybe that's why Reuben's faculties seemed to deteriorate so quickly. Sure, his friend was clean, well-fed and absolutely safe, while Mrs. McConnell probably missed a meal or two, didn't wash her hands as often as she should, and if she took medicine at all, probably screwed up the dosages. And, yes, she did blow up her home and herself by igniting a kitchen full of natural gas leaking from a faulty burner. But....

He looked over at his friend. Just two short years before, Reuben had the spunk to run away from The Willows rather than give in to the routine and lose his identity. In the whole scheme of things, George knew that facilities like this institution were a must. The demented and the infirm needed a place to be kept safe with dignity.

George glanced at Reuben, detoured and placed himself in the equation. Given only the two alternatives as he aged, he would eagerly accept Mrs. McConnell's declining years over Reuben's anytime.

On a previous stop at The Willows a month or so before, Reuben had actually been quite chatty. Unfortunately, he also kept calling him, Sam. At the time, rather than agitating his friend by confronting him and turning a halfway pleasant visit into a nightmare, he'd gone along with the name change. Later, during one of their conversations, Reuben began a long narrative about his new friend, Ralph, who lived upstairs and came down to talk with him each day. Though the *Reuben and Ralph Show* was convincing and feasible enough, George assumed Reuben's assertion was a fiction. Still, the doubt gave him a choice. He could accept his assumption or get to the bottom of it. With that thought in mind, on his way out of the building, George stopped to speak with a familiar face who was working the front desk. Without telling her why he wanted to know, he asked, "Can you tell me if there are any Ralph's living on the second floor?"

She studied him. "I'm not supposed...."

He smiled his most charming smile.

Returning his smile, she said, "How can it hurt?" She quickly turned to a computer screen and gave the keyboard a few pecks. "There's one," she said with finality.

"Oh, thank you. I'm never quite sure if I can believe my friend, Reuben Goldstein, but this time I can. This must be the Ralph who's visiting him."

The woman shook her head. "Oh! I don't think so."

"Why?"

"I'm not allowed to tell you, but trust me. This Ralph is NOT visiting your friend in his room."

He'd thanked her for the information and left the building. Since his doubts rode with him on the trip home, he decided to follow his curiosity and call Reuben's son. As much as he hated running the risk of stirring up the son's ire over such a petty issue, George figured it was mid-week and mid-day so his chances were good the man wouldn't be home when he called. Assuming he was correct, if anyone did answer the phone it would be the man's wife, and they'd gotten along fine the one time they'd met. If she had a clue, she'd surely give him the information without any guff.

However, just as in poker, pat hands don't always win. What were the odds that Sheldon would have stopped home to pick up a forgotten folder full of notes for the meeting he was going to attend that afternoon and be standing by the phone when it rang? At least this was what the son told George when he registered his surprise at hearing his voice.

"So, what do you want, Mr. Konert?" he asked in his usual blunt way.

"I just saw your father, and he told me a man named Ralph lives upstairs at The Willows and comes to talk with him. Could that be true?"

"My father has lost all contact with reality. He lives in a fantasy world. He probably thinks an orderly or a maintenance guy is his childhood friend, Ralph. I think when they were kids, he lived upstairs in the same apartment building in New York. Or, maybe he's just hallucinating and thinks Ralph is talking to him. I just don't know." George heard him sigh and repeat slowly, "I just don't know. However, I do know I feel sick every time I see how his life is ending. It may sound awful, but I wish he'd die soon, so I can recover the memories of who he was and forget all of the images of who he's become."

Although he and Sheldon had a run-in the first time they'd met, George felt empathy for the younger man. Watching a father lose his wits had to be a painful ordeal for a son. However, since he, himself, was ancient and might eventually take the same fork in the road as Reuben had, George found the experience more than painful. It was chilling.

"I'm sorry you have to suffer through all this," George said.

"I have to. You don't, Mr. Konert. Why do you visit him and try to make sense out of his ramblings?"

"I keep thinking I can make his life better, yet I know I can't. Still, if he were giving me some sign, I wouldn't want to miss it."

"He won't."

"I'll keep hoping." George then slipped in another question. "Lately, he's also been calling me, Sam. Any idea who that is?"

Sheldon said, "It's probably someone he made up."

"I was afraid of that. Yet, that fact doesn't diminish your father in my eyes. When I visit, I'll just continue to play the role he gives me."

"Only a true friend would go to that extreme. Thank you, Mr. Konert. Now, if you won't be offended, I have to get to my meeting." And that's how the phone conversation ended.

With his reminiscence concluded, George looked out Reuben's window at the worsening conditions. While no snow was falling, the wind whipping small trees into arches convinced him it was time to go. He glanced at Reuben who continued to sport a blank expression as he sat with his back against the headboard still gripping his knees. Rather than try to enter his private world, George rose from his chair and retrieved his sweater, coat and hat from the end of the bed where it had been parked for the last hour. Taking a few steps toward the hallway, he stopped and turned, hoping for some reaction from the old man like a grunt or gesture to acknowledge his stay or his leaving. Instead, nothing. Giving up, he edged toward the door. When he did find his voice, he turned and called back, "Goodbye, Reuben."

"Goodbye, George."

Shaken, he said, "What did you say?"

This time there was no reply. George shook his head. Had he heard right? Had his friend said goodbye and called him by name, or had he only imagined it? As he pondered the answer, he backed from the room and into the walker of an elderly man scraping up behind him. "I'm sorry," George said. "I didn't see you."

The man laughed. "Don't you worry yourself none, mister," he said in a scratchy voice. "Not many humans have eyes in the backs of their heads. Been seein' Reuben, have ya?"

"I'm George Konert. Yes, Reuben's a friend of mine."

"Mine, too. I'm Ralph."

CHAPTER THIRTEEN

"...Todd had to be an Immaculate Conception,.."

George knew that *suspicion* lurked in a dark corner of his psyche. Most of the time the beast was content to snooze away the days and nights, freeing him to be Lovable George, or Cranky George, or Wise Old George or whoever else controlled his spirit at that particular moment. Sometimes, however, the caged beast clawed at its shackles and demanded his attention. Unlike some who grooved on the potent emotion like an elixir, George hated its howls because, if the cursed beast broke loose, he was powerless to catch and restrain it until its prey was hunted down.

His most recent incursion with *suspicion* occurred when Roundy came into Gert's life. For reasons George never understood, he hadn't trusted the man. This distrust parlayed into a fear that Gert might end up being hurt by the relationship, and that dread led him to accompany *suspicion* on a thorough hunt for the truth. During that foray, he and *suspicion* observed Roundy, interacted with him and checked him out with others. George even interviewed Roundy's demented father at the assisted living facility. However, when the hunt ended and all the facts were uncovered, the only thing he discovered about Roundy was the embarrassing fact that his feelings about him had been totally wrong. Roundy turned out to be the salt of the earth and the perfect mate for Gert. Thankfully, *suspicion* was content to snooze when Todd entered the arena.

They had just left Gert's large dining room table following a traditional Christmas dinner. Besides Catherine and himself, the cast of characters included the hostess and Roundy, Gert's son, Todd, and his partner, Charles. Also joining them were Roundy's daughter by his first marriage, Sara, and her new friend, Ryan Parker, a burly, former college fullback. Earlier, Gert, with some help from her mother, had prepared the turkey and fixings. Then Roundy had carved the bird at the table and piled multiple slices on each plate. Following that, everyone selected and replenished empty plates from a rotating array of side dishes consisting of peas, beans, sweet potatoes, cranberry sauce and a fresh green salad. As was typical of such eating orgies, the main meal was followed by apple or pumpkin pie and ice cream, coffee and drowsiness.

Afterward, Catherine, Gert, Roundy and Todd cleaned up the kitchen and dining room. While Ryan, the football player, could be heard arguing with someone on his cell phone from the front hall, George, Sara and Charles staggered into the living room and began measuring their own digestive discomfort against one another. Before long, George dropped out of the competition and listened as the other two talked.

Sara, a petite brunette in her mid-twenties, was comparing notes on higher education with Charles, who was a full professor at Washington University in St. Louis. Although the vivacious young woman had been working in her father's company when George first met her the previous year, she was now studying toward a PhD in Botany at Ohio State. This pleased George because he admired Sara and was happy she was now back on her chosen career path. After all, how many young women would take two years out of their lives to help out at home during a mother's last illness and offer support to her grieving father following her death. In his mind, such dedication was rare.

Tuning out their conversation, George began working on a thesis of his own. Are our words and mannerisms honed by the professions we choose, or do certain types of personalities gravitate toward particular occupations? Actually, at that moment he didn't really care about finding an answer, nor even exploring empirical data on the subject. The curious question had just popped into his head at the very time he'd wanted to be an observer rather than a participant in their exchange. Moreover, focusing on Charles and Sara gave little credence to the validity of his central observation. Charles was a professor, Sara a wannabe, and each was as different from the other as day was from night.

Sara was a chatterbox, while the tall, lean professor always appeared to choose his words carefully. He'd listen to Sara, question her logic, even her syntax, and debate her answers in a quiet, yet authoritative tone. Occasionally he'd support her position with a nod. However, the professor's constant frown baffled him. That is until he realized Charles wore the frown to show his neutrality.

George chuckled to himself. How different he was from the professor. While Charles seemed fixated on the details of Sara's ideas and the precise words she used to present her thoughts, George was totally captivated by her expressive face, the constant movement of her hands and the emotion she exuded.

With his stiff demeanor and underwhelming sense of humor, George had originally felt put-off by Charles. However, with the help of Todd's solid defense of the man, he'd come to grips with their differences. "George," he'd said, "underneath that cool facade, lies a struggling human like the rest of us. The difference is he just can't let anyone penetrate his armor. Many researchers are like that." He smiled and added, "Please, give him a break."

"You're doing research, Todd. You're easy to be around."

"I'm just mediocre, George. I have to do it now to get ahead. My real strength is teaching."

"You're my kind of guy, Todd."

"I doubt that, George."

They'd both laughed over that.

After their discussion, George took Todd's plea at face value and worked to understand Charles. His attitude change didn't come as a result of feeling coerced. Instead, it came from the realization that he didn't have much experience with researchers and other solitary thinkers. During his working career, George had moved up the ladder at Kerr Manufacturing to plant superintendent, because he was capable of providing leadership to a variety of personalities that helped get things done. On the other hand, he had never contributed to mankind's store of knowledge like Charles and his peers. Since it was apparent to him that each of us had to be wired differently to achieve in his chosen field, George felt no envy toward the professor, just respect. Each made his own solid contribution to society. George found that comforting.

Drowsy from overeating and pleased with his observation, George flashed a quick smile at Sara and closed his eyes. Polite or not, it was time for a little nap.

When he awoke, Sara and Charles were still talking except Todd had joined them and the subject under discussion had changed. They were now talking about Charles' sons. Suddenly, the beast began to strain at his chains, and George closed his eyes again to give the impression he was still asleep.

Todd was telling Sara, "Like many latecomers to the openly gay lifestyle, Charles lived the *'big lie'* for quite awhile. He was married to a fine, intelligent woman, and they had these two sensational boys. "How old are they now, Charles? Twelve and ten?"

"Thirteen and eleven and a half, to be precise."

"Geez, time flies." Then Todd said, "Charles had an internal medicine practice in St. Louis where he was considered a brilliant diagnostician. He had a large older home in Olivette, one of the nicer suburbs, and as far as the straight community knew, he was living the American dream. Except, he knew better because he was miserable."

Sara said, "I can relate somewhat. Before I came back to Carlisle, I was working on my Masters and living with a guy in Columbus who was more interested in snorting his next line than he was in me. Yet, I was totally immobilized. To tell the truth, I think my mother's cancer saved me."

Charles has kids? Sara lived with an addict? Holy cow, George thought! I must be having a nightmare.

Charles picked up the conversation. "You see, Sara, loving one's wife and not wanting to be intimate creates endless conflicts. Added to that was the self-knowledge that I was misplaced as a physician. Excellent primary care physicians treat the whole person, not just their disease. The best of the best can alleviate their patients' fears by being a good listener and having a caring demeanor. While I did care about my patients, I had a tendency to treat them like case histories. I'd do my best to help them, but I didn't have the interpersonal skills."

"So, that's why you went into research?" Sara asked.

"Precisely, except I made that move before my wife and I separated and subsequently divorced. You see, by then I'd determined exactly why my wife stayed with me even after it was obvious our love could never be more than plutonic. She was infatuated with the concept of being married to a physician and willing to make the necessary sacrifices to maintain the relationship. So, when I left my practice and ceased to be an internist, there was nothing to bind us together."

Except to provide a home for the children, you fool, George thought.

"Did the divorce negatively affect your children?" Sara asked.

George smiled to himself. This telepathy stuff is pretty slick.

"Of course. Divorce is always terrible for kids, and it's been especially tough for the boys to get their heads around their dad being gay. But, we work hard at it. They seem well-adjusted and happy, and they have a home, a very fine and loving home. Theresa was remarried within the year."

"To another MD," Todd announced. "Charles has full visitation rights and sees his boys often. You and the boys get along great, right, Charles?"

He sighed. "About as well as can be expected when you've been replaced, and they live elsewhere. I love them, and they seem to respect me. At least my ex-wife hasn't turned them against me. I'm thankful for that. Now, do you suppose we could talk about something else? I'm uncomfortable going on like this."

"I didn't mean to drag all that out of you," Sara said.

"You didn't. It was Todd's fault."

Todd laughed. "I'm good at that. So, let's plan a fishing trip."

"Now, that's something I like to talk about," Charles said.

"Why not bring Kurt and Bobby along when we go fishing with George. It would be fun for the boys, and all the guys could get to know one another."

Charles ran his hand through his thinning hair. "That's a fine idea, except they can't miss school. We'd have to fish over a holiday weekend or wait until their summer vacation. We'll ask George about it when he wakes up."

Even though hearing his name rang an alarm, George decided to stay undercover for a bit longer. Why join in the conversation when he could learn a lot by just listening? Although his information gathering technique might be considered unethical by some, he was getting all his questions answered, and the beast was now content to snooze.

When Gert, Catherine and Roundy rejoined the group, the conversation quickly switched to the types of studies the two researchers were involved in. Todd began an overview of his project. "For a long time scientists have known that the mind plays a huge role in how a person deals with pain. For example, many studies have shown that the same kind of pain can be felt more intensely by some people because of emotional aspects like fear and stress. We also know that if people are given a "dummy" pill that they think is a pain relieving medication, they often feel relief similar to those who actually took the real drug. This is called the 'placebo effect.'"

"I've heard of that," Sara replied.

"We know the mind is heavily involved in producing this phenomena. My project will look at pain as a complex sensory and emotional experience which can lead to coping skill interventions a patient can learn. Just like a recent British study, we're monitoring patients who have knee pain caused by osteoarthritis. Since this is a common cause of pain, particularly in older people, we have a large trial group."

George opened his eyes, yawned and stretched. The first person he noticed was Ryan Parker, who was now sitting next to Sara on the couch playing put and take. Every time he put his hand on her thigh, she reached down and took it off. Other than playing their game, the guy looked bored to death.

George entered the conversation by saying, "I'm leaving my body to science. You can study my creaky old knees after I'm gone."

"Thanks, George, but, I'm afraid you won't do us much good if you're dead. We're studying brain function."

Catherine smirked. "In that case I doubt he'd do you much good, even now."

"Don't be a skeptic, mother," Gert added. "Todd's such a fine researcher, he might even find something useful in Georgy boy's head."

"George fits our profile perfectly," Todd said. "We're always looking for healthy, older people. I'd use George in my study anytime, if he was interested." He paused for more wisecracks. Seeing only lingering smiles, he plunged back into his research. "Our study uses high-tech imaging scans to monitor brain activity as a participant experiences knee pain caused by arthritis or pain caused by the heat we subject the person to. It also scans the participant when he or she is not experiencing any pain whatsoever. What we found was the arthritis and heat-induced pain activated a network of brain structures known as the pain matrix."

George began to squirm. Good heavens, Todd has a case of Researcher's Disease.

Todd paused until Ryan Parker finished yawning, then continued. "The pain matrix contains two parallel systems: the medial pain system, which processes the emotional aspects of pain including fear and stress, and the lateral system, which processes the pain's physical location, intensity and duration. What we found was the arthritis pain may have more of an emotional impact and a stronger association with fear and distress than heat-induced pain, because the activity in the medial system was much greater."

Now it was Roundy reflecting on what Todd was saying. "And, I thought engineering jargon was difficult to understand, and I am one."

Todd laughed. "I'm sorry. I am getting a little carried away. In a nutshell, if our findings are correct, our attitude about pain has as much to do with emotions as the cause of the pain itself."

George smiled at Gert after what he assumed was the benediction. She rolled her eyes.

Instead, Charles waded into the fray. From his exasperated demeanor, George could see he was intent on providing this group of deadheads the definitive explanation, one so clear that no one could possibly miss the point of Todd's research. "What the study demonstrates is the importance of the medial pain system while experiencing arthritis pain, and it suggests it's a likely target for pharmacologic and especially non-pharmacologic interventions."

"Now I've got it," Roundy laughed. "It's as clear as mud."

The room turned silent. George peered at Charles. He was stone-faced. His arms crossed his chest in a bear hug, and his foot was tapping at the speed of sound. He then glimpsed Todd fidgeting with his hands and casting furtive glances at his partner. For the first time in his life, George couldn't think of a thing to break the silence that didn't run the risk of offending someone and making the situation worse.

Suddenly, Charles brightened and began laughing. "Here's the down and dirty answer. We think this research will encourage the drug companies to come up with more and better drugs, and we hope patients will be encouraged to learn self-management, pain coping skills. How's that for a layman's summary?"

That's when George led the group in applause.

Following some light banter, and against all logic, Catherine asked Charles to tell them all about his research. George glanced at Ryan. He was asleep, just like he'd been earlier. Apparently, that was Ryan's defense when nobody ran any plays from his play book.

Charles began in his monotone. "I'll summarize it this way. We know that older people seem to stay sharper mentally if they engage in physical exercise and challenge themselves daily by reading, playing bridge or laboring over puzzles like crossword and Sudoku." Then he launched into the details of his study. "It has been hypothesized that these activities can even ward off Alzheimer's or dementia."

After listening to his limit, George grinned and said, "Now you have my full attention. And to think, I was going to suggest we all take a walk."

"George!" Catherine said sharply.

Charles smiled. "I agree with George. Let's do it, or talk about something else."

When no one stepped forward with an alternative, Charles said, "I'll finish up by saying, since we know our nation is aging, our study is attempting to determine which activities are most beneficial for the largest number of older adults."

"I like to garden," George said.

"That's one of the areas we're looking at," Charles replied. "We know it's extremely beneficial, both physically and emotionally. Obviously, gardening requires physical activity which gets older people off the couch and into range of motion exercise. Hoeing, planting, weeding and picking requires stretching which helps keep muscles and tendons flexible. Although there isn't a great deal of aerobic benefit, the times a gardener carries bags of fertilizer and lifts baskets of vegetables does increase strength. Also, if one has ever used a tiller, he'd know that's extremely hard work."

When George discovered the dour professor smiling, he made a calculated guess. "You must be a gardener, Charles."

"Actually, I am. I have a small plot where I plant what I like to eat. You know, the usual home garden fare like tomatoes, sweet peppers and cucumbers. Also, I grow the vegetables I can't find consistently in the produce departments of the supermarkets, like kohlrabi, parsnips, beets and leeks."

George said, "Then, I'm sure your study will confirm that gardeners benefit from being outdoors in the fresh air."

"My personal anecdotal evidence proves they have better mental acuity compared to non-gardeners. I think it comes from constantly trying to outwit the crop perils Mother Nature throws at them." With a wry grin, he added, "We haven't proved that theory, yet."

George said, "I also think gardening promotes togetherness for married folks. That's why Catherine and I are going to test my theory. We're planting a garden together next spring."

"I haven't bought into that," Catherine said. "Anyway, you've hired Jim to help you. You don't need me."

He held her in his gaze with an over-the-top explanation. "Oh, I do need you, Catherine, and I want *so* much work with you in our Catherine and George Garden. Remember, a few weeks ago when you told me how miserable you were when I wasn't with you?" George turned from Catherine to the group, "I believe she said, she was almost as miserable as when I was around." After the laughter died down, George turned to Charles and said, "Tell Catherine how she'll benefit emotionally from gardening. She'll learn about growth cycles and the effects of weather on plants and especially about gardeners. Tell her, Charles."

"George, unless I'm rambling on in an area where I have some expertise, I'm typically a man of few words. Therefore, since I have a limited knowledge of marital bliss, I choose to remain silent."

"Wise move," Roundy said.

They all laughed, except for Sara's ex-jock. Ryan Parker just yawned.

Later, after they were settled back in the great room following a short group walk, George saw Todd look quizzically at his partner. Charles answered with a shrug, and moments later Todd said, "Charles is peripherally involved in another study that interested both of us. It's called "The Molecular Genetic Study of Sexual Orientation." It's controversial because it explores a genetic basis for homosexuality. This would fuel the current fire in the cultural war between scientists who suspect sexual orientation is at least partially explained by biology as well as choice, and the religious groups who believe only choice is involved."

Charles said, "The scientists hope to gather one thousand DNA samples from one-thousand sets of brothers and test them for differences where one of the brothers is gay, and the other isn't. Since I have a brother who is straight, we're perfect candidates. I would expect the researchers to find some differences in our genes, although I have no idea what. We were certainly raised with all the same variables. So, that wouldn't account for the differences in the way we turned out.

"Unfortunately, Todd can't be a subject in this study, unless, " he nodded toward Gert, "unless he has a straight brother out there that he isn't aware of."

With a straight face, Gert quipped, "Since Todd had to be an *Immaculate Conception,* no one would ever believe it could happen twice."

After the laughing subsided Catherine asked, "Why brothers?"

"Because scientists already know that having a gay-straight sibling combination occurs too often statistically to go unstudied."

"Anyway," Todd said, "one of these days these linkage studies may shoot holes in the 'choice' theory."

"That's good," George said. "Unless they also find out you guys have some special gene that helps you catch all the fish. That just wouldn't be fair."

In the late afternoon, George had an opportunity to spend some one-on-one time with Sara's friend, Ryan Parker. He came away from his chat with the handsome, former running back totally unimpressed. While Ryan had the gift of gab, he had a singular topic of conversation, himself. As if that wasn't bad enough, he also had an annoying habit of acting bored whenever the spotlight shone on someone else. Before long, even with George's restraining hand holding him back, *suspicion's* growl began assailing his ears. Fortunately, with all the negative feelings he had about the young man, George did find out that other than playing college football, they also had something else significant in common. They were both wishing Ryan was somewhere else.

In the early evening, Ryan made an impressive display of announcing his intention of leaving the party and heading back to his apartment in Columbus. He thanked Gert and Roundy heartily, shook hands all around and told each individual how much he enjoyed meeting them. With Ryan in mid-chatter and showing no signs of an imminent departure, George slipped out of the great room where everyone was gathered and quickly walked down the long hall to use the guest bathroom by the foyer. There, while drying his hands, he heard voices.

Sara was saying, "I'm glad you could join us, Ryan."

"I am, too." Then he heard Ryan laugh. "I still can't believe I just spent Christmas with a bunch of old farts and two queers."

Suddenly the beast roared, and George had to hold him back to keep him from charging. He still had his hand on the knob when he heard Sara say, "Don't worry, Ryan. You'll never have to go through that again."

"Super. Then, I'll see you in a few days?"

"Ryan! You've got to be kidding. Get out!"

"What are you saying, Sara?"

"I'm saying I have no place in my life for anyone who'd voice a comment like that about my family. Even if you didn't care for them, I'd expect you to show some respect."

The silence that followed kept *suspicion* riled. Was he missing some whispered excuse, some apology that might result in Sara rescinding her condemnation? Was the guy so smooth, he'd won her over with a farewell kiss? When he couldn't stand the silence any longer, the beast burst forth from the john. Instead of the two of them sharing an embrace, George saw Sara standing triumphantly by the closed door. The wiseacre was nowhere to be seen.

Initially, she seemed startled by George's sudden appearance. Then, spotting his thumbs-up sign, her face lit up in a broad grin. Without a pause, she walked the few steps toward him and let George gather her slight frame into his waiting arms. "What a jerk," she said.

"My sentiments exactly."

The beast purred in agreement.

CHAPTER FOURTEEN

"If only we could stop the clock for awhile."

As was normal for the dead of winter, George awakened at six to darkness. With Catherine sleeping at his side, he slipped out of bed as quietly as possible to avoid waking her. Then, carrying his clothes from the bedroom, he dressed in the hall and tip-toed down the stairs. Ever reluctant to face the prospect of another gloomy winter day, he entered the living room, plopped into the recliner and closed his eyes.

An hour or so later, the first slanted rays of sunshine streamed through the living room window. Instead of feeling exhilarated by the light, he greeted the intrusion with despair. Why should he applaud the sunlight when he was groveling in the blackness of his thoughts? How could he be uplifted by the brightness when the dawning of another New Years day might be the first day of his last year on earth. His eyes were filled with tears.

Fortunately, Catherine was still sleeping. Why spoil her New Year with his rotten mood. Even if he chose to share his deepest heart with her, he doubted she could raise his spirits because she wouldn't understand the reason for his depression. Then again, maybe she would, since any casual glance at the calendar would explain it. Both of them were deep into the final stages of their relentless march toward eternity.

As depressing as it was to focus on the inevitable finality of life, in a way it also buoyed him to realize that to this point, the campaign had been quite successful when he compared himself to many of the comrades who'd begun the march with him and dropped out along the way.

So, why be afraid of the future? He'd had his bypass surgery, and he'd had his knee replaced. What else could break down? That was the scary part. He didn't know. It could be anything: a stroke, an aneurysm, deafness, blindness or senility like Reuben. Each step toward his demise could and probably would be accompanied by a yet unnamed life altering physical or mental breakdown. Actually, that's what he feared more than the end itself. He sighed.

He'd made the same statement some years earlier following his retirement from Kerr. The kids were on their own, he and Grace were in love and healthy, and they also had the time and resources to fulfill their dreams and experience all that they'd left undone. "If only we could stop the clock for awhile," he'd said, and Grace, who always understood the sentiment behind his words, had patted his hand and smiled and was diagnosed with breast cancer two weeks later.

After she died, he left all his unfulfilled dreams scattered on her grave with the rose petals. Instead of facing up to his changed circumstances, he chose to sit out an entire decade of his life by hiding in his house, holding seances with his deceased wife and planting himself in his garden. What a fool! If he'd only acted sooner, all the joy, the sadness and the love he'd experienced since he'd met the Alexanders, Gert, and especially Catherine, could have been his. But, no, he'd elected to pay an exorbitant price for his unwillingness to release his first wife. Ten whole years. No wonder he was depressed. It was tough enough facing an uncertain future without carrying the burden of this past regret.

While his old choices seemed foolish from his current vantage point, his actions in a way validated his love for Grace following her death. Even today he couldn't explain to Catherine the depth, breadth and lingering effects of that old love. How could any man explain to a woman he loves, just how much he missed another woman he once loved passionately. Only a fool would try.

That winter after Grace's cancer had raised its fist in victory, George found subsequent winters to be a heavy burden to bear. Finding no joy outside his home, he had felt trapped for the duration with nothing to do but read his seed catalogues, scan the obituaries and mourn Grace. Once in awhile for relief, he'd talk to his daughters on the phone, visit them at their homes or welcome them to Carlisle. Still, while he loved Jill and Anne and took comfort in connecting with them, they couldn't replace the memories of the wife he'd loved and the woman he'd lost.

Other than these short respites, driving to the store for enough provisions to sustain himself for another week and attending a few visitations and funerals for departed acquaintances, George seldom left his home until the spring weather beckoned him to work in his garden. While most aspects of this extended mourning period proved detrimental, there was one lasting benefit, and it sat in his junk-filled garage. The ancient Buick he'd purchased just before Grace's diagnosis was still a low-mileage diamond.

Eventually, subtle changes crept into George's attitude toward closing himself off from others. As a result, he began to resent *being* closed off from others. The winter weather that had kept him inside and protected from the hazards of human connection now entrapped him. It also was clear that since he alone had wandered down the path into the darkness, he was the only one with the ability to find a way out. Thus, by the time he found himself at the Alexander's door with a child's wagon full of cabbages, he was open to any relationship that could help him escape the dark endless tunnel. Then the Alexander kids led him out of the blackness, and Catherine eventually took over and reawakened his soul. Ever after, except for his seasonal grumbling, he and Catherine had thrived.

So, why was he feeling so morose this New Year's day morning? Although he'd already discovered the answer, he still wanted to confirm it with his deceased wife. He raised his eyes to the ceiling and pleaded, "Come on, Grace. Help me out here." Instead of a reply, silence filled the room. He sat amongst it waiting for the longest time until he finally concluded that he was totally and utterly on his own.

The squeak of a far off door caught his attention. Then the rattle of the window pane behind him. Excited by this novel approach, he turned to face her. "Is that you, Grace?" However, there was no answer. As the pervasive stillness engulfed him, he had to face a new reality. His deceased wife was not about to pay him a visit. The stark realization returned him to the gathering gloom of his thoughts. Moments later a toilet flushed and a noisy rush of water ran through the copper pipes. The sound brought an instant lift. Then, it turned into a high when a cheerful voice called from the top of the stairs, "Happy New Year, George."

Hallelujah! Catherine has awakened. Let the new year begin. So, maybe Grace hadn't shown up, but now it didn't matter. Catherine had the will and the resources to help him improve his mood. Moreover, her insights were far more reliable than those he'd glean from an ephemeral chat with Grace. He leaned forward in his chair and hollered back, "Happy New Year, Catherine."

"I'm gong back to bed for awhile longer, okay?"

"Okay!" Then raising his eyes toward the source of his joy, he chuckled and whispered under his breath, "I guess I shouldn't be expecting any immediate help from you, should I Catherine?"

George grunted as he rose from his chair. Once he was standing, and once he could walk without passing out, he shuffled to the kitchen to rustle up some breakfast. Later, parked at the drop-leaf table with a plate of toast smothered in orange marmalade and a mug of coffee, he focused on the hills rather than the valleys of his journey so far. The births of his daughters, their growing years and the magnificent women they'd become, and his wonderful extended family. Also, his career at Kerr, his marriage with Grace, all but the end, and his new life with Catherine as well as all the gardens he'd harvested. Each memory raised his spirits until he found himself at the edge of a high precipice overlooking a vast expanse. He was momentarily chilled as he took it all in. So, was this all he could see of the future? An endless horizon, a blank canvas, but no bungee cord to pop him back up if he fell. Scary? A little. But, he'd faced the future before, and it had turned out well. So, not seeing any signs of the grim reaper hiding in wait, and not feeling a need to check his pulse with his fingers on his neck or wrist, George decided to get a grip as he recalled Jim Alexander's all-purpose word of wonderment which perfectly fit the scene. "Awesome!"

Catherine finally joined him in the kitchen about nine-thirty. Dropping into a chair, she rested her elbows on the table and held the coffee mug he'd slipped in front of her with both hands. Between sips, George felt her eyes lingering on him as he rounded up granola for her strawberry yogurt and made her some toast. He liked the feeling.

"You're certainly bright and cheerful this morning," she said.

"I am now that you're up."

"I can't imagine I'm the catalyst. The Bengals must be on TV this afternoon."

"Catherine, the Bengals played on Sunday and lost. Today is full of college bowl games. You know the Rose Bowl, Cotton Bowl..."

"So that's what has you on a high?"

"I'd rather watch *The Sound of Music* again than those dumb semi-pro games. No, being with you, Catherine, is the reason I feel so good."

She yawned. "I feel the same way, George."

"Except, I'm sincere."

"I am too. You make my life sing."

"For heaven's sake. I'd like a recording of that."

"CD, George. They don't make records any more."

For the next few minutes George gazed at his wife while she nibbled at her breakfast. They returned smiles during the pauses between bites, but said nothing. Although he wondered what was going on behind his wife's Cheshire grin, being a cautious man, he didn't risk asking.

They cleaned up the kitchen together. Then, before Catherine trudged up the stairs to get dressed for the day, she called Gert. To George the one-way conversation sounded like this. "Happy New Year, Gert...Thank you, I'll tell George...Not much...No, we couldn't...No, you should be with Roundy's family...Oh! Well, maybe...Let me ask George, and I'll call you back..." Laughing. "Don't bother asking him because he's in love with you? Okay, then. We'll be at your place at five. See you then." With a smirk on her face, Catherine hung up the phone.

Seconds later, George groaned. "You're terrible. You just wangled an invitation from Gert for dinner, didn't you?"

"It's better than having to cook a meal for just the two of us."

Since the day was sunny and in the forties at noon, they bundled up and began the new year with a neighborhood walk. Approaching Gert's former house, Catherine spotted Jim and Jenny careening around the corner where Kevin was killed. "Look at that, George."

"Look at what?"

"Up there at the corner! Jim is peddling his old bike, and Jenny is riding on the handlebars. Don't these kids ever learn?"

"I can't see them clearly. Tell me they're wearing their helmets."

She squinted. "Yes, George, I believe they are."

"Well, at least Jim learned something. I pray it's enough."

They continued on to the corner, made the turn and were in full stride as they passed the Alexander's. Soon thereafter, George took his wife's hand and held it. Before long they were swinging their joined hands up and back and giggling like school children. "Why are we doing this?" she asked. "Because we love each other?"

"Yes, and we're happy. Unlike this morning when I felt depressed while you were sleeping, the new year is full of promise. Your cancer is in remission, my health is good, our families are prospering and they enjoy our company as much as we enjoy theirs. We're cruising in March, and I'm fishing in April with Todd, Charles and maybe his boys. Then in May, Jim will be planting our garden unless he finds a better job. Catherine, we are very lucky people. That's why we're swinging our arms."

"George? You know what? Maybe when we get back home, we should start the new year off right."

He grinned. "What did you have in mind, my sweet Babu?"

"Oh, I don't know...maybe a little lovin.' What do you think?"

Instead of answering, he stopped in the middle of the street, pulled her toward him and planted a long lingering kiss on her lips. When they parted, he said, "There, that's a good start."

"I can handle more."

"I'll give you my best, Babu. But, just to maintain the mood, I'm going to say a little prayer of thanks that we can do so many other things really well at our...at my age."

"I'm all for that." That triggered a laugh, and she grabbed his hand. For the remainder of the trip to the house, they resumed swinging their locked hands up and back.

There were times in the past when George found it more blissful to avoid the truth than face it. A few days later, Dr. Martin, his ophthalmologist, reinforced the validity of this behavior in just forty-five minutes. "George, you have a rather large nuclear cataract in your left eye and a tiny one in your right."

"I know lots of people with cataracts. They just get them fixed. What's the big deal?"

"That's true, George, and I'm sure your left eye will be improved with surgery. The cataract in your right eye is so small, we'll just continue to watch it."

"Good. Should we do it right now?"

The perplexed look on the doctor's face gave him pause, but only for a second. George had been aware of some worsening in his vision since his last appointment. Such tasks as reading fine print had become more difficult and the glare from oncoming high-beams drove him crazy. Also, at times it seemed that a perpetual haze hung over any distant object. Still, these changes weren't worrisome since he had no pain or discomfort, and always before, minor problems like these were easily improved with new glasses and a stronger correction. This time the treatment was a bit more complicated, but at least Dr. Martin could fix him up.

"Go for it, Doc."

"George, even if the cataracts were my only concern, we just don't yank them out like an abscessed tooth. We have to schedule the surgery, and make you aware of the risks and the aftercare."

"Of course, and I understand, but my wife and I have a big cruise scheduled for March. I don't want to miss that."

"Ordinarily I'd say you wouldn't, but I want you to understand you have a more serious problem brewing. There is evidence of atrophic macular degeneration in both eyes." The doctor paused, letting the news sink in. When his patient didn't react, he began a detailed explanation. "This is an age related eye disease where the macula, or central portion of the retina responsible for fine visual detail, degenerates. A person with MD has trouble seeing through the center of his eye and is forced to view things through the periphery. Close-up work like reading and writing become blurred, and the eye progressively gets worse. Eventually, blind spots form within the central vision."

As Dr. Martin spoke, George felt his anxiety level rising. He was well acquainted with macular degeneration. Several of his acquaintances had the problem. However, instead of backing off and giving him a chance to react, the doctor interpreted his blank expression as a desire for more information. He droned on.

"The problem with the atrophic or dry macular degeneration which you have, is there's not a darned thing we can do about it. There are aides such as magnifiers and machines that help you read a newspaper, write letters and pay bills, and we can teach you ways to live with poor sight, but for the most part we can't stop the disease from progressing."

George finally broke his silence. "How bad will it get?"

"Some patient's eyes deteriorate faster than others, but the answer to your question primarily depends on your longevity. The longer you live, the more sight you'll lose."

"Now, there's an incentive to keep going if I ever heard one."

Dr. Martin placed his hand on George's shoulder. "You never know, although I first detected signs of MD last year, your disease may not progress rapidly. Plus, research may come up with some cure or better treatment. You must try not to let it get you down."

"What else must I do?"

"Stop driving."

"Not drive?"

"When your license renewal comes up, you may not pass the eye test, but until then you shouldn't drive, especially at night. You have a wife. Let her drive."

"Have you ever ridden with my wife?" George asked. Not waiting for an answer, he kept on. "She's pathetic. She creeps, she speeds and if she's out of the driveway, she's lost. The world is better off with a blind man behind the wheel than Catherine."

"Nevertheless, George, even after the cataract surgery clears things up a bit, I'd suggest you start making other arrangements."

"Like what? Ride a unicycle? Have the neighbor kids pull me around in their wagon?"

"I know this news is very upsetting, but you're a good man, George. You'll do the right thing."

"I will. I'll go up to my attic and get my shotgun and...."

"George!"

"...And shoot...Oh shit!...If I'm blind, I probably couldn't find the gun."

"You won't be blind, George. Your sight will be impaired. You'll be able to discern objects through your peripheral vision and with magnification you'll be able to play cards, and...."

"...cut out paper dolls." George groaned. "Oh, hell, what am I bitching about. I'm in pretty good shape for the shape I'm in. Let's fix the large cataract. Just make sure you schedule it so it doesn't interfere with our Panama Canal cruise in March."

Dr. Martin nodded. "My nurse will call you in a day or two with the date, time and details." Then he raised George's ire with his next comment. "It's pretty bright outside, and your eyes are dilated. Would you like us to call someone to come get you?"

"I'm the primary driver in our household. I was able to drive here. I'll drive home, thank you very much!"

"Then, on the way out have the receptionist give you a plastic sunglass insert to put under your glasses for the drive home."

Instead of thanking him, George stormed out of the office leaving Dr. Martin shaking his head. After grabbing the rolled up dark glasses, George marched out of the waiting room, down the elevator and out into the afternoon sun. Then, with glare penetrating his tinted glasses and the insert, he turned the ignition key to on, revved the motor and peeled out of the parking lot onto the busy thoroughfare.

CHAPTER FIFTEEN

*"East is right. West is wrong. Unless I'm heading south,
in which case it's reversed."*

Immediately following Dr. Martin's diagnosis, Catherine had agreed to take over the bulk of the family driving chores. She hadn't been driving much since moving to Carlisle and even less since their marriage. Unfortunately, her license was up for renewal, and the importance of passing it moved George to enroll her in his personally administered remedial driving course. Although at times he felt it might be easier to teach a giraffe to ride a bicycle, he acknowledged Catherine was progressing nicely. He conceded she could handle the ignition key, the gas pedal, brakes and gear shift. She also knew how to operate the windshield wipers, the door locks and the buttons that turned on the radio. After several road sessions, he was fully satisfied she'd mastered the physical challenges of guiding a moving vehicle down a street.

However, teaching the finer points of arriving at a predetermined destination without getting lost proved far more difficult. One example was her inability to read a road map. He might as well be trying to teach a kindergartner Sanscrit for all the progress she was making.

"The top of the map is always north," he told her. "That means the setting sun is to your left, and if you were ever up early enough, the sunrise would be to your right. You do know the sun rises in the east and sinks in the west, don't you?"

"Of course, I do," she said with an air of certainty. "East is right. West is wrong. Unless I'm heading south, in which case it's reversed."

"Huh?" George shook his head and said, "I guess that's right–if you were driving on the map."

"That would be ridiculous. Maps are too small to drive on."

After a momentary pause to see if he was being ribbed, George smiled and continued the lesson. "So Catherine, if you were driving south, and I told you to turn left at the next corner, what direction would you be facing?"

"Where are we going?"

"It makes no difference where we're going, Catherine. I'm only concerned about the direction."

"That's easy, George. You told me that left is always west."

It was at this juncture that George made a disturbing discovery which he'd long suspected. Unless Catherine was deliberately acting stupidly to annoy him, he now knew for sure his wife was directionally challenged. This meant he would have to accompany her in the car at all times, a health risk he'd prefer to avoid. Furthermore, since his visual challenges matched her mental shortcomings, getting from point A to point B was going to be filled with far more frustration and danger than either should endure. Then he hit on the perfect solution.

Before each adventure, he and Catherine would pull a little paper arrow from a package of colored arrows he'd bought at the stationery store and place the point on their starting place on the map. Then they'd place a different colored arrow at their destination. With the map lying on the seat beside her as she drove, George would tell her to twist the map so the street on the map always pointed in the same direction as the one they were traveling. If they were driving east, the top of the map became east. If they turned right, she'd give the map a quarter turn right and the top became south, and so on. Using the map in this unique way, George kept his sanity, and Catherine got them to their destination without the burden of knowing north from south.

When the time came for her to solo, George had a knot in the pit of his stomach the size of a coconut. They carefully went over the map and placed a blue arrow on the supermarket although it was less than two miles away. He also made sure she had her cell phone for emergencies. Then, fearing the worst and hoping for the best, he'd kissed her passionately just in case she never returned. After the success of her inaugural run, he began encouraging his wife to take the car on her own to other familiar destinations like Gert's, the drug store and the mall. Although his anxiety reappeared before and during each mission, he prided himself on breeding some driving success in this previously hopeless woman. In fact, after each safe return, he'd feel a combination of relief and joy, relief that she was back home in one piece, and joy that the map idea he'd taught her turned out to be foolproof.

It wasn't until she'd celebrated a number of successful journeys that Catherine burst his bubble with a confession. She never used the map. At first, she'd memorized the route to the supermarket. Next, her daughter had written out directions to her house and the mall which she also memorized. Finally, by using landmarks like the Shell station on the corner of Fifth and Temple and the brown two story at Main and Forsythe, she could safely tuck the map into the glove compartment and still find her destination. "Anyway," she told George, "I never did feel safe trying to read a map while I was driving."

Upon hearing her confession, he'd tried to disguise his hurt feelings and apparently hadn't done a very good job of it. The truth came out when Catherine tried to kiss him on the cheek, and he'd flinched. Then in what felt to George like a condescending voice, she'd said, "Thank you for helping me get back into driving."

"You're welcome," he'd said in a tone dripping with insincerity.

Perhaps it was his mounting frustration with Catherine's navigational shortcomings, or maybe his deteriorating eyesight, but the fact was George began revisiting other alternatives for living out their lives. Topping the list was a move to The Willows because many of his acquaintances had already done so, and most appeared pleased with their decision. While he'd become familiar with the layout of the upscale retirement facility because he'd visited Reuben so many times, he discounted that knowledge. Reuben was in a separate two-story assisted living wing, and he had no intention of living there–yet. His interest was in the apartments that surrounded the main building.

The more he thought about it, the more he conceded the time may have come when he should sell the house and make a permanent move. After all, having a car wasn't necessary at The Willows, so his inability to drive and Catherine's dubious in-car driving skills wouldn't be an issue. The facility had a bus to take the residents shopping, to the doctor or on many planned outings to see plays, movies and sporting events. Moreover, The Willows bustled with enough daily activities to keep the most manic person busy from wake-up to bed-time. Plus, everyone raved about the meals. So, if a resident didn't feel like cooking, he or she could sign up on the spur of the moment and eat in the dining room.

During a conversation over the breakfast table a few days before, he'd fed Catherine all the positives and negatives about living at the place while being careful not to reveal his intentions or ask her for an opinion. This afternoon he bounded into the living room and brought the subject up again while his wife was reading in the side chair by the couch. "I just went over our finances and made some calculations, and I'm shocked, Catherine. A move to The Willows is affordable. When I add up all the current costs we'd no longer have and subtract them from our new costs, there isn't much difference. I always thought upscale retirement complexes were prohibitively expensive."

She laid her book in her lap. "I thought so, too," she said. "But, I suppose maintaining the house, filling the car with gas and keeping it in good running order really costs a lot."

"And the property taxes. They used to be a pittance. Now they're horrible. Damned politicians."

"George!"

He watched as she turned back to her book. Actually, figuring expenses was a carryover from his previous life when he needed to worry about such things. Now that the years ahead were fewer, he knew there would always be enough for both of them with plenty to spare. So what if he emptied the cookie jar? Any excess was going to Jill and Anne, and they needed more money about as much as an overweight man needed a handful of jellybeans.

In a way, knowing he could afford the move disturbed him. It removed the largest roadblock in his fight with himself to retain the status quo. Without financial concerns, he'd have to beef up his other arguments.

He started with the garden. Even though his physical limitations were mounting and his strength was on the wane, he was excited about planting this year's garden with Jim. However, when he checked with The Willows, he discovered they didn't have any plots where he could plant vegetables. While considering his desire to stay put, that was certainly helpful news, yet not being able to garden wasn't his primary fear. In fact, it paled compared to losing other important pieces of his life.

"You know, Catherine, while moving probably makes sense, I can't stand the thought of leaving my porch and all the memories it harbors. Or the Alexanders and O'Haras. I have so much invested in all of their lives, I can't imagine losing touch with them on a regular basis."

"I know, dear. I feel the same way. But, we've got to do what we've got to do."

George hesitated a second before bending down and kissing his wife on the forehead. Then he stretched out on the couch. What he avoided saying to his wife by leaving her to her book was lately he felt very aware of his own mortality. Yet, what was the point of troubling his bride with his maudlin feelings.

A few minutes later he interrupted her reading again. "Catherine, do you realize how much stuff we've got packed into the basement, attic and two floors of this house? If we do move, how the heck are we going to sort through all of my accumulated belongings and decide what to take and what to leave behind?"

"I don't know, George. From my vantage point it's the biggest deterrent to moving. Even if Gert pitched in, and we work for a week sunup to sundown, we'd barely get it cataloged. Then, assuming we can actually agree on what to take with us, we'd still have to decide how to dispose of the rest."

"We could have an auction or giant garage sale."

"Yeah, right. Who wants to work like a slave just to salvage a few bucks from a lifetime of accumulating. I don't want to do that, George. Do you?"

"Just the thought of perfectly good items being purchased for pennies on the dollar goes against my grain." Then he suggested, "We could let the family pick through the bones and take what they wanted, but with the exception of a few personal mementos like pictures of their mother and me and a few items belonging to their grandparents, what would Jill and Anne want with the surplus? They have enough junk of their own without adding to it."

So, he thought, if he and Catherine did choose to move, and that possibility was becoming slimmer and slimmer as he mulled over the obstacles and found them all daunting, how would they ever downsize? Since nothing else seemed doable, he'd probably call Goodwill or the Salvation Army and let them truck the stuff away.

All at once he started grinning.

"What?" she said.

"I have the solution. We'll invite everyone we know to help haul all our junk out into the yard and take whatever they want. Then we'll pile up the rest, douse it with gasoline and have the city's biggest bonfire. Following a few drinks and snacks, we'll watch the kids roast marshmallows over the embers."

"Sure, and after the cops arrest you as a pyromaniac and throw you into the clink, instead of moving into The Willows, I'll take your checkbook and slip off to Mexico to live out my life sipping Tequila and Dos Equis and subsisting on tamales and tacos."

"Sounds good to me," he said. "Just so you come back if they let me out."

George sighed. While decision making wore him out, avoiding a decision he needed to make took a far greater toll on his energy. Although he'd pretended to let Catherine in on most of his thinking, the truth was he was desperate to uncover any excuse that would keep him out of The Willows.

To start with, he held out hope that he'd be able to drive safely again after his cataract surgery. Or, maybe Dr. Martin's macular degeneration diagnosis was bogus. Moreover, if he did have it, maybe he'd outlast any serious ramifications. He was even willing to believe Catherine could handle all the driving. Held in reserve were other viable options such as taking cabs, hiring a driver or maybe Jim in the summer or having Gert ferry them around.

While he'd collected enough evidence to present a case for staying right where they were, there was still one aspect of moving he feared the most. Once folks moved in, they never got out alive. By contrast, as long as he clung to his current lifestyle, he had the freedom to do what he pleased, whenever he pleased no matter how foolish or dangerous, including a later move to the retirement complex.

The next morning after breakfast, he decided the whole issue needed to be finalized with Catherine before his surgery the next afternoon. Unlike his working years at Kerr when George enjoyed handling tough decisions, making them now made him uncomfortable. Now that he was older and wiser, he was more aware of the consequences of taking the wrong route and his limited ability to make corrections like The Willows move. To compensate for this new vulnerability, he'd developed a manic need to get the decision over with.

He glanced at the clock on the wall and groaned. Nine-thirty. Would his wife ever come down for breakfast? He forced a smile. Moan and groan all you want he told himself, but unless you're willing to go upstairs and wake her, you're not going to talk about The Willows with her until she's damn well ready to come down.

He hated waiting; for a bus, a plane, a table at a restaurant and especially Catherine. However, as long as that was his fate, he'd pass the time by closing his eyes and taking a little snooze in the lounger. After all, he should at least be as rested as his wife when it came to settling a tough decision.

When they sat down next to each other and George presented his case for staying put, Catherine smiled and said, "George, I'm content to remain here where I've spent the happiest year-and-a-half of my life." If her words hadn't fully convinced him, the lingering kiss that followed did the trick.

The next morning when George awakened, the weather was terrible. It had been sleeting all night, and now a steady drizzle was turning the streets into an ice rink. The TV weather guy read off a list of school and business closings. The guy also strongly recommended everyone stay off the roads until at least noon. By then, the storm should have ended and the street crews would have the major thoroughfares salted and sanded.

For George, all this weather-related chaos translated into a nightmare. His cataract surgery was scheduled for one-thirty. If he canceled the appoinment, who knows when he'd get another. Still, that was his most sensible option, since the ice on his short street would be low on the list of priorities for the city crews, and unless the sun made an unscheduled appearance, he'd have to throw some salt on his blacktop driveway just to reach the street. Also, since he couldn't be sure Catherine could or should drive on ice, he'd have to drive them to the doctor's office and pray for a quick melt so she could drive him home.

By the time his wife joined him, he was sitting at the kitchen table threatening the small TV with extinction if it didn't come forth with a brighter forecast.

"Pretty awful out, isn't it?" she said. "You should reschedule your appointment."

"I already have."

"Good."

"They had a cancellation so they could push it forward to four."

"I meant, do it another day."

"Don't you think I asked about that? Other than today, the earliest one I could get would be while we are on our Panama Canal cruise. I'm not missing that. Otherwise, it would have to be May. Jim and I should be planting our garden in May."

"I hope you aren't expecting me to drive you there."

"No, I'm driving there. You're driving me back home."

"George! I can't."

"The way I figure it, the streets should all be salted by then. It will be a piece of cake for you."

"An ice cake! I'm afraid to drive on ice." Then she brightened. "Why don't you call Gert. She'll take you."

"I don't think she'll fly back from Charlotte."

"I forgot she went there with Roundy. So, call a taxi."

"Catherine, those guys drive worse than you do. I only want surgery on my eye, I don't want to end up in the orthopedic ward." With that he pounded the heel of his hand on the table. "At three we're leaving for Dr. Martin's. I'm going to drive there, and you're going to drive me home. End of discussion."

She matched his intensity. "You are a stubborn man, George Konert, but I'm not budging from this place. You're on your own."

"We'll see about that!" he said, glaring menacingly at his wife. When she didn't back down from his threat, he stood up and headed for the closet for his heavy winter coat and galoshes. From there he grabbed one of several small bags of salt from the garage and began snaking down the driveway tossing the white pellets from side to side.

Later at three, after they both maintained their icy attitudes all afternoon, George again bundled up and with the cell phone in one hand and the car keys in the other, headed for the garage. "I'll drive both ways then."

"Good luck on your surgery," she called, not moving from her seat on the couch.

Knowing the doctor would not let him drive home after the surgery, he dressed for the weather, entered the car and backed carefully out of the melting driveway onto the unsalted glare ice of the street. Shifting into low gear, he crept down the street, fishtailing with the slightest pressure on the accelerator, skidding when he touched the brake. He managed to enter the curve by the Alexander's before losing total control of the vehicle, sliding sideways off the road and landing in their front yard. He pounded the wheel in exasperation. A couple of futile wheel-spinning attempts at backing out, and he was convinced he was stuck for the duration. More upset at missing his appointment than worried about his predicament, he dialed the eye surgeon's number to cancel. The receptionist told him another appointment had just opened up for ten the next morning. "If you really want it."

"Of course, I want it," he growled.

"Remember, nothing but water for three hours before."

"I know, I know. This is the third time you've told me that. Do you think I'm senile?"

"I just wanted to make sure, Mr.Konert."

"That I'm senile to be out on a day like this?"

"No, sir. That you remember not to eat."

"Okay, I remember." He punched the END button with his finger and got out of the car. Then he traipsed up to the Alexander's front door and pushed the bell. When no one answered, he grimaced and picked his way down their driveway, zig-zagged his way through the neighbor's yards and eventually reached his house. Since the garage was closed and the opener resting in the glove compartment of the Buick, he carefully mounted the stoop and rang the doorbell.

He could hear Catherine fumbling with the deadbolt. When she finally opened the door, he was shivering from the frigid walk up the street. Still, he managed to put on a happy face.

"Hi, dear, I'm home."

CHAPTER SIXTEEN

"I don't know how you keep your sense of humor."

Instead of bounding out of the queen size bed the next morning, George lay quietly on his back recalling the previous day. It sickened him. Although he wanted to curse the winter weather for all that had happened, he knew unequivocally that he was totally to blame. It was his stubbornness that resulted in the Buick resting in the Alexander's icy yard. In addition, it was he who had rejected Catherine's pleas to postpone his surgery and left his wife with frayed feelings he'd have to repair. Worst of all, he only had a few hours before his surgery to appease her. He groaned. How could one man wreak so much havoc?

To avoid a repeat of his past mistakes, he began making a plan for the day. Assuming the predicted forecast actually turned out sunny and forty, the wrecking company would have his car out of the Alexander's yard and back onto his driveway by noon. Also, assuming the taxi company didn't forget him, a cab would be at his door on time to take him to his 10:00AM appointment with Dr. Martin and also be on call to pick him up following the surgery.

The one unresolved item from the previous day's list of disasters lay next to him on her side with her back toward him snorting away as always. He'd never be able to smooth her feathers before he left, because she wouldn't be up. That meant following surgery he'd have to make amends when he was in a dependent state. Even worse, she might store her hurt for a later time and bludgeon him with silence. Damn, if he'd only heeded one of the Top Ten Rules of good marriages. *Never go to bed angry.*

Lying there in bed in the pre-dawn darkness with his regret egging him on, George began grasping at any solution that would assuage his guilt and defuse her anger. Since she was only a foot away, he rolled over onto his side toward her and placed his hand lightly on her hip. Snuggling closer, his lips found a home near the crook of her neck a short kiss away from her warm cheek. Meanwhile, his hand began gently exploring a larger and larger area. Although it had not been his intent, he soon found himself pleasantly aroused. He moved closer, pressing against her.

Suddenly, the rhythm of her breathing changed and her hips moved ever so slightly. Then her hand caught his and brought it to her waist where she held it tightly against her nightgown. He scrunched closer until her movements ended, and she lay still. With a mixture of exhilaration and regret he removed his hand, rolled onto his back and eventually got up.

After that, the morning continued with a series of surprises. First, Catherine pulled herself out of bed and proceeded to the kitchen much earlier than usual. Then, without his resorting to begging, she volunteered to accompany him to Dr. Martin's. Soon they were smiling and chatting, and like a windy autumn day, all of yesterday's fallen leaves had miraculously blown away.

Sitting across from each other at the kitchen table, he watched as Catherine spooned cereal and strawberries and smiled at him. Not knowing the exact purpose behind the smile, he accepted it as combination *sign of peace* and *best wishes on your surgery* smile. Without confirming her intent, she continued spooning and smiling her way through the rest of her breakfast. Then, placing the spoon in the now empty bowl, she looked up at him and smiled once more. Only this time he could see she was blushing slightly. "I had a most enjoyable dream this morning," she said.

He nodded knowingly. "What a coincidence. So did I."

She dropped her gaze to her hands. "You were in it." A long silence followed. Then she blurted out, "I love you, George Konert."

He grabbed her hand. "What a coincidence. I love you, too, Catherine."

On the way across town to the doctor's office, they were chatting in the back seat of the cab. "Aren't you nervous, George?"

"Not really. Compared to the way we drive, this guy does pretty well."

When the driver eyed him in the rear view mirror, George grinned, and his wife said, "I was thinking about your surgery."

"Why should I be nervous? Dr. Martin says it's the most common surgery in this country. More common even than gall bladder surgery, or heart surgery or even vasectomies. I'd thought about the latter, but at my age I came to the conclusion that seeing was more important."

She shuddered. "I don't know how you keep your sense of humor. Just the thought of someone cutting into my eye gives me the willies. I'd be scared."

"They give me drugs, Catherine. As I understand it, I'll be completely conscious on some level, but I won't feel or remember any pain. They say it's easier on the patient than having a cavity filled. I may be in La La Land, but I'll think I'm completely lucid."

"That's nothing new," she said. "I've seen you that way many times."

"That's not nice, Catherine, especially when your poor husband is about to go under the knife." Then as they moved ever closer to the clinic, he continued on with his nervous jabbering. "You are aware that for several months after I get my new lens, I'm not allowed to lift really heavy objects. Like you, Catherine."

"A hundred and twenty-eight is not heavy."

"It is for four foot-six." George saw the driver grin as he glimpsed at them in the mirror.

"For the record, I'm five-six."

"Maybe I can drag you by the hair, then."

She pretended to bop him on the head. The whole bit of nonsense brought smiles from all three and distracted George for a few more blocks. Then he said, "If you wake up in the middle of the night and see a pirate lying next to you, don't be afraid. I understand I have to wear an eyepatch for awhile when I sleep so I don't scratch my eye unintentionally." He raised his voice a little to make sure the driver would hear. "And, no sex, Catherine. It will be at least a month before I can get back to doing it every night."

The cab driver shook his head, and a few more blocks passed.

"Also, before I ever agreed to the surgery, I made sure it was okay for me to handle the luggage when we go on the cruise. I'd never want to miss that trip with you."

He reached over, found her hand and placed it in his. They rode on in silence. Suddenly, George pulled his hand away and began searching through his jacket pockets. With a note of panic he asked his wife, "Did you bring my sunglasses?"

"No."

"I need them for the ride home. I understand that right after surgery the glare will be a killer."

"Sorry, George, this is the first time I've heard about it."

"I'm sure I mentioned it."

"Maybe you did, but it didn't register. I have mine. They're not prescription, and I'm not too happy about you stretching them out with that big head of yours, but you can wear them."

"There's no way I'd ever wear sunglasses with all that gold trim and design work."

"I'm sorry, George. Maybe you should have remembered yours."

The truth stung, but he was past the point where he could retrieve them. So, considering his alternatives and as embarrassing as wearing female designer glasses might be, he quickly accepted her offer. He'd just have to look the fool.

That's when the driver reached into the glove compartment, pulled out a pair and handed them back to him. "Wear these," he said, "I always carry an extra pair. You can return them after I take you back home."

Arriving at the clinic, George paid the fare and tipped him on the heavy side as a thank you for the glasses. "We'll have the clinic call you when I'm ready to leave." He grabbed Catherine's arm and took a few steps toward the building. Suddenly, he turned back to the taxi driver and hollered, "I don't know your name. When the clinic calls, we may get someone else."

"It's Herb. But, don't worry about it. I'm the only one working this morning."

Waiting for the elevator, Catherine said, "That was sure nice of him to lend you his sunglasses."

"I'm never surprised at the inherent kindness of people."

"Me either, George. I also believe that thoughtful people attract kindness."

"Well said, Catherine. It worked to attract you."

Entering the elevator his wife said, "Before the driver lent you his glasses, I was going to suggest you ask the nurse for another one of those dark rolled up plastic things you wore under your glasses the last time. That would have worked fine until we got home, too."

"Good thought. Now you have two things to remember. Ask the nurse about the plastic things and remember to give Herb his glasses back. Don't forget, because I'm leaving you in charge. I may be out of it when we leave."

"When we leave?" She snickered. "How about now?"

"I'm fine."

"Sure you are. Push *Two,* George. Haven't you noticed the elevator isn't moving?"

"Oh!"

Eventually, he left Catherine in the waiting room and followed the nurse into the outpatient surgery suite. When they were seated in a small windowless room, she began running through her pre-op checklist. "Mr. Konert, you'll be having surgery on your left eye today. Is that right?"

George nodded.

"Mr. Konert, please answer the question for me. Mistakes can happen."

George looked at her quizzically. "Yes. Right."

"You're saying, the left eye is the correct one?"

"No, the doctor is going to correct the left one. The right one isn't bad enough yet."

She looked skyward for divine inspiration. With her pen poised above her clipboard, she repeated very slowly, "Mr. Konert, today you are going to have Dr. Martin operate on your left eye. Yes or no?"

By now, George was as perturbed with the nurse's persistent questions as she was with his answers, so he responded slowly and deliberately, "Yes, that's right."

She shrugged her shoulders and mumbled, "I sure hope the surgery goes better than this."

"Right. At least we're together on that," he said.

She then began to preview the upcoming procedure. "After the doctor administers the anesthetic to numb your eye and sedate you, he'll wait a few minutes and then begin the surgery. He'll make a small slit in your eye and insert an ultrasonic probe into the slit. This converts the lens with its cataract to paste. That is then sucked out of the intact lens capsule. After this, an inter-ocular lens is inserted to replace the removed one. The new lens is shaped to focus on medium to far distances so glasses are only required for reading. The incision is so small it doesn't even require sutures. Do you have any questions?"

"Yes. Will this help me drive again even though I have macular degeneration?"

The woman began searching through the charts she was holding. Finally, she said, "I'm afraid you'll have to ask Dr. Martin about that."

"So, it won't."

"Mr. Konert, I don't know."

"Or, won't say?"

In exasperation, she exclaimed, "Please, I'm the nurse. I don't have a crystal ball and only Dr. Martin can answer those questions."

"Well, I bet you have an opinion!" As she backed out of the room, he said, "I'm sorry, Miss...?"

"Don't even think about it, Mr. Konert. Everyone gets edgy before surgery. Good luck."

They were home by one-fifteen and a short time after Catherine called her, Gert appeared with sandwiches from Subway. They chatted as they ate.

"I can't believe you feel so good, Georgy boy."

"I'm not sure I see any better, yet. I guess it takes awhile for it to clear. The doctor told me I'd feel fine when the anesthetic wore off, and he was right about that. So, I'm sure I'll be seeing better soon. The whole process was certainly easier on me than other things doctors have done to fix me."

"That's amazing. I'd have thought you'd have some discomfort."

"I don't. Nor do I have any memory of the surgery. I remember talking to Dr. Martin. Then, the next thing I knew I was walking to the taxi with Herb, the cab driver, holding my arm." He turned to Catherine. "By the way, did you return his sunglasses?"

"Yes, dear."

George patted her hand. "Thank you, sweetheart."

Catherine grinned at Gert. With George listening, she said, "I've never seen my husband so mellow. I wonder if Dr. Martin would give him a prescription for everyday use."

"Bad move, mom. He's fine the way he usually is. A doped up George might get on your nerves."

"You're probably right. At least he's not usually an ogre, so I better leave well-enough alone. Still, it would be nice if he was occasionally solicitous of me. Maybe I could get something to give him on an *as needed basis.*"

Then Gert stood up to leave and gave him a gentle hug. "Forget the personality change, Georgy boy. I'm just pleased you're not suffering."

"Me, too, but I do think I'll take a nap when you leave. I'm getting sleepy."

After a two hour nap, George hauled out the playing cards and challenged Catherine to a game of gin rummy. After losing three games, he packed up the deck and accused her of taking advantage of his weakened condition. "George, I beat you regardless of your condition." Then she slipped out of insult range by moving toward the kitchen to start dinner.

A few minutes later a knock at the front door announced a new arrival. George looked out and saw Mike O'Hara shivering on the stoop, wearing only a sweater and holding two bottles of beer. When George opened the door and let him in, his friend said, "I thought we should celebrate your surgery."

"I'm not sure it's successful yet," George said.

"I've never personally heard of a cataract surgery that wasn't successful. But just in case, I wanted to be the first lawyer at your door to offer my services for the lawsuit."

"But, you don't know a thing about malpractice suits, O'Hara."

"You weren't supposed to know that. Or, that I'll get a big fat finder's fee from some lawyer who does."

Once they were seated in the living room, the lawyer held up the two bottles. "Before I get seriously involved, I have to give you a vison test. What am I holding?"

"Two bottles of Becks."

"Good. Now I want to test your brain function. What do you do with these?"

"I have a gross answer for disposing of the empties, but I believe the correct answer is, you drink them."

"Very good. Now to check your deductive reasoning, I need to know what you will do if I should leave right now and take the beers with me."

"I will strangle you with my bare hands."

"Ah, but you are weakened from your surgery."

"Exactly, that's why it's the perfect alibi when the cops question me after finding your body lying in my front yard."

With that, George placed his bottle in the fridge for another day and poured himself a glass of water. Then they chuckled and guzzled until O'Hara finished his beer and left. At that point, George tried on his eye patch. Parading into the kitchen, he sighted Catherine at the range. He tiptoed up behind her and suddenly threw his arms around her waist and pulled her toward him and asked in a gruff voice, "Aye Matey, what's for dinner?"

"Meatloaf."

"Aaargh."

CHAPTER SEVENTEEN

"How do you stand it?"

After a couple of reassuring checkups with the eye surgeon over the next two weeks, George was proclaimed "good to go." The only proviso was no heavy lifting until just before the cruise which was still a month away. Since the doctor hadn't defined heavy lifting, and George being a male hadn't asked, he tested his wife's patience by ringing every last drop from the surgeon's omission. His first request seemed reasonable enough. "You'll have to pull the trash can to the curb, Catherine. It's too heavy for me."

"Of course, dear," she replied. "I'll be happy to do that."

A later demand took the form of, "It's awfully cold here by the TV, Catherine. Would you mind going down to the basement and bringing up the space heater? I don't want to take any chances with my eye." This brought grumbling. Griping all the way, she grudgingly clumped down and then up the stairs carrying the small appliance. After plugging it in, she announced, "Anything to make you more comfortable, my precious, but for the record you could have carried it. The space heater is quite light."

The turning point finally came two weeks after his surgery when he shook his head at her request to stand on the step stool and take down a small, seldom-used double-boiler from a top shelf of the pantry. Since she only wanted the pot to melt the chocolate for the eclairs he requested for dessert, instead of showing her anoyance, Catherine hopped into the car, drove to the supermarket and returned home with two chocolate cupcakes covered with coconut.

Later that evening when it was time for dessert, she trotted out the second-rate, store-bought cakes. That led George to have a snit. "You know I hate coconut, Catherine."

"Really, dear? I'm sorry. I forgot." Then in a sweet voice dripping with sarcasm, she said, "I was going to make the chocolate eclairs you wanted, but I couldn't reach the double-boiler."

"Oh," was his whispered response as he quickly took a bite out of the cupcake. That night he decided it was time to relax his stringent lifting standards.

A few days later in mid-morning, Gert stopped by. After removing her coat and hanging it in the hall closet, she came close enough for George to give her the once over. She was all dolled up in a new pants outfit. At least it seemed new to him. Then again, maybe it was actually an old one. He shrugged. He wasn't much good at remembering the clothes women wore. What he did notice with his better vision was her new, svelte figure. Women's figures he could remember, and hair. She'd been letting her old buzz cut grow out, and he liked her longer, curlier hairdo."

"You look fabulous, Gert."

"Thank you, Georgy boy. I've lost forty pounds. Some women let themselves go after they get married. It took me so long to snare someone, I figured I owed Roundy a reward." She struck a pose. "Ta Da! Gert-Lite! "

Since Catherine was upstairs recreating herself, he escorted his stepdaughter into the living room. When she was seated, he stood over her and asked, "Coffee?" She shook her head.

"Tea?"

"No, thanks."

"Me?"

She laughed. "Now you're talking, Big Boy. Let's get it on!"

He frowned and pointed toward the second story.

"Oh, yeah, Mom. She's so quick to find fault and slow to forgive."

"Do you think?" he said, plopping down on the couch next to her. "Knowing how she is, perhaps I could serve you in a more realistic capacity?"

"Actually, you can," she replied turning serious. "I need some of your brilliant advice before I go stark, raving mad."

"Like the shrink on TV says, 'I'm listening.'"

"George, you've been retired for a long time...."

"Sixteen years."

"...How do you stand it?"

"You adapt."

She threw her hands into the air. "Oh, thank you so very much! Roundy told me the same thing and he's never been retired." She glanced skyward and shook her head. "Men!"

George grinned. "Gert, I'm sorry. I thought the quick fix might work, but I can see I was wrong."

"It's not cute, George. I'm really not making it. I'm so bored that once in awhile I'm tempted to take that first drink just so I can overcome the consequences of drinking it. I'm that desperate for something worthwhile to do. Ever since high school, I've been striving. Striving to stay sober, striving to build my commercial cleaning business, striving to overcome my conflicts with mom. Now that I'm past those battles, I need some new ones. At the least I need to find something meaningful to do." Stalling until the right words popped onto the screen in his head, he reached over and gently touched her arm. Quickly filling the void, Gert cried, "Why did I sell my business, George? My life is too easy without it. Heck, I can't even clean my own house because the Polish lady who's always cleaned it for Roundy and his first wife does it for me. When you retired, how did you handle it, George?"

"Poorly. I mourned my wife's death for twelve years. In reality, I replaced my job with memories and tears. However, I always had my garden. It not only gave me something to focus on, it gave me a job that was physically taxing, required planning and nurturing and provided tangible rewards for any success I achieved. I still stagnated in the winter, but at least for the rest of the year I was involved in something living that needed me." He studied her face a moment. "Then, I lucked out. I stopped by your old house, handed you a quarter and ended up buying your mother. That's when my life started back up hill."

Gert smiled. "If I hadn't been so desperate to get rid of her, I would have held out for a dollar. Normally, I'm a better business person than that."

"Whatever she cost would have been a bargain. I never let a day go by without thanking God for overcharging you for the cabbage you bought. Not only does Catherine's love fortify me, but I developed a friendship with her daughter, one of the most thoughtful, intelligent and funny women on the face of the planet. That was the icing on the cake, the toy in the Cracker Jack box, the...."

"I got it! I got it!" she said through her tears. Then, as usual, rather than wait for the tears to dry up on their own, Gert wisecracked, "You could have mentioned natural beauty and, slim, yet voluptuous figure."

"I was just coming to that part, Gert."

The silence that followed gave him a few moments to consider his options. Certainly, examples from the life he'd lived weren't relevant for Gert. Perhaps if he drew on the lives of others, it might help her more.

"My daughter, Jill, retired early and joined her husband's business. They've had their growing pains, but she seems happy."

"Jill is an exceptional woman with big time skills in marketing and finance. I cleaned offices. Sure, I marketed my firm's services, hired and fired employees and kept tabs on the profits, but my business was small potatoes. Another firm in a different arena wouldn't have any need of me." Once she started, the words poured out. "Roundy has suggested I work for him at Gerlach Machine, but what could I offer his company. I'm mostly qualified for a job on the production floor. I'd enjoy working at something different like that, but can't you just hear the chatter from the other employees if the president of the company were to place his first lady on the assembly line or had her sweeping the floors? It would seem so weird to them, they'd surely assume I was either a spy or a nut case."

He shook his head. "I really get upset when you typecast yourself as a manual laborer, Gert. Just because you've always done it, doesn't mean that's all you can do. You need to break out of your comfort zone."

"You're right, George, and I agree. That's why I've been thinking about volunteer work. Maybe ringing a bell at Christmas or driving around in a truck picking up used clothes for the Salvation Army."

"Don't be pathetic, Gert. There are all kinds of groups looking for members to be on their committees. Job counseling groups. Education groups. Arts groups."

She rolled her eyes. "Yeah, I'm so artsy, fartsy, and I just love committees. Everyone beats their gums, and no one does any work. I'd rather clean toilets than serve on a committee."

George groaned. "This is going to be harder than I thought."

"I hear you. Roundy thinks I should take a few courses at the community college, and I might, but none of the courses jump out at me. I was hoping for a self-help course on lobotomies."

George laughed. "Come on down to the basement. I'm a little out of practice, but in my prime I was pretty good with the electric drill, but weak with the chisel." He frowned. Sighing, he said, "Let's get serious." He stroked his chin. "How about taking some psychology courses. You already help drinkers in AA. Maybe you could expand on that?"

"That's a good thought, George, but I do more of that now than I want. I need to move on. I need a new passion, and I don't know what it is."

"I'm afraid I can't help you with that, but you're right on. If you're not getting a paycheck and you don't have a passion for what you're doing, almost any kind of work becomes frustrating and pure drudgery. That's why they call it *work*. I learned that the hard way right after Grace died. I attended grief therapy classes at church for several months, and it helped me a lot. Then a year or so later, when no one else would step forward to lead the class, I agreed to accept the responsibility. That was a mistake. By then, I didn't want to relive all the emotions of my wife's death, so I was a terrible leader. I kept the class emotionally sterile and nobody benefitted. You're right, Gert, to feel good about volunteering you need a passion for the mission of the organization."

Gert sat quietly through his short dissertation. When he finished, she remained contemplative so he said, "Come on, Gert. Certainly you have something you want to do. Some passion?"

"You're my only passion, my love, and you just taught me something."

"I hope I didn't discourage you from community service."

She shook her head. "You just made me realize that when I grow up I want to be wise, just like you."

"But, aren't there some anatomical issues?"

She shook her head and laughed. "Egad! It's scary how we're two peas in a pod. We're always making inane cracks at inappropriate times." Then she sprung a surprise. "I think I'll begin by taking that psychology course."

"Really?"

"Yeah, maybe I'll learn how to deal with all the guilt I feel over Todd."

Assuming her meaning, he answered quickly. "Hey, you were a teenager. Lots of things can happen to kids that they may regret later. You gave your baby a better chance by giving him up. Yet, you never forgot him, and when you finally reached a time when you were ready to find him it coincided with the time he was ready to let you into his life. So, why the guilt?"

"Because he's gay."

The suddenness of that foreign thought sent a shock through his system. He dropped her hand and looked up to the ceiling for inspiration. Grace wasn't listening, or if she was, she didn't come forth with the words he needed to express his thoughts. He plunged ahead anyway.

"Is it really so bad that he's gay, Gert?"

He watched her as his words sunk in, and she struggled to come up with an answer. Finally, she said, "No, I don't think it's so bad, but I feel bad about it."

He smiled. "Well, I don't. He seems like a high achieving, sociable and fulfilled human."

"But, it makes life harder for him. It's not normal."

"So, he doesn't enjoy sex with women. The world doesn't need another man adding to the population explosion. He's kind, fun to be with, and he doesn't tote a gun or harm people or bilk old ladies out of their bank accounts."

"But, maybe if I'd...."

"You'd what? You did one key thing. You gave a good man his life." When she didn't answer, he added, "You could have had an abortion."

She took a quick swipe at the perspiration forming on her forehead. "I couldn't do that even though his father, my father and both of Todd's paternal grandparents wanted me to."

"So, that left you two choices. Adoption or play mother. You weren't fit to care for a child on your own, and from what I've heard about your home life, it would have been criminal at that time to bring your baby into the poisoned atmosphere of your parent's home." He added softly, "You made the right choice, Gert."

"But, would he be gay if I'd kept him?"

George shrugged. "The jury's out on that one, Gert. Nobody knows for sure. But, considering your maturity level at that time, there's a good probability he would have developed into something far worse. Without parental guidance, it would have been easy for him to become a drug addict or even a criminal."

She was thoughtful for a second before answering. "Yes, George, I'm sure that would have been far worse for him." She scrunched farther back into the couch and hung her head. "Here I am talking about what is or isn't normal, and I'm an alcoholic."

"You were an alcoholic," he corrected.

"No, I'll always be one," she said with finality.

"Then so will Todd," George said. "But, at least he inherited your strength to control it. Now that's something to feel proud about."

The silence that overtook their conversation gave George a chance to take a few deep breaths and relax. The short break allowed him to shut off some of his concern for Gert without feeling like he was abandoning her. There were times, although infrequent, when he wondered whether he ever had any impact on anyone's decisions. Yet, at the same time, a part of him wondered if he had any right to think he should. In Gert's case she was, after all, the grown child of a woman he'd only recently married. She was not his child to influence. She was in her fifties and married, for goodness sakes. He smiled at the silent figure sitting next to him on the couch. He could be so damn presumptuous.

"Sometimes, Georgy boy, I get this eerie feeling you know me better than I know myself."

Before he could protest, she continued, "What I'm trying to say is your little message about Todd hit home. Bull's-eye! Maybe, I can move on now. I'm going to work with animals."

He sat back and gaped at her. "Where in hell did that come from?"

She craned her neck and kissed his cheek. "From you, George."

His first thought was, how did I do that? I don't especially like animals. Still, he grinned and added, "Well, good for me."

"Don't pat yourself on the back, yet, Georgy boy. I haven't a clue what form it will take, or if it will ever come about, but it's a start."

"We do have a lot in common, Gert. I'm still not sure what I'm going to do for the rest of *my* life, either "

CHAPTER EIGHTEEN

"Loser!"

The day George caught a glimpse of what he was going to do for the rest of his life dawned cloudless and cold. It was a perfect day to have a fire in the fireplace, play a little gin with Catherine and read the new seed catalog that just came in the mail. His plans also called for a trip to the cleaners to pick up Catherine's gray skirt and drop off his favorite beige slacks. Dry Clean Only the tag said. Although he would have thought the gravy stains could have been dabbed clean with soap and water, his wife, who was far wiser than he about such things, disagreed. So, as long as he was going to the cleaners anyway, he might as well take them along.

Ferrying clothes to the cleaners was just one of the many short excursions he'd attempted since his cataract surgery. He'd soloed to the grocer, the gas-station and cross-town to Gert's. But, he never drove after dark anymore. Even though the surgery had improved his vision, he knew that dusk was the trigger to move over to the rider's side and let Catherine handle the wheel. So far, the plan hadn't backfired.

Maybe it was silly to be uplifted by such mundane experiences, but these little jaunts with the wheel in his hand and his foot on the pedal helped him face a bleak future where such pleasures might not be possible. If the doctor was right, and he was going blind, being the commander on these daylight missions helped manage his fears. After all, he was driving to the cleaners, wasn't he? Typically, that wasn't something a man with vision problems did. This led him to the possibility his dire prognosis was wrong, or if he was developing it, maybe his disease would progress so slowly, life as he wanted to live it wouldn't be affected until the rest of his body checked out.

George turned onto the main arterial for the last lap to the cleaners. Humming along at a steady clip, he heard a rhythmic whisper, "Enjoy it now, George. Enjoy it while you can."

About two-thirty, Catherine and George finished a three game set of gin rummy. After losing the last nine sessions, George was ecstatic to win all three games and a buck and a half. While he didn't strut around saying, "I'm the man! I'm the man!" like he had following his most recent victory weeks before, he couldn't resist some gloating. Over and over he chirped about how he was back on top, and how skill always wins out over luck in the long run.

With Catherine accepting defeat with a degree of aplomb unfathomable to him, George tried to goad her into another three games. "What's the matter? Are you afraid to play me now that your luck's run out?"

When he could see she was wavering, he stopped his chattering and began shuffling the cards. That's when she said, "I'll play all afternoon if you want, George. However, I was going to bake your favorite dessert for dinner tonight, lemon meringue pie, and it takes awhile."

"Oooh!"

"And, I don't have enough eggs. One of us needs to go to the store."

"Oh!" he said, hesitating a moment before beginning to deal. "We'll play one more game for fifty cents, and the loser drives to the store, okay?"

"Okay, but when it's not dark out, you normally insist I let you drive. If you're planning on losing on purpose, I don't want to play."

"Are you crazy? Winning this game is worth far more than driving the car anywhere." He began sorting his cards. "Now that your luck has run out, Catherine, I'm going to capitalize on it."

George did end up winning a close game. He also bragged so much, Catherine said, "I have half a mind to just buy you a pie instead of going to all the trouble of making one."

And he'd replied, "Loser!"

After dressing for the cold, she'd marched out the door to the garage without kissing him goodbye. As it happened, that was the first thing he thought of a short time later when the two policemen came to the door and told him Catherine had been broadsided by a car that had run a red light.

George squelched a primal scream. Replying rhetorically, he said, "How could that happen."

The older officer, who'd broken the news and done all of the talking after George had invited them inside, took him literally and detailed the answer. "The driver of the other car was texting on a cell phone, didn't see the red light and crashed into the driver's side of your wife's car."

With fear quavering his voice, he asked, "How bad is it?"

The younger man backed away leaving the unanswered question for his partner. "When they put her in the ambulance, she was badly injured. I'm not so sure she was conscious, but she was definitely alive."

On the trip to the Mercy Hospital Emergency Room, George quelled his initial terror. Sitting alone in the back seat of the squad car, George felt so anxious the thoughts that should have been coursing through his brain had been pushed aside by those that didn't belong there. Instead of asking the police officers to call for an update on Catherine's current condition, he silently berated himself for all the events leading up to her ill-fated trip to the store. He stewed about the idiocy of crowing over winning a stupid card game and, worse, forcing his wife to play another so he could taunt her some more. Most of all, he felt sick that he'd let her get away without a kiss goodbye, or spouting the saying they consistently used as a parting ritual. "Don't embarrass the family, Catherine."

Back when they were newly married, she'd used the phrase for the first time when he was about to leave home to give the Buick dealer "a piece of his mind" for getting grease all over his upholstery following a tuneup and oil change. She had touched him gently on the arm and smiled before she said, "Don't embarrass the family, George." After that, he'd revived the admonition many times, especially after she began driving again on her own and displaying a penchant for getting lost. Yet, on this dreadful day, when he'd won at gin and sent her to the store without the benefit of the farewell warning or a goodbye kiss, his negligence had turned into a disaster. How could he ever forgive himself for that?

The patrol car was entering the final leg of the brief journey to Mercy Hospital. Ever since he'd seen the officers at the door, he'd been dreading what he'd find there. Moreover, since the police didn't have any up-to-date information to share with him, he was left to conjure up his own images of what he'd see. He knew the accident was serious. They'd told him that. The older cop had also told him she was alive when she was being carted off in the ambulance. Therefore, he began visualizing her in a bed with white-coated staffers hovering around her, sticking tubes in her and checking her vital signs. Although he feared the worst, that was the way he wanted to find her.

Not knowing what else to do until he could see for himself, he folded his hands and bowed his head in prayer. "Please, God, don't let her die." Then, while he was at it, he added, "And please forgive me for my stupidity."

Moments later, the older officer who'd been eyeing him throughout the trip, turned and said, "Is there anything we can do for you, Mr. Konert? Maybe, make a call to someone?"

"Could you find out how my wife is?"

"I could make that call, too, but by the time I'd get a report, we'll be there. I think it would be better to let the doctors tell you."

"You're not holding back, are you? She is alive?"

"Mr. Konert, I've been the bearer of bad news too many times over the years to hold anything back. Everything I know, you know. My gut feeling is she is alive but in serious shape. You'll know soon. We're almost there."

George leaned back and recalled the only other time he'd been at Mercy. It was following his heart attack. On that occasion he'd had no memory of the Emergency Room. He had driven himself there, collapsed at the ER door and awakened in a private room with Jill and Anne at his bedside. Following his grand entrance, someone apparently parked his car, wheeled him off to surgery and bypassed four arteries. Since he'd been asleep through that whole ordeal and had come out better than when he went in, maybe, he hoped, Catherine would experience a similar fate.

Suddenly, he caught his breath. Until that moment, he'd never considered who had triggered Jill and Anne's journey or how they got to his bedside. He only knew their presence comforted him, and his recovery was hastened by the joy of hearing their voices and feeling their loving presence. Now that he thought about it, he realized that only Catherine could have been responsible for contacting his daughters. Or, possibly Gert was involved. Either way, he now needed to inform Gert about Catherine's accident and let her know where her mother was.

George leaned forward and got the officers' attention. "Do you know if my wife's daughter has been contacted?"

They looked at one another before answering. "I doubt she has," the driver said. "Would you like us to contact her?" The other officer picked up a clipboard and pen. Since they had pulled up to the Emergency Room entrance, George said, "Would you? I'd be so grateful. Her name is Gert Gerlach, Mrs. Harold Gerlach." Reaching into his wallet, he pulled out a torn scrap of paper and handed it to the older officer. "And, here's her cell phone number."

"Great. Pete here will call while I take you inside."

"Is that the Harold Gerlach from Gerlach Machine?" the younger man asked.

"Yes." But before George could question him on how he'd made the connection, the older officer began helping George from the car and leading him toward the Emergency Room entrance. Along the way, he answered the unasked question. "Pete's father and older brother work for Gerlach." Then he added, "You know, Mr. Konert, that's one of the reasons why I never wanted to leave Carlisle. You're never completely alone here. Everyone knows someone who knows someone, and most people want to help if they can." He smiled at

George. "My name is Oscar Blankenship. And, now you know me. By the way, all my friends call me Ocky."

Inside, George saw a line of people waiting at the reception desk and fell in behind them. Ocky grabbed him firmly by the arm. He whispered, "You're not going through all that rigamarole. I know a few of the ER docs. They'll tell me what's going on." He pointed to the waiting area. "Take a seat. I'll be right back." While George numbly complied, Ocky marched down a short hallway and barged through a door marked, *STAFF ONLY.* George felt momentarily better. Evidently angels came in all shapes and sizes, and they didn't all carry harps. Some carried holstered guns and nightsticks.

He picked up a health magazine from the table and mechanically turned a few pages before tossing it back onto the pile. It was going to take a lot more than a well-worn rag to distract him from his thoughts. He leaned back until his head rested against the beige wall. Although he was practically bald now, he could still imagine his first wife, Grace, saying, "Don't lean your head against that nice wallpaper." Catherine, on the other hand, would have admonished him differently. "Don't do that, George. You don't know who's filthy head was there before you." It was weird how his brain had stored away so much mundane female guidance. Eighty-one years and two marriages worth.

Suddenly, he shivered. A cold draft from the front door announced another emergency being wheeled in on a gurney pushed by an orderly and led by a nurse. They proceeded down the hallway and through the door where Ocky had disappeared. George's terror followed them. Was the cop taking so long because he was afraid to face him with some deadly news? Or, if Catherine hadn't expired, why was he making him wait so long to know the truth?

His anxiety grew, and other questions begged to be answered. Had the young officer reached Gert, and if he had, was she on the way? Would she call her sister, Marianne, or was that his job? Of course, he'd have to call Jill and Anne, the Alexanders and the O'Haras. In fact, once he received the verdict, all kinds of people needed to know, and there would be much to do like canceling the cruise, and who knows what else. He scanned the hallway. Where was that officer? He had all these things to do, yet he couldn't do a darn thing until someone told him whether Catherine was okay, or if he was planning a funeral.

George stood up and began pacing. The line at the receptionist dissipated. Apparently, timing was everything. It was just his luck that the place was packed when he showed up. Now, anybody could wander in with the sniffles and get immediate attention. Hopefully, his beloved didn't have to wait.

He walked to the window. It was getting dark, dinner time for all but the unlucky. Other than an ambulance waiting under the portico, and Pete still sitting in the cop car that brought him here, the parking lot was as quiet as the waiting room.

He wanted to scream. "WHERE IS OCKY?"

George was heading back to the hard chair when he saw the heavy-set officer striding toward him. Something in his quick steps comforted him. Like a maternity nurse announcing the arrival of a new child, everyone hurries when they're bringing the gift of life. Only a cruel person would rush to tell him his wife was dead. However, not until he saw the cop grin or felt himself being engulfed in a giant bear hug, was he totally sure. Ocky's actual words were almost anticlimactic. "Mr. Konert, your wife is alive."

"Can I see her?"

"It's a zoo in there, but I knew you were going to ask. The Emergency Room doctor said your wife is stable and sedated for pain. You can stay with her for the time being until they move her out of ER to run some tests or perform procedures that can't be done there. At that point you might as well go home and get some rest. Meanwhile, you'll have papers to sign and questions to answer like what insurance company carries your Medicare supplement, or does Mrs. Konert have a living will, etcetera." George nodded and stood up and let Ocky take his arm and lead him toward the entrance to the Emergency Room. He said, "When you return in the morning, she'll be admitted to the hospital." Patting George on the back, he added, "They'll call you before morning if it's necessary."

Ocky opened the door and pointed him toward his wife's cubicle on the far side of the large room. A nurse came by and led him the rest of the way.

When she pulled back the curtain, he was shocked to see Catherine lying there with her eyes closed. The bed had the sides pulled up. Her left arm was immobilized and covered with dressings, and she was draped with a sheet except for her left leg which was raised slightly in a sling-like traction device. Ominous tubes ran from hanging bags to her right arm and hand. While the view was shocking and not at all what he'd expected, a few things he saw comforted him. Although he had no idea how to interpret them, the heart monitor showed a steady beat, and the blood pressure monitor gave off readings that seemed normal to him. Maybe most reassuring was Catherine's breathing. It came complete with the snorts he'd learned to love while lying next to her in their bed at home. He pulled a chair up to the side of the bed.

A half-hour or so later when his head began to droop, and he found it hard to keep his eyes open, he rose to his feet. He'd been hoping the doctor would show so he could question him. However, the last time the nurse had checked up on Catherine, she'd made it clear the doctor was swamped and probably wouldn't be able to see him. Reaching over and touching his wife's right hand, he whispered her a good night, pulled back the curtain and left.

To his surprise, Ocky was waiting for him when he returned to the waiting room.

"Why are you still here?" George asked.

"I kind of thought you might need a ride home. It's a long walk."

George cracked a smile. "I didn't know the police ran a cab service."

Ocky grinned and nudged him toward the exit. "We only take the good guys home, Mr. Konert."

Once George was in the backseat of the patrol vehicle, his body began to rebel. His head ached, his ears rang and just like a kid screaming for attention, his lower back exploded with pain from all the stress. Despite these physical distractions, his mind stayed the course focusing on Catherine, the uncertainties of her situation and all the things he had to do because of it. Suddenly he asked the driver, "I'm surprised my wife's daughter never showed. Did you ever get hold of Mrs. Gerlach, Pete?"

"No, I called several times, and then awhile ago I asked another squad to drive by the Gerlach home. They reported back that the place was dark, and there didn't seem to be any activity. Could they be out of town?"

"They could be, but Catherine never said anything about it. I saw Gert two days ago when she came over to chat. Could you try again now?"

"Of course. I know you'll want to fill her in about her mother before she hears it on the TV or radio or reads it in the newspaper."

George said, "I never thought of that. She'd never forgive me."

"Yes, she would," Ocky said softly. "In situations like this all you can do is try to do the right thing."

"Thank you for saying that, Ocky," but what he really heard was the echo of his earlier taunt. "Loser."

CHAPTER NINETEEN

"If you remember what she says, you can always tell me later."

The phone started ringing off the hook the evening of the accident. Acquaintances and friends who'd listened to the local six o'clock news on TV, their car radio, or in one case a police scanner, all bombarded him with questions and sympathetic sentiments. Mike O'Hara, who'd heard about the accident on his car radio while coming home from the office, immediately showed up at the door to offer support. What a friend! Even without a beer in his hand, O'Hara was able to raise George's spirits to a level where he felt he could make the tough calls to his daughters, Jill and Anne, as well as Catherine's older daughter, Marianne, in Seattle. To his own children as well as Marianne, he explained that as far as he could tell, she was badly beaten up but stable and getting lots of medication for her pain. However, barring any sudden change, she was going to survive. Then, he promised to keep them informed by calling regularly.

That left Gert. He tried her cell phone again. No answer. He tried her house with the same result. That's when he came up with the idea of calling Ann Marie, Roundy's assistant and his old friend. Using his magnifying glass, he began pouring through the phone book for Ann Marie Johnson's number and came up empty. Usually under those circumstances, his next move was searching for her by address. However, that would be fruitless because he had no idea where she lived. That left him with one hope. Since the number was obviously listed under her husband's name, perhaps looking for it would dredge it up out of the distant past. He did remember several other things about her husband–that he was tall and thin and spoke with a decided Swedish accent–but these wouldn't help him find the number. He also recalled the fellow didn't sport a common name, but after reexamining six columns of Johnsons, he was no closer to their number than before. Evidently, he decided, the listing used initials or the phone number was not in the book. He decided to scuttle his plans and call Ann Marie at work in the morning.

After taking the phone book back to its spot in the kitchen drawer, George went to the refrigerator and fueled up on cottage cheese out of the carton and a few slices of ham held together by two saltines to keep his fingers from getting greasy. When he was finished, he moved to the sink. While his hands were dutifully washing out the empty cottage cheese container, something he'd never do on his own except Catherine didn't like to recycle anything that had food stuck to it, his eyes focused on the now darkened side of the O'Hara's house. Suddenly, in white letters, S-V-E-N, passed before his eyes like the streamer at the bottom of the ESPN screen. Quickly drying his hands on his pants, he raced to the phone book. With the magnifying glass poised over the columns, he scanned the names until he found an S. Johnson on Hickory. Then, without wasting a moment he dialed the number, and Ann Marie answered.

"I heard what happened, George. I feel awful about it. Is she... is she all right?"

"She's making it, but it's too soon to know for sure what's ahead. Where's Gert?" he blurted out. "I've been trying to reach her all day."

"She accompanied Mr. Gerlach on a business trip to Cincinnati. They left early this morning, attended the meeting and as far as I know, went to a matinee of a musical in the afternoon, then had dinner and are driving home tonight."

"That explains her whereabouts, so as far as you know, Ann Marie, she doesn't know anything about her mother?"

"I haven't talked to Mr. Gerlach."

"Hopefully, she doesn't hear it on the radio while driving home."

"I agree. Although it's a burden for you, George, I hope she hears it from you first."

"Thank you, Ann Marie. I think I'll wait until morning to call her at home."

"I'll keep you in my prayers."

About nine, when George felt sure no one else would call, he took a shower and crawled into a lonesome bed. In the battle for his attention, his anxiety over Catherine's ordeal defeated his exhaustion. Fears that hadn't exposed themselves previously began creeping out of the darkness. Now that it appeared she was stable and most likely going to survive, he had to worry about how badly she was hurt. While it was obvious from his brief visit that her left arm and leg were badly injured, he didn't know what else was affected. Did she have internal injuries such as a ruptured spleen? Years ago, a friend of his was in an accident and had one of those, and he recovered. Were her ribs broken? He'd heard that was terribly painful, and sometimes a broken rib would puncture a lung. That wasn't good. He was sure of that.

Running through his limited litany of potential injuries left him frustrated. Unlike others who grooved on all things medical, George had always been content in his ignorance of such things. Until now, the sum total of his medical knowledge was based on the maladies he'd personally experienced: a heart attack and four bypasses, a chronic knee problem that eventually led to a replacement and the cancers that killed his first wife and so far only scared Catherine and him half to death. Still, based on what he had observed during his short visit to the Emergency Room, he now knew he needed some advanced study. Hopefully, he could depend on his wife's doctors to educate him. However, that fantasy was based on his ability to capture their attention long enough to tap their knowledge. Patting the empty space in the bed next to him, he said, "Thanks to God, you haven't left me yet, Catherine." He sighed and glanced at the clock. 11:38.

While determining the severity of Catherine's injuries was the logical first step, how she was going to recover from them was more important. That would determine what her life–their life–was going to be from this point forward. If her injuries turned out to be as serious as they seemed, their future life might never resemble what it had been before the accident. Instead of being the caretaker, he might have to become the caregiver. While he'd certainly devote himself to her needs, he, like most men, had never been tested for skills in that area. Heck, he had his own limitations. After all, he was almost eighty-two years old. He didn't have the strength or the stamina he once had or the patience. Although he knew he was rushing to judgement, if Catherine became an invalid or lived with chronic pain, no matter how solid his intentions, he might not be up to the task of caring for her. Or, what if, as predicted, his eyesight deteriorated? He could end up just as disabled as his wife.

George tore off the covers, struggled to his feet and began pacing. All the pressures of the disastrous day were taking a toll on his sleep. How would he ever solve the mysteries of the future if he never slept again? Each step around the room, each failed attempt at pillowing his head brought new anxieties into the fray, each glance at the clock a new frustration.

Midnight. First thing in the morning, he'd call his family practitioner and get a prescription for some sleep medication.

1:16. A strong one.

2:10. Swinging his legs out of bed for the umpteenth time, he began pacing again. After deciding that wandering aimlessly around the room was ridiculous, he sought out the stairs and ended up in the kitchen. Once there, he snooped around until he found the whole wheat bread, stuck two slices into the toaster and watched as the filaments reddened. When the toast popped up, he placed both pieces on a large plate, slathered them with butter from the fridge and munched until they were gone. With no newspaper to read, no desire to turn on the radio or TV and no energy for the climb to his empty bed, George shuffled into the living room and plopped down onto the recliner.

When he awakened, the sun was streaming through the blinds. For a moment he had to consider where he was, and when he figured that out, remember how he'd arrived there. Once he was fully oriented, he began to laugh. Day or night, he could always depend on his magical chair to carry him off to dreamland. Maybe, if he was lucky, years from now he'd even take his last breath in that same chair. Although the errant thought ordinarily wouldn't be his first choice for an eye opener, for some odd reason, this morning he found it comforting. He glanced at the clock on the mantle. 7:44. A record for late sleeping. Just five hours sleep, but he felt refreshed. Although it was not part of any regimen, he began a series of isometrics, some neck and arm stretches and a few leg lifts. Then he stood up and tried a few more from a standing position. When he finished the exercises, he felt so energized he resolved to do nothing but focus on Catherine's well-being all day–even without stopping for a nap. And, oh yes. He remembered and shuddered. Call Gert before she called him.

Rather than calling Gert first or preparing his breakfast while the coffee perked, George phoned the hospital for a report on Catherine. He learned that during the night Catherine had been moved from the Emergency Room to Intensive Care. "Why did they do that?" he asked the female voice on the other end of the line.

"I don't know, sir."

"Have things gone wrong, or what?"

"Sir, I couldn't answer that if I knew. You'll have to contact the doctor directly."

"You're scaring me. I don't know who the doctor is."

"Sorry," she said in an flippant little-girl voice.

He raged. "Well thank you very much for all your help," and he slammed the phone back onto the cradle. So much for feeling more in control.

He dialed Gert. When she answered, he skipped the salutations and launched directly into bringing her up to date on her mother's accident. When he finished, a hushed silence took over the line and then sobs. After another period of quiet, she began bombarding him with questions. "Do you know something you're not telling me? She isn't going to die, is she?"

He suffered through the interrogation for a few moments longer. Then, he interrupted her. "Gert, you're asking the same questions I want answers to. If you'd stop questioning me and get your butt over here to pick me up, we could be at the hospital learning the answers together."

"You don't have to snip at me, George. I just want to know what's going on. I'm worried sick."

"So am I, Gert. Why else would I bark at my best buddy?"

"Sorry, Georgy boy," she said softly. "I'll be there within the hour."

"I'm sorry too, Gert. About everything."

He quickly shaved, showered again and was in the process of dressing when the phone rang. A male voice said, "This is Albert Trammel from the Security Insurance Company. Is this George Konert?"

"Yeah, but my insurance program is in good shape, and I don't have time to talk."

"But, Mr. Konert...."

"I said I'm busy. My wife has been in a terrible accident, and I'm getting ready to go to the hospital. I'm going to hang up now. Goodbye." After cradling the phone, he mumbled, "Damn pushy salesmen!"

Seconds later the phone rang again. "Good heavens, I'll never get out of here!" he griped. "I can't even get dressed without being interrupted." He grabbed the phone on the third ring. "Konert's!"

It was the same male voice, only this time his words came on at machine gun speed. "Mr. Konert, before you hang up on me again, you need to know I'm calling about your wife's accident."

"What about it?"

"We insure the woman who hit her. We are well aware of the accident details. Therefore, I just want you to know we will work with you and your insurance company to make sure all her medical expenses are covered, and your car is replaced."

George remained silent.

"Have you contacted your insurance company, yet?"

George was dumbfounded. "Why would I do that? Your client hit my wife. She's at fault. You pay."

George heard him sigh. "Of course, that's essentially correct, sir. However, for your protection, we suggest you contact your own insurance company. While our organization will do everything possible to properly settle the claim, your company acts as your advocate and helps with the paper work and such."

Something in the man's voice put George on alert. "That's what my attorney is for."

The momentary silence from the other end was his reward for making the statement. "As you wish, Mr. Konert. Just remember, we're here to help you."

Hanging up the phone, he said to himself what he really wished he'd said to the insurance guy. "I'll bet."

When they arrived at Catherine's room in the ICU, George didn't notice anything alarming. In fact, he found her condition to be similar to the way he'd left her the previous night. She was sleeping, her left leg was in a sling, and she was hooked up to a bunch of tubes. The only discernable difference was her left arm was now immobilized in what he would soon find out was a device called a sugar tong. Since none of his grisly premonitions matched what he was seeing, George let out a sigh of relief. By contrast, Gert responded to her first sighting with a howl and a rain of tears.

Since he was past the point of initial shock, George was content to stay in the background and let Gert become acclimated to her mother's condition. After spending a few minutes aimlessly shifting his weight from leg to leg, watching Gert gently hold her mother's hand and wind down her sobs, he considered sitting. Scanning the cubicle, he realized his stepdaughter had confiscated the only chair. Knowing he shouldn't sit on the corner of the bed for fear of disturbing something, George decided to do some exploring. He peeked behind the drawn curtain that divided the room to see if there might be another chair in that cubicle he could borrow. He located one by the window. He also glanced at the aged black woman in bed there. Like his wife, she, too, was sleeping, except unlike his wife, she was hooked up to some kind of breathing machine. To his untrained eye, she looked very sick. Still, her arm wasn't in a cast and her leg wasn't hanging from a pulley like Catherine's.

Suddenly, he felt foolish. Who in his right mind makes comparisons between patients in the Intensive Care Unit? The woman wouldn't be there unless she was critical. For many, ICU was the last line of defense in the war against death, and the woman appeared to be losing her battle. That set him to wondering. When a person like this woman nears the end, does she let go and let her faith carry her into her next life, or does she keep fighting to hang on until the very last gasp. He guessed he'd have to wait to find out the answer to that one for himself. Hopefully, that would be long after he helped Catherine through her current crisis.

George slipped behind the curtain and quietly stole the chair. Then, sliding it near the bed next to Gert's, he dropped into it and began gazing at Catherine. While she was certainly banged up, and probably doped up, too, Catherine didn't have the look of death like her neighbor. Although her eyes were closed, she still radiated life. However, George wondered if it was fantasy to consider a full recovery. While so far, no one in power had stated his wife wasn't going to return to full health, no one had promised him she would, either. In fact, no one had even talked to him at all. The good news was she was still alive after a very long night.

Although Catherine hadn't stirred, Gert now seemed fully composed. During the same short time frame, he'd also emptied his head of worries for now. He was sitting comfortably when a thin, middle-aged, unnatural blonde nurse entered the room. She consulted the chart she was carrying, ignored Gert's imploring glance and nodded toward George. "I presume you're Mr. Konert?"

He smiled. "You presume correctly."

She glanced at the clipboard and then back at him. "Good. You are the person listed in Catherine Konert's medical power of attorney."

"That's right," George agreed.

"I'm Carolyn Osgood. Would you come with me, please? I need to talk with you." Like a battle sergeant, she started toward the door fully expecting her subordinate to follow.

Instead, George didn't move. He said, "This is Gertrude Gerlach, Mrs. Konert's daughter. Anything you have to say can be said in front of her."

The woman paused in the doorway. Her body language showed aggravation. "I wouldn't mind, Mr. Konert, but it's against protocol." She nodded toward the bed. "I need to talk with you outside of the room about your wife's condition and treatment alternatives. According to the law, when she can't make decisions for herself, you are the legally responsible party."

"And, I'm telling you I can't make any decisions without consulting Gert. So, you might as well start talking."

"Please don't make this any more difficult than it is. Come with me, Mr. Konert."

"You're the one making it difficult. Let her listen in."

The nurse put her hands on her hips and said with a deep sigh, "It's the law, Mr. Konert. We all have to live with these privacy issues."

George was just about to blow a fuse when Gert entered the fray. "It's okay, Georgy boy, go with the nice lady and let her tell you what's happening. If you remember what she says, you can always tell me later."

Nice lady? As far as he was concerned, the nurse was being an unreasonable bitch, and he'd be damned if he was going to give in to her stupid protocol. He glared at the woman to show his contempt. Then he switched his glare to Gert. And, where did she come off saying, "If you remember..." Why wouldn't he remember? There wasn't a damn thing wrong with his memory.

When he finally cut off his silent rage, he noticed a sudden change in the nurse's attitude. It took him a moment to understand that as totally absurd as Gert's statement was, he could see the woman considering his age and buying into his senility. That pissed him off, too, and so did her condescending smile. She nodded toward Gert and said, "Under the circumstances, I'll break the rules and let you join us." Then her tone softened. "But, we will have to step outside the room."

Trailing after her to a vacant office, both George and Gert listened as the nurse began explaining Catherine's condition. Apparently, Catherine had multiple fractures of her left forearm, a break in her upper left arm, a fractured clavicle and a segmental fracture of the femur in her left leg.

"So far, it doesn't appear that any organs were injured, and remarkably, the X-rays show no damage to her head or spinal cord, most likely because the air bag deployed. Considering the force of the collision, she's actually quite fortunate. Still, it's a little early to know what the future holds. I'm sure she'll need several surgeries to set her broken bones and extensive rehabilitation after that. Right now, we have her on a pain management regimen to make her more comfortable. That's why she's sleeping so much. Incidentally, she would normally be in a private room, but we had so many admittances to ICU last night we had to place her with another patient. She should be moved to a private room shortly.

"The next step is to have an orthopedic surgeon look at her and figure out what needs to be done first and in what order." She paused. "We're not a large medical center, but we're blessed with a great trauma specialist, Dr. Will Thomas. He does the bulk of the surgeries that follow accidents."

George interrupted. "Dr. William Perry did my knee replacement. He did a great job, and Catherine has met him several times. I'm sure she'd like to have someone she knows do the operations."

The nurse flashed him a smile. "Then, Mr. Konert, you might want to give Dr. Perry's office a call. My opinion is he'll probably refer your wife's case to Dr. Thomas or another general orthopedist, because he usually just does knee and hip replacements. Nevertheless, I've always trusted Dr. Perry's opinions. He's a straight shooter. I'll guarantee he'll recommend the best person to you."

"Shouldn't they get going on this?" George asked.

"Yes, I think the surgeon will want to get started soon. He probably won't do all of the surgeries at the same time."

"I'll call Dr. Perry as soon as we're done," George said. Then he smiled at the nurse and extended his hand. "Although we got off on the wrong foot, I want to thank you so much for clarifying my wife's condition. I really appreciate all your time, young lady. You're certainly a very knowledgeable nurse."

The woman smiled. Then he thought he saw her expression change slightly, and he wondered why. "You are a nurse, aren't you?"

"Actually, I'm the emergency room physician in charge of Mrs. Konert's care. If we weren't so busy last night, I would have had this discussion with you then."

"I just assumed...."

"Don't think anything of it, Mr. Konert. Many people mistake women doctors for nurses. Just like they think any male nurse with a stethoscope hanging around his neck *is* a doctor." She smiled again. "I think it's called gender bias."

After Dr. Osgood walked them back to Catherine's room, said "Good luck" and left, George whispered to Gert, "That was embarrassing."

"Forget it, Georgy boy. You won't be the last one to make that mistake." Then, she placed her arm around his back and said, "I thought she was a nurse, too."

Before reentering Catherine's room he said with finality, "I'll gladly play the fool if your mother is awake."

Sadly, she wasn't, so they took turns kissing her gently on the cheek and slowly backing away from her bed. Then, after glancing at her one last time from the open doorway, George took Gert's arm, and they walked down the corridor toward valet parking.

Later, after helping him pick up a few subsistence items like bread, milk, fruit and some frozen meals at the grocery store so he wouldn't starve, Gert dropped George off at home. Once inside, he immediately called Dr. Perry's office. He spilled out what he knew of his wife's condition to the receptionist and asked for a return call from the doctor. "He usually returns calls at the end of the day," she told him. "Will you be home then?"

"Absolutely," he said, not bothering to tell her he didn't have a car and even if he did have one, he couldn't drive anywhere after dark.

Ten minutes later the phone rang. It was Dr. Perry. "I'm sorry to hear about Mrs. Konert. I'm going to the hospital in a few minutes to do a knee replacement. If you'd like, I'll look in on her. Who's going to do her surgeries?"

"I don't know. I was going to ask you if you wanted to do them."

"George, I do hip and knee replacements. You need a trauma specialist like Dr. Thomas."

"That's the name that Dr. Osgood gave us."

"Well, he's the right man for the job. When it comes to trauma, he's the best in the state, and that includes the Cleveland Clinic. Right now I'm in a hurry, but if you'd like, I'll call him for you. I'm sure he'll take your wife's case anyway, but it might help if I give him a heads-up. Stay close to the phone, George. I'll be calling you back."

Hearing the dial tone, George said, "Okay. Thanks."

A few minutes later, Dr. Perry called back from his cell phone. "I reached Dr. Thomas. He'll round up the emergency room report and X-rays this afternoon and call you in the morning. It may be quite early, seven or seven-thirty."

"Most likely, I'll be up." George mumbled replacing the receiver. "If it's anytime after five."

CHAPTER TWENTY

"We'll get through this, George."

Four days following the accident, Gert dropped George off at the hospital for an afternoon visit. After taking the elevator to Catherine's second floor room, George was sitting by her bed talking to himself, because, as had been the case for the two days since the surgery on her leg and clavicle, she'd been doped up. Although Dr. Thomas said she was healing, and the nurses told George she was responsive between rounds of pain medication, George was frustrated because he never saw her awake. Like today, she'd been sleeping for the whole hour since he arrived. Although he'd been jabbering at her, he was getting tired of it. Finally out of patience with the situation, he squeezed her hand and exclaimed, "Come on Catherine, talk to me." As usual, there was no response.

Finally, to keep from dying of boredom, he launched into a story about a woman who'd dropped off a casserole at the house that morning. "Catherine, do you remember meeting Agnes Fowler? She's the heavy-set woman about my age I introduced to you at The Tea Room awhile back." He glanced at her closed eyes, picked up her limp hand and accepted her non-answer. Still, he continued. "Well anyway, she stopped by the house and dropped off an exact duplicate of the casserole she'd made for me sixteen years ago after Grace's death." He smiled at his wife. "How do I remember that?" His smile turned into a grin and then a little laugh. "It had to be the worst gosh-awful piece of garbage I'd ever tasted. At the time, I'd chalked up the failed effort to her grief over her own husband's recent death. Now, I'm not so sure she isn't trying to poison me because she failed the first time."

George shifted in his chair and listened to his wife's breathing. Even if Catherine wasn't listening, at least he was amusing himself by repeating the anecdote. "Anyway, rather than accommodate her and face a certain death, I took the dish with a smile, proffered some polite conversation and thanked her sparingly. Then immediately after she left, rather than taking a chance and verifying my fears, I heated a small portion, sniffed it and immediately fed the lethal goo down the disposal."

He glanced at Catherine. There was the hint of a smile on her face. Instead of snapping a picture to capture the Kodak moment, George stood up, kissed her and left.

On the following Monday morning, after explaining all the risk factors, Dr. Thomas operated on Catherine and placed an IM rod in the humerus bone of her arm. The next day he put plates on the ulna and radius bones of her forearm. According to the trauma surgeon, everything had gone well and now all she needed was time and physical therapy to heal and return to normal. Armed with that knowledge, George and Gert were unprepared for the sight that greeted them when they arrived in Catherine's room. She was propped up in bed, with her left arm in a dressing held by a sling. Moreover, she seemed to be awake, and what was even more amazing, she wanted to talk.

As usual, Gert confiscated the only chair leaving George standing at the foot of the bed. Unlike that first day in the semi-private room, there was no chair behind a drawn curtain to borrow, so he was forced to remain on his feet. Still, that earlier experience created a fleeting thought about Catherine's former roommate. Had the woman recovered, or had she ended her journey? He hoped the former was the case if that was what she wanted.

Still standing, he and Gert took turns interrogating Catherine about her pain and any needs she might have. By prearrangement, they skirted any issues that might cause her anxiety. In short, they volunteered little information and filled the air with small talk.

After listening to their babble for awhile, Catherine raised her right hand to her mouth to stifle a yawn. Seeing that as a sign for them to leave, George began to button up his jacket, and Gert stood up.

"Wait!" The suddenness of Catherine's order forced Gert to reclaim her chair. "You're not attending my visitation, you're visiting me in the hospital." She pointed toward the traction device holding her arm. "I know why I'm in here. I know I was in an accident. What I'm waiting to hear is was my surgery successful, and what's going to happen to me?"

Gert glanced at George, he returned her appeal, and still no one spoke to the patient.

In disgust, Catherine said, "You two dolts are no help. You're as bad as the nurses."

That was the first time George ever recalled feeling good about being chastised by his wife. Instead of presiding over a battered body in a comatose state, he had just received his first glimpse of her returning spirit. While her words stung a little, they wilted in the wake of the jubilation he felt over her sudden reappearance.

In the minutes that followed, he proceeded to tell her everything he knew about her prognosis, the length of her rehabilitation and when it might begin. To George's relief, the disclosures didn't throw her into despair. Instead, they seemed to calm her, which led him to believe she already had some insight into her fate. Before she closed her eyes, she sighed and reached out for his hand. Speaking just above a whisper, she said, "We'll get through this, George."

And then, he cried.

Much to George's surprise, long after the initial media blitz, the phone calls continued. Whether the calls came from old friends, marginal acquaintances or total strangers, each called to register concern. Some offered prayers for Catherine's quick and full recovery. Others tried to help in some practical way, like driving George to the hospital or the grocery store, and one or two presented him with open dinner invitations "when he felt like it."

He appreciated every one of these calls and expressed his genuine gratitude.

Mixed in with the thoughtful callers were a few who pissed George off. These were the ones he suspected of having ulterior motives. There were the nosy types whose main interest seemed to be a ghoulish need to know the details of Catherine's injuries and her latest prognosis. Even more irritating were those whose singular purpose was stealing an opportunity to rehash experiences similar to hers within their own family and acquaintances. Since most of these calls were innocuous, George's overly negative reaction bothered him. Why was he condemning the caller just because he found a few flaws in their message. Better to let their words roll in one ear and out the other than let his anger pile guilt on top of his concern for his wife. Although he was trying hard, these incidents blasted him with a terrible truth. He wasn't very good at letting go of anger.

Nevertheless, there was one group of callers that especially triggered his ire. These were the advice-givers. Admittedly poor at accepting advice under any circumstances, George found it particularly galling to be told he should have taken Catherine to Cleveland or Cincinnati because the bigger cities practiced better medicine than Carlisle. One even chastised him for not using Dr. So and So in Columbus to operate on Catherine's leg because "the surgeon is so good she'll be up in no time."

The unsolicited advice wasn't just confined to medical treatment. About a week after Catherine was admitted, he stopped with Gert to fill her tank at the convenience store where he usually bought his gas. There he received another jab to the solar plexus. The proprietor, an outgoing Pakistani man, began admonishing him in his broken English. "You should not let Missus drive sedan. If she drive big SUV, she be fine."

Fortunately, he didn't erupt like a volcano at the moment of impact because he might have hurt his hand banging it against the guy's skull. However, as they drove away, and even with Gert trying her hardest to point out the humor in the proprietor's poorly-conceived comments, George said, "That's the last gas I'll ever buy from that s.o.b."

Actually, another comment bugged him more than the foreigner's SUV remark. He and Gert were picking up a few items at the grocery store when they bumped into a guy who used to work for him at Kerr. Since time had obliterated his name, and the man didn't volunteer it, George couldn't comfortably introduce Gert. While the fellow may have felt just as awkward as George did about the chance meeting, he was kind enough to utter, "I'm sorry to hear about your wife." Unfortunately, instead of quietly moving on while he was ahead, he added with a laugh, "I know it's a little late for you, George, but I took the keys away from my wife years ago."

Gert wisely took his arm in a vice-grip and dragged him away.

Despite these few anomalies, George was overwhelmed by the generosity of most folks. Starting with the day following the accident, friends and neighbors began showing up unannounced with casseroles and other foods. They even gave him gift certificates to a variety of restaurants. Since he was eating his main meal each noon at the hospital, not only did he set the gift certificates aside for later use, George divided each of the incoming delicacies into serving-sized portions, froze them and called the gift-giver to praise the meal and make arrangements for returning the container it had arrived in. Then each night, when he got home from visiting Catherine, instead of pecking away at a sandwich or sipping canned soup, he'd microwave a serving to eat with his beer chaser. In most cases, he'd been given enough food to last a week or more. Since his German heritage wouldn't allow him to leave a bite uneaten, by mixing and matching from night to night, he managed to keep from being bored with a repetitive menu.

Unlike the poisoned food and the gas station guy's untimely remarks, there were also lots of pleasant surprises, like Pam Turner calling to schedule a visit late the next morning. At eleven, when she and her infant son, Timmy, showed up at his front door, he was overjoyed. After Pam put the baby's car seat on the floor, Timmy began to wail. While attempting to quiet the child, he and Pam began a juggling act of massive proportions. While she held the baby, George cradled the medium-sized box and large envelope she'd handed him. Then, they worked together to remove her coat and scarf and the baby's snowsuit, all of which George elected to toss over the bannister rather than hang in the closet.

"I was shocked when my husband told me about Mrs. Konert," she said as she ran her hand through her hair to smooth out the damage caused by her knit hat. "I'm so sorry. I'm assuming she's getting better?"

"The doctor says she is, but her progress seems imperceptible to me."

Still carrying the box and envelope, he ushered them into the living room. When he made an attempt at peeking into the face of her reticent baby, Timmy promptly buried his head in his mother's neck. As a consolation, George received a one-armed-hug and a kiss on the cheek from Pam.

With mother and child seated on the couch with him, George began opening the box. Pam interrupted and said, "Open the brown envelope first."

George went to the desk and returned with a letter opener. He then slit the end of the packet and carefully pulled out the contents. "Oh my!" he said upon viewing the watercolor. "What a magnificent painting. An eagle soaring over a red-rock canyon. And look at the purple mountains in the background and the clear blue sky. Spectacular! Do you carry pictures like that around in your head?"

She grinned. "No, I painted it from one of my father's photographs. I'm learning quickly, don't you think?"

"I should say."

"I've been taking an art class at the community college on Wednesday nights. The teacher is great, and Jack gets to spend an evening alone with Timmy. It works well for everyone."

George returned his attention to the cardboard box, "And, what have we here?"

"It's just a smoked ham, a small one. I didn't have the time to fix anything fancy for you."

"My dear, my refrigerator and freezer are full of *fancy*. What I'm longing for is *simple* and *good*. Thank you so much." He peeked at Timmy who was now sleeping peacefully on his mother's shoulder. "It's almost lunchtime. How about a ham sandwich?"

"That would be great," Pam said.

"Then follow me into the kitchen, and I'll make a couple."

As George helped her to her feet, Timmy gave a small protest before settling back into his mother's arms. "Do you recognize Timmy's outfit?" she said quietly.

He didn't, but he figured it must have been the one he'd given her, otherwise she wouldn't have asked the question. He pointed to the pictures on the fabric. "Are these the trucks I drove over to your house?"

She smiled. "Yes, and I'm surprised he's grown into it already."

"You've been pumping him full of nutrients."

She wrinkled her forehead and nodded thoughtfully, considering his comment. "I think you're right. Nursing Timmy has been a wonderful experience for both of us."

They ate their lunch at the kitchen table with Timmy sleeping in the car seat at his mother's feet.

"So, George, tell me how you're coping?"

"I cope by worrying about Catherine and visiting her every day and looking toward the future even though nothing is clear." He shook his head. "Actually, there's not a whole lot I can do for her, yet. Right now her fate lies in the hands of the medical profession. Dr. Thomas placed an IM rod in her upper leg and fixed her clavicle with a plate two weeks ago Monday. Two days later, he put a rod in her upper arm and set the ulna and radius bones of her forearm with plates."

"Wow, that's a lot to go through. Did all the surgeries go well?"

"So far, so good." He sighed. "The one thing I notice is following each surgery they pump her so full of pain stuff she sleeps all the time and can't communicate with me like she usually does."

Pam frowned. "That doesn't sound good for either of you. We women like to share our feelings."

"I know. That's one of the few things I've learned about women in my eighty-one years."

"And, you're a master at listening."

"I doubt that," he said smiling.

Pam bent over, smoothed the wrinkles from Timmy's shirt and then sat quietly for a moment or two. Then she said suddenly, "Do you believe in kismet, George?"

"Maybe, if I knew exactly what it meant."

"I'm not sure I know the definition, but I think you and I were destined to be involved with each other. I've been thinking about that a lot lately. First, your wife is diagnosed with breast cancer just as I'm about ready to have Timmy, and we meet quite by chance at the doctor's office. Then, she gets a clean bill of health, and I deliver and you contact me. Then, I mess up because I think you're some salesman and hang up on you. Still, you forgive me and get lost trying to give me a baby gift which you end up leaving in the car so we see each other again. Now, I'm here because your wife has had a bad accident, and I can share the art I'm working on." She shook her head. "There's just something about all this I don't understand, but it feels good, not the accident part, but do you believe it's somehow meant to be, George?"

"I'm not sure it isn't all chance, but we do seem to help each other. If our friendship is the result of some grand plan, I'm just going to relax and enjoy the pleasure it brings me. It's kind of like poetry. I can internalize the feeling, but trying to figure it out can spoil it for me sometimes."

"Well, let's raise a glass and toast the result."

George laughed and raised his water glass. "To us."

Pam mimicked his action. "And, to Mrs. Konert's full recovery." She looked down at Timmy and smoothed his hair without waking him. Then her smile faded, and she looked up a George. "Now that she's had her last surgery, what's going to happen to Mrs. Konert... and to you?"

"Who knows? After enduring all her surgical ordeals, she'll soon begin rehab. I think that's going to be especially difficult. Because of her leg, she'll need a walker or crutches to get around. My concern is she won't be able to use either until her arm and clavicle are healed and her arm is strong again. To me, it's a vicious circle. My worst nightmare is she'll still be in excruciating pain. What do we so then? No professional will speak to that. My fear is, worst case scenario, she'll be on heavy drugs and wheelchair bound the rest of her life. If that's the case, I'm not sure I can take care of her."

Pam said, "They say, 'God never gives us more than we can handle.'"

"*They* can say it all *they* want, but frankly, at the moment, I'm not convinced it's true."

While George was talking, Timmy began stirring and then fell back to sleep. Pam reached across him and touched George's arm. "You're not thinking of giving up?"

He smiled. "I doubt it. I get depressed, but I never quit. Catherine and I will stick it out to the end."

"You better. Not only will she need your support, but you're a wonderful cheerleader."

George sighed. "Yeah, I'm just one big walking inspiration."

"Hey, man, you're the coolest guy I know. If I sound condescending, I'm sorry. But, I feel that way. When I was so confused, both mentally and emotionally, you were there with your grandfatherly insights. You jump-started my new life by helping me understand that my destiny was motherhood, and I should embrace it. You said, 'You can be a business woman later if you want, but nothing is more important than being a mother.'"

George grinned. "I said that?"

"Something like that. At least that's what I heard. Regardless, it helped me focus, and I'm grateful." Suddenly, she began to cry and the tears flowed down her cheeks. George reached into his back pocket for the clean handkerchief he'd place there that morning and handed it to Pam. She dabbed at her eyes until she replaced the tears with a nervous laugh.

"I sure get worked up lately. It must be the hormones."

George tilted his head to one side. "Hormones?"

"I'm pregnant again. Two months."

George laughed. "I don't remember that being part of my free advice."

"It wasn't. Having two kids in two years was totally my idea."

"Well then, I'm excited for you. Congratulations!"

"Thanks, George. I'm excited, too, and so is Jack."

While the generosity of friends caught George by surprise, Mike O'Hara's gift won the prize. Not only did he lug over a case of German beer, he gave George carte blanch to drive either of their cars whenever necessary. The gesture was so thoughtful, George startled both of them by giving Mike a rare hug and thanking him profusely. Not surprisingly, after the spontaneous show of emotion, George backed off quickly and resumed their normal byplay. "Only an Irishman would give a friend enough beer to raise his blood alcohol to obscene levels before offering him the keys to his car."

When Mike's comeback was a meek, "I hadn't thought of using the two together," George, instead of gloating, cringed at the thought of the possibly lethal consequences. After taking a moment to regroup, he thanked Mike again for his kindness and, because it was mandatary, offered him a cold beer from his fridge—with one proviso. Mike had to hang around and keep him company. Since the gesture was akin to offering his four-year-old granddaughter candy so she would let him read her a story, Mike accepted. Thus, for the next hour they laughed, chatted and guzzled, and the impromptu party gave George a much-needed break from worrying about Catherine.

During the visit George did have the presence of mind to share his concerns about the mounting hospital and physician bills. "Do I ignore them and have Catherine thrown out into the street, or do I pay them and hope that the insurance company reimburses me? Since I don't trust insurance companies, maybe I should hire you to get some action?"

"First of all, there's no question of liability. The other driver hit Catherine. Her carrier is more concerned about you suing them for millions than paying a few medical bills. Just call your insurance agency, explain your concerns and ask them to get them paid pronto. In my opinion, they'll take care of everything right away without an attorney mucking it up. Just make sure you don't sign off on the claim prematurely, because Catherine's treatment may go on for some time."

The blunt honesty of Mike's response allayed his fears. To repay him, he fetched two fresh brews. One for the guest, and one for the host. After opening them, he raised his to Mike, and they clinked a toast. "To a good friend," he said.

The party ended suddenly when Cheryl O'Hara called to tell Mike he had ten minutes to get ready for a dinner engagement at their club. That brought Mike to his feet and out the door with George harassing him the whole time about being henpecked. After he'd closed the door behind him, George returned to the living room and experienced the biggest surprise of their long relationship. Instead of chugging down his beer as he ran out the door, his friend had left a half-filled bottle on the end table. He'd never seen Mike do a thing like that before.

The other result of O'Hara disappearing so quickly was George never told the lawyer he was no longer driving at night. If the truth be known, his omission was deliberate. George didn't want to diminish the value of the gift. Since the evening was the time when Mike and Cheryl would usually be home, that's when their cars would be most available.

Fortunately, the time spent with O'Hara and his visit with Pam helped to momentarily cleanse his mind of his obsessions. Still, they hovered under the surface and competed with his sleep time.

The next morning he awoke with another issue. Although not on a par with his concern for Catherine, the need to have his own car was a problem to ponder. Since he couldn't impose on Gert forever, or use one of the O'Hara's vehicles unless he could return it during daylight, he had to consider buying one soon. The question was, should it be a new, problem-free vehicle that would last as long as he would, or a beater that he could get rid of easily. If Catherine recovered and was able to drive, or he didn't go blind, they'd want a new one. However, if he or his wife couldn't drive, or the car was gathering dust because they'd moved to The Willows and didn't need one, selling a new car meant taking a big loss. By comparison, he could spend less on something used that he could get rid of quickly if he needed to do so without losing all that first year depreciation. Under these gloomy scenarios, which made the most sense? Dilemmas. Always dilemmas. Based on the way things had been going lately, whatever he decided would be wrong. He needed some divine guidance.

For once God answered him. "George, why are you obsessing over these issues when you aren't doing anything about the things you can handle today. Call your insurance company and get your bills straightened out. Then, call the travel agent and cancel the cruise." George was impressed. God made a lot of sense.

Initially, he hadn't canceled the cruise because he lacked definitive information about Catherine. Then, when he did know enough about her condition to realize they'd never make it, he'd held out canceling for a miracle. Finally, when there was absolutely no hope, he'd just plain forgotten to call. He hadn't blanked out for financial reasons either, because he'd purchased trip insurance. It also wasn't for lack of time, because other than going to the hospital and greeting a few hand-holders at home, he didn't have much to do. No, forgetting to call was a damn senior moment.

That was the problem with getting old. He'd been so caught up in what he couldn't control, he'd screwed up the few things he could. No wonder seniors got depressed. At times it was hard to find enough successes to balance out the lapses.

Immediately following breakfast, George did what he should have done weeks before when the guy on the phone gave him the same advice. He called his insurance agency. After getting a promise of immediate help and control of the situation, George hung up the phone shaking his head. Sometimes he was just too suspicious for his own good.

Here it was three weeks since the accident, and he'd finally accomplished something. It felt good, and it even felt better when he scratched off *Call the insurance agency* from his to-do list. Next on the list was *Call the travel agent and cancel the cruise.* After that was accomplished, he consulted the list again and found it blank.

Surely he had more important things to do than just those two. He thought for a moment and then jotted down *Don't let yourself get depressed, dummy.*

That made him laugh out loud, and he was still laughing when the old ditty he used to recite at work popped into his head. *Get off your ass and onto your feet. Get out of the shade and into the heat.*

CHAPTER TWENTY-ONE

"What to do? What to do?"

For the most part, George dealt with Catherine's plight quite well. However, at times, he felt like stress was building in him like steam in a teakettle. Even that analogy was mild compared to the helplessness he felt. He could almost hear the whistled warning that he was about to blow, and he still couldn't pull his vessel from the flame. In addition, he realized he was exhibiting a milder version of some of the same perverse traits he'd hated in his father. While August Konert was a hard-working genius in the factory and admired for his creative skill with metals, he was a tyrant at home. Cold and exacting, he demanded perfection from his wife and only son. Worse, he had an explosive temper when things didn't go his way. Although George admitted to occasional fits of anger, that's where the similarities between his father and him ended. His old man was mean, cruel and vengeful, whereas he was just *Lovable George* with an angry streak.

When George's first wife, Grace, became part of the family and was exposed to August Konert, she'd tried to put a good spin on his overbearing presence. As an outsider, she'd make excuses for his behavior. Nevertheless, George knew she despised his father's ways as much as he did. By the time he died, she'd altered his perception of the man with an insight that still haunted him. "George, your father may have been cruel to you, but he was probably trying to make you an obedient son. Stick with me, and I'll make you a good man."

Lately, though, he'd found himself slipping into his father's mantle whenever he thought about the details of the accident. That was the case this morning as he was getting dressed for the day in the bedroom. Remembering his own youthful driver training, he could vividly recall his father's early lessons. For one thing, August Konert was adamant about avoiding mistakes.

"You vill be a goot driver, George. You vill not speed, and you vill always slow down at cross-streets. And you, for certain, vill never take your eyes off the road to shift gears or talk to anyone."

He'd heeded those early lessons even as automotive technology advanced over his lifetime. With the advent of automatic transmissions, speed controls and anti-lock brakes all making driving easier, it also seemed to George these advances made him safer as well. However, the driver still needed to stay vigilant and drive responsibly.

"You vill not ever make a mistake, George," rang in his ears. While some drivers did and many didn't, he never dared to waver from his strict training. Even as automobiles morphed into comfortable entertainment centers with distracting buttons and levers that adjusted reclining seats, air conditioning and AM/FM radios with CD players, he continued to remain steadfast to his father's driving demands.

George placed his thoughts on hold to traverse the stairs and scare up a little breakfast. Then, as he was spooning granola into his mouth, his brain returned to the subject of driving. Typically, his unfinished thoughts on any topic disappeared into the nether regions where old people's thoughts go to die, so, in a way, he was relieved to find his way back. However, returning to driving and responsibility and his father's voice also gave him a glimpse of how fixated he was on the woman who caused Catherine's condition. As much as he might want to forget and forgive her so he could move on, he kept hearing his father pounding away at him to get even, to make her pay for her transgression. While he'd put his record up against almost anyone who'd been driving as long as he had, he still never entirely lived up to his father's exacting standards. He'd glided through a few stop signs, and on occasion, he'd turned on the speed at the sight of a yellow light at a busy intersection. Also, he'd eaten many a sandwich and downed a lot of sodas while barreling back to work, but never anything alcoholic.

George stood up and carried his dishes to the sink. Then, as if answering to an inquisition, George admitted his usual speed on an interstate was seventy rather than the posted sixty-five. Plus, he'd been involved in a few fender benders, several of which were his fault, and he'd been responsible for as many dings as he'd received from nearby cars while opening his door in crowded parking lots. But, he'd never been hurt nor had he injured anyone else. That's when he slammed his fist onto the counter and in a rush of emotion said, "And I sure as hell never caused a freaking accident while I blabbed, or worse, sent a text message, whatever that is, on a damn cell phone."

Just like that, standing there in the kitchen, his grief over Catherine's accident turned to venom. He'd go to his grave hating Samantha Garfield, the woman who'd injured his wife. Glancing toward the hall, he was startled by an ethereal figure nodding toward him from the doorway. Maybe for the first time ever, George saw his father with a smile on his face, and it emboldened him to act on his feelings. Suddenly, he felt the power of a vengeful God course through his being. He would get even, and he'd show the old man what he was made of.

To start with, if he'd had his way, the perpetrator's injuries would be far more devastating than just a few scratches and sore muscles. Not only would he punish her to the full extent of his imagination, he'd even elicit the old man's help. After all, who was more accomplished at making people miserable than his father.

Since her sending messages on the cell phone caused the accident, he'd make sure it became the focal point of his reprisal. If he could reconstruct the facts, her cell phone, instead of falling to the floor at impact, would have landed in her mouth, traveled down her throat and ended up lodged in her gullet. To remove the instrument from her belly, a sadistic quack would need to rip her torso apart with a chainsaw. All without anesthesia. His dad would enjoy watching that.

He began to pace. With a little effort, he thought of a more subtle punishment. Why not doom the woman to a life of continual internal phone ringing. Since her gabby friends would never stop calling or texting her, he'd call off the chainsaw surgeon. Oh, the joy of that constant ringing driving her crazy!

He kicked the pantry door slamming it shut. Sadly, the plan had a shortcoming. At some point, the battery would have to be recharged. In which case, she'd just let the instrument rot in her stomach, buy another cell phone and go on maiming and killing a few more helpless citizens while she stayed connected. George fretted. "What to do? What to do?"

Going to the closet, he pulled out a light jacket and headed for the porch. Once outside, he eyed the chaise, but a wind gust warned him away from great expectations. A glance at the remnants of winter covering his gardens and the bare branches of the maples convinced him he'd find no solace there. Nor would he let the frozen landscape distract him from his preoccupation with destroying Samantha Garfield. He moved back into the kitchen. Just as he was stepping over the threshold, he felt a helping hand on his elbow followed by a voice in his ear that told him August Konert was about to come forth with something even more insidious to add to her misery.

In the end, their joint decision was even better than insidious. First, he'd attach a device onto the phone that would cause intense pain whenever the woman's battery wore down. Then, to obtain relief the woman would have to charge it. Now, the brilliant part. From hell, he'd summon forth a skilled surgeon to permanently attach a charger to the embedded phone. Thus, when the pain began notifying the woman she was in need of a charge, she'd have to plug herself into a wall outlet or an extension cord. Think of the inconvenience, the embarrassment. What a diabolical way to remind the woman that she ruined Catherine's life. Although she deserved even more punishment, George felt ecstatic. Until now he'd never initiated such unbridled creativity.

All at once it occurred to George that his own battery had run out of juice and was about to go dead. All his scheming was punishing him more than Samantha Garfield. He lifted his head hoping for some applause to urge him on, but there was no father, no "ataboy son," nothing but dead space. He tasted bitterness. The bile in his throat and the emptiness in his gut announced his revenge against the woman was over, and he felt no better for it. His flight of fancy had accomplished nothing except some faux communication with his father. Not only was there no plan, he now wasn't sure his victim ought to be treated so severely. He'd be satisfied if he just knew she'd suffered some consequence for needlessly crashing into his wife.

Still, before letting her totally off the hook, maybe he should alert the media to her crime. Some reporter could write some biting text about being distracted while driving a car. They could even take pictures of her standing beside Catherine's hospital bed, ignoring the patient as she sent text messages. Maybe for once, something good would come from the media's rush to tell a story to the world, and maybe the story of Samantha Garfield would throw the fear of God into all cell phone addicted drivers.

While he paced, George wandered into the living room, spotted the lounger and dropped into it, exhausted. He wiped his eyes with his handkerchief. As usual, his connection with his father came to nothing, but at least his anger toward the woman had subsided to the point where he could smile about his tirade. That's when he realized he wasn't alone. Standing by the coffee table, he spotted Grace in her white bathrobe. "It's been a long time, Grace. What's the occasion?"

Her face broke out in a sardonic grin. "I came to congratulate you."

"For what?"

"For turning into your father."

He answered sheepishly, "That whole rant was awful."

"Yes, it was, George."

His eyes sought the glowing apparition. "It won't happen again. I promise," he said earnestly.

He waited for her response with the hope she would mollify him, or even better, forgive him. He didn't care. Just so she said something to prolong the visit. He even reached out to her and pleaded, "Please don't go, Grace," but her light faded and the smell of her perfume dissipated, and she was gone as quickly as she'd appeared.

"I promise," he whispered, and then burst into uncontrollable, gut-wrenching sobs.

CHAPTER TWENTY-TWO

"Wow!"

For George, the major problem with being alone was the lack of distractions. Without places to go and people to see, he spent far too much time in his head. That was his gripe this morning. How could he get excited over shaving, bathing and placing dishes in a dishwasher? For some, morning TV was the answer, especially if they grooved on news broadcasts or soaps. He had a jaundiced view of both. Soaps were insipid, and the news seldom related to his world. Why would any normal person listen to an intense reporter tell the tale of a rape or murder? He supposed it would be the same kind of person who was attracted to an accident scene, fire or flood. The same was true with the wannabe experts who blabbed on about political maneuvering or economic concepts he didn't care about or want to understand. In his opinion, the only purpose in televising the typical junk, other than selling advertising, was to scare people back into their cocoons or make them so angry they'd rush out to see the latest Oliver Stone propaganda movie. He went to see one once and walked out after fifteen minutes. What a waste. Usually, when he hated a movie, he'd at least stay and sleep to get his money's worth.

Rather than allow the electronic media to force-feed him, George enjoyed reading what he wanted to read in the newspaper at his leisure. Unfortunately, for some reason, the newspaper carrier had skipped him this morning. When he called to complain, he explained to the woman that while for some, a missing paper was probably no big deal, for an old man like himself it was a catastrophe.

"How am I going to get through the day without it?" he whined. Still, by the time he cradled the receiver he was confident his plight would soon be remedied. What he wisely left out of the call also probably helped his cause; that the paper was the vehicle that chronicled the two most important issues in his life. It told him who died, and whether his favorite teams won or lost.

Results from his effort bore fruit within a half-hour of ending the conversation. When George opened the front door and examined the stoop, the newspaper was lying on the mat.

As he was bending to pick it up, George glanced off toward the east where the Alexanders lived. Since he hadn't been able to see anything at that distance for some time, the attempt was mostly symbolic. Nevertheless, he held out hope that he might catch a glimpse of some activity that would let him know they were all doing well. As expected, he didn't.

Actually, the entire Alexander family had been conspicuously missing from the hoards of concerned supporters who'd lined up at his door following Catherine's accident. Except for the short phone message that Mary left on his answering machine after hearing about the accident on her car radio, he hadn't heard a word. True, Jim did show up following a light snow to fulfil their contract to shovel George's driveway and walk. Since the snowfall occurred just after the accident, he now wondered if his handling of that transaction may have created a rift with the sensitive teenager.

When Jim finished shoveling, he came to the door to be paid. Deep in his own thoughts, George had broken with his usual pattern and not invited him in. Instead, he handed Jim his pay through the partially opened storm door, fully expecting him to run off to his next activity. However, the young man surprised him by hesitating. Instead of leaving, he shuffled his boots and even wiped the sleeve of his heavy coat across his eyes and nose. Since none of these actions registered on George, he stared at him blankly waiting for him to leave.

"I hope Mrs. Konert will be okay," he said.

"I hope so, too," he absently answered before abruptly closing the door.

Sadly, it wasn't until he'd passed the living room window and peeked out at the young man trudging home that it dawned on him he might have just made a poor decision. One that was too late to rectify.

Although he'd invested a ton of emotion in all of the Alexanders following Kevin's death, it didn't surprise him when Mary hadn't reciprocated. Nor was he disappointed. He didn't need a casserole to know she cared about Catherine and him. There could be space in their relationship without him feeling slighted. Plus, he never believed for a moment that kindness and inspiration were intended to even out. Thinking about it, there actually wasn't a thing she could do at this time that would equal what she'd already done for him. After all, she and her kids had inspired him and renewed his faith in his own future when he needed to wake up from his long and deep withdrawal following Grace's death. No one else, not his own kids nor his old friends, ever provided the spark to lift him out of his depression like she had. In fact, it was Mary who had found a way to tap his spirit and set him on the path that ultimately led him to Gert's doorstep and a desire to vie for Catherine's heart. For that he'd always be grateful.

Even before Catherine's accident and his unfortunate snub of Jim, the space in their relationship had been widening. He'd known for several months that Mary's marriage with Dan was in crisis mode, and George had used every excuse he could think of to stay uninvolved. Since he didn't know Dan well or understand the dynamics of their marriage, he felt staying away was better than sticking his nose into something that he might only make worse. Nor did he even want to know if they were splitting, in counseling or how the kids were reacting to a potential breakup, because, hopefully, it would never come about.

Throughout his adult life, George had been painfully aware that virtually every family struggled following the death of a young child. He supposed it was because each parent grieved differently, and even though each desperately needed the other at that critical time, neither had anything to give. Stresses that ordinarily wouldn't factor into their day to day existence came to the surface. Often, the common escape from pain became divorce.

Now, with Catherine in the hospital, he had problems of his own he couldn't solve. This widened the space between the two families. However, he never once expected their separation to be anything more than temporary. Given some time to figure out his own future, he'd seek out Mary to discern hers. Mostly, he wished he hadn't dismissed Jim so abruptly.

The next morning, he finally got around to returning several calls from his oldest daughter, Jill. When she answered the phone, without thinking he said, "Hi, Jill. How's business?"

There was a pause. Then in a voice tinged with irritation, she said, "Is that all you think of when you call me?"

For some reason her response ticked him off, so he hung up and then immediately felt guilty enough to call her right back. After consulting the cheat sheet of numbers taped on the wall by the side of the phone, he quickly dialed her cell phone. When she answered, he said with fake enthusiasm, "Hi, Jill. This is your father. How are you and Curtis and the boys? I'm sorry I haven't called, but with Catherine in the hospital, I've been..."

Her laughing cut him off. "I'd say you dug us both out of that hole in record speed. That was quick thinking." Then she added, "How is Catherine?"

"I'm fine."

"Daddy!"

"Do you know how many times a day I have to answer that question? She's in the hospital for gosh sakes, she's not outside jumping rope."

Jill said, "Sorry. The stress must be worse than I imagined."

"I'm the one who's sorry, and, yes, the stress is getting to me. I don't know how long it will be, or even if Catherine is going to fully recover, so I have all these scenarios running through my old brain. If *A* happens then it's one plan. If *B* happens it's another. I can't even decide what kind of car to buy, or where we should live. I hate it. I wake up, shower, shave, go to the bathroom, eat a few meals and visit Catherine. Then I go home, have a beer, pull a piece of casserole out of the freezer and nuke it. Then I twiddle my thumbs for a few hours and go to bed dreading the next day, not because of what I have to do, but hating the fact I have nothing to do but wait."

"Wow!"

"That's why I hung up on you."

"Daddy?"

"Yes."

"Let me rearrange a few things. I'll fly to Cincinnati and be at your house by tonight to tuck you in, okay?"

"Would you?"

"Yes, or in the morning at the latest if I can't get a seat on the plane." Dabbing at the corner of his eye with a knuckle, he heard her laugh. "And, Daddy, in answer to your original question, Curtis and the boys are great, and business is just dandy."

When Jill arrived in the rental car at his house in Carlisle, it was close to eight. Since neither of them had eaten, he whipped up a lettuce salad and pulled a chicken, spinach and noodle dish from the refrigerator, threw two sizable portions onto a dinner plate and microwaved them. With Jill spurning his offer to open a bottle of wine, he passed on beer number two, and they drank water.

"This casserole is really good," Jill said with a half-full mouth. "Did you make it?"

"Are you kidding? I know how to broil fish, cook vegetables and make a salad. The meal is a gift from someone. I'd have to consult my list to see who gave it to me."

"Don't bother."

He sighed. "I still haven't sent out thank you notes for all the food I've received since the accident."

Jill smiled. "Well, if it's been as good as this, we'd better get started writing tonight before we go to bed. Maybe they'll bring you more." She touched his arm. "I don't suppose you have any note cards."

"As a matter of fact, I do. I bought a couple of boxes when the gifts started arriving. What I haven't done is write on them." He shook his head. "Why haven't I written any. I've had the time, and I'm capable of writing a few thank you notes. I just don't seem to be able to get organized and get things accomplished." George pushed his chair back from the table. "With Catherine in the hospital, my life seems so topsy-turvy. I know I have lots of long term decisions to make, and depending on what I decide, I'll have enough work to do to last a lifetime. Instead, I'm locked into this state of inertia. He glanced at his daughter for understanding. Then he stood up and took her empty plate. "More hot dish?"

"Yeah, it's so good, but before you get it, listen to me for a second."

"Okay."

"Dad, when one is depressed and worried, being unable to act or take charge of situations is perfectly normal. That's why I came. I figured your pistons might need firing up."

George looked at her fondly for a moment before saying, "I know you're right, but I feel like such a loser." Then he moved toward the counter. "I'm going to shape up, and I'll start by getting you some more casserole. Then, we'll write some notes." George nuked a plateful from the Tupperware container. Returning to the table, he set the steaming plate before her. With his eyes glistening with tears, he said, "Gosh, Jill, I'm glad you're here."

For dessert he cut up two pears that were bordering on extinction, and served them with a couple of small chocolate chip cookies from a bag Gert had given him.

That night while he wrote notes and Jill addressed, stamped and sealed envelopes, they talked until just before midnight. Leading her up the stairs to the guest room, he hugged her to him. Then, he retired to the master bedroom, and for the first time since the accident, fell asleep at once.

The next morning he was up at six, and after showering and shaving, he trudged downstairs. When he passed through the door to the kitchen, he witnessed the day's initial surprise. For the first time in at least twenty years, a woman in pajamas sat at the kitchen table drinking coffee at that early hour.

"I couldn't sleep," Jill said.

"I'm sorry."

"There's nothing to be sorry about. I wanted to come to Carlisle to see Catherine, offer support and help you problem-solve. After last night, I think I understand your situation. Now the tough part begins; weighing the alternatives and deciding which are the best under what circumstances."

"No wonder you're so successful in business, Jill. You have an innate ability to look at all facets of a problem and then make a reasoned decision."

"I talk a good game, Daddy. The truth is, there's a reason I couldn't sleep. I discovered that personal decisions like you'll have to make don't fit neatly into my methodology."

"So, you haven't a plan?"

"Daddy, I don't know shit."

George laughed. "That's a business term?"

"It's an all-purpose term that fits the pickle you're in."

"Then you and I are in sync. That's more comforting to me than you could ever imagine."

While George was making omelets and toast, Jill volunteered a solution to his vehicle problem. "With all the imponderables, I don't think you should buy a new car," she said.

"Okay, I agree. Since I can't depend on Gert or the neighbors forever, I'll just have to hit the used car lots, listen to a lot of spiels, and hope I don't end up driving away with a piece of unreliable junk."

"Why don't you tell me how you really feel, Daddy."

He grinned. "I think, I have. I'm not very good at picking out used cars." He put an omelet in front of his daughter, sat down with his and began eating.

Moments later Jill said, "Okay, then. If I have a better solution, you'll accept it, hands down, no questions asked?"

He looked at her Cheshire Cat smirk and waffled. "I guess if the price is right."

"Oh, the price will be right!"

Something about her expression and the tone of her voice told him he was going to like her solution. Still, he said, "Then my answer is a definite maybe."

"You're either in or out, Daddy."

"All right, I'm in...unless..."

She tossed him a fake scowl.

Not willing to confront the inevitable, he said, "I'm in."

"Good. Do you remember the old Lexus I had when Curtis and I got married?"

"That wasn't old. My Buick is old. I bought it fourteen years ago."

"Actually, Daddy, my vehicle is six years old, and it only has thirty thousand miles on it. It sits in our garage, and no one uses it. Curtis and I use his new SUV, or we have Carlos drive us, and since I don't want the boys banging it up, we bought them an Intrepid to share. I won't sell the car, because I love it—plus, I can't get anywhere near what it's worth even if I wanted to go through the bother of selling it. Meanwhile, even though it just takes up space, we have to pay for the insurance and the license and an occasional oil change."

"So, you want me to buy it."

"No, Daddy. I want you to drive it. It will be a great car for you and, hopefully, Catherine, and if you come to a point where you don't need it any more, you can give it back."

He stammered, "I don't know what to say."

She laughed. "I think saying, 'I'll take it' would be a good start." Then she reached out and took his hand. "And, you could follow that up with a big hug like last night."

George did what he was told but made Jill stand up so he could feel her in his arms and kiss her hair and tell her much he loved her, and how proud he'd always been of her, and how her gift was the finest he'd ever received, and how sorry he was that her mother couldn't witness her generosity.

That's when Jill said, "She's probably smiling down on us right now."

And George said, "I'm sure you're right," and they both sat back down to finish their omelets.

Later while they were cleaning up, George asked, "Does Curtis know about the Lexus?"

"He knows I was going to offer it to you. He just didn't know whether or not you were going to be too proud to accept it."

"Tell him my motto is practicality before pride. I'm German, you know."

Still later, George asked her when he could get the car.

"It will be here in a few days. After I explained my plan to Carlos and had him road test the car, he insisted on driving it here."

"Carlos also knows I have no pride?"

"He doesn't care about your pride. He likes you, Daddy."

"No, he likes you. As I see it, 'Your wish is his command.'"

Jill grinned sheepishly. "Be that as it may, he wanted to do this for you. He already has his return plane ticket from Cincinnati. You might want to save him the cost of a hotel room by putting him up for the night."

"Right, and I'll take him to Anthony's for a thick, juicy porterhouse to show him how grateful I am. Maybe buy a bottle of Chianti. Carlos has always been very kind to Catherine and me."

"I guess that shows me where I rank. Carlos gets steak at a fancy restaurant, and I eat salad and casserole at the kitchen table."

"Considering your lack of cooking skills, I thought it might be a treat for you."

"And, as always, you are absolutely right, Daddy."

Later, as they were sipping coffee in the living room, George asked, "How is Carlos getting from my house back to the airport."

"I assumed you'd take him back in the morning. That's okay, isn't it?"

"Of course. I just didn't know the plan. As always, it's a good one. Along the way I can learn the Lexus' quirks while Carlos is onboard. He might even enjoy being chauffeured by someone else for once."

Jill grinned. "I doubt it, but knowing how Carlos feels about you, he might even go along with it." Her words drifted behind her as she hustled up the stairs to get dressed. Before leaving for the airport, she still wanted to see Catherine at the hospital and visit with Gert. George wasn't bothered by Jill's short visit. He knew how busy she was. Had they continued talking, he might have damaged his case for driving Carlos to the airport by admitting he was no longer driving at night. In fact, he might have jinxed the whole car deal.

On Friday, after keeping George informed of his progress by cell phone, Carlos pulled into the driveway in mid-afternoon. After taking time to drink a cola and "get the road out of his head," Carlos showed George all the features of the car and let him road test it both in town and out on the freeway. Then, at Anthony's, George said, "Thank you for driving all this way to deliver the car. My daughter told me you even paid all your expenses. You certainly went to a lot of trouble to help me out."

"I wanted to do it for you because you and Mrs. Konert have always treated me with kindness. You must understand, Mr. Konert, that because I'm Mexican and a driver, some people I meet don't show me respect."

"You might drive us around, Carlos, but my wife and I don't consider you a driver. We look forward to seeing you because you are a friend. As for the Mexican part, I never knew that was your family background until you told us one day. I actually thought you might have been Italian."

"Who knows, George? I could have some Italian in me. Are any of us one-hundred percent sure of our heritage?"

CHAPTER TWENTY-THREE

"Now, that's worth giving up a nap for."

After what seemed like a month or so of snow, rain and gloom, George's spirits began to rise with the first sunny March day. Perhaps it was the budding of the silver maples, or maybe the jonquils popping through the mulch that gave George a lift. Possibly, the premature birth of summer was all that was needed to give him some hope when there weren't many other joys at the moment.

For one, Catherine's recovery could hardly be called miraculous. After four surgeries, the only improvement he could discern was a reduction in her discomfort along with a corresponding decrease in the use of her pain medication. At least she'd been able to wean herself of that potential addiction and was far more alert and talkative. However, each time he heard Dr. Thomas crowing about the success of his work, George cringed. Humpty Dumpty still languished in the Stephano Rehabilitation Center and seemed destined to remain there.

Catherine had suffered through a rod being inserted in her broken leg as well as another one in her upper arm. In addition, she had a plate holding together both broken bones in her lower arm. The good news was the repaired collar bone seemed to be responding to therapy. In theory, because all of the injuries occurred to the extremities on her left side, healing the collar bone was the first step to making her a mobile woman again. With the pain in that area subsiding, each day brought her closer to using a walker or even crutches to move about. That meant the end of her confinement to a bed or wheelchair. It also meant that after awhile she'd be able to transfer herself from spot to spot without needing a muscular aide at her beck and call. Nevertheless, because George wasn't all that strong, she'd have to recover considerably more before she could be without some professional help.

The problem for George was not knowing when, or if ever, she'd be herself again. That negative thought then led to other worries, and those worries pressured him into thinking about their future together. It was the anxiety surrounding that last unanswered question that beat him down during the day and kept him awake at night.

Recently, he wondered if he was capable of managing their uncertain futures. While he'd proven he could physically take care of himself, he never remembered being a good caretaker for another at any time in his existence except briefly before Grace died. Now, whether he liked it or not, he was being given an opportunity, and he was determined to do his best. Although his insight wasn't accompanied by a clap of thunder or flash of lightning, he suddenly realized that by helping Catherine through her ordeal, he was making the final payments for the wonderful life he'd been given.

Since the day was beautiful, George decided to attend to an annual rite of spring. He slipped into a windbreaker, marched down the stairs to the basement garden room and out the door to the back yard. Although the turf was soft from the snow and rain, he began a tour of his gardens. He started with the flower beds near the house. What surprised him more than the daffodils approaching full bloom were the purple and yellow crocuses dotting the beds. Even though they didn't rank high in his hierarchy of favorite spring flowers, they were the heralds of the glorious royalty to come. In previous springs, he used to search for them on a daily basis from the kitchen windows. However, this year he'd neglected looking, almost letting them wither away before he could be thrilled by their appearance. All at once, he began wondering what else he'd missed out on, so he began a squishy trek to his vegetable garden.

The first thing he observed was a beginning crop of dandelions and a few other weeds. He also spotted a few hoof prints from one of the deer that appeared periodically along the edge of the woods over the winter. Although a daunting adversary during the growing season, he was glad the handsome animal found a reason to visit his plot. Hopefully, the deer would be so grateful for the winter forage, they'd respect the confines in the summer when it was at its bountiful best. George let himself be entertained by that fantasy. Another pipedream was the Catherine and George Garden. Or, maybe it was going to be the George and Catherine Garden. He didn't remember who had top billing, nor did he care. Although Catherine admitted she wasn't serious about the idea of helping him with the gardens, he'd held out hope he could change her mind. Now, with her out of commission, the whole idea was as dead as a possum on a highway.

Realistically, the best he could expect from Catherine would be moral support. Even if she developed any interest in the project at all, she would never be able to work on it. As for the heavy work, he was almost as helpless. It was quite clear that if there was going to be a vegetable garden, Jim was going to put in the majority of the effort and all of the backbreaking labor. Therefore, if Jim were forced to break the contract he'd made over the winter, there would be no garden. He'd just buy the produce they wanted at the farmer's market and let the land lie fallow.

Sadly, it was possible the Alexanders were in so much turmoil the family might move out of town, or their finances could require Jim to get a higher paying full-time summer job. While Jim's word was his bond and George trusted him implicitly, Jim might have to break his promise. Under certain circumstances George still might get a little work out of him, but reality suggested otherwise. When the young man finished his day job, he'd be hanging with the cute young thing with the bare belly that lived down the street. George laughed. If he was a teenager again, he'd be doing exactly the same thing.

The irony of his current situation was the promise he'd made to his wife the year before. About this time, he'd told her there wouldn't be any more gardens. Then, with her blessing, he'd reneged on that promise in order to help the Alexander kids get through their grief. That experience had proven so therapeutic for every one of them that he conned Catherine into a joint venture that stirred his blood and filled part of each day with dreams of their cooperative effort, plans for the spring groundbreaking and reading seed catalogs. He was even looking ahead to a joyous spring on the day the Garfield assassin decimated his partner, ruined her life and killed his dream.

Suddenly, his eyes welled up and making no attempt at wiping them, George turned away from the plot of black earth. Sloshing slowly, he picked his way through the damp ground to the back door of the house. Then, with a hand on the door knob, he turned and gazed back at the familiar sight. All at once he realized what was adding to his pain. It was jealousy. An insane jealousy at that. Still, he verbalized it. With a sigh he thought if young people lose out on one dream, another pops up to replace it, and they never give their loss a second thought. By contrast, ancients are expected to willingly give up an activity they once loved when they can no longer perform at peak efficiency. George shook his head. To add to his pain, he realized that each day on his march toward decrepitude, there were fewer and fewer replacement options available to him.

After making a ham and Swiss sandwich for lunch, George felt a bit better. He'd thought about having a beer when he'd returned from the garden, but decided it was not only too early in the day, but it might make him even more morose. One beer worked well to relax him when he'd been active and enthused about his day. However, sometimes it further depressed him when he was already wallowing in self-pity like he was today. During his eighty plus years, he'd learned a few rules about managing his attitude. So instead of a brew, he drank a glass of cranberry juice. While it didn't chase away his blues, it didn't drive him further into the dumps either.

George usually called Catherine at Stephano after she'd finished her morning therapy and had returned to her room to await her lunch. Typically, they'd chat awhile, then in the late afternoon he'd drive over in Jill's Lexus, eat an early dinner with her and chat some more before leaving for home before dark. This morning as he passed the answering machine, he noticed the message light blinking. Since the early crush of well-wishers, this had become a rarity. In fact, lately he feared some new disaster, so he hesitated before listening to the message.

"Hi George. This is Gert's son, Todd. I know from talking to Gert that you and Catherine have been having a rough time, but Charles and I have come up with a couple of dates in April to go fishing, and hope you can come along. It would be great to have your company, and catching a big salmon might give you a boost. Please call me as soon as you can."

Instead of calling Todd back immediately, he dialed Catherine to get her take on the trip and, hopefully, her blessing. Since she would most likely be in her regular therapy session, he'd probably have to wait until lunch time to ask her. Still, what did he have to lose by trying? If she didn't answer, the time spent wouldn't effect his busy schedule. He didn't have one.

When she answered, instead of being pleased, he felt a knot immediately form in his gut. "Why are you in your room? You're okay, aren't you?"

"I'm in as good a shape as I can be in for the shape I'm in, George. PT is just running a little behind today. They'll be getting me soon."

"That's a relief. At least there's no setback."

"George, I won't allow any setbacks. Some day soon I'll be walking out of this joint."

"On my arm, I hope." George paused, then said, "I need to talk to you about something. What time will you be eating if your therapy is running late? We can talk then."

"The *something* you want to discuss wouldn't happen to involve Todd, would it?"

"Yeah, it does."

"Call him back this morning and get your fishing trip all set up. Then come on over later as usual."

"But, Catherine...."

"I want you to go. Gert wants you to go. You have to go. There is no discussion."

George laughed. "Well, all right then. I'll be over to see you this afternoon."

With Catherine making the decision for him, George felt like two giant hands had picked him up out of the muck and raised him high above the clouds. With his attitude adjusted, he began making a mental list of all the things he needed to consider before calling Todd and committing. His one-track mind led him back to the young-old comparison.

The young didn't have his problems. They'd just pack up on the spur of the moment and go without thinking of the various contingencies and *what ifs*. They'd take the cheapest flight regardless of the departure time or how many times they had to change planes. They'd haul their luggage on a bus or other public transportation without a thought to the physical toll, and if they didn't plan ahead on a place to stay, they'd spend the night in a hostel or on the floor at some acquaintance's apartment.

Old men couldn't travel that way. Trips had to be planned. Where was he staying? Would the bed be comfortable so he'd get a good night's sleep? How would he get to and from airports without having to drive at night? Packing the luggage had to be efficient so he had everything he might need without the bag being so heavy he couldn't handle it. Plus, he had to remember his drugs, money for tips and to leave for the airport early enough to be patted down by the TSA guy because his knee replacement set off the alarm. In truth, there was so much to worry about, he sometimes wondered why he looked forward to traveling at all.

Still, whatever the price, he shouldn't bitch. This was a welcomed invitation. It bordered on giving a dying man a last whiff of oxygen. He flexed his right hand. Just the thought of once again feeling the tug on the line as a fish pulled the tip of the pole to the water's edge was a gift of renewal. Not only did it come at the perfect time after a stress-filled winter, it stirred his imagination. For the first time ever, he might catch a big salmon. What an event to look forward to and savor if it really came about.

Fishing in his usual spots over the years, he'd caught most of the common species. He'd caught bass, crappies and pike in the large impoundment over in Kentucky and catfish and carp in the river that ran through Carlisle. He'd also caught some ocean fish in the estuaries off Florida and taken stocked rainbow trout from a quarry near Columbus. However, all these achievements were recollections from the past. He'd hung up his poles twenty years ago. Now, he'd have a new saga to add to his memories.

Besides the potential for catching the big one, the trip was highlighted by an opportunity to bond with Todd. While he'd only met him twice, he really liked the lad, and not just because he was thoughtful enough to invite him fishing. First of all, George respected Todd for being ambitious and successful in his career and appreciated how willing he was to share his research with people not as sophisticated or educated as he was. Maybe it was old-fashioned to think this way, but George still ascribed to the theory that a truly great man should be able to relate to anyone on some common level. That applied to researchers as well as skilled tradesman or business leaders.

Secondly, he enjoyed being with Todd for all the reasons he liked any man's company; shared interests, like fishing, and to a lesser degree, gardening. Finally, he was Gert's son. Take away all the other reasons and that was enough to accept him and find things to like.

George glanced at his watch. Since St. Louis was an hour behind, he should be able to easily catch Todd before he took a lunch break. Thus, with Catherine removing any potential guilt for his abandoning her for a few days, he called Todd back and accepted the fishing invitation for April seventeenth.

In the early afternoon, he called the airline and placed a ticket to Chicago on hold, called Jill to make sure he could stay with her and easily begged a ride to and from O'Hare. A bit later, after realizing his original plan had him leaving Carlisle in the dark before sunrise to catch his plane in Cincinnati, he called the airline back and scheduled a later flight. Then, he called Jill back to see if a later arrival made any difference to her.

Finally, with his work completed, he plopped into his recliner and accessed the snooze button in his head. Fifteen minutes later, with his eyes still wide open and his synapses still cranking out information, he realized the travel virus had invaded his sleep mode and made it non-functional. He had to call Todd back.

"I'm all set with the airline, and I'm staying with my daughter, Jill, in Winnetka, but I can't remember where the fishing charter leaves from so I can plan to get there."

"It leaves from Waukegan, George. But, not to worry. Charles and I will spend the night at a friend's condo in Evanston. We'll be picking you up at your daughter's and bringing you back from the boat."

"That seems like a lot of trouble for you."

"It's no trouble at all. It's on the way, according to my map. All we need are specific directions to her home. Besides, I'd like to meet your daughter. From what I've heard, she's a very special person."

"True enough," he gloated. "But, who did you hear it from?"

"My mother...I mean from Gert."

George caught the uncertainty and chose to share his own views on the matter. "My stepdaughter is so proud to be your birth mother, she'd be thrilled if you called her mother or mom or anything like that. Until you came around, she never had a soul to call her anything but Gert." George added with emphasis, "Even if it's a little awkward at first, do it."

He waited a few moments for a reply that never came. George sounded a laugh and added, "Please don't call me grandpa, though. You're a little too old for that."

The continuing silence from the other end of the line perplexed him. Had he said something wrong? Something offensive? While his mouth could run away with him on occasion, it didn't seem this was one of them. Then it came to him. "Of course, don't call her mother in front of your adoptive parents. There's no reason to hurt them."

That brought an immediate response. "There's not much chance of that happening. They've been wonderful parents, and I love them, but my choice of lifestyle doesn't match their religious beliefs. They can't accept it. Unfortunately, they've pretty much written me off as a lost cause."

"That's sad."

"I know. I hardly see them anymore, and it breaks my heart."

George continued in a thoughtful tone, "You know, Todd, when the line went dead, I was worried I'd said something to offend you."

"Oh no, George. I was trying to control my emotions. I was touched by your willingness to accept me and promote a mother-son relationship with Gert..mom." George heard what sounded like a sigh. "I want you to know, George, in my adult life, I've never met an older person quite as open as you."

George laughed and said, "Maybe you should call me grandpa, after all." When no response came, George filled in the gap with, "I have a rather disparate group as it is, two young ones, one directly related, one by adoption. Two step grandsons, from Catherine's other daughter, and two teenagers through Jill's second marriage. Still, I always have room for one more, especially since you came by way of Gert."

"Okay, grandpa it is. But, I wouldn't think you'd be comfortable with my calling you that."

"Todd, I'm comfortable with everything about you. Would I let you take me salmon fishing on Lake Michigan if I weren't?"

"I really don't know you *that* well, George. Would you?"

"Of course I would. I'm an old man. This may be my last chance to catch a salmon."

After he hung up, George went back to his lounger intent on contemplating his conversation with Todd and hopefully catching a few Zzz's before heading off to see Catherine. He'd just about met his second objective, when the ringing phone brought him out of his chair. It was Todd again.

"If you remember from Christmas, I asked Roundy to come fishing at the same time I asked you. At the time, he declined because he was too busy. Since we still have room for more, do you think he'd go?"

"I really don't know. You'll have to ask him again."

"Better yet, do you think my mother would like to fish with the three boys?"

"Todd, I don't know about that either, or if she fishes, but knowing Gert and how she feels about you, I have a hunch she might like to come along if only to sunbathe."

"With that in mind, I'll call my mother and see if either of them are interested."

"I'll call and give her a heads-up."

When they were through talking, George placed the phone back on the cradle. Poking his head into the living room and glancing longingly at his recliner, George returned to the kitchen and called Gert's cell phone. When she didn't answer, he left a message and returned to the living room to resume his nap. He'd barely closed his eyes when she let herself in the front door and startled him from his lounger-born stupor. He glanced at his watch and sighed. Three o'clock. "No rest for the wicked," his mother used to say.

Gert was standing over him with her hands on her hips. "So, did Todd actually invite me, or did you wangle an invitation for me, George?"

"He brought it up. I'm just a conduit carrying messages between beleaguered souls. No input, no output, just a human telegraph working twenty-four hours a day keeping lives in order."

Her pensive expression slowed him. "Did he really seem to want me along, or was it kind of like he felt obligated, if Roundy couldn't go."

"I honestly don't know his mind, but I think he was afraid to ask because you'd feel like you'd have to go. Typically, a man doesn't invite his mother on an all-male fishing trip, especially when she doesn't fish."

"I fish. My motorcycle buddies liked to fish down at the reservoir, and I used to go with them. I'll bet I've been more recently than you. When's the last time you went fishing, George?"

"Well, if you must know, I went just last century."

"Well, I went five or six years ago, but I've never fished for salmon."

"Me either, and I want to catch one before I croak. So, Gert, are you in or out?"

"In."

"Do you want to call Todd or have *me* do it?"

"Have *me* do it."

"Okay then, I'll call," George said.

"For an old guy you still catch on pretty quick."

He laughed. "Most of the stuff that comes out of your mouth isn't exactly rocket science, Gert. Even if I'm not smarter than a fifth-grader, I can usually figure out what you're saying."

"On that note, I think I'll call Todd."

"Of course you will," he whined. "Have yourself a nice little chat with your son while I spend the rest of my afternoon begging Jill for another bedroom for you, getting you a plane ticket and then calling Catherine to tell her it will be too late for me to come see her today." He shook his head. "Stepchildren are such a bother."

"Well, *Little Boy Blue,* Gert has come to the rescue. I haven't seen mom in a few days, and Roundy's out of town on business, so what do you say I pick you up about five-thirty, we'll visit my mother, and then I'll take you to Chason's Restaurant for a steak. After all the casseroles you've been eating, your arteries must be begging for some fresh cholesterol."

The offer brought George out of his chair to give Gert a hug. "Now, that's worth giving up a nap for."

CHAPTER TWENTY-FOUR

"Lucky, like me?"

It had been over two months since the accident, and the news from the rehab hospital was positive. Catherine's leg fractures were mending on schedule. She could stand without pain and take a few steps if she was supported by a muscular therapist. Her arm also was progressing well. She could hold a book, drink from a glass and pull up the covers on her bed.

Thinking about Catherine drinking from a glass started him thinking about his own drinking glass sprouting germs in the bathroom. It hadn't been washed since Catherine's accident. Since that time he'd remembered its potentially lethal condition at least twenty times. Doing the math, that meant he'd also forgotten to take it to the dishwasher twenty times. Not today. He buttoned the last button on his sport shirt, marched directly into the bathroom and grabbed the offender. Holding it up to the light, he grimaced at the sight of whitish residue clinging to the sides and covering the bottom. He smelled it. Sewer gas might have been more fragrant. Then, holding the glass aloft, he said triumphantly, "Today's the day, sucker," and picked his way down the stairs to the kitchen.

Once the oft-forgotten vessel was dispatched to the dishwasher, he began the process of brewing coffee, pouring himself a bowl full of granola and thinking about Catherine. One recent sign of progress had pleased them both. The doctors had taken her off anti-coagulants. In Dr. Thomas' professional opinion, her risk of a blood clot was so minimal, taking them wasn't worth the bother.

However, what George had feared from the beginning hadn't been resolved. With all the damage confined to her left side extremities, her mobility became problematic. How could any person, especially one past the spring chicken stage like Catherine, be expected to use crutches, a cane or even a walker with an arm broken in several places on the same side as her shattered leg. While the doctors were optimistic, to this point, no one had dared to predict whether she'd ever be able to get around on her own without a wheelchair. Over the last month he'd been trying to convince himself she'd eventually be okay, but he felt pessimistic enough to doubt it would ever happen in his lifetime.

George distracted himself for a moment by filling his coffee cup. More and more often he realized the answer to their joint futures seemed to lie at The Willows where she could have the therapy and daily help an old fart like himself just couldn't provide. Sure, they could try to live at home, have therapists come in periodically, maybe a nurse, too, but what if there was an emergency? Realistically, he didn't have the strength to pull her up from the floor if she fell. Or, what if he had a problem? She couldn't care for him at all. It would be a struggle for her just to get to the phone to call 911.

Competing with all the potential catastrophes that were dancing around in his brain was another black thought. Even if nothing dire did happen, was staying at home cooking and arranging for cleaning, playing gin rummy and welcoming the rare guest the way to play out the string? While he loved Catherine and would sacrifice everything for her, there had to be something more to each of their lives than staring at each other and bemoaning their fate. Heck, unlike some married couples who enjoyed spending their remaining days recalling stories of their shared past, he and Catherine had less than three years to talk about. That was about a week's worth of conversation. Then what? At least at The Willows there would be others around to meet, talk with and possibly share some interesting adventure or activities. In addition, because someone else cleaned up after them, he wouldn't get poisoned and die from the mold in his drinking glass. Also, at those times when he didn't want to cook, he and Catherine could always eat in the dining room. That was far better than packing Catherine into the Lexus and driving to a restaurant for an "early-bird special" during daylight hours or for lunch. Sadly, change never comes without a surcharge. Sacrificing all of their current living space would be painful. In fact, for awhile at least, they wouldn't even be together. Catherine would be in the assisted living section, and he'd be holed up in a two-room suite. Although the arrangement would allow him to see her every day and eat his meals with her at noon and night, they wouldn't be sharing a bed. While he didn't like that idea very much, he could probably handle it because they hadn't exactly been cozying up at the rehab center or before that at the hospital. Even so, he sure hated to think of the stretch of time before he'd feel the warmth of her body next to him again.

Of course, the price tag for this new arrangement would be more dear, but nothing he couldn't afford. After he hit up Jill and Anne and talked O'Hara into having a *Bring a check for poor old George charity party,* they'd get by. George laughed. He'd love to see the look on O'Hara's face if he were to suggest such a thing. Actually, with the insurance company paying all his wife's medical bills for her surgeries and continuing care plus a possible settlement for her suffering, his financial position was as good as ever. In fact, if he wanted to, he could even hold on to his house for the first year or so after moving to the retirement home. However, he did realize the *why* of that strategy was driven more by his emotions than intelligent financial planning. The way he saw it, hanging onto his home was a safety net of sorts. In the event Catherine returned to a semblance of normal, it would guarantee they could resume their lives in the home he loved, and she had adopted. Plus, it gave them an easy way out if the move to The Willows didn't prove satisfactory. Although each excuse was an acceptable rationale to feed the curious from the outside world, George knew in his heart the real purpose.

He took his cup of coffee and meandered through the open door to the screened porch. Although it was only seven, the morning sun was warm and the slight breeze welcoming. Such were the vicissitudes of early spring days. Yesterday was rainy. Tomorrow might be chilly. The next day windy. Still, so far at least, the day was glorious, and that brought him back to the authentic reason for holding on to the house. His garden. While it was questionable whether Jim would or could fulfill his contract, George still held out hope. He even had a backup plan if Jim bailed. He might be able to work the plot by himself if he planted a smaller version of his usual garden. Or better yet, what if by some odd quirk of fate, a neighbor, a stranger or even an alien from a galaxy far, far away agreed to share his gardening chores for one more glorious year. That would be perfect.

George laughed. What a headstrong old Kraut he was. Fifty dollars a pound and sore back muscles for a mere pound of beans. Ten dollars and a sunburn for an ear of corn. Those were the costs to harvest a crop when he considered taxes and upkeep on the property. And for what? Vegetables he'd eventually give away. Go to a jury with that alibi, and he'd be condemned to a mental hospital.

He lingered a moment longer sucking in a chestful of fragrant air and slowly letting it out. Then, he repeated the action several more times and in the calmness that remained, he decided his thinking was that of a sane man. At his age there was nothing wrong with keeping the house so he could garden. Gardening was tied to his deepest heart. In fact, it would be sacrilege to jettison his passion just to save a few bucks.

After returning to the kitchen, George picked up his full cereal bowl, drowned it with milk and sat down at the table with a fresh cup of coffee. His ever-shifting thoughts drifted to the insurance company that continued to pay Catherine's claim. Unlike his unfounded perception of such organizations, this particular company had been so humane and understanding, so generous and responsive to his and Catherine's needs that it had earned his highest praise. When he recalled his earlier misfire with the company's claim adjuster, he felt embarrassed. Especially the part where he threatened the man and his company with a lawsuit he had no intention of filing. Considering that their reaction to his threat continued to be a steady stream of personal kindnesses, he concluded they'd marked his folder "crackpot" and ignored his acrimony rather than been swayed by it. In spite of his negative involvement, the company established the procedures to settle Catherine's claim amicably rather than being put off by him and paying it contentiously. Considering the costs involved with their potential move to The Willows, George felt grateful for that.

Still, he knew enough about insurance policies to know they had limits as to how much they would pay. Fortunately, according to the adjuster, Samantha the Terminator, carried an umbrella policy that would take over once her limit was reached. That should cover all the rehab costs for a long, long time.

Ever since he'd become convinced he couldn't handle Catherine's physical problems at home and begun researching every aspect of the move to The Willows, he'd been reluctant to discuss his thinking with his wife. While it was probably a mistake to hold back, he didn't want her feeling responsible for his decision when the truth was, he'd been thinking about a move long before her accident. Even after deciding in favor of the retirement home, signing the papers and giving them a deposit for their spaces in the main building, he still kept everything to himself. Suddenly, he felt foolish for waiting so long. Sure it had made sense not to distract her while she was in the hospital and a foreign idea might throw her into a tailspin, but she was much stronger now. She didn't need to be protected. She needed to have something positive to focus on and look forward to other than her recovery. Certainly, a move to The Willows was a good thing for her and himself as well. Plus, with the house to fall back on, why would she object?

That afternoon when he walked into Catherine's room, he was thankful he'd taken his windbreaker off before entering. It had to be ninety in there. As he approached her chair, he tried to catch the title of the hardcover book she was reading, but couldn't. He assumed it was the same novel Gert thought might entertain her, and it probably was because she'd been reading it for the last week or so.

He bent to kiss her. "Whew! It's warm in here today," he said.

"Not if you're just sitting here in a light robe. But, go ahead and turn it down if you want."

George trudged to the thermostat. It was set at seventy-five. He turned it down to seventy and sat on the edge of the bed facing her. He decided to begin with small talk. "Enjoying the book?"

"It's just okay. Kind of gory for my taste, but exciting."

"That's the kind of stuff Gert likes?"

"Yeah. As long as it has a motorcycle in it." She laughed. "Typically, I prefer a bit more plot and literary quality, and this ain't it."

"But, you're still reading it?"

"Like I said, it's exciting. At this point, I'd rather be riding through the desert on the back of a Harley with my arms around a muscular guy wearing leather and a handlebar mustache than lingering in this place."

George smiled down at his wife. When she gazed up at him, he directed his eyes toward the lunch tray resting on the end of the bed where she'd stashed it. Although a quick glance at the half-eaten remnants gave him his answer, he still asked, "How was lunch?"

"The vegetable soup was good." She shook her head. "But, another ham sandwich? That's twice this week. I keep telling them I'm Jewish and can't eat pork, but they must know I'm lying. Tomorrow they'll bring ham salad."

"I suppose the crucifix on your necklace tipped them off."

"I suppose," she answered, but without a hint of mirth.

George had hoped he'd find her a bit more upbeat so he could discuss The Willows proposition. Instead, she pulled her cotton robe tighter across her chest and asked, "So, what have you been up to today?"

Even though it was an opening, the question came out of her mouth in such a flat monotone, he'd be a fool to answer honestly. "Not much," he replied.

His wife responded by not responding, so he climbed down from the bed and pulled the second chair from the corner of the room so he could face her. By the time he was seated, she'd returned to her reading. So instead of delivering his message, he sat in the chair watching her read and waiting to pounce at the slightest opening. When it never came, he felt his anger growing. It bugged the hell out of him that she obviously preferred reading a book she didn't even like to talking with him. What even pissed him off more was the fact that he, like a fool, was sitting on his butt watching her read a book she didn't particularly like.

As the silence continued, his anger, instead of escalating began to subside. That's when he felt his eyes becoming heavy, and he made no effort to keep them open. A quick glance at his watch told him it was a little after one. The next time he took a reading, it was almost two. After stretching his arms over his head, he gazed at Catherine and surmised she was not about to close her book for something as frivolous as discussing the rest of her life. He stood up, kissed her goodbye and started to leave.

Placing her finger in the book, she closed it and said sweetly, "Thank you for coming, dear."

He responded with a grim smile, struggled into his windbreaker and walked the corridor to the desk by the front door where he signed out. Then, he crept through the Burger King drive-thru to pick up two Whopper Juniors with extra pickles and no onions to take home for a lukewarm late lunch or a early dinner in need of a toaster oven.

The next afternoon as he slipped through the door to her room, Catherine smiled up at him from bed. That encouraged him to explain his whole Willows decision before she could intimidate him into another day of silence. So, he laid out everything; the living arrangements, the meals, the activities and how they'd both have an opportunity to meet some new people. When he interpreted her blank stare as non-committal instead of negative, he found the courage to forge ahead and admit that he'd already made the down payment and signed the lease. "We're tentatively moving Memorial Day weekend," he added, "and I hope you'll agree that it's the right thing to do."

He braced himself for the reaction. Instead, she struggled with the controls to raise the back of her bed and scrunched up into a sitting position. Then, using her good right hand she tugged at the light blanket and top sheet until they covered her. She still said nothing. Just when he was sure the knot in the pit of his stomach was going to strangle all his internal organs and kill him on the spot,

Catherine did the improbable. She tossed him a smile; a mysterious, cryptic smile that untied the knot but left him confused.

"What?" he asked.

"Nothing, George."

The end game was about to begin, so he called her bluff and raised the bet. "Come on, Catherine. I need a reaction. Are you happy, sad, delighted...mad as hell? Please, just some reaction."

"Okay...ah, I guess I'm surprised. No, overwhelmed. I never dreamed you'd place my needs first and give up your house and garden." She wiped her tears with her hand. "I've been petrified thinking of the future. I don't know what to say." Her tears kept falling.

Never one to let a positive response pass without an accompanying wave of guilt wash away his hero's mantle, he began doubting his motives. What if the move to The Willows was designed to make his life easier rather than hers. Furthermore, if he was so darned altruistic, why was he looking forward to making new friends and involving himself in new activities instead of focusing on her recovery. Wisely, he stopped trying to discover more reasons to berate himself for fear his ego might shrink to insect-size. Instead, he summed up his decision by saying, "It just seemed like the right action for us at this time, Catherine." With that he stood up and sealed the deal with a kiss. They were going to The Willows, and that was that.

When he was back in his chair, Catherine smiled at him and said, "Thank you for loving me, George."

He faked a frown, "Don't gush, Catherine. It makes me uncomfortable."

"I know, dear. That's why I do it."

They spent the rest of the afternoon attempting to play gin rummy, even though Catherine couldn't shuffle or deal and had trouble getting her cards out of the cardholder. While they didn't bother to keep score, they both agreed if they had, she would have won.

The day Samantha Garfield chose to visit Catherine at the rehab center, George and Gert were off fishing with Todd and Charles. He didn't hear about it until he returned. The stunning announcement came after he'd regaled Catherine with the details of the trip. "I had a great time, and I caught a nice salmon." He held his hands about two feet apart and said, "It was huge so I needed Charles' help to boat it."

"And, Gert?"

"She had fun, too. Todd doted on her the whole trip." Then he added, "That boy's the genuine article, Catherine. He's so pleased to have connected with his birth mother and to be part of her family."

"I know. He's a delightful young man." She grinned. "But, did Gert catch a fish?"

"Well, yeah."

"One big one like yours?"

"Maybe more."

"More like two or maybe five big ones?"

He glared at her. "Exactly five, and you've been talking with her." He groused. "Women! Even when they fish, they're so darn lucky."

"Lucky, like me?" she said, gesturing toward her injured extremities.

"I was talking about fishing," he said softly.

"I know you were, George."

The silence that followed gave George a chance to regroup. It wasn't like he tried to snarl their relationship by his thoughtless comments. However, given his penchant for saying the wrong thing at the wrong time caused him to admit he'd perfected that skill to a professional level. Then again, why should he accept the whole blame? Catherine didn't have to emasculate him for catching only one fish.

He eased out of his embarrassment by saying, "Todd says he's coming to see his grandmother some time after we move."

"That will be wonderful. I like Todd a lot, so I hope he finds his way here." Using her good arm, she lifted her other from her side and rested it in her lap. Then she glanced at George. "It seems I'm becoming quite popular. The woman that hit me, Samantha Garfield, stopped by while you were gone."

"That wretched bitch. She's called at home a few times, and I've sent her scurrying. I'll bet the insurance company wants her to soften us up so we don't sue."

"I know your feelings, George. I just don't happen to share them. Samantha wants our forgiveness so badly that I feel sorry for her."

"Forgiveness. Here you are in a rehab facility swinging your arm around like Dr. Strangeglove and you feel sorry for her? That woman's a Svengali. Why would any normal person expect you to forgive her after she demolished you with her carelessness?"

Catherine reached out and caught his hand. "George, that *woman* is a girl in her thirties with a husband and two young children. She's so miserable about what she's done to me, she's in grief counseling with her minister. Most people would run from their victims like a scared rabbit. Not Samantha. She has the courage to face up to her mistake, or in this case, face the person who's suffering because of it. Since I've chatted with her, I've undergone some soul-searching. I know she can't undo what's already been done. However, I can't find any joy in crucifying her for her mistake. Forgiveness may not even help her, but, in my heart, I know that it will help me...and you."

"You're rationalizing, Catherine."

"I could be, but she has her whole life ahead of her, and I want it to be a good one. I told her she was forgiven."

He gazed at her and slowly shook his head. "You are really something, Catherine."

"You know I'm not."

"In my eyes you are, but..." He sighed. "I just can't forgive her that easily."

She squeezed his hand lightly for emphasis. "I'm not sure my forgiving comes as easily as it should."

CHAPTER TWENTY-FIVE

"So, what's bugging you, kid?"

Catherine was released from the Stephano Rehabilitation Hospital on the Wednesday morning after Easter in the third week of April. While this was a positive sign, it created some turmoil because their move to The Willows wasn't scheduled until the last weekend in May. To allow her to rehab for that month in a home featuring steep stairs, narrow hallways and tight door openings, George orchestrated some modest changes. With Gert and Roundy helping with the heavy lifting, they revamped his older two-story home to meet her current needs. Since Catherine would spend much of her day in a wheelchair and obviously couldn't go up and down stairs, they rearranged the living room furniture to accommodate a rented hospital-style bed and provide a clear path for her to wheel around for meals and get to the bathroom.

While living in this foreign environment was confusing at first, George quickly adapted. The joy of watching his bride's gritty determination to improve made up for new annoyances, like not having an end table by his lounger to hold his drink or having a light bright enough to read his newspaper. As frustrating as these piddly problems were, they disappeared with each of Catherine's successful trips up and down the hall using only her walker. Then, there were the few steps she took totally on her own while he walked next to her for reassurance. Plus, there was her attitude toward pain. True, her intense pain had subsided, yet each day she willingly accepted more by submitting to the therapist who worked with her to retrain her unused muscles and help her rebuild her strength. As the woman said, "At first, working with Catherine was like teaching a board to dance. Now, it's like teaching a bird to fly."

"Like an ostrich?" Catherine quipped.

One day after a particularly tough therapy session, Catherine insisted on continuing to practice her walking after the woman left. Starting in the foyer, she trudged down the narrow hall to the kitchen where George was sitting at the table marveling at her persistence. Then she turned and reversed her labored steps. When she was finally out of breath and perspiring, he stood up, took her arm and guided her into a chair next to him. While she rested, he poured her a glass of water and watched her down it in a series of gulps.

Shaking his head he stated, "I can't believe how hard you work, Catherine."

She looked over at him and scowled. "I have to do this. I refuse to be an invalid." Then her determined expression softened and she said, "Anyway, George, this isn't so bad. This is good pain."

Following his wife's return home, along with the physical changes to the house, they also added a new wrinkle to their breakfast routine. Instead of George eating early and Catherine later, they prepared breakfast together. One morning they'd eat at eight-thirty. On another day, it might be eight or nine. It all depended on what time Catherine got up. While this new scheme added an additional measure of togetherness at the beginning of their day, it didn't always add to their marital bliss. On occasion, she protested his penchant for burning her toast and always buttering it, even though she kept telling him she liked light toast, hated butter and preferred orange marmalade. In addition, he usually splashed milk onto the counter whenever he poured it into their cereal bowls. When this happened, he typically wiped it up with the clean kitchen towel instead of using the dish cloth, and she'd register a complaint. Eventually, the sum total of all her complaints caused George to nickname her, "Miss tidy-bowl cleaner," a name that made no sense for the circumstances except to point out her neat-freak tendencies.

With only a few weeks left before their move to The Willows, they had both come to the conclusion their mornings would be more civil if they returned to separate breakfasts. However, in the spirit of camaraderie, they devised a new plan. From that point forward, George retrieved the bowls and cereal from the cupboard, something Catherine couldn't do. He also fetched the bread, the milk, strawberries and marmalade from the fridge and placed them on the counter. Then his wife, using her walker, would toddle over and carefully fix everything the way her occupational therapist taught her before sitting down. When she was settled at the table, Catherine signaled George, the waiter, to carry the food to the table for them to eat. After they finished, George returned the dishes to the sink, rinsed them and placed them in the dishwasher. Since this arrangement proved mostly successful for both of them, Catherine asked George to take over another task that had been plaguing her. For their final few weeks in the old house, he became the strawberry slicer.

While to some, sharing a breakfast preparation might seem insignificant, for George and Catherine, it was like learning a new dance. George found out he could lead without trying to take control, and Catherine learned that by following she could regain some control over her life. This realization was a major breakthrough on their march into the future. Not only did it help them peacefully perform a common task, but they proved to themselves that by blending their abilities they could get through a difficult period. While they were getting all of the kinks out of this sharing process, Catherine chided her husband, "I think we work best when you're the body, and I'm the brains."

"Exactly, Catherine, because at the moment, I'm the only one with a working body."

"And, I'm the only one with a working brain." She smirked. "Each day, my body is getting better, George. Can you say that about your brain?"

In response he could only laugh, because, of course, he couldn't.

On Monday of their next-to-last week before the move, the physical therapist was scheduled to arrive at eleven. The late start allowed George and Catherine to linger at the breakfast table. During the conversation he asked, "Catherine, what would you think about

Anne driving down to see us some day soon with Lily and Gregory George? Would the kids running around be too much for you?"

"Too much for me? Why do you even ask? I'd love having them. We could read together and play games...." Suddenly she looked horror-struck. "Wait a minute, George! Do you think it might scare them to see me like this?"

He laughed. "Catherine, you're not scary. True, you used to be scary. Now you're a pussy cat."

"I meant, would seeing their grandmother in a wheelchair or with a walker upset them or give them nightmares?"

"I'm the one with the nightmares," he moaned.

"George, you *are* a nightmare. For goodness sake give me a straight answer."

"All I meant was when they're tearing around, they might unintentionally bump you or knock you down. After all, they are children, and Gregory George is all boy. I just want you to be safe."

"Well, George, that's a risk I'm willing to take. Tell Anne to come anytime."

He grinned sheepishly. "I already did. She's driving from Columbus on Thursday."

"Such a considerate man. Thanks for asking, though."

Later, after the therapist left, they made a joint decision to air out the house. Accomplishing this was simple. George opened every downstairs window so the gentle spring breeze could drive away the winter stuffiness. Then he traipsed up the stairs to open some strategic panes to provide a cross ventilation. By design, this airing out was therapeutic. Of equal or greater importance, it was metaphorical. It not only confirmed the arrival of a new season, but with Catherine improving each day it signaled her successful assent from the chasm of despair. With her grit and determination she'd climbed up and over the edge of the precipice. Soon she'd be fit enough to join him on a whole new journey to The Willows and beyond.

The change of seasons had also brought sadness. Several days earlier, Mary, Jim and Rachel Alexander had stopped by to inform him they were selling their house and moving to Dayton, Ohio. Dan, her husband and the children's father, had accepted a permanent transfer there. According to Mary, rather than continue living separately as they had been for several months, she decided to give up her job, join him and reunite the family.

"The kids aren't too happy about changing schools, but they thought it was better than shuttling from parent to parent." She put an arm around her son and daughter. "Right, kids?"

At the time, George had thought their nods were a bit too automatic and their smiles a little weak, but who was he to tell a family trying to avert a crises how to behave. With his eyes staring at the tops of his shoes, Jim said, "So you see, Mr. Konert, I can't work for you this summer."

Although she'd never been asked, Rachel added, "Me neither, Mr. Konert."

"I understand," he said calmly although his stomach churned at the unwelcome news. "What I'll really miss is seeing your cute smile, Rachel, and our man-to-man talks, Jim." Suddenly the tears made an appearance, and he said, "You all mean so much to me."

Mary stepped forward and threw her arms around his neck. "You and Catherine have been so kind to us. We'll never forget you."

"I just hope we'll see each other again sometime," George said.

When Mary slowly moved away, Rachel rushed to hug him and with all the drama an eight-year-old could muster, said," I looove you, Mr. Konert."

Then Jim stuck out his hand and said, "Goodbye, Mr. Konert."

George not only shook his hand but held onto it to pull him forward and hug him. "I'm going to miss all of you."

After releasing Jim, he smirked and said, "I'll bet there's someone else who's going to miss you, Jim." Jim's puzzled look caught him by surprise, so George cleared up the question by saying, "What does Jenny think about your moving?"

"Oh, her. She dumped me for another guy. We're still friends, though." Then he grinned. "I thought you were asking about Krista, and I was wondering how you could know anything about her since we've only been going out for three weeks."

I'm sorry I asked, George thought.

Wishing them well, he reluctantly ushered them out the door and watched them pile into the car. Then, he waved and they waved back, and he turned back into the house to tend to the lump in his throat. Worst of all, he knew he'd have another emotional breakdown about their leaving after he told Catherine when she returned from a car ride with Gert.

George refilled his cup and carried his coffee to the chaise on the porch. He stared at the panorama and shook his head. He'd miss it all: the flowering rows of zinnias he planted amongst his vegetables, the baskets filled with shiny red tomatoes he hauled to his basement sink and even the tilling and weeding that stressed his back muscles and wore him out. Each year his gardens told a story of the seasons. The plot twisted and turned as the characters sprang from the rich black earth or wilted and died at season's end. Yet, each in its own voice described a place where nature and humanity worked in harmony and kept him engrossed and whole.

If he was an artist, now that his workers had been taken from him-Kevin the previous year and now Jim-instead of a vibrant palette of strong rich earthy colors to savor, he'd have to be settle for a pastel of swaying maples, green grass and fast-moving clouds playing shadow-games before his aging eyes. Although the day was rapidly warming, he shivered. If he could only return the ripped off pages of the calendar, he'd willingly relive those joyful days when his Victory Garden was paramount, or his prime years when he tilled the soil on Grace's watch. Even returning to the lost years following Grace's death when he hid amongst his plants to avoid facing a life without her was better than facing a growing season where he'd have no personal stake and his ground would lie fallow.

George wasn't surprised when Gert showed up that afternoon. Since she'd sold her business in the fall of the previous year, she'd been in and out too many times to keep count. He loved Gert and was always glad to see her. Each of her visits was typically unique. Plus, since Catherine's accident, she'd been a rock.

He was resting in the living room when he heard her turn the key in the lock and watched out of the corner of his eye as she slipped into the hallway. He waved when she spotted him lying back in the lounger to let her know she wouldn't startle him. As she approached she began an elaborate pantomime. George quickly figured out the first question and mouthed, "She's in the bathroom."

His response brought her closer. She whispered, "I need to talk with you, alone."

Since her request seemed to be tinged with a degree of urgency, he answered, "We are alone. Talk fast. She'll be in there for awhile." When Gert hesitated, he added, "I know because she does everything slowly these days."

"I can't do it now. I have a lot to say."

He was about to remark, "You always have a lot to say," but the tenseness in her voice and her imploring look kept him from saying it. "And, you can't say whatever's on your mind in front of your mother?"

"Exactly."

Moments later they both raised their heads like startled animals when they heard the toilet flush. To stop her from fleeing, he reached out to her and said, "Sit down, put a smile on your puss, and I'll take care of everything."

"You will, Georgy boy? How?"

"Who am I, the man with the plan? I haven't a clue, but I'll think of something."

Catherine emerged from the hall doing a steady point-five miles-per-hour. Her face brightened as she said, "Oh, hi, Gert."

"Did everything come out all right?" George asked.

She turned toward Gert and shrugged. "That's gross, George, but as a matter of fact it did, and according to the doctor that's quite important."

Gert went to her mother and kissed her on the cheek. "I'm glad to see your relationship with George has come full circle, and you're back to the 'potty talk' stage."

"I never should have married a tasteless man."

"Well, Mother, you did it once before."

"The first time I was stupid and paid a big price."

George interjected, "And, the second time you were desperate but got lucky."

Catherine smiled at him. "I'll buy part of that. I was extremely lucky." Then she arched her back slightly and looked directly into her daughter's eyes. "Still, without that first marriage I wouldn't have you to love, Gert, and you mean the world to me."

Gert struggled with tears and embraced her mother.

That should fix whatever's ailing her, George thought.

Around three, Catherine shifted locations from the couch to her hospital bed. "If you guys don't mind going somewhere, I need a nap."

Gert said, "No problem, I was just leaving anyway." She kissed her mother goodbye and started toward the door.

George intercepted her. "Before you go, how about a spin around the yard?"

"Well," she said with a wink. "I guess I have time for that."

They walked out the front door, down the stoop and around the burning bush at the end of the house. George let out a yip of surprise when he thought he saw a tinge of red. Since its leaves usually didn't turn fiery red until early autumn, this was a strange anomaly. He turned back and took a second look, didn't see any red and concluded it was his imagination.

As they were meandering toward the tulip bed in the back yard, George said, "So, what's bugging you, kid?"

Gert withheld her answer at first, so George urged her on. "You said you wanted to talk to me alone. We're alone. So talk." Then he caught her pensive mood and softened. "I really want to know what's bothering you, Gert. It isn't Roundy, is it?"

"Absolutely not. I love the 'Round Mound of Joy' so much, and he loves me. We couldn't be better."

"Good. Then if it isn't marriage, the only other serious problems are war and pestilence. Which one is it?"

She grinned. "Thank goodness you can make me laugh. Lately, I've had trouble because everything seems so depressing. First, I worry about you and mom. She's all banged up and neither of you are adolescents."

George said, "So what? We're making a comeback."

"Still, it really shakes me up to see both of you aging."

"It depresses you. Think how I feel." George took her hand, and they stopped to look at the tulip bed. He guided her gaze to a pocket of large red and white blooms. "See all these flowers? We can learn something valuable from them. They have their season, which happens to be now when they are a blaze of color. Then they fade and fall apart. Finally, we deadhead what's left of the blooms and let the leaves collapse and turn brown. But their spirit lives on, and next spring, God willing, they'll flower again, and we'll be able to bask in their glory."

"That's poetic George, but not very relevant."

"Why not? I'm telling you to enjoy every season while you can and not worry about it ending." He grinned. "After all, nature teaches us that life is a never ending circle. My personal concern is my body will outlast my brain like my friend Mrs. McConnell. Fortunately, there doesn't seem to be any evidence of that happening so far."

"I can only think of a few instances," she cracked.

He shook his head sadly. "I know. Your mother does seem a little ditzy at times."

She acknowledged his remark by rolling her eyes. While they walked on toward the vegetable plot, Gert said, "Do you want to know something else, George?"

"Go ahead. You're the plum. I'm the prune."

"What in the heck does that mean?"

"Who knows? Just another brain cramp."

"And I confide in you!" she said laughing. "And the worst part? I hang on your every word as if you're spouting wisdom."

"I am, my lass, but it's in code. You have to be brilliant enough to decipher it."

They were gazing out over the budding silver maples that surrounded the property. Two jays calling to each other momentarily distracted him from the real purpose of their little walk. "So, what's so awful you can't discuss it in front of your mother?"

"George, I was so bummed out the other day I drank a half glass of white wine."

"You what? You can't do that. You're an alcoholic."

"I was so hysterical that even after being sober all these years, I was hoping that having a buzz on might be better than the way I felt. So, I emptied the glass in one slurp. Fortunately, I swished it around in my mouth for a few seconds to savor the flavor, and that gave me time to come to my senses. Instead of swallowing the poison, I rushed to the bathroom and spit it into the toilet."

"Good god, Gert. I'm glad you stopped, but why would you even consider doing that?"

"I've already told you. It's worrying about you guys and thinking about my future and...."

"And?"

"If I don't find something that's satisfying to replace my work, I may do something else equally stupid."

She was crying now, and to comfort her George took her into his arms and held her awkwardly. He wanted to say something profound to end her tears. Instead, he berated himself for failing to gauge the depth of her despair. For months she'd been sending out warning signals that he'd passed off as the laments of a strong, expressive woman in transition. He'd assumed, wrongfully as it developed, that with her high-energy and talent she'd quickly find something fulfilling to do. However, unlike his daughter, Jill, who could move smoothly from one assignment to the next and make the most of it, apparently his stepdaughter needed to be pointed in the right direction. Unfortunately, his reluctance to take her seriously was based on a misconception. Since she'd already overcome so much, he'd misjudged her. Never in a thousand years would he have pictured her as the fragile little girl he now held in his arms.

When she was composed, she forced a smile and said, "Sorry to dump on you like that, Georgy boy, but I really scared myself."

"Don't worry about me. I'm glad to see a smile on your face."

"I'm afraid it's only on the outside."

"Now you're scaring me," George said. "I'm going to walk you back to your car, and you're going to call your AA mentor." He turned on his heel and watched to make sure she was following.

She quickly caught up with him and said, "George, I've already talked to my AA mentor, twice. He thinks I'm just a little anxious."

"A little anxious? I don't think so. If that's what he thinks, you both should see a shrink."

Gert said, "I already saw her once, too."

"Oh, my!"

"She thinks I'm justifiably depressed."

"What's the matter with these people?" George raged. "Even I can see you're depressed. What I want someone to do is help you get out of it. NOW!"

They were at the burning bush again. Suddenly, she grabbed him and pulled him to her and embraced him in a bear hug. It wasn't until he began trying to escape that she released him. As he was catching his breath he watched in amazement as she threw her arms into the air and cried, "Hallelujah, I'm cured!"

He shook his head in mock solemnity. "You're not cured, Gert. You are beyond help."

"I know," she said laughing, "but being able to trust you with my demons seems to make me feel instantly better."

"Then, promise you won't ever wash your mouth out with booze again?"

"I promise, George. I don't want to see you go all apoplectic over my stupidity. Are you tired?"

"Never when you're around, my love."

"Good. Then let's take another stroll. I may want to dump on you some more. Anyway, I'm not ready to leave yet."

George sighed and led Gert around the perimeter of the yard near the first row of maples. With Gert seemingly her old self again, it was like taking a walk in the sun after waiting out a sudden thunderstorm.

Spotting some wild honeysuckle, he explained how he must constantly cut back the fearless invader to keep it from encroaching on his hosta beds and other shade plants. Then he spotted three of the many wild turkeys that roost in the woods separating his home from a nearby subdivision. In recent years it seemed that greater numbers of the outsized birds were on display pecking around his gardens for grubs and seeds and whatever else they needed to fill their bellies. As they slowly approached the turkeys, he watched Gert's amusement as she gawked at their antics. Then suddenly, even though they surely knew by now he meant them no harm, one of the birds fanned his tail, and he and the others beat a path into the denser underbrush.

"I've never seen wild turkeys before," Gert said. "They're so interesting to watch. I just love birds and animals."

"One time I counted thirty-eight in my yard. They're my friends. They don't cause any serious problems, and they're always entertaining. But, just like those three, they're quite wary. So you can't get too close."

Gert nodded. "I never realized your yard was so exciting. What other creatures do you have back here?"

"I have deer, racoons and squirrels, of course. Plus rabbits and ground hogs. From my standpoint, the latter have no redeeming qualities. They eat my vegetables, dig holes and physically they're ugly as sin."

"With that attitude, I hope you don't have a lot of them?"

"Not anymore. A few years ago I hired a trapper, and he removed seven of them."

"Does he kill them?"

"I never asked. Maybe he trains them for the circus."

She scowled at him. "I hope he doesn't kill them."

"Me, too, I guess. I'm pretty sure he relocates them. All I know is, since then, I only see the one that comes out of that darn O'Hara's yard in the early morning to feed on anything and everything green."

They moved on until George spotted a neat round hole under the horse chestnut tree. "Did I mention we have chipmunks? They're a nuisance, too. When they multiply they can turn a yard into Swiss cheese, so I trap them periodically and take them for a ride. We also have a flock of geese that keeps my yard fertilized, and once in awhile a coyote wanders by. Oh, and did I mention we have lions, tigers and the occasional kangaroo?"

"Someplace in there I stopped believing you, George, but I'm amazed at all the wildlife you have right here inside the town limits."

George chuckled. "Some guys are chick magnets. I'm an animal magnet."

Gert said, "I wish I gardened. I'd love having all the animals around."

"Well, I am a gardener, and I can assure you that most of them are actually a curse. For example, the deer. When they're munching on my shrubs or hostas or playing soccer with my tomatoes, I don't get a kick out of having them around." He shrugged. "Still, I guess I can see your point. They do add to the ambiance."

He and Gert were standing next to the fenced-in plot of black earth sprinkled with emerging weeds. It broke his heart to look at it. He'd kept an escape route open by not putting the house on the market, but that was just in case the two of them hated The Willows or the lifestyle there. Moreover, with Catherine's progress to date, the need for them to live separately–he in one section and she in assisted living–was becoming more remote by the day. They might start out that way, but sooner rather than later if all went well, they'd be living together in a larger suite or in one of the outlying apartments or homes. Once that move was made, and they were settled and happy, there would be no reason to keep the home or the garden he tried unsuccessfully to pretend he didn't care about.

"George."

Gert's voice startled him from his reverie.

"I want to have my own garden."

"Really? It's a lot of work. A lot of sweat."

"I love manual labor. I like to sweat. I feel good when I'm tired from physical effort."

"Then, go for it."

"I would, except I see two obstacles."

"Like what?"

She grinned. "Like, I don't have enough land at home to plant one, and I don't know anything about gardening."

Her smile gave him an inspiring idea. If a garden always lifted his spirit, why shouldn't it help put an end to Gert's blues. He spun and faced her. "Have I got a deal for you, my lady!"

"I'm open to about anything. What've you got in mind, Georgy boy?"

"I'll rent you my little plot here and be your consultant. You work. I advise."

"What's the rent?"

"I just told you. I get to tell you exactly what to do."

"That's pretty cheap. I need your advice anyway."

George thought for a second. "You're right. It's not enough. Directing you will be next to impossible."

"Actually, I'm a fast learner, so don't make it too steep, Georgy boy. I may back out."

George responded quickly. "Okay, the new deal is, I get first dibs on all the veggies." He stuck out his hand. "That's the deal, Gert. Take it or leave it."

"I'll take it." She slapped at his hand and taunted him. "I'm shocked that you're such a terrible negotiator. You could have asked for more than just the vegetables. Believe it or not, I don't give a darn about 'em. You can have them all, if you want."

"Then, silly, why have a vegetable garden?"

She gave him a classic eye-roll. "Because, silly, I want to attract the animals. It's maintaining a place for them that excites me and, of course, planting beautiful flowers everywhere."

George was amused at the naive idea that flowers and animals could coexist, but heck, she was still young and dumb. Let her find out the sad truth for herself. "Whatever works for you, my princess."

"You may think I'm kidding, but I've been reading about a local garden group that's pushing the city for beautification. They say it's good for the psyche, the local economy and actually reduces crime. Although I know nothing about the group other than what I read in the paper, their ideas feel right to me, and I want to get involved."

George was not only blown away with her grasp of the concept of beautification, but he was struck by the importance of his role in her new interest. He smiled at her.

"Don't laugh, George. When I get enthused about a project, I put a lot of back and mouth into it. In fact, I discussed this with Roundy and talked him into dividing up his ugly blacktop parking lot at the factory with concrete beds of blooming shrubs and ornamental trees. He surprised me by liking the idea so much he's going ahead with it in a week or so. Besides that, he promised to talk it up with some other business leaders, and I'll bet they'll follow his lead. What do you think of that, Georgy boy?"

"I'm impressed, Gert."

She grabbed his arm for emphasis. "Yeah, and think how much more I can dream up after you teach me all you know about gardening."

"With your enthusiasm it won't be hard. It will be fun." As an apparent afterthought he mumbled, "And, I still get all the vegetables."

Walking back on the path toward the basement door, they were silent until George tossed her a skeptical grin. "I can't believe you really want to encourage the animals to feed on my veggies?"

"Your veggies. I thought the garden was mine."

"It is yours, but you agreed the veggies were mine. Don't you realize it's sacrilege to feed my mortal enemies?"

"I think Someone long ago suggested we do that."

"But no one every confused me with Him." He took a deep breath and said, "All right! All right! I'll let bygones be bygones. Let the critters eat some of my goodies. This is going to be so much fun."

Gert threw her arms around him, squeezed him to her and kissed him on the mouth.

When he was able to pull away, he gasped and said, "What if Catherine saw that?"

"I hope she did. Then she'll know she's not the only woman in the world who loves you."

Instead of going in the basement door, George led Gert around the garage side of the house toward the driveway where her car was parked. While they were negotiating the rise, George asked plaintively, "You really want me to feel good about welcoming animals to my yard?"

"Yes I do, George."

"Even the ground hogs?"

She grinned. "Good Lord, no ground hogs!"

"Good. I want to see how successful you are at keeping them out. And, you want to plant more flowers and less food crops?"

She nodded.

"It will seem strange at first, but I guess I'll learn to accept it."

When they reached her car, he said, "Since you aren't going to plant many vegetables, I may not have enough to eat. Do you suppose petunias are edible?"

Gert punched him lightly on the arm. "I think you boil them, Georgy boy."

CHAPTER TWENTY-SIX

"Oh no! Another one!"

Catherine was involved with her physical therapist in the living room when the doorbell rang. George hollered, "I'll get it," left his coffee cup on the kitchen counter and sauntered through the hall. When he opened the door he immediately found himself face-to-face with an unfamiliar young woman holding a pineapple upside-down cake.

She handed it to him.

George thanked her politely.

She then asked if she could see Catherine.

He said, "She's busy right now." Then, feeling the pressure of her continued presence on the porch, he beckoned her inside. While standing in the foyer gripping the cake plate, he finally came forth with the words he'd been harboring since he first laid eyes on her. "I don't believe I know you."

She shied for a second, then answered with some reluctance, "I'm Samantha Garfield."

The airing of the hated name and a quick glance at the gift brought by the young woman standing near him set up a sudden clash of emotions that he found nearly impossible to quell. Eventually he was able to say in a taught, even voice, "She's working with the therapist right now. Let me tell her..."

"Who is it, George?" Catherine called from the living room.

"It's Samantha Garfield, and she's brought you a cake." He finished the discourse by averting his eyes and fixating on her shoetops.

"How nice. We're almost done, dear. Take her into the kitchen and pour her some coffee. I'll be there in around five or ten minutes."

Responding like any normal person who suddenly found himself forced to entertain a manslaughterist, he kept a stone face and silently led Samantha Garfield into the kitchen. Pointing to a chair at the table and placing the cake on the counter, George poured her a cup of coffee. Then, with his own cup topped-off, he joined her.

Sensing his obvious animosity, she said, "Perhaps I should come back another time."

George shook his head. "No, this was bound to happen eventually. It might as well be now."

Sitting across from her, George surveyed the cause of Catherine's altered state. Her hands were trembling so much she needed both of them to raise the cup all the way to her lips. His first reaction was satisfaction, that his hatred for what she had done to his wife was inflicting pain. Then Catherine's words, that forgiveness could be healing for all of them slipped into his consciousness. Catherine was right. The young woman was not a monster. True, she'd made a serious mistake, but instead of running away, her remorse was bravely driving her to make amends. Why else would she be here facing him, obviously frightened, her cup shaking precariously a hand's length from her mouth?

George studied her and finally said, "I hung up on you every time you called."

"I understood why, but I had to keep calling, do something, anything to...I didn't really want to trouble you more than I already have, but..."

He smiled at her and said, "Samantha, I'm sorry for doing that. Now calm down and drink your coffee before you spill it on that pretty yellow blouse."

Whether it was the suddenness of his apology or her inability to perform simple tasks in such an emotion-charged atmosphere, the cup she was holding never made it to her lips. It slipped from her hand, tumbled off of her breast and onto her lap before crashing to the floor leaving a trail of dark splotches at each stop along the way. "Look what I've done now!" she cried.

George was on his feet immediately. He rushed to the cupboard and returned with a new roll of paper towels. After ripping off the cellophane wrapping, he handed Samantha a large wad of paper. Then, he stood by helplessly. Because of his prosthesis, he couldn't get down on his knees easily to clean up the mess, nor could he very well pat down Samantha's blouse. So, he fed her fresh toweling while she frantically picked up shards of shattered pottery and blotted up all the spilled coffee she found on the floor and herself. He also listened to her running commentary of self-loathing. For him, that was the clincher. His remaining enmity disbursed with each utterance. When the job was finished, he went back to the cupboard and returned with a large plastic garbage bag. She began filling it with used towels and pieces of the cup while he held it open. As he was accepting the last of the mess, he caught her hand and said softly, "It's all right now, Samantha."

"But, I broke your cup."

"You're forgiven for that, too," he said simply. She shuddered and said, "I am so sorry."

After procuring a new cup for her and filling it with fresh brew, they huddled over the table. In time the topics of conversation drifted from one to the next as they waited for Catherine to make her appearance. From Catherine's progress, they moved to gardening and on to the problems Samantha was having with her young son's potty training. About all George could contribute to her concern was a willing ear. After all, he'd never sired boys, and his daughter, Anne, had never discussed Gregory George's achievements in that area.

"I'm sure he'll eventually get the hang of it on his own," she said.

"They usually do," George offered sagely. "Sooner or later."

When he heard the therapist leaving, George nodded toward the door to alert Samantha to Catherine's entrance into the kitchen. Although he was well aware of her progress, he was thrilled each time he saw her walking without the aid of a walker or any other device. To greet her, he began an off key rendition of the Miss America theme song. "Here she comes..."

Samantha looked up and gushed, "You really are progressing. I'm so glad."

Since Samantha's comment came in mid-stride Catherine didn't acknowledge her words until she'd drawn a deep breath and collapsed into a chair at the table. She wiped her brow and said, "Yes. I am doing quite well. I may make my goal, yet."

"What's that?" George asked, surprise escaping from his lips with the question.

"By the time I get to The Willows, I want to sleep with my husband."

George grinned. "Sounds good to me."

"As cheeky as that sounds, it beats the heck out of being stuck in assisted living."

"I should hope," he said. Then to bring his wife up to speed on his conversation with Samantha, he decided to tell the tale of the broken cup to explain the huge stain down the front of her blouse. He gestured toward the young woman and said, "Samantha had an accident."

"Oh, no! Another one!"

"I mean she spilled her coffee," George said.

"Oh, my! I thought she..."

"Just coffee," he reassured her as Samantha began to cry.

George was sitting on his garden stool weeding the plants and shrubs around the foundation in the front of the house. The weather was perfect for such an endeavor, not so cool as to require a jacket and not so hot he'd expire in a pool of sweat. He was resting on his spade when he spotted Rachel whiz by on her under-sized bike. Her long, almost white hair trailed like a jet stream. He waved as she passed, but apparently she hadn't noticed him, or at least she hadn't returned his friendly gesture, and though he tried not to feel a little hurt, he did. She was wearing her helmet, however. That helped compensate for his being invisible to her.

He continued to eye her as she rounded the circle at the end of the street. Pumping furiously, she entered the straightaway that ran past his house. By now he was waving in earnest. Seeing him, she slowed and whipped into the driveway before skidding to a stop. After catching her breath, she said, "Hi, Mr. Konert."

"I waved, but you were going so fast you must not have seen me," he said.

"I saw someone, but my mom says not to make eye contact with strangers."

"But, I'm not a stranger."

She giggled. "I know that. But, I didn't know you were Mr. Konert when I wasn't looking at you."

George nodded. "That makes sense."

By then she was standing by her bike, so he shuffled closer and asked, "Why were you going so fast?"

She put a hand on her hip and said in a little voice filled with a lot of impatience. "I was working out."

"You're eight years old. What are you doing that for?"

"That's for me to know, and you to find out," she said, giggling.

Even though he knew it was a playground comment that had been around as long as he had, George recoiled. "You're getting quite a mouth on you, young lady," but his tone of voice held more amusement than condemnation, and she continued giggling.

Still, he regretted his words because he'd learned long ago with his own girls that the worst way to fight a smart mouth was a frontal attack. Even an eight-year-old would end up winning that battle. His experience prepared him for the inevitable. No man, regardless of age and experience, could go mouth to mouth with a female and win. So, if a man wanted to win, and what man didn't, and he couldn't out-verbalize them, he had to play to his own strengths and exploit their biggest weakness. That meant he had to out-think them. With that hopeful, irrational thought in mind, he flashed a smile and grabbed her handlebars. "We need to talk. Want some lemonade?"

She didn't respond immediately, but she did slip to the ground and carefully lay her bike down on the blacktop driveway. Then she looked up at him and said, "I can't. Too much sugar. I don't want to get fat."

He studied her slim frame and frowned. "Who says you're too fat?"

"Nobody. But I want my new friends to like me, and kids don't like fat girls."

An alarm went off in George's head. What regular kid wouldn't drink lemonade for fear of losing friends? "I'm not so sure I agree, Rachel." Then, feeling inadequate to force her continued involvement in the conversation, he resorted to subterfuge. "When people exercise I've always heard they should drink lots of water." He caught her eye. "Since I was just going to have some right now, why don't you come inside, and we'll have a drink together on the back porch." Then he came up with the clincher. "I know Mrs. Konert will want to see you. It's been such a long, long time between visits, what with school, and her accident and everything."

She eagerly grabbed his hand and let him lead her up the stoop and into the house. Seeing Catherine dozing on the couch when they entered the living room, George managed a loud throat-clearing as they passed. Her eyes flew open, and her voice echoed surprise. "Who have we here?"

"Hi, Mrs. Konert," Rachel replied.

"Hello, dear."

Placing his hand gently on her helmet, George filled in the details. "Rachel was riding her bike, and we both decided we needed a drink of water, so I suggested we sit on the porch a minute and chat. But, do you know what, Catherine? I think I'd even like a chocolate chip cookie if we have any." He cleared his throat again signaling his wife to action.

"I think I'd like one, too, dear. Why don't you two get your water, and I'll toddle along with the cookies and join you on the porch. What do you think of that, Rachel?"

The little girl beamed. "I like to sit on your porch."

Once Catherine joined them with a plate full of cookies, and she and George each took one off the plate, Rachel grabbed a cookie, gobbled it down and then took a second. Moreover, she didn't shrink from the conversation which George began by saying, "Rachel was telling me that her friends don't like fat girls, so she's watching her sugar intake."

Rachel corrected him. "Mr. Konert, I said I didn't want to get fat, because I wanted everyone at my new school to like me."

George scratched his head over her reply as he tried to discern the difference between her meaning and his.

Fortunately, Catherine adroitly slipped into the discussion. Glancing at the rapidly disappearing cookie in Rachel's hand, she replied, "I understand, dear. You don't want to eat too much sugar because you want to feel good about how you look, right?" When Rachel kept munching, Catherine continued. "The best thing is to be just about right, don't you think? You don't want to be too heavy, and you don't want to be too thin." She paused as George reached over and wiped a smudge of chocolate off Rachel's cheek. "And, of course, you don't believe for a minute that how you look will determine whether your friends like you or not."

"My mom says if I'm nice to them, they'll be nice to me. That's what I was trying to tell Mr. Konert."

While he searched for the words to defend himself, Catherine smiled sweetly and said, "Men sometimes don't hear everything we're saying, Rachel."

He kept his ire to himself as well as his manly rebuttal. Instead, George gave an exaggerated blanket approval. "I agree with everything Mrs. Konert said. She is very wise."

"Don't worry, Mr. Konert," Rachel said, patting his hand. "*I* think you're smart."

She was reaching for a third cookie when she glanced at Catherine and pulled her hand back. "I think two are enough, don't you, Mrs. Konert?"

"Two are perfect."

"I thought so," she replied.

Then Catherine smiled and added, "Just like you."

When it was time to leave, George walked Rachel to her bike. Her eyes danced as she said, "I'm going to visit Daddy at his apartment tomorrow. All day. He's going to cook spaghetti. My mom says it will come out of a jar. Sometimes she makes Spaghetti Os. I don't care. I know they both love me. We'll watch a DVD and play video games and have lots of fun."

He smiled at her. "How could anyone not love you, Rachel?"

George watched her adjust her helmet and smooth her hair onto her shoulders. "By the way, when are you moving to Dayton?"

"I don't know. I'm not in charge," she snipped, putting her small hands on her hips and striking a pose. George stared at her as he tried to frame a reaction that would let her know how he felt about her comment. Evidently she sensed an incoming chastisement, because George noticed an immediate visible change in her attitude. Still, he withheld his smile until he saw her hands come off her hips and heard her giggle. "My Daddy's moving into a new house next week, but my mom, Jim, and I aren't going until after school is out."

"I'm glad," George said. "Then, you can stop by and see us again."

"I will, Mr. Konert," she said as she climbed onto her bike and began pedaling away.

The difference between her leaving and her arrival came when she glanced back for an instant and waved.

CHAPTER TWENTY-SEVEN

"Time changes our outlook on a lot of things."

Two-year-old Gregory George, whose name in George's eyes had been relegated to the dung heap of common names when his parents chose to drop the *George* from his given name and call the tike Greg, sat on the couch next to Catherine. From the time he'd entered the house, the child had treated her with the deferential treatment usually reserved for a queen. Remarkably, his grandson seemed aware of her fragility and her proximity to him even as he bounded around the room bumping every other object that blocked his path. At the moment there was a reason for his quiet demeanor. She was reading to him. Still, there was something eerie going on. On the few occasions when he read the child a story, Gregory George-Greg-was all over him, jostling him and jumping up and down on the cushions. The only reasonable conclusion? The child was either intuitive or Catherine had some kind of magical hold over the kid.

By contrast, if the child listening to Catherine read with folded hands and a beatific smile had been Lily, Greg's older Asian sister, he would have been spared the shock. From the moment she arrived from China, she had been the epitome of calm perfection. She was bright, curious and friendly without being demanding and overly precocious. She was sweet without being saccharin and always solicitous of her grandmother. To date, the only blot on her record was a shyness toward men, which in his mind would have been a good thing if he hadn't fit snugly into that category.

George took off his glasses and held them up to the light. When nothing of substance seemed to be distorting the picture posed by his wife and grandson, he returned them to his nose, pulled himself up from the lounger and trudged up the stairs to the second floor.

When he found Anne and his granddaughter in the spare bedroom, Lily was trying on clothes from a small pile on the bed. "That's a cute dress," he volunteered after spotting her tiny body in a blue and white striped outfit with a large white collar that set off her dark hair. Then, in an attempt to impress his daughter with his vast knowledge of children's apparel, he added, "And, it fits her perfectly, Anne."

Lily corrected him in her sweet pre-kindergarten voice. "It's not a dress, Grandpa. It's a skirt and top."

He took a step closer and acting surprised, exclaimed, "Oh, so it is."

"And, it's actually a little big," Anne added.

He shrugged. "Well, anyway, I like it."

"We do, too, don't we Lily?" When his granddaughter nodded and began to remove the top so she could try on another, Anne decided its fate. "We'll just put it away until you grow into it."

"Makes sense to me," George agreed.

George chuckled to himself. Displaying his ignorance about children's clothes was becoming a habit. When his wife commissioned Gert to purchase the "grandma gifts" for Lily, he'd been coerced into viewing the results after his stepdaughter had returned from the mall. Despite protesting his lack of knowledge of children's garments, the two women continued to invite his opinion on each item as it was pulled from the bag. After a few showings, when the totality of his replies consisted of, "They're awfully small," their combined disgust drove him to the refrigerator where he retrieved a beer and stayed out of sight until Gert left the premises.

Since he had no intention of missing this opportunity to connect with Anne and Lily, he sat through the modeling session silently smiling his approval from the chair in the corner of the room. Still, he had to acknowledge that watching Greg play with his new trucks was more up his alley.

When all the clothes had been tried on, Anne suggested to Lily that she trot downstairs and join Greg and her grandma. "Maybe you can read to them." When the child eagerly rushed off toward the top of the stairs, Anne warned, "Careful!" Then she added, "Hold on to the bannister so you don't fall."

"Okay, Mama."

Anne turned to her father and said lightly, "You know how kids are. You have to be on them every minute so they don't kill themselves."

George turned morose. "I'm all too aware of that," he said.

It had been weeks since Kevin had crept into his consciousness, but once installed there as he was at this moment, his presence placed an immediate damper on his festive mood. Anne must have noticed it, too, because she reached out a hand to his arm and asked, "Are you all right?"

Rather than go through the torment of explaining his feelings, he denied them entirely which as a rule wasn't too smart, but with Anne ready to worry about him, it seemed a better choice. Why drag her down with his load and ruin her visit? Who knew how many more moments they'd spend together?

"You seem so sad."

He forced a smile and said, "I always look this way when I'm happy to see my family." When she frowned at him, and he knew she hadn't bought his flippant answer, he confessed. "I just had a fleeting thought about the neighbor boy who died last year."

"And, my comment caused it?"

"No...yes...no...actually I think about Kevin often. It's nobody's fault. It's just hard when a child dies. The feeling creeps in at unexpected times. And, now the family is moving away."

He put his arm around her waist and led her into the hall toward the door leading to the attic. He opened it and started up the steps, signaling her to follow. "There's some stuff up here I want you to look at."

When they were standing in the middle of the large room among the bare wooden rafters, he pulled up a small stool for her to sit on. Then he loaded her lap with a large brown cardboard box containing a number of smaller boxes piled one on top of the other. "These all belonged to your mother. I packed them away before I married Catherine. I just assumed my second wife wouldn't want to wear my first wife's jewelry. Or rather, I decided it wasn't right. I guess I always felt your mom would want you and Jill to have first crack."

Anne reached down and pulled out a small white box. She opened it and removed a pearl necklace. "Wow! I don't remember seeing this before."

"I think we bought it when we went to Majorca after you kids were in college. Your mom didn't wear it much. I don't know why."

Anne cradled it in her hand and studied it. "I don't know why, either. It's beautiful, and I don't have a necklace just like it."

"Take it. I won't be wearing it."

"It's not your style?"

"Not enough glitz."

Anne grinned and started to reach for another box. She straightened. "If you're really giving the necklace to me, I'd love to have it. But, don't you think Jill should get a chance to go through Mom's stuff, too?"

George nodded. "I do. There are pins, bracelets and some more necklaces in there and quite a few earrings. I think some might fit your taste. Others may have some sentimental attachment for you guys, and some could be junk for Lily to play *dress up*. A few might be valuable. I just don't know which, and I don't want to take any of this stuff with me when we move." He put his hand on hers. "Except for the wedding rings in the safety deposit box. You'll have to fight over those when I die."

"So, what are you saying, Dad?"

"I'm not sure. I'll confess that every once in awhile I still come up here and paw through the boxes just to connect with your mother. Now that we're moving...you know...I can't..." He took a finger to the tear that appeared in the corner of his left eye. "What's the point?"

Suddenly he reached down and picked up the whole box and moved it to a table near the door. "There's still so much to do here. Take the box of jewelry and work it out with Jill, okay?"

Peeking into another larger box, he groaned. "Work clothes. Too good to throw out. Too many to keep. They go to the Salvation Army." He opened another. "Your mother's old skirts and fancy dresses. You may want some of them." He marked the first box with a large black SA and pushed it aside so he could get at more. He carried the skirt and dress containers and placed them next to the first box on the table. He also kept up a running commentary. "I can't look through each one of these, and I can't throw them out sight unseen. Save me, Anne." He glanced at his daughter who had moved on to yet another box. "Anne?"

She had pulled her stool into the light from the single reflector covering the bare bulb that hung from a cord and lit the greater part of the attic. The cylinder of light rained iridescent dust particles stirred up by their activity. She was sitting on the small stool, looking at a picture. When he returned to her side, she looked up at him and grinned. "You were quite the dude. All dressed up in your football uniform."

"With all there is to do, and you're into the picture box?" He reached out and took the five-by-seven shot from her hand and grinned. "I was, wasn't I? Do you know how you can tell this picture is over sixty years old?"

She chuckled. "Because you look like a teenager?"

"Well that, too. But look at the leather helmet." Suddenly, without warning the word *helmet* triggered Kevin back into his thoughts. Sometimes he was warmed by his visit, but most of the time like now, he could get by just fine without that recurring sadness. He returned the picture to Anne and asked, "Did you see the one of your mom in the oversized sailor suit?"

"I'd seen that before. But, so many of these are new to me." She handed a colored snapshot to her dad. "Like this one of Jill and me. I was probably eight or nine. Jill, at the most, eleven. Judging by the fancy spring outfits, it might have been Easter."

George shook his head. "I can't help you there. Too bad your mother isn't here. She could clear up all the mysteries." He pointed at the sister's joined hands. "However, I do remember the hands. Your mom and I used to laugh about it. She once said, 'If Jill was a cop and Anne was a criminal, Jill wouldn't need handcuffs because Anne would never get away.'"

She sighed. "I never wanted to get away. Jill was like a second mother. I did whatever she told me. I doubt I would have survived my childhood without my big sister. She led me around and protected me from that mean Alfamo kid who liked to pick on me. She's still my best friend, although we don't see each other nearly often enough anymore."

"You'll have to find a way now, because along with everything else, you're taking all the pictures with you, too." Between the dim light and his diminishing sight, George wasn't quite sure he properly interpreted her facial expression, but she sounded sincere when she said, "Thanks." Nor did he much care if her attitude was cynical. There were more boxes that needed inspecting. As long as he was the foreman, he'd have to keep his only worker from slacking. He slid another cardboard box over to her stool.

"There's more?"

"We've hardly started." Pointing to a neat stack of boxes that lined one wall of the attic, he grinned. "We have all those."

"We can't finish those today!"

"Then you and the kids will just have to stay overnight."

"Dad, I can't. I told Brett I'd be home tonight."

Then he stopped his kidding, and said, "Those are all earmarked for the dump or the Salvation Army. I'm going to try to get Gert over here some day soon and have her carry them downstairs. While you paw through that carton, I'll begin moving the ones you're taking with you to the foyer."

After carrying the relatively light box of pictures down two flights of stairs, George stopped to check on Catherine and the kids and started back up. He paused on his return at the foot of the last flight to the attic. Although stopping allowed him to gulp some air to calm his heart and continue his ascent, it also filled him with awe. When he was two years younger, he would never have attempted the trip. If his knee hadn't collapsed or thrown him into spasms of uncontrollable pain, the angina he tried to ignore would have driven him to the medicine cabinet, the bed or both. But, all that changed with his knee replacement and bypass surgery and the rehab from both. He glanced up the stairs where more boxes lay in waiting, then he put his leading foot on the first tread and slowly lifted his following foot to the next. At nearly eighty-two, he was an extremely fortunate guy. With God's blessing and the medical profession, he was as physically fit as many healthy, younger men. Wiping the perspiration from his forehead with the sleeve of his shirt, he gasped for breath and rethought his comment. The only healthy younger men as decrepit as he was were probably eighty.

When he came upon Anne, she was waving a piece of paper at him. "What's this? Did you write it?"

He took the paper and cringed. "I thought I threw this out. Don't hold me responsible. I wasn't faring too well back then."

"Maybe not, but it is a pretty good pep talk. Listen to it."

He covered his ears, but he smiled so Anne knew he was listening.

"What do you do
When you're seventy-two
And life is a wintry-mix?
You think of the guys
Who've closed their eyes
Who'd love to be in your fix."

She handed him the paper. "It's short, but it certainly sounds like your practical wisdom," Anne said.

George grinned. "I have to admit, it doesn't sound as bad now as when I wrote it."

"Time changes our outlook on a lot of things," Anne said.

Before his daughter and grandchildren left for Columbus with six boxes of "stuff" filling the back of the van, Anne insisted on snapping a series of pictures with her digital camera. Some included the children in various poses with George and Catherine, others only the adults. After taking a series of shots, Anne passed around the camera so each could view the results. This produced a few giggles from the children when they saw themselves. However, in Anne's practiced eyes, the best shot was a photo of her father and stepmother standing in the foyer with George's arm around his wife's waist.

"This one should be framed," she said. "I want one for my library, and I know Jill will want one. What do you think?"

"I don't know why you'd want a picture with an old guy like me in it, but I doubt you'll ever get a better one of the two of us together."

"I'd love to have one, too, Anne," Catherine said.

CHAPTER TWENTY-EIGHT

"It strikes me that you came to The Willows to die."

Dr. Thomas, Catherine's surgeon, surprised them both by proclaiming at a follow-up appointment that she had progressed so far she was overqualified for assisted living. "She doesn't need to be in that environment. It is more expensive and takes nurses away from others." With a wink at George, he said, "Mrs. Konert can now be back on her feet cooking and doing *women's work* in moderation." When Catherine started to flare, he smiled at George and said, "You'll be glad of that, won't you Mr. Konert?"

Realizing it was not a good time to gang up on his wife even in jest, he said, "Oh my, yes! No assisted living? Won't that be wonderful, Catherine?" Without waiting for her answer, his brain immediately began working on a new plan for The Willows.

However, Dr. Thomas insisted on continuing his lecture. "Mrs. Konert, you need to get out now, meet people and involve yourself in activities. I understand they're always looking for bridge or Scrabble players at places like The Willows."

Catherine kept a straight face and said icily, "How can I do that when I'll be busy doing women's work?"

George studied the surgeon's surprised expression. Then, the man forged ahead and made the salient statement that brought each of them a smile. "Mrs. Konert, just continue your PT and daily exercise, stay active, and you'll soon be back to where you were before the accident."

After they left the doctor's office and with George at her side, Catherine was pushing her walker through the corridor toward the entrance of the clinic. She was still bristling. "Is he chauvinistic, or what?"

"Look how well you've done. Let's just give him a pass."

"I suppose, but *women's work*? That's archaic."

"I think it's his attempt at humor."

The extent of her agreement was a nod.

After the valet parked the car under the front portico of the building, he helped Catherine onto the bench seat and placed the walker in the back. Then, once they were out of the driveway and heading for home, George said, "I think I'll take a run out to The Willows this afternoon. Do you want to come along?"

Catherine's reply revealed her lingering pique. "That's manly work. You go, dear. I need to rest up for the kind of work required of me."

When they arrived home, and he'd had a bite of lunch, George called The Willows and arranged a meeting with the facilities manager at three. Since his new plan consisted of a request for a change of venue from the cramped one bedroom apartment he contracted for, with Catherine in assisted living, he practiced pleading his case for a larger two bedroom apartment in an outlying building where they could live together.

As it turned out, all his last minute preparation was unnecessary. An apartment had just opened up, and they could move in whenever they wanted. "It's just a simple matter of drawing up a new contract and transferring your deposit, Mr. Konert."

After he and the manager had taken the short walk to explore the new first floor apartment, George flashed an enthusiastic thumbs up. Although compared to his spacious home, the apartment still seemed a bit small, it was a paradise compared to the original arrangement.

Surprisingly, the move itself was a snap. Over the ensuing two weeks, George and Catherine made several trips to The Willows listing everything they wanted to move from silverware and canned goods to medicines, clothes and linens. Then, with Catherine directing from the lists, George gathered the articles for Gert to pack, and they eventually boxed all the smaller items they would need to begin their new life.

On moving day, with Catherine directing the action at the receiving end and George stationed behind at home, the heavy work began. To handle the furniture and packed boxes, Roundy had produced a company truck and two husky young employees in need of some extra money. When they arrived, all George had to do was consult his list and point to the item that needed to be put on the truck. Later, when the truck reached the other end, the young men brought the items into the apartment and Catherine directed them so everything ended up in the right place. The afternoon ended with Gert organizing the small kitchen and making up their bed. Roundy put the finishing touches on the move by taking them all out to dinner. The following day after Gert and George put all of their personal things away, they moved in.

Once they were settled into their new digs, they placed the eight-by-ten framed portrait Anne shot on the dresser in their bedroom. In George's mind, the picture had taken on additional significance since he'd first viewed it in the camera. What pleased him most was the fact that the larger copy didn't reveal any of the stress his wife had been under since her accident.

Catherine, on the other hand, claimed the picture flattered them both. That comment came before she revealed her deeper feelings. "I'm just thrilled that your daughters have reached a point where they want the world to see me posing with their father's arm around me."

"But, they've always loved you, Catherine."

"I know, just as Gert has loved you. But, this is further confirmation."

Once Catherine's therapy schedule was established, George used the time to meander over to assisted living to visit Reuben. While the empty visits didn't take a big bite out of his day like they had when he used to drive to The Willows to play cribbage with him, he found chatting with the blank screen that Reuben had become terribly depressing. When he thought of the erudite poacher he'd discovered in his garden eighteen months before, and compared him to the mute lump propped against the headboard of his bed, his mind couldn't comprehend the deterioration. Since the results of his visits never varied, he began spacing them to longer intervals and shortening his stays to a minute or two.

The O'Haras, on the other hand, brightened a number of evenings after George and Catherine were settled in their apartment. They'd arrive around six, have a drink on George in the room or patio, and then walk to the dining room in the main building for dinner, or drive to a nice restaurant in Carlisle. George looked forward to these events because he could keep his barb-tossing skills sharp with Mike, while the women chatted and laughed, often at them.

Several times each day George encouraged Catherine to make the trip from their apartment to the main building with just her cane and no walker, as long as she waited until he was at her side. Not that he could do much more than break her fall if she started to topple, but he did serve two useful purposes. He could go for help if she did fall, and he knew the way to the *Big House,* the resident's name for the main building, which she didn't.

"Why can't I figure out which way to go, George? It's so frustrating."

"You've put your cancer behind you, and you've come back from a terrible accident. You expect too much. While I have heard of a few cases of people being cured of Disfunctional Directionitis, it's quite rare."

"So, even the great Dr. George can't cure me?"

He studied her closely and answered in mock seriousness. "Sadly, no, Catherine. In my humble opinion, I believe you're totally incapable of developing a sense of direction. You'll just have to live with it."

"But, I don't like feeling lost."

"Think how I feel. I can't make a bed or pick up dirty clothes and put them in the hamper. Those are your talents. I'm good at directions. That's why men and women get married." Her grin encouraged him to continue. "I will give you one tip, though. If you should ever try to walk to the main building on your own and realize you're lost, just keep making right turns. Eventually, you'll end up back at the apartment or get dizzy trying."

Lucky for George she still wasn't at full strength. The blow from her purse just glanced off his forearm.

On occasion, Catherine had a tendency to dawdle while adorning her body for the day. This would drive George to distraction, particularly if he thought she'd be late, like for today's therapy session. Usually, he'd parade back and forth outside the bathroom door threatening her with myriad consequences if she didn't hurry. While his nagging did little to move her along, at least it made him feel like he was helping.

Today, when it appeared she'd be late, he insisted she use her walker to make up the lost time. While she resisted going back to the aid, his demand had enough merit for her to condescend to its use.

"A little reminder of what I've been through?" she asked him as they walked along the winding concrete path.

"That, and a reminder that most people try to be on time for their appointments."

She acknowledged his dig by glancing at the sky and saying, "It's a shame to waste a gorgeous day like this doing therapy."

"Or, waiting for you to finish," George responded glumly, not considering the effect his thoughtless words might have on his wife. "If I were home, I'd be in the garden. In fact, I may see if Gert is going to be there and go help her this afternoon."

Catherine shook her head sadly. "Every day you wake up in this place, you must hate me for forcing you to give up your old life."

He responded immediately by taking a few quick steps to stand in front of her and block her path. Reaching out, he grabbed the walker forcing her to stop. Looking at her intently, he said, "Catherine, the day I met you, I began giving up my old life. The move to The Willows was just part of the process. My joy comes from you, and now that you're doing so well, we're going to have a great time together for as long as it lasts."

"Oh, George! I love you."

"Not any more than I love you."

Catherine spent the remainder of the walk alternately moving the walker and dabbing at her eyes. When they reached the door to the *Big House*, he held it for her and ushered her toward the therapy room. A few steps along the hall, he said with a twinkle, "And, Catherine, the best part about your doing so well is I can die knowing you'll be okay."

She stopped in her tracks, a look of horror on her face. "You die, and I'll kill you."

He smirked. Then, with a voice filled with shaming disapproval, he said, "Why is it women are always so violent?"

He led her through the door of the gym and up to the untended appointment desk. A young woman spotted her and came running. "Ah, here you are, Mrs. Konert. We've been waiting for you."

Rather than share any blame for her tardiness, George retreated toward the door to the hallway. With his hand on the knob, he said, "When you're done, you'll find me sitting on the couch in the waiting area. Have a good session."

Once he was into the corridor, he ambled toward the card room intent on finding a game to play or at least some company to help fill the time. He peeked through the glass door and saw two couples playing Scrabble. Since he didn't expect to be welcomed by the strangers, nor did he particularly enjoy playing Scrabble, he continued his search. In the corner, he spotted his new friend, Charlie, playing cards with three women—single women, he presumed, since Charlie was a recent widower and a target for any and all the unattached ladies. He opened the door and quietly approached them. "What are you playing?"

Three pairs of eyes peered up at him and then just as quickly returned to bathe his friend in adoration.

"Bridge," Charlie answered. "Do you want to play?"

"I don't play bridge that well," George said as the eyes reexamined him. "Plus, I only have forty-five minutes before I pick up my wife."

As the women turned back to their cards, he heard their collective sigh.

"You can take my place for a few hands," Charlie said. "I can use a break."

"No, Charlie," his partner said. "You can't quit until we finish the rubber."

His friend looked up and shrugged. "Maybe another time, George?"

He nodded and floated from the area on the breeze from the other player's sudden exhalation.

Out of boredom, he stopped at the Scrabble game to kibitz. While he wasn't made to feel uncomfortable, he realized his presence wasn't generating any genuine warmth, either. No one even stopped playing long enough to say, "Hi," or initiate an introduction. After a few more sterile minutes, he left the game room altogether.

Once he was back in the large hallway, he sauntered to the library. The place was empty. At first he wasn't sure what to make of it. Since he'd seen others in there on several occasions, he was sure the emptiness had a lot to do with the time of day. Then, too, it could be a statement about the interests of the resident population as a whole. Either way, he had the room to himself. He glanced at a few titles before finding an article in a *Smithsonian Magazine* about Arctic climatic changes. He read through it and left.

Walking through the hallway, he was struck by the contrast between his current experience and his pre-Willows expectation that projected hundreds of residents eagerly seeking him out for conversation, companionship and friendship. So far the facts were proving otherwise. On this morning, with the exception of Charlie, the residents seemed either in absentia or otherwise too preoccupied to bother with him. Still, it was far too early to conclude that he and Catherine were doomed to a friendless existence. He'd just have to try harder to involve himself in activities that would connect him to others with fellowship needs.

While walking past the front office, George glanced at the women filling the desks. At one time or another he'd met all three while they were answering his questions or honoring a request. Each was efficient, helpful and friendly. However, since he had nothing major to request of them this morning except a moment's pause or a passing smile, he gave them a quick glance, found them busy and moved on.

By the time he wandered back to the therapy waiting room and flopped onto the couch, he'd given up any thought of filling in the remaining thirty minutes with a pleasant distraction. If he were lucky, he'd fall asleep.

He was twiddling his thumbs and still musing on the topic of retirement home living, when a woman approached. After viewing her surgically rendered face, his initial thought was disbelief. In an ambitious attempt to make an aging person appear youthful, some plastic surgeon had pulled her facial skin so tight, she was left with a perpetual smile on a featureless landscape that began at one ear lobe and stretched across to the other. In addition, she had the high-riding, perky breasts and chemically lightened hair of a faded Hollywood star.

While he studied her face, he heard her say, "May I join you?"

George flinched. Watching a person speak without moving their lips sent him into a temporary paralysis, one so severe it made him forget his manners. Instead of welcoming her by attempting to stand or saying something, he scrunched closer to the arm of the couch to avoid any contact.

"Don't bother getting up," she added.

While she was mooring, George glanced at his watch to determine how long he'd be subjected to her presence before Catherine reappeared. Twenty minutes. Unless his initial impressions were deceiving, that could be a lifetime.

"I'm George Konert," he finally offered.

"Abigail Wainwright." He was relieved when she didn't offer her hand, but that didn't mean she was going to leave him in blissful silence. The irony of the encounter wasn't lost on him. After a morning of being ignored by potential friends, he was being set upon by Mrs. Frankenstein. Yes, he knew he should be more accepting of the poor woman and her predilection for surgery to sustain eternal youth, but given his current mind set, he'd sooner be breaking rocks with a sledge hammer in a penal colony.

"My husband was James Wainwright," she said with pride in her voice. "If you're from around here, you've undoubtedly heard of Wainwright Technologies?"

"I have," George said.

"We lived in a large home on the bluff overlooking the river. I was so happy there."

"I know the home. It was famous as the center of Carlisle society, I believe."

She smiled. Or, at least George assumed that was the purpose of the slight raising of the corners of her mouth. "That's what they always said. Then you are aware of my history, Mr. Konert."

"Everyone knew the Wainwright estate. The parties were legendary."

With a far-off look in her eyes, she murmured, "Those were the days."

Bringing the conversation back to the present, he said, "I believe your son is running the company now?"

"All too true. Plus, the little bastard kicked me out of my house and stuck me in this dreadful place."

George laughed to himself. Apparently, Abigail Wainwright's facade had been breached. Assuming her mind hadn't been altered like the rest of her, he might enjoy exploring its inner workings. "You don't like your son or your room?"

"He's okay. He just did what he thought was best. The estate was too much for me to manage." She tapped her chin with a bony finger. "As for my relationship with my son, we get along all right. He's not really a bastard. It's just that my daughter and I were very close and ever since she died of cancer, nothing seems to have meaning for me anymore. I'm afraid I've distanced myself and become somewhat bitter."

After hearing her tale, he was about to reach out to her when she added with a possible grin, "Just for the record, Mr. Konert, I live in a house on the grounds, not a room."

George found a speck of humor in her reply. "Of course, I should have known." He glanced at his watch. Fifteen minutes to go. Maybe the old gal was worth his remaining allotment after all.

Recalling one of his own pet sayings, *Everyone has some redeeming qualities,* he decided to devote the remaining time to discover Abigail Wainwright's. "If we're going to be friends, I think you should call me George." The shockwaves from his blunt demand caused her head to recoil like a startled turkey. "And, if you don't mind, I'd be more comfortable calling you, Abigail."

"What is your motive in being so personal, Mr. Konert... George."

"Well, Abigail, it's like this. My wife and I moved to The Willows to have some fun, make new friends and live. Now, forgive me if I offend you, but it strikes me that you came to The Willows to die."

Her reaction was instant and not totally unexpected. "Of all the effrontery. I've never been so insulted....how could you be so rude?" She began to cry.

While his natural reaction was to comfort her or make some gesture of remorse for his bluntness, for some reason he held back. Maybe Abigail was truly offended because people just didn't say such things to her, or maybe his own misgivings about living here had led him to go way overboard. On the other hand, he might have hit the nail on the head, and she was reacting to it. While the former might be the case, he assumed the latter was the real cause of her tears, and the more she cried, the worse he felt for speaking up. Still, rather than apologizing, he waited quietly for her to stop. He also peeked at his watch. Ten minutes more. Pray that Catherine would not be released early so he'd have to explain to her why this stranger was crying, and how he'd been the instigator of her tears.

"George?" Abigail's piercing voice interrupted his thoughts.

"Yes."

"What's your wife's name?"

"Catherine. Why do you ask?"

"Because I wanted to know. How else would I find out?" she said bluntly. "What I really want to know is will you and Catherine join me for dinner at Vale Hollow Country Club tonight? I'd like a change of ambiance, and I know you'll find the food and the presentation far superior to the fare they serve here at The Willows." The whole invitation came in the form of a plea.

"My wife is recuperating from a serious auto accident. She might not be up to it. Let's ask her when she comes through those doors in..." he glanced at his watch, "six minutes."

"Actually, I appreciate what you said to me about dying here, George. You might have spotted the truth. Right or wrong, your comment took courage. I admire courage."

He grinned. "I think I might have gone way past courage and ended up in gall."

"You didn't. Most people are afraid of me. You obviously aren't, and you got my full attention." Just like getting a horse's attention by hitting it over the head with a two-by-four, he thought.

She lowered the intensity of her voice. "I really don't want people being afraid of me." Shrugging, she added, "At least not all of the time."

"That's where we differ. I don't want anyone to be afraid of me. I need all the friends I can get."

"I know. I truly don't want to put people off, but at the same time, I'm reluctant to let them get too close. I've always been that way."

"Abigail, when we come to a place like The Willows, we are all pretty much equals because we know what the ultimate ending of our story will be."

She nodded to show she understood.

"So, Abigail, I think we need to unburden ourselves of our earlier chapters, toss in some unpredictability and spice up the ending."

She was still nodding when she engaged his eyes with hers. "Well said, George," she responded with enthusiasm. "You make a lot of sense."

Just then Catherine entered the waiting room. Apparently Abigail didn't notice her at first, because Catherine was able to give George a quizzical nod toward the stranger sitting on the couch with him.

That was his signal to pull himself up and give his wife a peck on the cheek. "How'd it go?" he asked.

"Very well, thank you."

He introduced the two women to one another.

"Abigail has invited us to dine with her tonight at her country club, Vale Hollow. Do you feel up to going?"

"How nice. I love eating there. Of course, I feel like going."

"You've been there?" Abigail acted surprised.

"Many times. My son-in-law, Harold Gerlach, belongs there."

"Roundy?"

"Do you know him?" George asked.

"Know him? I love him. My daughter was married to him, until..." she dropped her voice. Quickly recovering, she added, "So, you're the wonderful new step-grandmother my family raves about? My, my! We are going to have a lot to talk about tonight, aren't we. I'm looking forward to every minute."

As they were leaving, George said, "How's that for unpredictability, Abigail?"

She grinned.

While George carried the walker on the trek back to their apartment, Catherine kept bombarding him with questions about Abigail Wainwright. In return, George kept shushing her until he was finished with his mental calculations. Why did she need to interrupt him when he was so close to zeroing in on Abigail's age.

CHAPTER TWENTY-NINE

"So, is this it, Grace?"

George didn't bother to call Gert on her cell phone to see if she was going to be at his old house tending the garden. He kind of expected she would be, but if not, he'd look over her work, pick a few snow peas, leaf lettuce and, if some green beans were ready, he'd swipe them, too. Then he'd head back to The Willows with his loot. Stealing fresh produce from one's own plot added a dimension to gardening he'd never experienced before. It was exhilarating.

When he pulled into the driveway, he made a brilliant deduction. If Gert's car was missing, she wasn't there. The assumption proved accurate as he strolled leisurely around the house to the vegetable garden. The first thing that caught his attention was the profusion of color that came from the perennial beds and the abundance of annuals that never existed on his watch. He felt a rush of excitement. Gert was actually serious about making the place a blaze of flowers. In a large bed by the back corner of the house the purple mountain bluets were just beginning to bloom. While the blooms on the peonies he'd planted nearby were mostly played out, the annuals were just coming into their own.

Further along on his trip, he spotted the first casualty marring Gert's hard work. The darn deer had gobbled up a whole patch of hosta. He smiled. Silly girl. He'd told her all about the fight she'd have on her hands trying to keep the deer from devouring her hosta, but apparently she had to learn the hard way. Now, he'd have to teach how to apply the product he kept in the basement. When it was sprayed on, it made the plants taste so noxious the deer left them alone. Then a sudden insight spoiled his thoughts of revenge against the herd. Gert wasn't a typical gardener. She probably considered the deer her pets and wanted to continue feeding them.

He meandered past another new bed planted in annuals. Some, like the dahlias and petunias had obviously been started with small plants. Others, like the zinnias, were well behind in their growth and had obviously been started from seed. He wasn't concerned. They'd catch up.

Upon reaching the vegetable garden, he suddenly clutched his chest in shock. Instead of a food crop, the whole first row facing the house was sprouting gladiolas. He shook his head. What was wrong with that woman? In the space it took to plant the bulbs, she could have had a long row of something edible. Not only that, she'd have to dig up all the bulbs in the fall and store them until the next spring. How ridiculous was that? It certainly defied his long-held belief that if you couldn't eat it, why plant it.

He made his way around the flowers and entered the garden. The first thing that caught his eye was the lack of weeds. While he considered himself a terrific weeder in his prime, he had to admit he'd slipped in his later years when back pain combined with poor eyesight forced him to settle for less than perfect grooming. But this garden, Gert's garden, was immaculate. It was obvious she took weeding seriously, and despite her planting quirks, he tipped his hat to her.

When he came upon the row of snow peas climbing the string fence stretched between two poles, his skilled eye noticed they were more than three feet high and flowering. Upon closer scrutiny he found a number of pods intermingled with the flowers. He began picking and filling a quart sized plastic bag he'd brought from home for just such a possibility.

Moving on, he picked off enough lettuce leaves untouched by the rabbits for a good sized salad and joined them with a few mature radishes and a handful of immature beet leaves. Better to pull the leaves and eat them in a salad now than let them crowd their companions. Had he forgotten to tell Gert about thinning the beets?

If so, it must have been one of his senior moments, because letting them crowd each other was about the only way a gardener could end up with stunted beet roots. To make it up to her, he bent to the task and received enough satisfaction from doing it to refrain from complaining to Catherine about his back being sore.

His last act before leaving for home was checking out the rows of beans. To his dismay, one whole row was gone. A few stubby stems marked the line of plants that at last inspection had been at least a foot high. He'd suspect a rabbit, but this devilish work was beyond the usual damage of the large-eared pests. Rabbits nibble at the leaves. Bigger animals devour whole rows right to the ground. From experience, he guessed the perpetrator was a ground hog. Moreover, since he'd never noticed another in recent years, it undoubtedly had to have been O'Hara's *live-in* rodent.

Suddenly, the joy he'd received from filling the plastic bag with edible goodies was replaced by rage. Hadn't he warned Gert about the ugly intruder and its evil ways? Now she needed to see the damage with her own eyes to confirm its existence. Hopefully, the horror of it all would motivate her to hire a trapper to remove the animal once and for all. Unfortunately, that was something he should have done himself in the last year or two. Or, O'Hara should have. After all, it was his pet. The problem was O'Hara didn't worry about the damn thing because he didn't have anything worth eating in his yard. Thus, anytime the ravenous hog came to his door begging for a handout, the lawyer just pointed him to George's vegetables and said, "Help yourself." The worst part was he couldn't sue for the damages. O'Hara was his attorney, and some of the finest moments in recent years were spent drinking beer with him on his porch.

When he was finished raving—and feeling a bit foolish for getting all worked up—George decided it was time to stroll back to the car. If Gert wasn't going to show, what was the point of his hanging around? He could go back to The Willows and wash the peas and salad fixings, maybe take a short walk around the grounds with Catherine and then lose a few games of gin rummy to her. Since they'd resumed play, he was down $4.80, and while losing to her was inevitable, he was feeling such a desperate need to get even that he'd even entertained the idea of doubling the stakes. The only roadblock was the thought of Catherine's maniacal laughing as she pocketed an even larger portion of her eventual inheritance.

He started up the path, retracing the steps he'd followed so many times over so many years. Today, while there was no reason to stay, a magnetic tug from the garden slowed his steps. Still, he marched ahead veering past the burning bush and on to the car. He opened the door, tossed the bag of veggies in ahead of him and slid onto the seat.

Typically, he'd have his car keys in hand so he wouldn't have to search through his pants pockets while he was crammed under the steering wheel. He looked in his hands. They were empty, and he found it spooky. Was someone making it difficult for him to leave?

He squirmed and tugged trying to dig the keys from his pocket, but they were so entangled, he finally realized he'd never be able to remove them while in a sitting position. Rather than displace a shoulder trying, he reopened the door and stepped out. Standing in the driveway, he easily fished out the medium-sized ring of keys and held them up, amazed they'd caused so much trouble. In the process, he squinted at the individual keys. The one that caught his attention was not the car key, but the house key. Suddenly the whole struggle took on meaning. For some reason, he wasn't suppose to leave yet.

As if being propelled by the strings of some giant puppeteer, he climbed the steps of the stoop, unlocked the door and entered the house. There, accompanied by the silence, he walked through the living room, the dining room and entered the kitchen. The door to the porch beckoned, but first a beer. Porch and beer. Beer and porch. The two words were conjoined like Siamese twins. He slipped into the garage and opened the refrigerator. It was empty. Darned if he hadn't shared his last two beers with the ground hog lover the last time he and O'Hara were together before he moved. Just as well, he thought. If he never returned again, he had no desire to leave a fridge full of beer as a legacy.

He opened the porch door, raised the back of the chaise lounge so he could see out over the garden and plopped down. While working among the plants in the garden was mostly satisfying, sitting on the porch overlooking the entire landscape was inspiring. The swaying silver maples framing the colorful gardens interspersed among a sea of green grass was the picture he'd paint if he had the talent. It also would be the view he'd measure against the best heaven had to offer. In fact, if he were to pick a place to die, it would be right here on a beautiful summer afternoon like today. But, not alone. He never wanted to die alone.

A voice from behind him said, "You're not alone, George. I'm always with you."

"Is that you, Grace?" He turned quickly and saw his deceased wife lounging in the open doorway. Feeling the calm of her presence, he smiled and said, "I had this strong feeling you might be coming for me today. I'm ready, you know." He reached out to her. "So, is this it, Grace?"

She laughed. "Don't be so melodramatic, my love. Heaven's not ready for you yet, and neither am I."

"Then, why are you here?"

"You know why I'm here, George. To remind you. More than anyone, I understand what nourishes your soul." Then she slowly faded from view.

George sighed, pulled himself up from the chaise and headed for the garage. If he remembered correctly, the old live trap was still stacked in the corner.